Spanish Seduction Trilogy

BOOK ONE: **EL MIRADOR**
BOOK TWO: **EL PRECIO** - THE PRICE OF PASSION
BOOK THREE: **INCENDIO** - THE FLAMES OF PASSION

by Jean Maxwell

ACKNOWLEDGMENTS

Thank you to my family for humouring me and allowing me the time and space to indulge in the creation of this work. For the interest and encouragement to finish it and for not laughing even once.

With grateful thanks to Dawn, Gracie, Debbie, Silva, Lisa and Rosanna, Chris Baty and NaNoWriMo, the helpful critters who inhabit the online creative spaces, the Toronto Romance Writers Association and MacEwan Writing Works.

Table of Contents

EL MIRADOR. . . . .

EL PRECIO:
The Price of Passion. 205

INCENDIO
The Flames of Passion 409

EL MIRADOR

SPANISH SEDUCTION TRILOGY– BOOK ONE

by Jean Maxwell

Prologue

July, 1972

"Don't do it, *mi amigo. Le ruego,* I'm begging you. *No lo hagas,* don't do it."

Tristan's hoarse voice echoed in the hollow concrete underground. He gripped Ari's arm, but his friend wrenched away.

Darkness and heat cloyed the space, the smell of petrol thick around them. Black tar oozed from the uneven ground beneath their feet. The flames would rage out of control if Ari set off the acetylene torch he clutched in his sweating hands.

"Ella no vale la pena, Ari. It's not worth it, *she's* not worth it," Tristan said, his tone desperate.

Ariel Torres was his friend, his mentor, the accomplished master showing his young apprentice the ropes of the hospitality business. Tristan couldn't bear to watch him destroy everything he'd worked for in a single moment of passion, rage. Jealousy. And for what? A careless woman who didn't love Ari or the unborn child she carried. Ari didn't even know if the baby was his.

"Damn you, Ari. I didn't bail your ass out of that backstreet cantina for this," Tristan shouted, his memory of the night they met flashing back to him. Was this how it happened when you were about to die, images of the past appearing in your mind at random? "I should have let that gypsy bastard kill you then and saved you the trouble!"

The interior of the tiny tavern in Madrid took shape in the young engineer's head, a picture of Torres amid clacking castanets and drunken revelry, ogling and ass-grabbing the red-haired flamenco dancer.

"You know nothing, *estudiante!*" Ari said with measured contempt, waving the torch at him. "Nothing about life or women."

What? Tristan Benjamin Flynn, top engineering graduate from Cardiff University, knew nothing? Tristan's fear meshed with anger as he pushed sweat-soaked locks of his blond mane of hair from his face.

Ari had taught him nearly everything about life since arriving at the Costa del Sol together after that night in Madrid. How dare he say such a thing? He admired Ari, his education, his thriving hotel and casino enterprise, his fast cars and even faster women. Had Tristan been wasting his time hanging about with the likes of him?

The memory pushed its way in again, the bright-colored swish of the dancer's skirt as she lured Ari into the crooked alleyways of Madrid to be ambushed by the big Romani.

Tristan swung his heavy backpack and cold-cocked the hapless brute from behind, saving Ari from a second black eye and worse.

No, Tristan thought, forcing away the parade of the past. *It can't end this way. Not over this.* They'd been friends too long, despite an age difference and Ari's perpetual recklessness, to give up on their dreams now.

They'd lived the high life here on the famous strip of white beaches, holiday resorts, and wild nightlife of the sunny Spanish coast. They'd learned from and trusted one another.

Just yesterday, Ari had pressed money into his hands to gamble in his casino—because Tristan had a knack for winning.

Never had he wanted to win more than now. He needed to persuade Ari not to set fire to the twenty floors of his own hotel above. He had to find a way to save this place and Ari, too.

"Tristan, *sale de aquí*," Ariel said with eerie calm, pulling the striker from his pocket.

Tristan didn't move. "You don't mean that, Ari. Come with me, walk away and leave this place."

Ari raised his voice, his eyes glazed with madness. "Get out of here, now! *Ahora!*" He raised the torch higher and began to open the valve, the escaping fuel issuing an evil hiss.

Tristan's lungs burned from inhaling the hot air and fumes. He backed away, staring at his friend in horror and defeat.

Then he turned and ran.

Chapter One

October, present day

Zara Marlena Flynn leaned forward in the back seat of the moving Mercedes, craning her neck to see better. Awakening from a fitful nap, she blinked away the sleep from her eyes and watched the monstrosity rise from the horizon like a charred skeleton reaching into the air. Black against the azure sky beyond it and the brilliant white beach upon which it stood, she half-wished it might be a mirage that would disappear in a shimmering wave of heat. Instead it drew nearer, enlarging itself unbidden in the car's window.

"This is my inheritance?" she asked. "It's not a hotel. It's hardly even a building." She stared in disbelief at the wall-less slabs of concrete suspended one above the other by vertical columns. Bent, uneven fingers of steel pointed aimlessly upward from its roof. "Someone's made a mistake."

"Es okay, Mees," Jorge said in his strong Spanish accent. He nodded toward the structure as he steered the Mercedes around the wide sweep of motorway that followed the shoreline. "No mistake. This is El Mirador, the property your father wished you to have."

Zara stared at the forbidding remains of the building. Clearer now, as their approach slowed to within a few hundred meters, she could see the degrading concrete, chipped and blackened with fungi from the moist air off the Mediterranean. She counted, sixteen, seventeen…twenty stories in all. She supposed there must have been a penthouse as well, which explained the flailing, loose steel poking out the top. She sank back into her seat.

"Oh, Jorge, are you sure?" she asked, her voice almost a whine. Jorge was nothing if not honest. He'd worked for Flynn Enterprises, her father's company, for as long as she could remember and now chauffeured her around the Costa del Sol to investigate this legacy left to her. Such as it was.

"Si, Miss. This is prime resort property. You must look beyond what is apparent," Jorge said, his voice matter-of-fact. "You must have *visión*, like your father. You are like him. You will see." He swung the car onto an exit ramp off the highway, circling toward the abandoned edifice onto a narrow road where the pavement gave way to crushed gravel and the ubiquitous white sand that surrounded them.

Beautiful, she'd give it that. The beach stretched for miles in both directions, equally breathtaking no matter if you looked left or right, east or west. Lapping waves of the Mediterranean Sea were ever-present. Beckoning, whispering, seducing.

She turned her attention back to the ruined structure. Though stark and sinister-looking now it must have been fabulous in its day, Zara thought. She imagined all sorts of scandalous escapades taking place here while famous celebrities vacationed with abandon. What records she'd been able to find told of the fire that gutted it decades ago, but she'd presumed it had been rebuilt at least once since then. She swallowed bitterly.

Looks like the joke's on me.

Why her father had acquired it remained a mystery. He'd

never spoken of it, at least not to Zara. It seemed she'd been left in the dark until the reading of his will. He'd purchased the property over a year ago, but beyond that, there was little information. She knew only that with the sudden loss of its CEO, Flynn Enterprises needed her.

And she needed answers.

Top engineers like Tristan Flynn didn't just have 'accidents' on the job. And he wouldn't have bequeathed a derelict old building to his daughter without good reason.

Jorge stopped the car. After their long drive, Zara stretched her stiffened legs out the rear door. As she stepped outside, the heat formed an almost physical obstacle barring her way. Her lungs balked at inhaling the superheated air. In a moment, the breeze off the water made its sinuous way toward them and she lifted her long hair off her neck to catch its cooling breath.

Sand slipped inside her sandals. Even her light-colored linen pantsuit felt uncomfortable in this hot, humid climate.

"We will stay only a moment, Miss. You are not used to the heat and we must get to our hotel soon," Jorge said, taking her arm as they stepped away from the vehicle and toward the dark hulk. There were no safety barricades or caution flags anywhere.

Zara stopped about fifty meters away, gazing at the gaping, non-existent walls, her eyes moving upward to take in the enormity of the thing. Impressive in its own way, it seemed to send echoes of seabird cries and crashing surf drifting over the deserted landscape.

Deserted. Dead. Like her father.

Dad had died thousands of miles away from his family. She'd not talked to him for months before the accident and felt robbed of the precious time she could have spent with him. The sting of tears returned, as it had so many times when she thought of her father over the past several weeks. Tears of anger as well as sadness. *He knew better than to put himself in danger on a jobsite.*

The irony of it made the news of his death on the Indonesian project very hard to take. She admired her mother for having accepted it with typical Spanish stoicism. Zara used to wonder if Mom had ever regretted leaving her homeland after marrying the dashing and enterprising Tristan B. Flynn. But of course she hadn't. They'd been deeply in love. Still, Dad had been away a lot over the years, and though heartbroken, Mom seemed to have known that one day he wouldn't make it home.

Zara stared harder at the remains, raising her hand to her brow to block the glare of the sun. She noted the way the sand drifted up the sides of the base, how the spiny steel points reached heavenward.

A few moments of silence passed with only the sound of the surf as backdrop. "Let's get out of here." *I have a hell of a lot of work ahead.* Turning abruptly, she made her way back to the cool interior of the Mercedes.

*

The car sped eastward, revealing a myriad of views of the Mediterranean coast. Shining beaches one moment, rocky cliffs the next. Villages occasionally dotted the hills to the north, their whitewashed buildings stuck like sugar cubes to the ascending hillside. Slender palm groves lined both sides of the road as they passed hotels and vacation properties.

"*Aqui,* here we are," Jorge said.

He gestured to a white archway looming on the road ahead. As they drew nearer, Zara could see the lettering carved into the archway. MARBELLA. White pillars flanked it, adorned with beautiful plantings of dwarf palms and dracaena, lush pink blooms and draping vines cascading over giant white planter bowls.

Through the partly open window she could smell their

intoxicating bouquets mixed with salty sea air as they passed. The clear blue sky made a striking background to the white, etching the name into the viewer's eye.

Once beyond the arch, they entered the town of Marbella. Resorts and residences were visible on either side of the road in continuous succession. White stucco and wrought iron appeared everywhere, as did masses of flowering plants and exotic greenery at every gatepost and doorway.

"This is beautiful," Zara said, shifting toward the window to get a better look. "What is this place?"

"Ah," Jorge answered, "Marbella. The Beverly Hills of Andalusia." He chuckled, waving his upturned hand at the townscape and tossing her a wink. *It does look a little Beverly Hills*, Zara thought. All that stucco and paving stone, sweeping staircases leading to grand entrances of homes and condominiums set into the rolling landscape. But an old-world graciousness existed here, that no made-in-America movie town could ever match.

The architecture fascinated her. She remembered with dismay the dilapidated wreck she'd just inherited. *Wouldn't it be something to restore it to its former glory?* She pondered the possibility and sheer scope of such a project. Daunting to say the least. She'd know more after the meeting with Flynn's operations manager and local development officials tomorrow.

Zara sighed. She'd given herself until Christmas to make a go of running Flynn Enterprises' operations in this area. She wasn't at all certain about leaving her familiar life in Montreal to take this on. *Have I bitten off too much?* Perhaps. But she needed to prove herself, challenge herself. She owed her dad this.

The highway began to curve inland, away from the coastline. The land to the south became more mountainous, revealing properties visible along the horizon. Jorge steered the Mercedes into the right-hand lane, preparing to exit off the main road. Soon, a sign appeared. 'Club Marbella, Zona Hotelera.' Jorge took this exit, and ascended the ridge into the hotel zone.

"Are we getting close?" Zara asked. The drive seemed long all of a sudden. It had been several hours since leaving the airport in Seville.

"*Si,* Miss," Jorge replied. "The gates are just up ahead."

As they reached the top of the road, the Flynn-built Club Marbella revealed itself in all its grandeur; elegant and exclusive with massive palm trees and elaborate topiaries bordering the surrounding white walls. The Mediterranean Sea provided a glistening canvas behind. They pulled up to the huge wrought-iron gates where huge hurricane lanterns mounted on either side glowed with welcoming light, beckoning the Mercedes forward.

They cruised up the stone driveway, bordered by beautiful green lawns and charming statuary of angels and animals that peeked out from well-placed shrubbery along its length. They stopped at the glass doors under a covered entrance, where concierges waited to retrieve their luggage. Zara got out of the car and walked into the sumptuous lobby. Ceiling fans revolved overhead in the vaulted interior, making the space humanly comfortable against the heat outdoors.

Despite the palatial environment, Zara wanted only to get to her room and a good night's sleep. While she waited at the desk for her cardkeys, a loud bang echoed from a nearby hallway followed by the rolling sound of wheels. A set of double doors swung open, and a huge flatbed cart appeared, loaded with audio speakers, instrument cases, and other equipment.

One of the two desk clerks ran toward it hollering, *"Utilice la carga."*

Thanks to her mother, Zara understood a reasonable amount

of Spanish and knew this referred to the loading dock. The clerk didn't seem pleased they were bringing in equipment through the main lobby.

"Here you are, Señorita," the female desk clerk said above the noise, handing her the newly coded cards. "Suite 1004. Elevators are *izquierda*, to your left."

"*Gracias,*" Zara said.

Turning to leave, she spotted a figure passing quickly on the far side of the equipment cart, a grey hoodie pulled over his head as if trying to escape notice. Two burly companions followed.

The desk clerk gasped. "*Dios mío.*" Wide-eyed, the girl gaped openly at the mysterious passer-by. "*Es él,* it's him! *Es Miguel!*" she exclaimed, clapping her hand to her mouth as if she'd said too much.

Chapter Two

Dave Parker paused in the doorway of Ernesto Alvarez' office, a bright and pleasant room which overlooked the garden between city hall and the market street. A long table in the centre lay strewn with blueprints, scale rulers, design notes, and drafting setsquares.

Ernesto, Flynn Enterprises' Operations Manager, stood at a light-table in the corner of the office, poring over a site plan of some kind. *At eight a.m., he'd probably been here an hour already*, Dave thought. The man seemed tireless, always arriving at the office before anyone else. Dave knocked on the open door frame. Ernesto looked up, pushing his eyeglasses into position.

"Hey, Ernie, you wanted to see me," Dave said as he entered the room, handing over a courier envelope. This came for you."

Ernesto smiled. *"Gracias,* David," he said, moving toward him to take the package. "Yes, I have a bit of a job for you."

Dave stood facing him, shoving his hands in his jean pockets. He shrugged at Ernesto's comment and flashed one of his comedic, deadpan expressions. "No kidding, Ern. I do work here, you know."

Ernesto chuckled aloud in response. Dave always seemed able to make him laugh and see the lighter side of things. He knew Ernesto liked him for this reason, among others. But then most people did. Call it a gift. He drew people to him with his disarming sense of humor and easygoing personality.

He'd worked hard to build good relationships with everyone here in the Malaga office of Flynn Enterprises. Had it been three years already? He hoped to move up in the company and had jumped at the chance to work abroad when they'd offered him a transfer from the Boston office. Though still young for an engineer, Dave felt he'd earned the respect of many senior executives and foremen on the job, including Tristan Flynn himself.

Their interactions had been few but the magnanimous Flynn left a big impression on Dave. Mr. Flynn called him 'Youngblood.' "*Hello, Youngblood, what do you know today,*" he'd say in his charming Welsh accent. "*Don't sit down, Youngblood, I've moved your chair.*"

He missed him. Sometimes painfully so. Dave was the only other person from the Malaga office who'd been to the Indonesian site. *Worse than that.* The only one who'd come back.

Ernesto repositioned his glasses as he opened the envelope and prepared to read its contents. "David, I would like you to meet with a new team member and help out with the El Mirador project. Are you busy on Wednesday?"

"I'm always busy, but I have the crews all lined up for this week so whatever you need, I'm sure I can spare some time," Dave said. "What's up at El Mirador?"

Ernesto's expression turned serious and he ran a hand through his steel-gray hair. His eyebrows knitted together as he read the delivered pages. The news didn't seem good.

After a moment Ernesto looked up, peering over the top of his glasses. "The site has a new owner, someone who's also coming to work for Flynn." He paused. "In fact, she *is* Flynn Enterprises now. She's Tristan's daughter," he said, staring pointedly at Dave as if expecting some unusual reaction.

Well, he wouldn't get one if Dave could help it. He drew in a thoughtful breath and folded his arms across his chest. "And?"

"She's also the new CEO of our division and will be heading up the restoration effort. I'm meeting with her in an hour," Ernesto said. "I'd like you to accompany her on a site visit."

"Really," Dave said, allowing a heartbeat of silence to punctuate his words. "So, now I'm a tour guide? I thought you said you wanted help."

Ernesto smiled. "You make it sound boring, David. I'm sure you'll enjoy a break from your desk. And yes, I need your help. She needs your help. Don't let her get too closely involved."

Dave frowned. "If this woman's the new boss, shouldn't she know everything? I mean, full disclosure and all."

Ernesto shrugged one shoulder. "She's travelled a long way and needs time to get settled." He glanced down at the documents he still held. "Just make sure you wear all the proper safety gear and keep an eye on her. She needs to be part of the operation, but from a distance. It's not safe."

"Why?"

"Let me show you." He motioned to the light table. Dave walked around the center table to join him. "See the foundation plan here, and here," Ernesto said, pointing to the drawing. "The mechanicals run east to west, steel studs north to south as usual. But here," he circled his finger around one corner of the building on the landward side, "this area is void of reinforcement. No pilasters or columns. This is where I think you need to look."

Dave scanned the blueprint. "Look for what?"

Ernesto pulled one of the papers from the bundle and handed it to him. "Just let me know what you find. Or, what you don't find."

Dave eyed him narrowly and took the page from him. *Oh shit, this again?* They'd talked about it many times, Ernesto's suspicions surrounding the Indonesian job and his fears that the same thing might happen again. He knew what he wanted him to look for.

"Okay, Ernie. I'll do it," Dave said with resignation. "Don't worry about a thing." Ernesto nodded as he adjusted his eyeglasses again. Dave turned to leave the room. "And make that damn optometrist appointment, man. You drive me nuts with those glasses."

Dave returned to his own office at the opposite end of the hall. Tristan's daughter. Great. A shiny new CEO stepping right off the plane and into the boardroom. She hadn't put in five minutes with the company let alone five years. How would this affect his plans for advancement? And how would he carry out an investigation while ushering her around? Some overfed, spoiled rich kid with Harvard credentials.

At least that's how he pictured her. It occurred to him he hadn't even asked her name.

*

The alarm clock next to Zara's bed began squawking at 7:00 a.m. She slammed the snooze button and dozed off again until it buzzed once more. She reluctantly rolled over and looked at the LED display, feeling the crisp linen of the sheets against her skin and the silky slipping noise of the satin bedspread as she moved. As she grew more alert, facts presented themselves one by one inside her brain. *Marbella. Spain. Costa del Sol. Meeting this morning.*

She heaved the covers aside and got up, heading for the shower. The luxurious, marble-tiled enclosure made a perfect, private incubator for her thoughts and within its confines could give free rein to the memories she'd been keeping at bay.

She missed her father terribly. He'd flown in and out of her life since the day of her birth. The Flynn banner waved on building sites, excavators and cranes all over the world. The company had a lengthy reputation for LEED-certified builds, producing high-tech designs with low-impact, earth-friendly methods. Something to be immensely proud of.

As a child she remembered marveling at Daddy's drawings, and how this fascination led to her degree in architecture from McGill University. But she'd disappointed him. He'd always expected her to take her place with Flynn Enterprises when she'd graduated, but being Zara, she'd wanted to make her own way and had chosen to stay in Montreal and work for a smaller firm. *Great decision,* she thought in retrospect. A company restructure had forced her into unemployment less than a year later.

Shit happens every day. It had nothing to do with her skill or competence. So why did she still feel so inadequate? She scrubbed her skin with the hotel-issue loofah as if to scrape away the feeling and wash it down the drain with the rest of the suds.

Her mother Marlena had insisted she come home to Barrie after she'd been laid off. She'd had no immediate options at that point anyway. Then came the day. That awful day they got the call.

Zara felt numb as the company lawyer read the will to them. The words 'El Mirador' had meant nothing to her then. When it became clear that she would need to make the trip to Spain, Marlena had chosen to let her daughter take on this new challenge of her inheritance alone.

"When you have taken care of the business, I will join you. I am longing to see home again," she'd said.

Mom still referred to Spain as home, even though she'd

lived more than half her life in Canada. A classic beauty, Marlena had done well as both a scholar and a part-time model. This at least, had been Zara's good fortune; blessed with her mother's lovely shape and features.

Too bad the good fortune hadn't extended to her hair. Unlike Mom's flowing brunette tresses, Zara's sandy-colored locks hung limp, refusing to take on even the slightest hint of curl even in the dry climate of home. As she shampooed, she feared the humidity here might drive her hair and herself to madness far sooner than the problems with her property.

*

Zara pushed the button for the elevator. Wearing black slacks and a crisp, white collared shirt, she felt sufficiently trade-certified for her meeting this morning. Waiting, her eyes focused on the gigantic urn set on the floor between the two elevator doors. At least four feet tall and constructed from glossy green marble, a spear like bundle of flowers and grasses protruded from it. *It's all about scale,* Zara thought, noting how the large arrangement commanded the rectangular space in the elevator foyer. The kinds of things a trained designer and architect would notice. The doors opened, and clutching her shiny red Fendi bag that doubled as purse and briefcase, she stepped inside.

She pushed the button for the mezzanine level where the conference rooms were located. Descending, the elevator came to a stop on the fourth floor.

The doors opened, but she didn't see anyone. As they began to close, a hand slammed between them forcing them to retract again. Zara jumped at the sudden movement, saw the flex of a man's arm and the connecting body come into view. Except for the hotel towel loosely covering his lower body, he was naked.

The man hopped into the elevator and whirled around to

look out the doors, as if evading a pursuer. Zara stared at his nude bottom right there in front of her. A great-looking one, too, rivalling some she'd seen on Ladies' Night at the Cove Club in Montreal. Still wet, probably having come from the pool or showers, droplets of water coalesced on his skin and ran in streams down his body and onto the floor.

Embarrassed, she turned her face to the wall but couldn't quite stifle a giggle. As the elevator doors eased shut he turned to face her, suddenly aware of her presence, and clutched the towel with both hands.

"*Señorita, lo siento,*" he said. "But I must get away from them." He tipped his head toward the doors, as if indicating a mob that chased him.

Extraordinarily handsome, his dark hair fell wet and dripping over his forehead. Then he shook his head like a dog, spraying her with water. She flinched and wiped her face with the back of her hand.

"Oh, *lo siento,*" he said again in a desperate voice.

He started to offer her the towel, but as she let out a short scream and put her hands over her eyes, he quickly covered himself again.

The elevator reached the mezzanine and Zara edged her way past him to the doors, shielding him from view with one hand. The man started to laugh. "*Verdad,* I am okay, really Señorita, I'm not dangerous."

"*No hay problema,*" she stammered, stepping out onto the mezzanine.

As she moved away, she heard him laugh again and shout, "What are you doing Tuesday night?" The metallic thud of the elevator doors cut off his voice. *Who the hell was that?* And where exactly did he think he would get away to, stark naked and riding an elevator on its way down to the lobby? The next people waiting for the lift were in for a big surprise.

Chapter Three

Ernesto laid his briefcase on the conference room table and began to open it when a large, balding man entered the room, making wide gestures and talking loudly in Spanish to the man following behind him. He greeted Ernesto with a hearty, *"Buenas días,* old friend. Good to see you again."

Ernesto looked up, pushing his eyeglasses into position and nodding. *"Buenas días,* Ignacio. I'll accept the friend part, but hopefully not the old,"

As the Planning and Development officer for the region, Ignacio Verrera was an irritating but necessary addition to the meeting personnel. Ernesto had dealt with him many times, as Verrera had nearly every project in the area under his direction in one way or another. A good businessman for the most part, he stood out of the way of progress and the potential for tourism dollars flowing into the Costa del Sol. But too talkative, in Ernesto's opinion. The man rambled incessantly, about everything and nothing. And he had a slimy way about him, always leaving Ernesto with the impression he'd just been in the presence of a talking reptile.

"I am told El Mirador has a new owner," Verrera said, shaking hands with Ernesto and seating himself at the conference table. "This is Bernardo, my assistant," he added, introducing the man who accompanied him.

Ernesto shook his hand. "*Sí.* Miss Zara Flynn from Montreal," he confirmed, digging out file folders, pens and his smartphone from the briefcase.

"Flynn?" repeated Verrera. "As in Flynn Enterprises?"

"The heiress herself, I suppose you might call her. Tristan's daughter. She's expected shortly," Ernesto said and nodded toward the door.

Verrera checked his watch. "Not still on American time, I hope?" He grinned.

"Canadian, actually," Ernesto said."

Verrera scoffed. "You're a funny man, Alvarez. American, Canadian. They both eat too much beef and drink the wrong wine with dinner." He chuckled outright, turning to Bernardo and encouraging him to join in the joke.

Annoyed, Ernesto peered over the top of his glasses at Verrera. It wasn't important what Verrera thought of Miss Flynn, but it would help if he had some measure of respect for her since she held the deed to the property they were about to discuss. "Thank you, Ignacio. I'm sure she'll take that as a compliment."

With a dismissive wave, Verrera turned back to Bernardo and began a conversation in Spanish. A slight, unremarkable-looking man with close-shaved hair, Bernardo wore a shirt and tie with a v-neck pullover vest. He seemed focused on Verrera's dialogue, but not particularly interested.

Ernesto glanced toward the door, wondering when Zara would make her entrance. He almost felt nervous. He hadn't seen her since she'd been a young girl, but heard Tristan talk of her many times, the pride in his daughter evident. Her excellent grades in school, her spunk at refusing to take the easy route and accept a position with Flynn Enterprises. He hoped she was equal to the task ahead at El Mirador. Her father had certainly thought so.

The door to the conference room swung open and Ernesto felt a lump in his throat as Zara walked in.

She looks so much like her mother. "Señorita Flynn," he finally said after an awkward pause, extending his arm as if to scoop her off the threshold and into the room. "Welcome. Did you have a pleasant flight?"

"Yes, thank you," Zara said, stepping forward and nodding to the two other men. She reserved a warm smile for Alvarez. "How good to see you, Ernesto. I remember you at my parents' anniversary party."

Ernesto laughed. "My, that was many years ago. You weren't more than thirteen or fourteen then."

Zara nodded in agreement. "I have a good memory. My mother and father talked of you often."

Ernesto returned a grateful smile. Her remark reminded him what a great loss they'd all suffered with the death of a man like Tristan Flynn. "I'm honored. It's wonderful to see you as well."

Ernesto began the introductions. "Miss Zara Flynn, this is Ignacio Verrera, chief development officer with the regional government and his assistant, Señor Bernardo." Ernesto paused, waiting for the man to volunteer his surname. He stood with his hands in his pockets.

"Cruz," he said, suddenly lifting his right hand from his pants pocket and extending it to Zara. "Bernardo Cruz," he finished. They shook hands, and Verrera followed suit, instead taking Zara's hand in his palm and raising it to his lips.

"Señorita," he said with admiration, "what a pleasure to meet you. I trust you are enjoying your stay so far?" He stared into her eyes, as though waiting for an answer before releasing her hand.

"So far," Zara said. "Which hasn't been long."

Verrera smiled in acknowledgement. "All in good time, then," he said, finally letting go.

As if to wipe away his sweaty touch, Zara brushed her hand on her slacks and moved toward a swivel chair at the head of the table near Ernesto. He pulled the chair out and when she'd been seated, motioned for the others to sit before taking the chair next to her.

"So you have seen El Mirador, Miss Flynn?" Ernesto said, placing a set of architectural renderings on the table in front of her. Quite taken by her appearance, he remembered Marlena as a young woman, and her daughter bore a striking resemblance. An old wound began to re-open in Ernesto's heart. *That was a long time ago*, he reminded himself.

Zara reviewed the drawings, the cover page showing a finished exterior view, complete with sunbathers and beach umbrellas in the foreground and parasailers in the blue sky above. El Mirador. In English, The Viewpoint, or vantage point. "I saw it on the way from the airport." She held up the drawing. "Are these the restoration proposals?"

Verrera spoke. "These plans were approved by my office six months ago, Señorita Flynn. Unfortunately, the project has been delayed due to certain…circumstances." She turned to Ernesto, who looked down at his papers on the table.

"Oh? What circumstances?"

Ernesto handed her copies of the papers he'd received. Sent from Vistamar Holdings, the first page described the site as an 'extreme ecological hazard,' with 'Methane and H2S gas present. Foundation considered unstable due to marshy substrate.' The existing structure had been deemed 'unsafe' and demolition was advised.

An offer to purchase filled the second page, for 2.5 million Euros, about fifty percent of Flynn's original purchase price of five million. Small change, by comparison.

Ernesto felt pity at her crestfallen look. "I know it is not what you hoped," he said. "But before we do anything, we should complete our own inspection of the site. Please don't visit there again without official escort and proper safety wear, you promise?"

Zara sighed. "Yes, yes, Ernesto, I promise." She gave him an assuring glance, like a good student deferring to the teacher's authority. Ernesto nodded and returned the papers to his briefcase, closing it with a snap.

"What is Vistamar Holdings?" Zara asked.

"A relatively new company," Verrera answered. "The municipality has used them to do survey work, generally on public and state lands. They specialize in health and safety assessments."

Ernesto coughed into his fist. "*Verdad,* that's true. But they also specialize in reclamation," he said in a flat tone. "Which is, I assume, why they are interested in acquisition."

"Who ordered this assessment?" Zara asked.

Again, Verrera interjected. "It is protocolo, for any government lands," he said. "Waterfront is ordinarily state property. A private sale is unusual." An ingratiating smile creased his round face. "Señor Flynn was very influential."

His attempt at a compliment appeared to give Zara a chill. "Why has the site not been redeveloped before now?" she asked, her voice icy.

Verrera's smile faded to a look of mild condescension. "Well," he said, tilting his head toward her. "Things here do not move as quickly as they might where you have come from, Señorita."

Zara regarded him skeptically.

Ernesto sensed her growing annoyance and decided to cut the meeting short. "That's all for today, gentlemen," he said. "Thank you for coming. We will be in touch."

Verrera seemed surprised at Alvarez' sudden dismissal. He glanced over at Cruz, but shrugged and said, "Very well. You can reach us at my office." Verrera stood and nodded to Zara. "Señorita," he said and turned to leave. Cruz followed him out.

Ernesto watched them go, then turned to Zara. "I've arranged for someone from our office to lead the site inspection on Wednesday. Why don't you go and have lunch now and I'll confirm the time with you before you finish a Spanish coffee."

"Thank you, Ernesto." She nodded toward the door. "Rather odd…that Señor Cruz, didn't you think?" She paused, looking thoughtful. "You knew my father a long time. I trust you. It doesn't seem like you trust *them*." She gestured after the two men. "I can't believe El Mirador's just been left to rot all these years. Did my father discuss his intentions with you when he bought it? Or his long-term plans for it?"

Ernesto drew a long breath and ran his hand over the leather surface of his briefcase while considering his answer. There was more to his relationship with Tristan than she knew. He thought he had put his feelings behind him when he had relinquished Marlena, his childhood sweetheart, to his friend Tristan. The better man, who had won her heart.

"Not in detail," he said. "I didn't question your father's motives, but of course we discussed his initial ideas about the restoration, how it should look, what structural concerns he had and so forth. I ordered the concept renderings you are holding at his request." Ernesto sighed before continuing. "But no, I didn't have a chance to talk with him much since. I wasn't one of the last people to see him before he died. I'm sure you would like some insight into his last words, thoughts. I'm sorry. I haven't any for you. I wish I did."

"When did you see him last?"

"About a month before he left for Jakarta, where the accident happened." Ernesto gave himself a mental kick. *She already knew that, estupid.* "He intended to go in September but…he went early."

"Who was with him?"

"Mostly the local workforce," he said. "Some of them were lost in the explosion also," he reminded her, hoping her compassion for others would help keep things in perspective.

She closed her eyes, furrowing her brow. "There must have been a foreman present? A supervisor or crew chief at least?"

"Zara," he said, his voice quiet with understanding. "Of course you want answers. We all do, but the Javanese government is making access to information difficult. It happened after-hours. Your father and the others were just in the wrong place at the wrong time."

Even as he spoke them, Ernesto knew these were unsatisfying words that didn't qualify as explanation. Silent for a moment, Zara appeared unable to think of anything else except to change the subject.

"I'll be in Marbella for a few weeks, before I go to Zaragoza," she said firmly. "I want to contribute to the company while I'm here. What is the office address?"

Ernesto reached into his jacket pocket for a business card. Taking out a pen, he wrote on the reverse side before handing it to her.

"The address and telephone numbers are on the card, but here are my home and cell phone numbers. Don't hesitate to call if you have any other questions. Why don't you come to the office after the site visit. Perhaps Thursday?"

He smiled and touched her shoulder in a fatherly gesture. He wanted to help her any way he could. As Marlena's flesh and blood, she was precious to him. "We must bring Tristan's vision to life, *si?* Don't worry, it will be *magnifico.*"

Zara smiled back. *"Si. Magnifico!"*

Chapter Four

Zara spotted Jorge reading a newspaper in the terrace café. *"Buenas días,* Jorge," she said, sliding into the seat next to him. "What's good on the menu? I'm starved."

Jorge let the top half of his newspaper flap down to look at her.

"Everything is good here. The lunch menu is always, as you say, 'a big deal' *en Espana."* He moved his coffee cup aside to make space at the mosaic tile-topped table.

Zara smiled. She remembered this from her last visit. Breakfast here consisted of not much more than coffee and a churro in anticipation of lunchtime. The locals began preparing the next day's lunch almost as soon as today's was finished. Lasting until perhaps two p.m., most everything would shut down until six or seven. Heaven help you if you were hungry before nine p.m., but booze? No problem. Beer was cheaper than water here, or even Coke. The Spanish liked to stay out late, often partying until dawn. No wonder caffeine and pastry were all anyone could stomach in the morning, she mused.

She perused the menu, and after ordering a light seafood dish and glass of white wine, she checked her phone for messages. Her mother must have texted her by now. Yup.

Land safe? How is weather, Jorge taking good care of u? Call me when you're settled, luv u. Zara replied that all was well and would touch base later. She slipped the phone back into its pocket inside her red bag.

"How was your meeting, Miss?" Jorge asked. "Did you find out much about El Mirador?"

"Yes," she said with a sigh. "And no." *I found out there are naked men running around this hotel, though.* So far, the incident was looking like the highlight of her day. "Had you seen it before, Jorge? Before yesterday?"

Jorge shook his head, folded his paper and rose from the table, as if deliberately ignoring the question. "I am off to take my cousin and her family to the beach for the afternoon, Miss. Is there anything you need before I go?"

The server approached with Zara's lunch. She shook her head. "Thank you, Jorge. I'm still a bit jet-lagged. I just need to relax for a while. You enjoy your free time."

"Si, lo haré. I will return this evening, but…perhaps you would like to come along?" he asked, as an afterthought. He seemed hesitant to leave her alone on her first day.

Zara picked up her glass of wine from the table. "No, but thank you for asking. You have a nice visit. I'm sure they're looking forward to seeing you."

Jorge donned his hat and strode away. She sipped her wine and, taking a deep breath, paused to admire the garden foliage surrounding the terrace. *So beautiful.* She wished she could enjoy it more, but after the news from the meeting she felt on edge; and more than a little nervous about the site visit.

Aside from Alvarez, she didn't know any of her father's business associates here. What would they think of her, a twenty-four-year-old rookie fresh out of architecture school waltzing in to try to run the business? Expecting her to make decisions and answer questions. She wasn't inexperienced, but far from an expert in corporate matters. She took another sip of wine and started in on her fish. As she ate, she heard a woman's brash voice coming from a few tables away.

"Wot, wi' this heat?" The woman spoke with a northern British accent. "On yer bike wi' ya. Bring me a G and T, luv." Zara looked over to see a slim, older gentleman shuffling his way toward the bar. "And some of them tapas, too, Diggy."

The man muttered in response. "Yes, yes, luv, I've 'eard you." Diggy's route steered by Zara's table. He spotted her and smiled. "What wifey wants, wifey gets!" he said, sending her a friendly wink. She watched him get a round of drinks from the bar and as he passed by on his return, placed a second glass of white wine on Zara's table next to her first.

"Young lady all on her own, eh? Well, enjoy another drink on old Diggy won't you?" he said when she looked up at him in surprise.

"Who's that you're talking to, Dig?" Zara heard the woman say.

"Just a lass needing a bit of refreshment, luv," he responded, making his return around the potted plant. "Nice-looking too, she'd best not be left on her own, I say."

Zara rolled her eyes.

"Well, why the hell didn't you invite her to join us, you absent-minded git."

Zara picked up the glass of wine Diggy had brought and followed him to his table to introduce herself. "Excuse me," Zara said and the couple turned to look at her simultaneously. "Thank you for the wine. You're quite right; I'm all on my own more or less."

She looked at the woman and smiled. Middle-aged, heavy set with bleached-blond hair teased up in a coarse beehive on the top of her head. Short tendrils of curly hair framed her face. She wore a bright floral-patterned blouse with a deep v-neck that showed off her ample cleavage. "Your husband is very kind."

"Well then," the woman said, slapping her hand on the table. "You must join us. Diggy, pull up a chair!" She made a swooping gesture at him with a pointy, pink fingernail, the shade matching her overdone lipstick. "Bette Ridley," she said, thrusting out a hand to Zara. "This here's Diggy, the love-o-me-life." Diggy nodded and smiled, as he pulled one of the wrought-iron chairs over to their table.

"Oh, I don't mean to intrude, really." She shook Bette's outstretched hand. "I just wanted to say thanks. I should be going. I've a lot of work to do," Zara said, taking a step backward only to bump into the chair Diggy had already placed behind her legs.

"Rubbish!" Bette said. "Work! Who comes here to work? You're on the beach girl, have a seat and another drink. Fancy sommat stronger than that wine, like a G and T?"

Zara sat as commanded. Bette did not appear to be the kind of woman you said no to.

"This is fine," Zara said, brandishing her wineglass. Zara hadn't anything that pressing after all and really could use some diversion. The couple seemed very familiar with the place. Perhaps she could ask them a few questions.

"What's you're name then, luv?"

"Zara. Zara Flynn. Do the two of you come here often?"

Bette and Diggy exchanged wry glances. "Oh yes, luv. Nigh twenty years now, isn't it, Dig?"

"Too right, luv. Twenty and then some, I expect," Diggy said, raising his pint glass.

"We fancy the weather here in Spain, like most folks from our neck of the woods. Mind you, not always been the Marbella, we've been all over this lot. Ibiza, Tenerife, Tangiers too. It's right upscale here though, we like it," Bette said.

"Where are you two from, then?" Zara asked.

"Egad, lass, we's from Liverpool," Bette said, swigging her Gin and Tonic with a flourish. "Paella's fine but," she leaned in a little closer, "I like to find a decent chippy, y'know… sometimes it's comfort foods you fancy, eh?" Another swig of gin. "You're from America, yeah?"

Zara took another sip of wine. "Do I seem American?" she asked innocently, always curious why anyone with a western accent was immediately assumed to be American. She noticed it often on her travels.

"Well, aren't you globe-trotting on your own, fancy designer bag and all?"

"I live in Montreal, but I was born in Ontario," Zara said, wondering what kind of reaction they'd have.

"Ah," Diggy said and brightened, cutting in between his wife's chattering. "You're from Canada then." He nodded and smiled. "Great country. Loyal to Her Majesty, bless them."

"Yes, yes," Bette said. "Royal watchers they are, follow the Tabs on the Royal family."

"So, you've stayed at Club Marbella before?" Zara steered the conversation back on track. "Which airport did you fly in to?"

"Charter from Heathrow into Malaga this time," Bette said. "And you?"

"Seville." Zara said. "I passed by something on the coast road on the way here. An old building called El Mirador. Have you heard of it?"

Bette raised her eyebrows. "Oh, yes, luv, I've heard of it and the stories 'round it, too."

"Stories? Like what?"

"Well," Bette said, glancing left and right as if she didn't want to be overheard. "They say a woman and her lover burned to death in it. Torched it was, struck by lightning I think." She looked over at Diggy, oblivious as he swilled his pint. "Dig, pay attention!" Bette snapped. "Lightning, wasn't it?"

"Naw," Diggy said, licking the foam from his lips. "Pirates, I heard."

Bette snorted. "Pirates. What are you on about, you silly mug. Lightning," she repeated, nodding with finality.

Diggy snapped his fingers. "Oh wait! Now I remember. 'Twas ghosts of Moorish sailors, avenging their conquest by the Spaniards. Sent flaming arrows from a ghost ship out at sea. Phoosh!" He raised his arms in an exploding gesture. Then he winked.

Zara smiled and looked down at her lap. *No help here.*

"Pay him no mind, luv," Bette said. "Pirates…" she muttered, rolling her eyes and shaking her head. "I tell you, a woman died there. That much is true."

At least they agreed on the fire, Zara thought. Maybe another tack. "Did you see anything…unusual…this morning?"

Bette downed the last of her G and T. "Unusual? Like what?" she asked.

"Unusual say, a naked man running from the spa to the elevator, for example?"

Bette nearly spit out her gin. "Say what? Naked man? I wish to God I had, missy! Ha!" Lowering her voice, she added, "Was he a looker, or just an old punter who lost his way to the loo?"

"Oh, he was quite good-looking," Zara said. "So was his rear end."

Bette's cheeks glowed pink on either side of her excited grin. "Why the hell didn't you chase him down, then? You let him get away!"

"I take it it's not unusual, then," Zara concluded.

Bette raised her eyebrows. "We're on the beach in Spain, dear. Wouldn't be normal without naked men around, or women and all!"

The server made an appearance just then, clearing their lunch plates and taking another order of drinks.

"Another round, sweetheart, and one for yourself," Diggy said to the girl, hoisting his empty pint mug toward her.

"Well, I really should be going," Zara said, pushing her chair back from the little table.

"Aww, we was just getting to know you, luv. Please stay."

"I promise I'll have a drink with you another time. Thank you for a lovely conversation."

Bette called out as Zara moved away. "Come to the stage show tomorrow night, dear. Sit with us."

"What's playing?"

"Don't you know? Bloody hell, it's only Mickey Mountain!" Bette said. "Miguel Montana, dear," she added, seeing Zara's blank look. "Eight o'clock."

Miguel. Where had she heard that name?

Chapter Five

It felt good on her face, the brilliant, constant Mediterranean sun. It warmed her chest, her thighs, and the backs of her hands. Zara knew she should have covered her head or worn a hat of some kind, but screw it. Back in Montreal Old Man Winter would be nipping at her heels. She'd take the sunshine as much as she wanted here and now.

She'd removed her bikini top. It dangled lazily over the back of her deck chair. The hot rays felt delicious on her bare breasts. *When in Rome,* she thought. *Or Spain.* The Mediterranean sun-seekers had no compunctions about removing their clothing, so why should she? *Five more minutes, then I'll start back to my room and get ready for tonight.*

Rested, her internal clock had finally reset itself. She'd spent most of the day lazing around the resort, venturing down to the fourth floor to use the workout room and whirlpool without running into any stray, naked men. She swam in the pools, walked around the gardens, read a book, and sipped Perrier at will. Now she lay on a deck chair on the beach. If there was any place closer to heaven, Zara couldn't think of it.

Reluctantly she reached for her top and put it back on.

Gathering her belongings and stuffing them into the shiny red bag, she departed from the beach and walked the stone path back to the resort. She found a message waiting for her at the desk from Bette and Diggy inviting her to meet them for dinner at the *Paraiso* dining room before attending the stage show.

She pawed through the clothes she'd hung in the closet, selecting a red silk dress and silver strappy sandals to wear. The dress was a deep-cut halter style top that showed off her shoulder blades, and Zara smiled as she examined herself in the mirror. Buckling the skinny ankle straps of the high-heeled silver sandals, she grabbed her trusty red bag and breezed out the door.

*

The *Paraiso* dining room afforded tranquil views of the hills to the north. Greenery and the fresh scent of flowers pervaded the indoor space and wafted out onto a long balcony. As dusk fell, thousands of mini-lights illuminated the walls and bejewelled the potted shrubs placed throughout the room. Zara saw Bette and Diggy waving to her as she entered. The dining room host escorted her to their table and pulled out a chair.

"Aww, don't you look a picture," Bette said, her voice a dove-like coo. "No more Miss Business tonight!"

Diggy stood and nodded his approval. "You look lovely, dear."

"Thank you," Zara said with a smile and ordered a lime margarita. "I feel lovely. I had a great day all to myself. Something I don't get very often."

Bette smiled. "You deserve it, luv. And it shows. Such a lovely frock."

The three of them ate happily, exchanging stories and toasting drinks. Bette revealed that she and Diggy owned a curiosity shop back in Liverpool, consigning everything from teapots to trading cards. Diggy had been in the army and enjoyed a comfortable service pension while entertaining his skeet-shooting hobby and keeping the shop running.

Before long it was show time, and the three made their way to the adjoining theater for the evening concert. The lush, padded auditorium smelled lightly of lemons and roses, the air circulating in refreshing waves from the overhead fans.

"I can't believe you've not heard of Miguel Montana," Bette said as they settled in their seats. "He's only one of the hottest acts on the continent right now."

"What are some of his songs?" Zara asked, more interested in observing the rococo-esque, pastel décor of the space than in Montana's repertoire.

"Oh, there's loads," Bette said as the lights began to dim. The rest of her words drowned in the overture music that rose from the stage pit. A tangible anticipation swelled in the room.

The emcee announced, first in Spanish then in English, "Ladies and Gentlemen, please welcome Spain's very own international singing star, Miguel Montana!"

The intro music grew louder, the audience swayed and clapped to the beat. Zara could feel an accelerating energy in the air. The curtains parted and her breath caught as dancers literally exploded onto the front of the stage, live fireworks igniting behind them as they leapt forward. Stunning girls and buff young men in sequined outfits whirled and moved to the music before pairing off, creating an entranceway for the headliner at center stage.

Excitement rippled through her as the sharp ozone residue tickled her nostrils and a riser at the back of the stage brought a silhouetted figure into view. The figure struck a pose, an arm raised pointing toward the stars on the backdrop.

The theater erupted in screams as the spotlight hit the stage and he turned his face to the audience. The star rotated his arm forward to point directly at the crowd and advanced to center stage, his athletic body moving seductively to the pounding Latin rhythm.

He wore white leather pants and a matching sleeveless tunic cut in a low V in the front, with laces criss-crossing his bronzed, sculpted chest. Grabbing the microphone, he belted out his opening song, eliciting even louder screams from the mostly-female audience.

Holy shit, Zara thought, *this guy's big news around here.* Her jaw dropped as she watched his magnificent physique writhing suggestively on stage, his appeal further heightened by the soul-ripping power of his voice. He strutted stage right, toward where she and the Ridleys sat.

Mesmerized, Zara watched him as he drew to the very edge of the stage in front of them. Her eyes followed the length of his body from his feet to his crotch, then and upward to his chest and neck. Framed by dark hair expertly gelled into place, she saw his face in startling clarity and something flipped over in her stomach.

Oh God, she knew this guy! He was the naked elevator man! She raised her hand to her mouth, a burning sensation rising in her cheeks. The ceiling fans might as well have been nonexistent as she felt the air grow hot around her. The singer kept moving to the right, the bright stage lights reflecting off his white outfit.

He continued to sing with punctuating gestures to the audience, until he looked directly at her. *He couldn't possibly see me with the stage lights on,* she thought. Yet he seemed to point straight at her, tilting his head with a flirtatious smirk on his face as he continued with his song. Reversing his steps he moved stage left, acknowledging the fans on the other side of the theater.

Girls swarmed to the front of the stage, reaching out to the sexy star. Miguel kept singing, smiling wide as he reached down to touch some of the outstretched hands at his feet. He retreated to center stage, replaced the microphone on its stand, and started in on a solo dance routine. The stage dancers spun and gyrated around him; but as good as they were, she couldn't take her eyes off the star of the show.

Intense and hypnotizing, his movements practically spelled the word *sex*. For a nanosecond, she actually thought she *smelled* sex. Zara shifted in her seat, to interrupt the feelings of arousal stirring within her.

His thousand-watt smile seemed even more brilliant in contrast to his bronze skin and shadow of dark beard on his chiselled jaw. Zara wondered what rock she'd been under to have never heard of this entertainer before. *He is drop-effing-dead gorgeous.*

The opening number ended and the dancers landed in a circle surrounding Miguel. He hit the final note while raising his hands in an almost saintly pose. He stood still in the spotlight, breathing heavily and basking in the applause of the audience. Then he lowered his arms and took a deep bow. Straightening, he waved and shouted *"Gracias!"*

The lighting changed to a fluttering aurora of color. The dancers parted as Miguel turned away from the audience and marched to the back of the stage. Zara watched his marvelously sculpted butt she had just seen in the nude a day ago swing seductively away from her. The orchestra segued into the next number and the dancers regrouped in the front of the stage.

Bette slapped a hand on Zara's arm, the applause still thundering from the opening song. "Wasn't that brilliant!" she exclaimed, doing a quick double take upon seeing Zara's face. "Dearie, are you alright? You look as though you've seen a ghost!"

Zara clasped Bette's hand and leaned in to speak in her ear. "That's the naked man I told you about."

Chapter Six

Bette sat next to Zara at a table in the late-night bar, sliding a gin and tonic toward her and insisting she drink it down. "What a shock, eh? I must say, girl, I'm right jealous of you. You've seen Mickey Mountain with his kit off! How many can say that, eh? C'mon, get that down you!"

With the events of the last few days and perhaps a little too much sun, Zara was well past caring how much alcohol she'd consumed. She took a big swallow from the glass in front of her.

"Does the body live up to the name, then?" Bette asked.

It was Zara's turn to nearly spit out her drink, as she caught Bette's joke. "Can't say. He had his meat and two veg covered with a towel," she said. Bette squealed with laughter.

Why didn't I catch on right away? Zara thought. It all made sense, now. Despite his best efforts to hide, he'd probably been spotted by some of his fans and had to make tracks out of the spa. The getaway car just happened to be her elevator. She took another gulp of her gin. Diggy sat at the bar a discreet distance from the two women, apparently content to give them a little girl time. He nursed his usual pint of beer, chatting with the bartender.

The cocktails kept coming until last call. Zara felt barely able to hold her head steady. "Oh, shit," she said, looking at her watch. "I gotta get up in the morning. I have a site visit at ten." She hiccupped and then clapped her hand to her mouth.

Bette laughed at her. "Best get you off to bed then, lass. C'mon," she said matter-of-factly and climbed down off her barstool to take Zara by the arm. "Dig, let's go, luv. Time for nighty-night." Diggy polished off his last pint, and came over to help.

"I'm fine, really," Zara said. "I can see myself out."

"Shush, girl," Bette said as she and Diggy guided her across the room toward the exit. Before they made it to the hallway, a duo of gentlemen approached. One a bit taller than the other, they both wore dark suits and bluetooth earpieces.

"Perdoneme," the taller one said. "We don't mean to intrude, but we have a message for Miss Red Dress." He gestured at Zara. She looked up, blinking, then straightened to her full height, a drunken smile pasted on her face.

"What message? It's late, gents," Diggy said, trying to warn them off.

"Lo siento, Señorita," continued the taller dark suit, the pair of them looking like secret agents. "It is late, but our employer wishes to invite you to a private party. It's very important that you attend." He held out his hand. *"Por favor,* Miss."

Zara swayed a little, supported on either side by her British guardians, and broke out in a naughty grin. "In that case, I accept."

Bette snorted and gripped her arm tighter. "No you don't, lassie. You know you shouldn't talk to strangers, and this lot's the strangest I've seen in awhile."

"It's my party and I'll spy if I want to," she giggled, jerking her arm away and stepping forward. "Lead on, double-oh-seven."

The men quickly replaced Bette and Diggy on either side of her, leaving the couple behind as they swept Zara toward the elevators.

"Mind your p's and q's, luv!" Bette called after her.

"Who's throwing this party, then?" Zara asked, looking from one dark suit to the other as the elevator rose skyward.

"A *surpresa, Señorita.* We are certain you'll be pleased with your host." They stood with their hands behind their backs, not saying any more. Zara sniffed and watched the floor numbers light up one by one as they ascended, trying not to let a spinning sensation take over her from the several gin and tonics she'd drank. The number twelve illuminated, then a letter P, where the elevator slowed to a stop.

A panoramic view of the sea greeted them as they stepped out onto the penthouse level. Starry skies and moonlit breakers shimmered through the wall of windows in front of them. The dark suits turned left and escorted her to the one and only door at the end of the hall. The shorter dark suit swiped his cardkey in the electronic lock and swung the door wide, motioning Zara to enter.

In the dimly lit room, she heard soft guitar music. She took a few steps forward, but the suits backed out into the hallway and closed the door, not accompanying her further. Zara whirled around as the door made an ominous click. She banged her hands against it. "Hey, what do you think you're doing," she shouted.

The door handle didn't budge as she pushed down on it. Panic wavered at the edges of her brain. *Doors don't lock from the outside.* Didn't seem like much of a party going either. She appeared to be alone. But then the suits did say 'private party'. *Shit.* Why did she leave the bar with those goons? *Stupid, stupid, girl.* She stood still in the vestibule, checking her surroundings. The music had a soothing effect on her gin-addled brain. Tiny pin lights in the ceiling around the perimeter of the room ahead sparkled softly. A pleasant scent filled the air. She had to do something. *Think.* She dug for the cell phone in her bag, fumbling with its contents.

"Entrez, mademoiselle," she heard a man's voice call.

"Que est?" Zara demanded, with what she hoped sounded like authority, her hand frozen around her phone. He stepped out from around the corner just a foot or so ahead of her, reaching out to clasp her wrist.

"C'est moi, mademoiselle," he said, drawing her close. Even with his face in shadow, she recognized Miguel. Showered, shaved, and dressed in something, ah, much more comfortable than his white leather outfit of earlier. "Did you *apprécier la performance?"* he asked.

Dumbstruck, Zara could do nothing but stare at him. *I'm in freaking Miguel Montana's hotel room.* Her mind went fuzzy. She should not have come, yet now wanted to stay. He had his hand entwined with hers and they stood chest to chest. He wore a spicy, sensual cologne.

"Oui, c'est formidable," she answered. "But you had better let me out of this room right now before I—"

He interrupted by pressing a finger against her lips. "I am sorry to sneak you here, mademoiselle. Please don't be angry. Won't you visit with me for a while, let me apologize for embarrassing you yesterday."

"You were the one with no clothes on," she said.

He smiled and removed his finger from her lips. *"C'est vrai,* I was. And I am sorry. I owe you an explanation."

"I accept your apology, you don't need to explain. Your fans tonight did it for you. But you should let me go now. I'm not feeling well."

He looked sincerely worried. "Then you must stay," he said. "I'll make you feel better. I'm very good at that. Please stay. Aren't you wondering how I found you?" Zara swayed a little, her resolve crumbling. He looked so vulnerable, his brown eyes brimming wide and pleading like a cocker spaniel. She had no doubt he was good at making women feel better. "I saw you in the audience," Miguel said. "But I began my research the minute you stepped off the elevator."

"Research? How do you mean?" she asked.

"I have many friends traveling with me who find things out when I ask. You *parler Francais,* then? I only made a guess when I learned you were from Montreal."

"Naturellement," she answered. "It is one of our national languages."

"Oui, of course," Miguel laughed softly, staring into her eyes. "You were very funny when I surprised you in my towel. *"Por favor,* please come in, sit. May I offer you something to drink?" Zara almost hiccupped but stifled it and realized she'd had quite enough to drink already. "Perhaps some water?" he suggested. Then he smiled and nodded. *"Si, agua.* You won't mind if I open some champagne?"

Zara shook her head slowly, taking a serious look at him, all of him. He wore a plain pair of beige khakis but no shirt. Her gaze panned over his well-defined abs, his arms, and his bare feet standing on the marble floor tiles. The most perfect male feet she'd ever seen. *Whoa, wait a sec.* Were his toenails… *painted?* She blinked, not entirely trusting her eyesight under the circumstances.

He led her to a fabulous black leather couch in the greatroom and sat her down. "Don't go away," he said, moving off to the galley kitchen. The room was huge compared to her suite and the furnishings more luxurious. Fatigue began to set in and she sank back into the comfortable couch, admiring the architectural details of the room in her mind, never quite able to shut the designer engine off completely. Miguel returned with three glasses, one of water and two of champagne. "In case you change your mind," he said, setting all three on the coffee table in front of her and offering her the water glass.

"Gracias," she said and sipped it down to help clear her head and ward off tomorrow's hangover. The liquid had the distinctive tang of mineral water.

He sat next to her and toasted his glass to hers. "Thank you for coming." He seemed a perfect gentleman. Zara tried to keep her guard up but felt her eyelids begin to droop. "I didn't have that much of a choice, thanks to your boys." She put her glass down as if to leave. "I really shouldn't be here."

"Are you truly so disappointed?" he said, looking deeply into her eyes while taking a sip of his champagne.

"Well," she said, thinking it over. She wasn't exactly guiltless in the matter. "Not quite yet."

A clever smile crept across his handsome face as he set his glass down. "I am forgetting my manners," he said, placing his hand on his chest. "My name is Miguel. I am honored to meet you, *Señorita.* I, of course, have already found out your name but want to hear it from your own lovely lips. What is it?"

"My name is Zara Flynn, architect, and as of yesterday, CEO of Flynn Enterprises," she said with a flourish of her hand.

"Welcome, Miss Flynn the architect, to my little universe for the evening," he said. "Smart as well as beautiful, I see. What will we build here tonight, do you think?"

She scanned his face at close range, noting a crooked, white scar on his face that traced a route from his upper lip to just past his left nostril. *Aha. Not so perfect after all; stage makeup goes a long way.* "Something unforgettable, I imagine."

Taking her hand, he rose from the couch, pulling her with him. "Let me show you the universe." He led her to the penthouse windows that looked out onto the waterfront. Here the beach arched into a shallow cove, the lighted windows from neighboring resorts reflecting off the water. Beyond that, the sparkling breakers of the Mediterranean appeared and disappeared against the blackness of the waves beneath them.

"This view is one of my favorites," he began. "You can see up the coastline almost all the way to Barcelona." He drew her to the fireplace opposite the couch above which hung a large painting, "This is a portrait of my home. I always bring it on tour, so that home can still be with me when I am away from it so much." The painting depicted a small harbor with fishing boats tied to a pier and seabirds floating above. Silhouettes of pine forests covered the surrounding hills.

"It's lovely," she said. "Where is home?"

"San Sebastien. On the north coast, in Basque country. Yes, it is lovely," he agreed. "Like your name. Zara. Tell me how you came to have this name."

Zara smiled, thinking of her mother. "I was named after a place near here where my mother was from."

Miguel's eyes lit up. "So you are partly Spanish, also? I should have known. *Donde?* Where?"

"Zaragoza. So she named me Zara."

Miguel smiled, apparently delighted they had a shared heritage. They stood near the wall by the fireplace. He brought his palm up to her chin and turned her face toward him. Taking both her hands in his he pushed her firmly toward the wall, flattening her against it. Then he covered her mouth with his and she felt his hand trace down her thigh, finding the hem of her red silk skirt. He pushed it upward until his hand met the curve of her buttocks.

Panic seeped into her brain, and her free hand rose to his chest in an attempt to resist. No good. Her muscles tingled and refused to work properly. Her eyes fell shut and she surrendered to the sweet pressure of his lips on hers. Then the spinning sensation returned and everything went black.

Chapter Seven

What the hell was that noise? The ringing came again. Zara unwillingly regained consciousness and recognized the sound of the telephone. Not daring to move her head, she reached for the phone and brought it to her ear. She didn't speak, but a familiar voice came over the receiver.

"Miss? It's after nine o'clock. We were to meet you at nine. Is everything all right?"

Zara winced at the sound of Jorge's voice as reality set in. She'd forgotten about the site visit today. Oh God, she felt awful. Her head pounded and nausea rose in her throat. "Jorge," she said, her voice croaky as a frog's. "I'm sorry, can you give me twenty minutes? Are you in the lobby?"

"Si, Miss. There's a Señor Parker with me. He is anxious to get going. Do you need help? I can ask the concierge to send someone up."

Oh, she felt like a four year old, having to be looked after. "No, Jorge, please—just give me a few minutes. I'll be down as quick as I can." She disconnected and turned her face into her pillow in disgust. *What have I done? How could I have been so stupid?* Brief flashes of the previous evening came back to her. How did she get back to her room? Whoever had brought her back here now knew her suite number and had access to it. She must change rooms immediately. For now, she had to make a supreme effort to look presentable in less than twenty minutes. She threw back the covers and attempted to sit.

Oh, she felt like shit. Shivering with the realization she was naked, she saw her red dress from the night before neatly draped on the back of an armchair. *How did that get there? I don't remember getting undressed. Don't think about it now--just move.*

She stood on the cold tiles and inched her way to the bathroom. Turning on the shower full blast, she let the hot water rush over her, steadying herself with one hand against the wall. In the steamy heat she tried to recall the events of the previous night as best she could. She found it appalling that she'd drank so much as to become reckless, incompetent. That wasn't her style at all. Maybe it was more than the drink. Then she remembered Miguel. So different in private from his on-stage persona—an irresistible combination of sexy and sweet. She could feel his lips against hers, the pressure of his body pinning her against the wall. And then nothing.

Did she faint? Had he slipped her something? Forced himself on her? No, impossible. He didn't seem the type. What did Miguel think of her? Had he brought her back here, to tuck his silly groupie into bed? *Groan.* How many times had he done that before?

Grasping the grab bar on the shower wall, Zara hunched over and vomited.

*

The elevator reached the ground floor and Zara stepped out into the bright morning light. She'd dressed in heavy cotton twill pants and a tank top. Steel-toed hikers covered her feet. She'd tied her wet hair in a ponytail and dashed on some makeup. Dark sunglasses concealed her red-rimmed eyes. Hardly model perfect, but enough to disguise her misery.

With her Fendi bag slung over her shoulder, she marched to the lobby where Jorge and another man waited. Based on his white skin and light brown hair, Zara didn't peg the tall guy with Jorge as a local. He stood casually, one hand resting low on his hip and the other holding a cell phone to his ear. He wore a white Henley shirt and jeans that stretched over lean, never-ending legs.

Jorge smiled in relief as he saw her approach. "Ah, Miss Zara, I was beginning to worry. Did you have a late night?"

Jorge had no idea what had gone on the night before and she felt comforted by his presence now, taking control of things. "Thank you for caring about me, Jorge. I know Mother will be pleased." She put an arm around him, truly glad to see him. When she let go, Jorge introduced her to Dave Parker, one of Flynn's construction supervisors.

Dave extended a hand to Zara. "Pleased to meet you, Miss Flynn. I worked with your father on several projects, I'm sorry for your loss."

As Zara looked at him, she couldn't remember ever seeing eyes such a shade of blue. Cobalt blue. She gave him her best business handshake, firm and confident. The last thing she wanted was to appear as hung over and out of control as she felt to this new stranger. Unlike Señor Verrera's, his hand felt warm and strong. A braided leather bracelet encircled his wrist and she caught a whiff of Lacoste cologne.

"Thank you," she said, breaking contact. The alluring fragrance made her feel even more wretched. She hoped the man—Dave, was it?–wouldn't really look at her at all, and she made a conscious effort to look away.

"Shall we?" Jorge prompted, ushering them out to the waiting Mercedes. He opened the back door of the car to let Zara step in, followed by Dave. A utility van bearing the familiar Flynn Enterprises logo idled in the entrance roundabout, carrying a crew of specialty-task team members. The two vehicles pulled in tandem out of the roundabout and down the long drive to the main road.

Heading west on the highway, Zara tried to settle herself enough to rest her head and close her eyes for the duration of the drive. Her thoughts trickled back to Miguel and how exciting the night had been until she passed out. With regret she thought of Bette and Diggy, how they'd tried to stop her from going along with the dark suits. She must remember to call them tonight and apologize for her abominable behavior and let them know she was all right.

She needed to see about getting another suite, too. *Damn.* There hadn't been time to deal with that this morning. She hadn't left any valuables behind, so a room change could wait until she returned. She should call her mother too, come to think of it. She'd almost nodded off when Dave spoke up.

"So how do you feel about stepping into your father's shoes?"

Zara started at the sound of his voice and turned to face him. "Pardon me?"

"Oh, sorry, I didn't mean to disturb you. Please, go ahead and rest. We've got at least a forty minute drive."

Zara leaned her head back on the plush leather headrest. "Thank you," she said, running her tongue over her lips. They felt so dry. "My apologies. I did have a rather late night." She reached in her bag for some lip gloss.

As she slicked it on, she felt Dave watching her intently. Her lips shined with the honey-colored gloss on them. After a protracted moment that fell just short of gawking, he looked away out the front windshield. "Jorge," he said suddenly. "Could you put on some music, please? Not too loud." He turned back to Zara. "Is that all right?"

She nodded. Dave relaxed on his side of the rear seat. Soft

Latin jazz began to play from the car speakers. They drove on for a bit. Dave sat with his hands folded across his stomach, his head turned away from her, concentrating on the view as the car cruised westward. "To answer your question," Zara said. "I feel great about it. I'm proud that he considered me worthy of following in his footsteps. I didn't work for him because I didn't want people to think I couldn't make it on my own as an architect. Now it's different, they have to respect me."

Dave turned to her. "That includes me. You're officially my boss now, as I report to the CEO of the company."

She kept silent for a moment then let out a light chuckle. "I think I like that idea." She looked straight ahead out the front window. "So where are you from, Dave, and how long have you worked for Flynn?"

Dave shifted in his seat, turning his attention to her. "Well, I've been with the EU division for three years now. Before that I started with the company in the Boston office. I moved to Boston to attend MIT, but originally I'm from Thunder Bay." She looked sharply at him. "You know Thunder Bay?" he asked.

"I was born in Barrie," she said, a smile tugging at her lips.

Dave smiled back. "Small world, eh?"

"Certainly is, eh?" They both laughed, sharing the private joke, neither admitting how the 'eh' phrase was both defining and insulting at the same time. Zara leaned back, enjoying the moment of comic relief. It lessened the throbbing in her head. "What do you know about El Mirador?" she asked.

"Well, from what I've read, it was a busy holiday resort for the jet-set of the day," Dave said. "It went out of business about twenty years later. It reverted to the government after that, but was never re-developed. Something about a succession plan, the land rights tied up in legal bullshit…sorry…red tape," he corrected. "For a long time. Flynn acquired it last year and as far as value, well, you'd have to talk to the local real estate people. Waterfront property must be quite valuable, though. You'd think the government would have forced some action on it, but things move pretty slow here."

Zara frowned. She'd heard that before. "So, what has Ernesto said? Why did he send you on this trip?"

Dave looked out the window, as if pondering how much he should reveal. After a moment, he inhaled deeply and then spoke. "I'm sure you've noticed the crew traveling with us? The reason El Mirador shut down all those years ago wasn't lack of business. It burned down and the structure is unstable. That team following us is forensic experts. They'll have priority over investigating the site, not us. We're to keep our distance and do what they say. Understand?"

Zara blinked at him. "Why wouldn't I understand?"

"I didn't say you wouldn't," Dave said, frowning. "Just letting you know there's something more than just a derelict old building there. Keep a safe distance, wear your safety gear, and don't go poking around where you're not supposed to."

Zara looked away, annoyed. Who did this guy think he was? This was her property, not his, not the company's. She had more right than anyone to go 'poking around.'

She bit her lip, stewing. Why would Tristan have put this burden on her shoulders? There didn't seem to be an upside to this deal, other than the location. The structure in ruins, potential trouble in the foundation, and millions in projected restoration costs. She almost didn't want to know any more. She had the whole of Flynn Enterprises to worry about, now. Perhaps this project could wait.

The cars slowed as they approached the turnoff to El Mirador, which swung to the right and beneath an underpass to the seaward side of the highway. Then they hit the gravel path that she and Jorge had taken just days before as they neared the site. In the morning light, the wreck looked a little different. The exposed steel glinted in the brightness and bits of exterior finishes could be seen on the lee side of the building. Patches of pink and aqua stucco remained, studded with mercury-glass mosaic tiles embedded in spots here and there.

The van parked closest to the building. The four men inside pulled out equipment from the rear and side loading doors. Dave opened the trunk of the Mercedes, which had pulled in behind the van to take advantage of what shade it afforded. Inside were hardhats, reflective vests, safety glasses, and gloves for each of them. Having read the report thoroughly, Dave also brought SCBA packs in case the air quality was compromised. He went to confer with the task team as they unloaded specialized monitoring equipment, hand-held scanners and sample containers. Everything fitted into packs that the team could carry on their backs. They moved to the base of the structure and scanned the entrance point. Signalling the all-clear, they waved the others to follow.

Safety gear in place, they crossed the threshold of the main floor. Zara noted the blackened teleposts laid out in a regular grid pattern and the central concrete column of the elevator shaft. As they approached the dark, open maw of the shaft, Chavez, the team leader, directed a high-powered beam into its depths. A flurry of coos and flapping wings surged from the opening, barely missing the heads of the seven people standing near it.

Dave and the task team ducked as the pigeons scattered past them. When the air cleared, the team began fitting up portable lights inside the elevator opening and a ladder to descend to the floor below. Pigeon dung stuccoed every visible surface. One by one they climbed down to the basement level, the dark and dampness palpable as they went. Chavez' handheld gas monitor showed acceptable levels and he gave the okay to remove the air packs. *Thank goodness*, Zara thought, releasing the mask and its accompanying air cylinder from around her face. *Uncomfortable enough in here without those.*

A barrage of odors assaulted them. Seawater and its fishy smell seeped in through the foundation and left puddles all over. The sounds of dripping water echoed all around them and there were underlying scents of sewage and sulphur. And something else. Zara couldn't quite put her finger on it.

The light-mounts on their hardhats activated in the darkness. Square concrete columns fanned out in every direction in the same grid pattern as the floor above, charred from the long-ago flames. The team moved toward the far corner where columns seemed to be missing. The outer wall on that side had narrow horizontal openings near the top. *For ventilation, no doubt,* Zara thought. As they were above grade, subdued daylight filtered through the openings.

Halting a few meters from the area the team motioned Zara, Jorge, and Dave to stop where they were. The four crew members advanced further, setting down their equipment packs and placing sensor stakes into the soft earth around the perimeter. The LED modules at the top of the stakes began to illuminate and cast a greenish light over the scene. The center of the earthen area appeared rough with an almost mushy surface, like oatmeal.

The team spread out, taking readings and samples and sealing them in containers. Zara watched them proceed in methodical fashion, moving from left to right, scanning the area. It measured approximately ten meters by twenty meters as best she could judge. She saw Dave from the corner of her eye, also watching the men's movements. The strangely familiar odor was stronger here. She closed her eyes and sniffed, concentrating on it. As the crew moved toward the corner farthest from them, Dave suddenly took a step forward.

"Chavez," he called out. "Hold up. What is that?" Zara looked toward Chavez, ahead of the other men and about ten meters away from where she stood. He reached down with a gloved hand to pull on an object sticking out from the lumpy earth. All of them drew in a gasping breath.

It looked like a human bone.

Chapter Eight

"Teléfono, Sr. Bernardo Cruz," the concierge announced. Bernardo looked up from his seat on the plush lobby couch, folded his magazine, and tossed it on a side table before walking over to the house phone by the front desk. Standing five foot six and slight of build, Cruz kept his head shaved, which exposed his protruding ears. He didn't care. The convenience of the close-cropped style made up for it.

He'd been married once to a local girl his parents had arranged for him, the daughter of family friends. But things did not go well. He discovered his interests were not suited to marriage and left her after only a few years together. His Catholic community openly disapproved. He shook off the memory, reminding himself that he was here now. He nodded to the concierge and, picking up the receiver, spoke softly into it.

A smile came over his face as he listened to the comforting voice on the other end. *"Si,* I will be off work by five. I will be there. Until then, *adios. "* He hung up the receiver, holding back his joy at hearing his lover's voice. It had been a long time and looked forward to resuming that relationship while they were both in the same city.

Bernardo took the elevator down to the parking garage. Driving out into the sunlight, he checked the time. Verrera didn't like his staff being late for anything. He made sure that his laptop case lay safely stowed behind the passenger seat. He relaxed into the driver's seat and exhaled, pulling out onto the main road that led to the business district.

He couldn't help but smile at the thought of his date later tonight. His thoughts trailed back to the last time they were together, so exciting, so intense, so dangerous. But for now, he had better think about finishing his report. He'd stayed at the resort for a few days, following and observing the Flynn girl, as Verrera had requested. He knew Verrera desperately wanted possession of El Mirador. The project had been expected to continue under general contract with Flynn, or put up for public tender. His boss became angry upon learning the property had been willed to a family member of the Flynn empire.

So far he didn't have much to report, other than a party had left for the site this morning. He recognized Zara of course and assumed the men in the utility van were Flynn employees, but wasn't familiar with the chauffeur or the other young man who accompanied them. He'd taken plenty of photos though, certain that Verrera would find them interesting.

He pulled into the parking lot of a small centro comerciale. A bay on the far end of the center housed the field office, where a number of businesses leased warehouse and office space. With his laptop case under one arm, he locked the car and walked through the glass doors into the dingy office. He moved past the unattended front desk to the two smaller offices beyond it.

"Ah, Bernardo," Verrera said, as Cruz entered. "Did you have a nice 'vacation,' up at Club Marbella?" he asked with a grin.

"It was very interesting." Cruz set his laptop on one of the chairs facing Verrera's desk. "You might even say intriguing."

"Oh," Verrera said, closing the newspaper he'd been reading. "Tell me more. Was the decor appealing?"

"Very much so," Cruz said, thinking of the photos he'd captured. He sat down in the other chair and from a side pocket produced a USB drive that he handed to Verrera. "For your viewing pleasure."

Ignacio cradled the stick between the thumbs and forefingers of both hands. "What other observations have you made? Does the heiress seem at all interested in the investigation?"

Bernardo scratched his right ear then folded his hands across his lap. "Señorita Flynn left this morning with a crew from the construction office, along with her driver and another gentleman. They headed west in two vehicles at around nine-forty. Before that, Miss Flynn stayed out very, very late last night, attending a stage performance after dinner. She seems to have made the acquaintance of a middle-aged couple from England. They don't appear to have any connection to her or her father's company."

Ignacio tapped the memory stick on the table, thinking. *"Esta bien,"* he said. "Anything else?"

Bernardo continued, "The daytime she spent indulging herself. The spa, the pool, the beach, et cetera. With the exception of last night, since our meeting on Monday she's laid pretty low. Hard to tell her intentions at this point."

Verrera seemed to consider this. "Well, all we can do is continue to observe. Will you return to the resort tonight?"

"Yes," Bernardo said. *But not for the reasons you think.* He zipped his laptop case closed and stood up. "May I use the other office? I have some paperwork to take care of before heading back."

"Yes, by all means. We'll see you back in the Malaga office on Friday, *si?"*

"Friday," Cruz replied as he crossed the hall.

Verrera rubbed the memory stick between his fingers as if unsure what to do with it. After a long moment, he slipped it into his breast pocket and gathered his things. He left the office without another word.

*

The team stood by the van, facing Dave and Zara. As the midday sun glared down on them, Zara removed a glove to wipe her forehead and upper lip. Dave ran his fingers through his tousled forelocks, sweat creating wet tendrils around his forehead and temples. Zara viewed him from the corner of her eye, grateful for her dark glasses. Not only to hide her bloodshot eyes, but so that Dave couldn't tell she was looking. She took a swig from her water bottle. *He's actually pretty cute.* Clean-shaven, with a nice straight nose and deep dimple lines set around his highly kissable lips. *Kissable lips? What am I thinking? I have to work with the man.*

She watched a bead of sweat trickle down his chest, exposed now that he'd undone the buttons on his shirt. His sleeves were rolled up, revealing well-muscled forearms.

This made her think of Miguel, his bronzed chest glistening in the dimmed lighting of his penthouse. *Oh God, I still have that to deal with.* Would his henchmen be looking for her again? Had they been the ones to undress her and put her to bed last night? The idea made her sizzle with embarrassment. She had to get that room changed right away.

"The core samples will tell us more about residual chemicals or trace elements that may have contributed to the structures' degradation," Chavez said. "The sensors showed no radioactivity. But as you all saw, the area had the characteristics of quicksand." He gestured to the bone sample they had pulled from the soggy earth, now encased in a sealed plastic exhibit bag. "All this will be taken to a forensic laboratory at the University and we should have some preliminary reports by the end of the week. That's it; we'd all better get out of this heat."

The crew piled in to the van and made ready to leave. Jorge waited in the Mercedes for Zara and Dave. The two climbed in, grateful for the air conditioning already running inside the car. They slumped into the back seat, feeling wilted from the heat. Zara reached into her bag and pulled out a facial towel from a small travel pack. Removing her sunglasses, she wiped her face with the soothing cloth.

"Mind if I try one of those?" Dave asked.

Zara looked at him in surprise. "Oh, I'm sorry, of course. Here," she said, reaching for the travel pack and offering it to him.

"Wow, those are quite a set of red-eyes you've got there. Allergies?" he asked, pulling a towel from the pack.

Zara quickly put her sunglasses on again. "Uh, no. Just…some new eye makeup I think I reacted to," she said, swallowing the little white lie.

Dave put the towel to his face. "Uh-huh. I must have tried the same brand, then. I think it was called Jack Daniels."

Great, she thought, looking away from him. *A smart-ass. Please, God, tell me I don't reek of booze.*

Dave grinned. "How about a drink when we get back to the resort," he said. "I'll buy."

Chapter Nine

The Ridleys stood at the front desk. "You see, she's not checked out, luv. Just out for the day, sightseeing or shopping or sommat. Didn't she have a work do this morning?" Diggy asked.

Bette looked unconvinced. "So she said. I don't like it, Dig. I felt awful leaving her to go off with them gents. Scary blokes; gave me the creeps and all, didn't you?" She stamped her plump foot and spun around to face the desk clerk. "Are you sure she's not left us a message, dear? The Ridleys, room 620?" She wagged a pink fingernail at the girl behind the counter.

"No, Señora," she replied in her soft, Spanish-accented English. "No messages. Would you like I call housekeeping to see if she leave 'do not disturb'?"

"Can you do that?" Diggy asked.

"Certainly, Señor," she said. "Just one moment." She went to a side desk and picked up a house phone.

"Thank you…Delores," Diggy said, reading the brass name badge pinned to her uniform vest, nearly bursting its buttons keeping Dolores' ample bust line in check. "Calm down now, sweetie," he said to Bette.

Bette scanned the lobby, as if expecting Zara to pop up from behind an armchair or pillar.

"Señor?" Delores had returned. "Housekeeping say they make up her room already. She not there, but all things are undisturbed."

Diggy sighed. "All right, can we leave her a message then, please?"

Delores brought out a pen and notepaper, foil-stamped with the Club Marbella logo. He scribbled a few lines then slid the note back to her. Delores filed it into slot 1004.

"I've asked her to call us the minute she gets in," Diggy said to Bette, putting an arm around her and steering her away from the desk. "Don't worry, luv."

Delores turned back to her computer and began typing. 'Señor and Senora Ridley asking questions. Flynn not yet returned. Housekeeping says room undisturbed.' She poised her index finger over the keyboard. Then she hit send.

*

The phone chirped a text message alert. Zara trudged across the tiled floor of the opulent lobby and ducked toward a couch at the sound of the message coming in. She plopped down on the overstuffed cushions and pulled out the phone. 'Everything OK? Not heard from you in two days, please text back ASAP.'

Feeling guilty she'd not contacted her mother sooner, she replied: 'Hi Mom yes all OK, very hot here had site visit today, explain more later, call you 2nite.' At one o'clock in the afternoon, Zara already felt exhausted. And hungry. Without any breakfast before her exit this morning, her stomach growled and her head pounded furiously.

She couldn't get out of the Mercedes fast enough. Mr. Smart-Ass had teased her then had the nerve to ask her out for cocktails. He didn't quite get the idea that Tylenol and a nap ranked higher on her list of priorities at the moment than his riveting company. She decided to order room service, but first things first. She headed for the front desk.

"Perdoneme," she said, attracting the attention of the desk clerk. Different than the one who'd checked her in. *"Hablas Inglés?"*

The girl nodded and said yes. Zara smiled, hoping to create enough rapport with her to get what she wanted. "I need to see about possibly changing rooms, would there be anything else available? I'm in 1004 right now."

The desk clerk blinked and frowned. "We are heavy booked, *Señora.*"

"Are you sure you couldn't move me a little closer to the fourth floor, nearer the spa and gym?" Zara asked. "I'd be happy to take something smaller." She checked the girls' name tag pinned to her chest. 'Marta.' "I'm Zara," she added, extending her hand and smiling the best smile she could muster. Marta blushed a little and returned the handshake.

"Marta. Let me check reservations," she said and turned to her computer. She appeared to be running the desk alone. "There is a standard room on five. Not as big as what you have, but with sea view."

"That will be fine. Can you send someone to move my things in about an hour?"

"Sí, Señora. One hour. I will send the new cardkeys at that time."

Zara tapped the desk counter with the palm of her hand and smiled. *"Gracias."* She felt instantly better having resolved her security concerns.

She turned to leave when Marta called out, "Por favor, you have a message, Miss." She plucked the card out of slot 1004 and handed it to Zara.

Shit. She chided herself inwardly for neglecting the

Ridleys. *"Muchas gracias,"* she replied and hurried to the elevators.

*

Dave settled himself in the front seat of the Mercedes after seeing Zara through the entrance doors to Club Marbella. "Thanks for agreeing to drive us today," he said. "I'm glad Ernie thought to ask you. Sure beats riding in the company bus." He thumbed over at the Flynn vehicle exiting onto the main road heading east.

"De nada," Jorge said with a tip of his chauffeur's cap. "I have worked for Señor Flynn for many years. It is my privilege to escort Miss Zara wherever she needs to go."

Dave thought about Zara as Jorge spoke her name. She'd been mostly silent on the ride back to the resort, having turned down his offer of a drink. More alcohol was probably the last thing on her mind. She looked hung over, but apparently didn't subscribe to the hair-of-the-dog philosophy.

Having a good view of her from behind as they left the resort that morning, Dave couldn't help remembering how nicely her hips fit into the work pants she wore. Not many women could pull off looking sexy in a pair of Dickies. And the tight-fitting tank top did little to hide her traffic-stopping figure as she'd trooped up and down the site with the rest of the crew. So much for the plump Daddy's girl he'd imagined.

He resolved to ask her out again another time. Her refusal only served to encourage him. That long silky ponytail. The smooth, creamy skin with tawny freckles dotting her nose and cheeks. And those mesmerizing green, albeit bloodshot, eyes. He'd never expected such a delightful new boss.

Whoa, big fella, Dave thought, his fantasy screeching to a halt. *Bad enough getting involved with a co-worker and here you are lusting after the boss.* To top it off, she was Tristan's daughter. A man he respected. And damn it, still felt responsible for. He jolted himself back to reality. "So how long would that be, your employment with Flynn Enterprises?" Dave asked, realizing what an opportunity he had in talking to someone close to her.

"Oh," Jorge said in a drawn-out voice. "Ever since Marlena recommended me, when Miss Zara was very little."

"You mean Mrs. Flynn hired you?" Dave asked, curious now.

Jorge tipped his head from side to side in an ambiguous response. "Not hired. Recommended. But Señor. Flynn never denied his wife anything, so here I am, twenty years later," he said with a chuckle.

Dave smiled, glad to be getting on with the likeable little man. "You were close friends with Mrs. Flynn?"

Jorge looked at him slyly. "*Naturalmente,*" he said. "We are cousins."

It was Dave's turn to laugh. *Jackpot,* he thought. A treasure trove of information on the lovely Miss Zara Flynn. "Does she plan to stay in Spain, now that she has a role with her father's company?"

Jorge shrugged. "I know Marlena plans to come here when Miss Zara is ready for her. They are going to Zaragoza for a while and visit family. After that, they planned to return to Montreal. Whether Miss Zara will choose to live here is up to her."

Dave looked out the front window, watching the scenery rush by. "Is that how she got her name, after Zaragoza?" he asked.

"Si, you are *muy perceptiva.*"

Dave laughed. He'd been called a few things before, but never 'perceptiva.' He glanced sideways at Jorge and saw the man smiling to himself. Did he surmise Dave's interest in his pretty second cousin? If so, he seemed to approve.

Chapter Ten

Ignacio closed the door to his home office. His wife and children were not home yet, but he pulled the venetians shut over the windows just in case. He had to think of a way to dislodge Miss Flynn from the El Mirador project. He'd waited too long and invested too much to lose it now. She seemed a nice, educated girl and he didn't wish to see her harmed or mistreated in any way. Who knows, she might even prove to be a good company executive. But El Mirador was his. It had to be. He sat down at his computer and looked through the photos on the USB that Bernardo had supplied.

A shot of the Mercedes driven by Flynn's man, Jorge Allesandro. Next. Distance shot of Allesandro and Flynn standing fifty meters away from the site. Next. Zara Flynn walking into the Club Marbella entrance. Next. Flynn swiping the cardkey of room 1004. Next. Flynn at lunch in Cafe Marbella. Next. Flynn now seated at another table with two unlikely looking characters. An overweight woman in a garish outfit and a thin gentleman with combed-back grey hair. This must be the English couple Cruz had mentioned. Were they friends, relatives? He zoomed in but didn't recognize either of them. He sent the image to a printer on an adjoining desk, then clicked Next.

Uninteresting photo of Club lobby. Next. Photo of stage entrance, the marquee above it reading 'appearing this week only, exclusive...' Next. View of suite balcony...presumably 1004? Looked like a long drop to the ground from there. Verrera's twisted mind formed potential scenarios by which to solve his little problem. The next several photos were of the hotel interior and he skimmed through them not seeing anything of note. He glanced over at the printer tray which now held three or four sheets, and rose from his desk to retrieve them. He couldn't afford to leave anything lying around.

He enjoyed his home office with its dark wine-colored walls, white trim, and deep bookcases. A humidor which carefully stewarded his collection of exotic cigars sat hidden inside a bar cabinet. His one weakness. He picked up the prints and returned to his desk. Scrolling through more pictures, he saw the same elderly couple with Flynn in the dining room. Eating, laughing, and drinking. Next.

Ignacio froze. There, in full view of the frame, was Zara Flynn, reclining in a deck chair, her hair flayed out across the towel on which she lay. The photo appeared taken from above, giving the image a voyeuristic edge. Save for her bikini bottoms, she was naked. He stared in disbelief at the almond-white skin, glossy lips, and most noticeably, the round, exquisite breasts in the center of the frame.

"Dios mío," he swore in a whisper. He wrestled with his emotions, knowing he should click to the next image immediately. But his mouse pointer stayed poised over the print command. In a weak instant, he clicked it. No sooner had he released the mouse button when he heard the latch on the front door give a click, followed by the swishing sound of it opening. With his car parked on the drive pad, they all knew

he was home. His family came bumping and crunching into the front room just outside his office.

"Padre! Padre!" he heard his daughter Daniela squeal as she rushed for his office door. He quickly shut off the computer's monitor and snatched the USB stick from its slot. The door burst open. *"Tu est aqui!"* Daniela exclaimed. She bounded into the room with her usual excitement whenever daddy came home early. He often worked late or went away on business. She jumped into his arms, nearly knocking the USB stick from his hand. In a moment his youngest daughter Ericka joined them, clapping her hands, anxious for her turn on daddy's lap.

"Niñas, niñas," he said. "One at a time. Come, let's go to the kitchen and help your mother." He lowered Daniela to the floor and slipped the stick into his pants pocket. He took Ericka by the hand and led them both out of the room, closing the office door. He'd come back to tidy up, he assured himself. In the kitchen, his wife Carmella carried shopping bags in from the car. The girls rushed past her into the back garden to play.

"Hola, my dear," Ignacio said, taking the bags from her. A short, portly woman, Carmella brushed a strand of curly dark hair off her forehead, looking flushed from the heat outdoors and from carrying the heavy bags.

"There's more in the car," she said in a monotone, breathing heavily from exertion. She set her purse down on a kitchen stool and began to unpack the first bag.

"I'll get them," Ignacio said, recognizing all too well the annoyance in her voice. Unlike his daughters, Carmella did not appreciate him coming home early. It seemed to upset her routine, so he was eager to do whatever she asked to avoid an argument. He retrieved three more bags of groceries from the rear seat of her little car, an economic Punta sedan he'd picked out for her two years ago. Carrying them to the kitchen, he set them down on the counter opposite to where Carmella stood pulling out cans and packages to be stored in the pantry. Ignacio did the same with his bags.

"What are you doing home at this time of day," she asked with her back turned to him. He thought for a moment how he should answer to elicit the least hostile response.

"Oh, well, we were working in the field office today, at the Centro. We finished early, but it became too late to drive all the way back to Malaga. So here I am." He paused. "The girls seem pleased."

Silence prevailed for a few minutes as the two of them worked in the kitchen without speaking. "I think you should work more," Carmella finally said. "I can handle things here. You're just in the way when you come home early."

Ignacio sighed. He worried about her being overweight and with high blood pressure. And being irritated all the time, as she seemed to be lately, wasn't helping her health. Like Bernardo, his family had 'arranged' his match for him. Carmella's father was well off, so the pairing should have been prosperous. However, apparently not so prosperous as she'd hoped, always hinting at getting a bigger house, better cars, better clothes and toys for her and her daughters.

She'd nearly died when Ericka was born. The pregnancy and delivery had taken a toll on her precarious health. His father-in-law being sick and elderly now, it was unclear how much estate might be left to Carmella when he did pass on. "I don't do it very often, cariña. I'm not in the way. I am trying to help you. You might have fainted carrying in all those bags. You should work less and let me do more," he suggested. This statement he felt smug with, having thought of it so quickly and coming off more brilliant than he'd intended.

Carmella set a can of tomatoes down on the counter, ever so firmly, making a statement without actually slamming it and turned to face him. "I said, I can handle things. I don't need you underfoot. I need you out there, earning more money."

Ignacio looked down at his hands, which he placed flat on the counter while he took a few deep breaths so that he could speak calmly. "I am at the top of my wage scale with the county. Until next year's budget, I won't see a raise. You know that. I am working on some things. I've only just started getting my own contracting business off the ground. It takes time, We have to be patient."

She tapped her pudgy fingers on the marble counter top. "*You* have to be patient, but I don't. I shouldn't have to be. My father can provide for me just as well or better than you."

Ignacio ran his hand over his bald head, knowing his efforts to avoid a quarrel were in vain. "Cami, your father is not well. I can provide for you and the girls. I always have and I always will. And it will be even better when I close some deals with my business. I don't want you to worry about this anymore and I don't want to argue. It's bad for you." She sniffed and turned back to her groceries. Ignacio put away the last of the items from his bags and went to find his girls. He hoped they'd not overheard their conversation.

He went to the garden, but they'd either gone back inside or to the park down the street. *They would have told us if they'd done that*, he thought. They were raised to always let Mama and Papa know where they were and to ask permission. He went around to the front of the house but didn't see them there either. He noticed some trampled flowers near the front steps. He bent down to straighten them and pick off the crushed blossoms when a scream echoed from inside. He bolted through the front door, vaulting toward the sound of his daughters who'd found their way back to the kitchen.

Carmella lay on the floor on her side, her eyes rolled upwards and hands pressed to her chest. Ignacio called out in anguish and Daniela knelt beside her while Ericka stood with her back against the kitchen cabinets, terrified.

"Madre, Madre," they screamed. He grabbed for his phone and dialed the police, fighting back tears.

Chapter Eleven

Sitting in an armchair in her new room, Zara hung up the phone. She felt better now, having assured the Ridleys of her welfare and apologizing for not calling them earlier. Under the circumstances, they understood she had a job to do and forgave her for rushing out of the hotel without contacting them that morning. She also let them know her new room number so they could call her any time or stop by. Bette sounded pleased at this news. She seemed to have taken a maternal interest in Zara that grew stronger by the minute.

She set her empty glass of Perrier on the room service tray next to the remains of her lunch. Having something to eat killed her hangover but made her sleepy. A nap wouldn't be out of line. Lying on the bed, she pulled her cell phone out of her bag and dialed her mother. It would be very early in the morning in Ontario.

"Hola," came her mother's pleasant voice, in spite of the early hour.

"Hi, Mom."

"Oh, darling, it's you, *gracias a Dios. Como esta?*"

"Fine, Mom. Sorry for not calling before—you got my texts?"

"Si, querida, I'm so glad to hear from you. How are things going, are you getting much done? What you wanted to?"

Zara sighed. "I'm working on it, Mom. And I'm going to Dad's office tomorrow to get familiar with everything. We went to the site this morning. You won't believe what we found. It's a wreck. The structure is decades old, looks like a bomb hit it, and, get this. It's sitting overtop quicksand. I don't understand why that could be. They'd know where quicksand was before starting construction. Did Dad ever talk about El Mirador, or explain why he bought it?"

"Not really," Marlena answered. "But you know your father, always 'the big picture.' He never did anything without purpose, even if it wasn't obvious to others. I knew you would inherit the business and with it a number of different properties, but remember, as a private sale El Mirador is yours outright. You can do with it whatever you wish. Dad had a reason and I'm sure you'll figure it out. You're a brilliant young woman. I should know. I raised you."

Zara laughed. "Can't argue with that, Mom. I'll keep you posted. Jorge says hi."

"Muy bien," Marlena said. "I hope he'll come with us to Zaragoza. He needs to see his mother. Juliana hasn't been well."

Zara hadn't thought about Great-Aunt Juliana for a long time. While true she was Jorge's mother, the family did not speak of it, Juliana being unmarried at the time of his birth. A bit of a recluse, she didn't attend family functions. All she remembered about Juliana were the burn scars on her face and arms and how they'd frightened her as a child.

"Have you booked your flight yet, Mom? Because I'm not sure how soon we'll be able to do that, get away to Zaragoza, I mean."

"I'll wait to hear from you. Dad has open tickets with the airlines, remember? *No hay problema*."

Right, Zara thought. *No problema.* "Okay Mom. We'll talk to you soon, bye."

"Adios, querida."

Zara disconnected. 'Dear one,' her mother called her. She thought of when she was a little girl, playing in the sandbox, going to the park, riding a bicycle. Before long she drifted off to sleep, her cell phone still cradled in her hand.

*

At six o'clock, Delores logged off her computer, tidied up her papers, and put fresh mints in the tray at the end of the reception desk. She called into the back room, *"Adios,* Marta, I'm leaving for the day."

A mumbled, "Okay," issued from inside. Finished her day shift, Delores took her handbag from under the counter and headed down the hallway to the staff lounge. A few people lingered there, watching soccer on the lone TV in the room. Two of the housekeepers giggled over a trashy magazine. Each said hello as she passed by.

Delores opened her locker and took out a duffel bag and sweater. She checked her makeup in the room's only mirror and slicked some extra lipstick on. Then she checked the duffel bag to ensure she had everything she needed for the evening ahead. Perfume, shoes, sexy outfit; all in place.

She zipped the bag closed, grabbed her purse and sweater, and left the room. She walked past the housekeepers again on her way out, hiding a smirk as she entered the corridor, looking both ways to make sure no one saw her before pushing the button for the service elevator at the end of the hall.

*

Seeing as his boss had left early, Bernardo shut down his

laptop in the scrungy cubicle across from where Verrera had been working. No reason not to get a head start on his evening. He'd tried hard to put it out of his mind for the afternoon, focusing on his work to pass the time. But no use. He felt he would scream if he sat still much longer. The temptation of what awaited him back at the Club made him itch in places that couldn't be scratched in public.

He looked forward to leaving the spare, stuffy workspace of the field office. The main office in Malaga was much nicer, much more appropriate for a savvy young executive on the rise such as himself. He planned to be a great deal more than Verrera's assistant. Only a stepping-stone to better things, he'd performed some distasteful duties already in the six months he had been at this job. Soon it would be time to move on.

He slipped on his blazer while looking at the pale, undecorated walls. *Yes,* he thought. *I will be moving on very soon.* He locked the metal and glass entrance door as he went out. He got into his car, started the engine and the air conditioning. Feeling uplifted, he peeled recklessly out of the parking lot, screeching his tires and leaving tracks as he started back to Club Marbella.

The sea looked lovely in the late afternoon sun. Salsa music boomed from the stereo and Bernardo tapped his fingers in time on the steering wheel, thoroughly enjoying the triple sensations of wind against his face, sun on his shoulders, and pavement disappearing beneath his wheels. He felt free and light, as bubbly as the breakers striking the beach below. He slowed as he approached the gates of the Club, but sped up on the long driveway to the hotel, just for effect. He entered the underground garage and cruised to his parking stall, braking abruptly to squeal the tires.

His studio room on the eighth floor boasted a terrific view, but it held no interest for him tonight. He showered and changed clothes, then went about arranging everything just so. A vase of red roses on the nightstand, chilled bottle of champagne set out on a console table with two glasses. He shut all the blinds and draperies, dimmed all the lights, and left the room. He discreetly dropped one of his cardkeys in the green urn by the elevators and went down to the cocktail lounge to wait.

*

The third floor didn't have any guest suites; mostly utility and storage rooms, a few salons, and a larger open space for hospitality receptions. Delores stepped off the service elevator and walked down a corridor toward an inconspicuous door at the end. She swiped her magnetic badge that hung on a lanyard around her neck in the cardlock. The room stored linens, pillows, and draperies piled in neat stacks on aisles of shelving.

At the end of the center aisles, a few shelving units had been removed, creating a hidden rectangular space against the back wall of the room. Draperies hung around it like Persian rugs in a marketplace. Parting the curtains, Delores stepped inside the little makeshift room where a low divan overflowing with satin-covered pillows of all shapes and sizes had been placed. The striped damask upholstery of the divan further enhanced the middle-eastern look. Delores set down her bag, withdrew an outfit, and began to change.

With the costume in place, she arranged herself provocatively on the divan, pleased with how the gauzy veils and skimpy, spangled, two-piece suit looked on her. She'd also brought a burner and some incense sticks, which she lit and set on the floor. Inhaling the heady smoke, she relaxed and waited for her guest to arrive.

*

Bernardo rubbed his palms together to dispel the familiar

sweaty fear that overtook him on occasions such as this. The ride up the elevator seemed interminable. He'd downed a few scotch in the lounge, and felt well-primed for his rendezvous. His guest liked to arrive unobserved. He approached the door to his room, took out his second cardkey, and entered. The lights were out, but a figure stood silhouetted in the window and he went toward it. Reaching out, he touched her on the shoulder and she turned to him, the face in shadows. Bernardo knew exactly who it was.

"Michelle," he whispered softly.

"*Si,*" the husky voice replied.

She'd changed her hair since last time, and wore a white gown with a deep split in the skirt, revealing a leg sheathed in gartered stockings that shimmered in the dim light. He touched her leg, ran his hand up her thigh, and pulled her upper body close with his other arm. He felt drunk just smelling the dark and spicy cologne, his lips searching in the dark.

They kissed, slowly at first. They moved toward the bed, where Bernardo turned her to face away from him. He unzipped the lovely gown, slipped the shoulder straps off, and let it fall to the floor. Then he pushed her roughly onto the bed on her stomach and began to undo his pants. His gaze fixated on the shapely buttocks in front of him as he ripped the condom from its package. Fully aroused, he ran his hands across her taut cheeks and placed himself between them. He held on to her somewhat bony hips as he fucked her hard in the ass, interpreting the low grunting sounds she made as feminine sighs of ecstasy.

*

"What do you mean, he's not coming?" Delores demanded. Her cell phone had rung after waiting about an hour in her drapery-walled enclave. He'd been late before. Not unusual, having to dodge photographers and reporters wherever he traveled. But never had she received calls from his bodyguards, expressing his regrets that he must reschedule their 'appointment.'

"Well, tell him he can go straight to *el Diablo,*" she snapped and hung up. *"Madre de dios,"* she muttered and punched one of the silky pillows on the divan. She threw another one across the little room where it struck one of the drapes and knocked it down. More than angry, she now felt silly dressed in this get-up, waiting for no one. Where the hell was he? After all she'd done for him. Did he think she appreciated being called so late last night, just to come back to work and tuck Little Miss Red Dress into bed? Silly cow who couldn't hold her liquor.

Delores had managed to usher her back to the tenth floor unnoticed, deposited her into her room, and undressed her. She'd even thought about stealing the pretty red dress, but reasoned that it couldn't possibly have fit her. *From now on,* she thought, *he'll be the one to dress up and wait for me!*

Chapter Twelve

Miguel waved to Zara from the boat. He wore his all-white suit that she'd seen him in on stage, his hair blowing in the breeze off the Mediterranean. She waved back to him as best she could, keeping one hand on the tow handle, skiing bravely behind the churning wake of the speedboat.

It was her first time on water skis. Miguel had taught her in just one afternoon, being an expert and having won many competitions. Suddenly she hit the cross-wake of another craft that passed by and tumbled into the water. She tasted the salt on her lips, heard no sound as her head slipped beneath the surface.

In an instant, she felt Miguel's arms around her. He'd cut the motor and dived off the stern of the boat to get to her, ensuring her safety. They bobbed up and down in the crystal blue sea, splashing each other playfully and laughing while he held her close. He kissed her and licked his lips, making a show of how good and salty she tasted. She splashed him again and they swam back to the boat together.

The next thing she knew, they lay naked on the swim deck of the boat, she on her back looking up at his face framed by the incredible blue of the sky. Under the hot sun, his hands stroked her nude body and she giggled, embarrassed that the driver might see them. Of course, he was paid not to see them. Why should she worry, or care?

His lips were about to touch hers, his face so close she could feel the heat from it when a booming claxon sounded. Startled, Miguel covered her body with his, bending his head down against the curve of her neck. Then she saw the boat driver clearly, looking straight at them. She felt guilty, brazenly lying here in the open air with this crazy man. Especially when the driver looked exactly like...Dave.

Zara woke with a rushing sound in her ears, like an ocean wave that receded as she gained consciousness. With her heart pounding, it took a moment to recall her surroundings. The room became lighter as she opened her eyes and realized she'd been dreaming. She expelled a long breath of air as if she'd just run a marathon. In those first few seconds, the dream seemed incredibly clear. The exciting touch of Miguel the Latin superstar followed by the stern reality of Dave Parker the construction boss.

Oddly, she'd felt guilt in the dream sequence, having the distinct impression she somehow belonged to Dave and shouldn't have been messing with Miguel or anybody else. In the next instant, the whole scene faded and she couldn't remember what she'd been dreaming about at all. She rolled over and checked the bedside clock. 5:05. Was that a.m. or p.m.? Pale light emanated from the windows. *Must be morning. I've slept for almost twelve hours.* She closed her eyes again for a few minutes before forcing herself out of bed and into the shower.

Knowing better than to skip breakfast this time, Zara went down to the café and ordered a plate of sliced fruit and a croissant. She'd filled a travel mug with coffee from the buffet and waved when Bette and Diggy entered the café. Bette bustled over, wearing a bright green print dress with matching green slingbacks. Diggy followed her in his ever-casual style, brown slacks and a short-sleeved cotton shirt. They joined her at the next table, pulling their chairs close so Bette could interrogate her on her whereabouts Tuesday night.

"So, what happened then," she asked in concerned excitement. "So glad you're safe, luv. Worried sick, weren't we, Dig? Who were them gents?" Bette even wore matching green-rimmed sunglasses, completing the English tourist look. Plenty of English people roamed the Costa del Sol. Only a short flight from Heathrow it made a popular destination for Brit vacationers. You could tell by the fish and chip shops in every little town on the highway. Zara sipped her coffee, knowing she would have to come clean with Bette sooner or later. No time like the present.

"They work for someone in this hotel," she said. "Someone very famous who apparently felt inclined to invite me to a party."

"Give over!" Bette said in a low voice. "Not our Mickey, surely. You're joking!"

Zara took another sip from the travel mug. "Let's just leave it at, someone male, and musical, and performing in this hotel. And no, I did not get taken advantage of."

Bette's mouth dropped open. "Why the hell not, if it was flaming Mickey Mountain taking the advantage!"

"Bette," Diggy cautioned. "Mind yourself, now."

Bette elbowed him. "I'm just having a little fun and all. What was he like, then, eh?"

Zara shook her head. "Nothing happened. We had some champagne and I…blacked out. The next thing I knew, I woke up in my room."

Bette looked genuinely alarmed. "Well who put you there then, if you passed out?"

Zara shrugged. "I must have walked. I'm fine; nothing happened, really." She left out the waking up naked part, which still made her burn when she thought about who might have undressed her. Jorge waved to her from the café doors. Zara pushed her plate away and stood to leave. "I've got to go, folks. My ride is here and I'm going to work today," she said, feeling quite proud. She had a purpose here after all, despite the shenanigans of the first few days.

Diggy stood. "Glad to see you're all right, lass. Call us anytime if you need sommat. Go build something pretty, eh?"

Zara nodded as Bette chimed in. "Let's plan a trip out to Gib on the weekend. Got some lovely pubs and shops there. We'll arrange it while you're at work."

"Sounds fine," Zara said as she hurried to make an exit from the café and her overprotective guardians.

The route into Malaga's city center veered away from the sea, and soon, tall buildings blocked the view. Jorge parked the Mercedes in front of a modern office building a few blocks off the main thoroughfare. Though not owned by Flynn Enterprises, the company leased an entire floor in it where Ernesto and others ran the Andalusian operations. Her father also kept an office here in which she could work.

In the back of her mind, she knew she really hadn't come to grips with her father's death. Too many unanswered questions left her unable to achieve closure. These people at Flynn probably knew more about him and the circumstances of his death than she did. They took the elevator to the eighth floor and saw the steel double doors bearing the Flynn logo cast in metal. Zara thought the hard-edged industrial look was quite impressive, despite being only a regional office. London housed the HQ, but offices similar to this one existed in Hong Kong, Sydney, Montreal, and Boston. Jorge pulled on the long vertical handles of the door, crafted from solid bar stock and polished to a fine sheen. The doors parted and Zara entered the room.

A half-dozen people surrounded the reception desk. All of

them turned as she walked in, including Ernesto. He started everyone in the room applauding. They were all smiling, apparently anticipating her arrival. Ernesto came over and took her hand. *"Buenas días,* Miss Flynn. I've been telling everyone about you and they're anxious to meet Tristan's daughter. We're a close-knit group here. A testament to him."

He began to introduce her. Armand, the accountant; Pilar, the round-faced receptionist with dark hair cut in a chin-length bob. Two draftsmen, Chico and Efren, sat next to each other at their CADD stations. A few younger women, file clerks and a proposal writer, also nodded in greeting. Dave stood in the doorway of an adjoining coffee room. His dimples creased as he smiled at her. He folded his arms and leaned against the door frame.

"Hi," he said simply, no further words necessary. An unspoken bond had already begun forming between them. She tilted her head as if seeing him in a new light.

"Hi." A good deal more than 'cute,' she liked his longish, sandy brown hair that curled up at the ends, making him look more like a surf bum than an engineer. And the neatly trimmed sideburns he'd given himself, she hadn't noticed those the other day. But she did remember those eyes. Cobalt blue, staring disapprovingly at her in a dream. The image fragment flashed in her brain, unsettling her. She broke her gaze away from him.

He spoke to Ernesto. "Well, let's give the lady a tour, shall we. I'm sure she'd like to see her office."

Ernesto nodded. "By all means. Zara? This way." He gestured to his left down a short hallway. Zara followed Ernesto to the room at the end, with Dave falling in behind her. She sensed him only a few feet away and found herself wondering if she'd dressed appropriately. She'd chosen a navy blue skirt, the kind with the flippy edges at the hem that swirled back and forth as she walked and a short-sleeved v-neck sweater. Did the neckline reveal too much cleavage? Her favorite silver necklace with the dolphin pendant dangled just above it. A smashing pair of navy pumps showed off her legs.

Dave nearly bumped into her as she stopped short inside the doorway of Tristan's well-appointed office. She floated to the center of the room, turning a slow three-sixty to view the walls, adorned with a strategic mix of paintings, awards and architectural drawings. A huge mahogany desk commanded the space, paired with an oversized leather swivel chair. A large flat screen monitor rested on the desktop.

Under a window sat a familiar-looking drafting table. On either side of it stood matching mahogany bookcases filled with volumes of reference books, technical manuals and architectural publications. She longed to sit at that table, as if the vellum sheets laid out on it called to her along with the large carousel of pencils and tools next to it. She walked over, reached out, and touched all the items. Dave and Ernesto exchanged glances.

"Can I get you a coffee, ma'am?" Dave asked, breaking the silence. He said it in a deferential tone, but tongue-in-cheek, underlining the fact she was now his boss. She laughed and spun around to face the two of them, a big smile on her face.

"Yes, please."

The three of them spent the morning reviewing project plans, each at various stages of completion. A nearly finished high-rise in Estepona. An apartment building here in Malaga, as well as a shopping complex. Renovations for two resorts on the Mijas-Costa, an upgrade to the stadium of the Plaza de Toros at Ronda...and El Mirador.

"The forensics reports are not yet in," Ernesto confided. He, Dave, and Zara sat at a long table surrounded by drawings and photos. Dave had taken a chair next to her and she felt his arm touching hers as they leaned their elbows on the table.

She tried to ignore it, but the heat spot it created kept drawing her attention, as did the return appearance of Rene Lacoste. *Damn, he smelled good.*

"What were your impressions of the site?" Ernesto asked.

"We stayed out of the way as much as possible, as you asked," Dave said. "But when we found the bones, we got a little closer. I'm not an anatomy expert, so I couldn't tell you if they were animal or human. The fact they were near the surface suggests the victim was recent, or the bones were placed there from somewhere else."

"And did you find evidence of explosives?"

Dave sent him a dark glance. He shook his head. "The team scanned for residual chemicals as well as live sets, mines. If a bomb went off there, it was a long time ago."

Ernesto looked at Zara overtop of his eyeglasses. "What were your feelings, Zara?"

She sat with her arms folded, taking in all the information. *Explosives?* Her lower lip protruded in thought. "It felt staged."

"How so?" Ernesto asked.

"The quicksand, it didn't fit. Who would build over top of it? And why? It's as if the quicksand was *put* there, although I don't know how you'd do that. To disguise something."

"Quicksand does occur naturally in a coastal environment," Ernesto said. "Particularly at low tide. Underground water, salt water separates the sand granules from each other making the surface unstable."

"Could it have developed after the original completion of the building? The water level might have been different thirty or forty years ago," Dave offered.

Ernesto considered this. "*Tal vez,* maybe. But it would still be possible to build around the area. The depth of quicksand wouldn't be great."

Zara leaned forward. "As I said, the question is why? There are miles of beach there. Why that spot?"

"A very good question, Zara. Now that you're in charge, how would you like to proceed?" Ernesto asked.

"Well, I thought I'd be in the resort business when I found out the property belonged to me. Can we find more information on what the place was like in its heyday? It looks so lonely and abandoned. It's fascinating to think about what went on there. I'd like to see it restored." She sighed, knowing how unrealistic that sounded. "But if you feel it's better just tearing it down for public safety reasons, I'm okay with that." She held up one of the project photos. "We can always build another hotel, right?"

"Some research would be prudent, in any case," Ernesto said, looking to Dave.

"You want me to do the research?" Dave asked, sounding surprised.

Ernesto nodded. "You have access to all the online archives. Try the tourism office, too. Zara, would you like to get started on some drawing projects in the meantime?"

"I'd love to."

"Good. I think Chico is running into some issues with the Estepona high-rise," Ernesto said. "Why don't you meet with him and see what you can do on that one to start with."

Zara nodded, but added, "I think Dave has more important things to do than fact-find. How about we do some internet searches first?" She looked over at Dave, who didn't seem too thrilled with his assignment. In truth, she wanted a little space from him. He was a distraction. She really needed to focus on some work right now.

"Honestly, Ern, I really should be checking in with my crews. Pilar can help with the web search," Dave said.

Ernesto turned back to the papers in a file folder in front of him and sighed.

"I thought I'd do the research myself," Zara said. "That computer does work, doesn't it?" She thumbed in the direction of Tristan's office next door to Ernesto's.

"Of course, wireless, too," Ernesto said.

She gripped the armrests on her chair and stood up. "I can have a word with Chico, get my feet wet in that, and get the background on El Mirador at the same time. You needn't bother Dave. I'm sure he's tired of babysitting me."

Dave stood as well. "You're the boss," he said, sounding relieved. "Ernie, I'll call in later and let you know if I'll be in tomorrow. I might have to go out to Gib and see suppliers."

"Well," Ernesto said, closing his file folder. "Looks like the two of you don't need any motivational speeches. *Seguir,* carry on." They both turned to leave.

As Dave held the door for Zara, she asked, "What's 'Gib'? Some friends of mine wanted to take a trip there."

"Oh, I meant Gibraltar. Have you not been there?" he asked.

"I think you know where I've been, Dave. I only got here four days ago and so far I've spent two of them with you," she said flatly.

"You mean it's your first time to Spain? I thought your dad would have brought you here on vacation. Gibraltar, you know, the Rock?"

Of course she'd been to Spain before. She'd never heard Gibraltar referred to as 'Gib' until today and felt a little foolish as the realization dawned on her. "Oh, right. To be honest, I never did stop there," she said, formulating a defence.

One corner of his mouth curved up in a half-smile. "That's a shame. One of the great wonders of the world, you know. Anyway, it's British territory and a major shipping port. So it's easy to get building supplies, electronics, booze, anything. And really good fish and chips. Maybe you'd like to come along. Plenty of boutiques there, too."

She shot him a patronizing look as she felt a mild burn rising in her cheeks. He appeared to take great pleasure in making fun of her. He backpedalled, saying, "But you could always hang with me at the timberyard if shopping's not your thing. That's always exciting."

Zara considered it, leaving a purposeful silence hanging in the air. "I really should get to work. I wouldn't want these good people to think I'm the Princess CEO."

Unaffected by the awkward pause, Dave cocked his head to one side, conceding her point. "I suppose not. Well, I'll be heading out first thing and I'd have to go right past your hotel anyway." He reached into his shirt pocket for a business card and handed it to her. "My cell number's on the card. Give me a call around eight a.m. if you change your mind."

She took the card and read it. It had the Flynn banner at the top, his name in the middle, and contact info at the bottom. 'David J. Parker, CET, B.Sc., Project Supervisor.' She noted 'smart-ass' was not part of his title. "I'll think about it. Thanks."

Dave smiled again, turned, and went down the hall to his own office. Zara made a mental note of which door was his. It might be interesting to see how he kept his work area. Neat freak or pack rat? Flapping the card thoughtfully against her palm, she watched him and his cute butt disappear into his office, then turned and went back into her own. *My office,* she thought. She'd have to get used to that idea. She could never replace her father, but she would damned well give it her best shot.

She sat at the drafting table and looked at the drawings still taped to it. Elevation views of a new project. The title block read '*Los Teides.*' A circular kind of building with three stories and a cone-shaped roof. A few loose sheets lay on one corner of the table. These seemed more like sketches, perspective renderings intended for proposal purposes.

To her surprise, they appeared to be residential plans. Large private villas that looked like homes for the very rich. Strange. Her father didn't ordinarily do private residences. The titles written in stylized architectural lettering at the bottom right of each drawing caught her attention. *'La Marlena'* read one. Her mother's name. *'La Dulce Zara'* read another. Were these her father's pet projects, designing homes for private clients? Or perhaps for the very people he'd named them after?

Beautiful, but no indication that the designs were actually under construction. Just ideas on paper. Great ideas; Eco-friendly. That was her Dad's work, for sure. She decided they would look great framed and on the walls of the office. She slipped the drawings inside a large envelope, placing it in the top drawer of the desk. Now she could have a chat with Chico and begin some real work.

Chapter Thirteen

Bernardo listened to his voicemail with alarm. Verrera left a choked message that his wife was in the hospital recovering from a heart attack and that he wouldn't be at the office until further notice. He'd taken his daughters to a relative's house out of town and had spent night and day at the hospital. He asked Bernardo to go to the Malaga office in his place. Too bad. He was having such a nice morning remembering last night's exciting events. He chose to have lunch at a favorite bistro across the avenue from the Club.

From the Malaga office, he wouldn't be able to monitor Flynn's private life for the next little while. But there were more important matters to attend to. He sipped the last of his coffee, then reached for his cell phone again and scrolled through his contacts to find 'Michelle.' His pulse quickened just seeing the name. He began to text. 'Gracias for last night, miss u already, can't wait til Friday.' Send.

Next, he called the office and left a message saying he couldn't be there until the morning to cover for Verrera. That way, he'd have time to pay a visit to El Mirador this afternoon. He placed his napkin over his plate, picked up his laptop case, and headed for his car.

*

Delores worked her afternoon shift, her anger still smoldering at being stood up the previous night. She supposed she should have expected it. She wasn't exactly the only doll in the toy box, after all. She'd been responsible for most of the 'play dates.' How many meetings had she arranged for him? Twenty? Thirty? Always a different girl, always exactly as requested. Perhaps his people would get in touch with her today, to explain and apologize and arrange an alternate meeting to make it up to her.

This made her feel a bit better. Despite her anger, being in the company of the fabulous Miguel Montana was not a privilege to take for granted. She knew she would make herself available whenever he asked. She appraised herself in the staff lounge mirror. What was not to like? Brunette hair, flashing eyes. Large breasts firmly displayed in a pushup bra, creating noticeable cleavage even in the plain-collared shirt and vest of the Club uniform. She undid just one more button, hoping the manager on shift wouldn't give her trouble about it and marched out to the front desk.

She greeted her co-worker, Linda, who had come on the morning shift to relieve Marta. *"Buenas tardes,* Delores," Linda replied. "I'd button up that shirt if I were you. Garcia is on today." Delores ignored her and logged in to her computer terminal, scanning the reservations for the day. Her instant messenger icon flashed and she clicked on it right away, hoping to see the news she wanted.

Instead, it read 'arrange meeting with Flynn.' This annoyed her. They wanted to know all about the Flynn girl but couldn't be bothered about her, Delores. Her 'dates' were in exchange for her not-so-ethical services to Montana's goons, yet they'd cancelled on her without a thank you or an apology. She opened the booking screen and scanned the room assignments. When she saw suite 1004 was vacant, she began to panic. Where was Flynn? Had she checked out? She searched for the surname and found it under 514. Who had made the room change? Marta? She sniffed.

An idea began to form in her head. Since Miss Flynn already occupied a new suite, they wouldn't have any idea that 1004 was vacant until she told them. If they wanted to know her whereabouts so badly, maybe she could set up a surprise for them and get a little revenge in the process. She typed a one-word reply. 'When.' She stared at the message window, fingers poised over the keyboard. She hit send and waited. Her mind raced ahead, thinking her idea through. They would go to 1004, expecting to meet Flynn. Instead, they'd find her. But what if they spotted Flynn somewhere else in the meantime? Well. Delores would just have to make certain that she wasn't.

The messenger window flashed. 'Weekend. Reply with details, call for escort if necessary.' Delores licked her lips and typed, 'Understood.' Now she could work out the details of her little plan.

Linda elbowed her to signal the manager's approach. Delores closed the chat window and returned to the reservation screen. She kept her back to Garcia, the evening manager, as he emerged from the back room. Hopefully he'd ignore her if she ignored him. "Linda," he said, lingering over the syllables of her name as he wiggled his way behind the counter.

A fat, boorish man with greasy hair and bad manners, few of the staff could tolerate Garcia. Fortunately, laziness numbered among his attributes, so while on shift he spent most of his time in the back room eating, watching TV, and occasionally checking the security monitors. Empty potato chip bags, candy wrappers, and at least three empty cola cans typically remained in his wake. If you wanted to be left alone, a bag of sweets or box of pastries placed in the back room would make him disappear for hours. Today however, he sidled up to Delores as she scrolled through various screens on her computer.

Leaning in he said, "Good evening, Delores," right in her ear. Too close, he almost made her skin crawl, smelling the sickening combination of hair grease and old-fashioned cologne.

"Señor Garcia," she said tonelessly, trying to sound professional despite her repulsion.

"I see you've worn my favorite outfit today," he said, peering over her shoulder to get a better look down her unbuttoned shirt. Nauseated, she shifted away from him.

"Just doing my job," she replied, moving away to refill the brochure rack in an effort to put some distance between them.

Garcia backed off. "And you look very good doing it. Don't forget to run the weekly check-in list. Tomorrow's Friday and a lot of timeshare people will be arriving." With that, he disappeared into the back room again. Delores and Linda exchanged looks, both finding Garcia equally distasteful, and went back to work.

*

A few kilometers away from the turnoff to El Mirador, Cruz concluded that Verrera's plan must be executed without delay since Verrera himself wouldn't be available while his wife was in the hospital. Hired as Verrera's assistant just six months ago, Bernardo Cruz played the part of an unassuming clerical aide well. He did his paperwork, made phone calls, conducted research. He supposed in a way, that's exactly what he was doing right now. But the work wasn't related to Verrera's day job as the regional development officer. Although Verrera had control over many project approvals, he wanted the one thing his desk job couldn't offer—real wealth.

On the side, Verrera had started up his own contracting business, buying up supposedly unwanted, unviable properties and proposing his own development bids, which he could quickly rubber stamp through the approval process. He could then build anything he wanted and reap the rewards of income-generating projects built on real estate bought for next to nothing.

Of course, to keep his government job he couldn't be known as the owner of the new company. A phony front became necessary. Enter Bernardo Cruz. A man of many talents, Cruz could secure investors. He could acquire business licenses under assumed names. He could remove obstacles that stood in the way of progress. A mysterious man named Salvatore Rodriguez legally owned Verrera's new company, Vistamar Holdings. And the properties it bought were unwanted because Bernardo made them that way.

A prime retail space lay abandoned because of 'structural compromise.' An apartment building in a desirable district suddenly became vacant due to 'pest infestation.' And an old hotel on a deserted strip of beach declared unsafe to rebuild? Sat on an unexpected deposit of bitumen sands, potentially yielding millions of barrels of crude oil once properly extracted.

Verrera had almost cried when Tristan Flynn bought the site, furious that his prize had been snatched away from him. Flynn became an obstacle to Vistamar's progress and needed to be removed. Cruz turned out to be very helpful in this regard, too. Yes, Verrera was being clever, but not as clever as his assistant. Once the projects were underway, Bernardo could pull the rug right out from under Verrera's feet. Because Salvatore Rodriguez was one of Cruz' many aliases. He had collected long ago the necessary credentials to simply appear one day and become Señor Rodriguez, leaving Verrera out in the cold.

Only one obstacle remained; neither Cruz nor Verrera had counted on the young Miss Flynn becoming involved. *No matter*, Cruz thought. She could be taken care of just as easily as her father had, if it came to that.

He parked his car at a viewpoint off the main highway. He approached the remains of the building on foot, the sun throwing its lonely frame into silhouette as it lowered itself to the west. Making poor El Mirador completely undesirable required an additional touch. The leg bones and ribs from the unfortunate Toro killed last month at Ronda were just the beginning of the scare tactics Cruz had up his sleeve. Posing as an eccentric tourist, he'd talked the local butcher into cleaning and drying the bones for him as a souvenir of the spectacular bullfight. They'd made convincing remains of a victim overcome by the quicksand.

But when he followed Flynn's little convoy yesterday, he'd known the team would soon discover the quicksand wasn't real. A pocket of bitumen lay close to the surface; no concrete foundation had been poured in that area. Cruz had done his homework. Years ago when they found it necessary to expand the original building, the supporting columns had simply been constructed around the troublesome patch of muck. Bernardo discovered that by pumping salt water from the nearby sea underground to the pocket, the sand and oil mixture became 'bloated', losing cohesion and causing the appearance and characteristics of quicksand.

Up to now, the ruse had kept most intruders away. But for Flynn to lose interest in it, El Mirador must die completely. He slunk closer to the columns surrounding the bitumen pocket, carrying his laptop bag. Moving into the shade, he set the bag down carefully and opened it.

He'd removed the computer from the case the night before. Six brick-shaped objects took its place. In another compartment lay a remote device and stubs of wire. He worked efficiently in the shadows, molding the putty-like substance on the surrounding columns and inserting the detonator wires.

One more of his many talents; he'd been an army cadet as a young boy and became fascinated with munitions. A kind of hobby, he learned the history of explosive devices and materials, exactly how they were used and for what purposes. The knowledge came in very handy.

By the time he'd finished, the sun dipped below the horizon. He planned to stay until full dusk before leaving, just in case. He sat down in the shade and leaned against a loose block of concrete. He wished he hadn't quit smoking. Now would be a good time for a cigarette, if he weren't surrounded by C-4 plastic explosive compound.

He thought about Michelle and when he would see her Friday night. When he became as rich as he planned to be with Vistamar Holdings, he could have a different partner every night, if he wanted. But none compared to Michelle. He would do almost anything for another tryst with her. As darkness closed in, Bernardo picked up his now empty laptop case and climbed the hill to the viewpoint.

Chapter Fourteen

Zara enjoyed giving her Spanish a workout in teaming up with Chico. Between Spanish, French, and a smattering of English, they communicated well. They seemed to understand exactly what the other wanted to achieve with the project and Zara proved helpful in solving his problem with the exterior detailing. She volunteered to do the final elevation views and spec out the finishes and materials while he concentrated on the mechanicals. Thanks to the networked computers, she could access Chico's files and work on them in the same CADD program that he used.

She saved the revised files into the proper directories and began a search on El Mirador. Her first keyword matches brought up articles on Flynn's purchase of the site. She printed those and tried different keywords to obtain more historical information. Typing in 'El Mirador Hotel' and 'beach resorts 1960s' returned some interesting photos. At last, she had some images of what the place had looked like and printed those off, too. Alongside the photos were a few entries about the fire, similar to those she'd read before leaving home. She scanned them, noting a repeated name. Businessman and owner Ariel Torres had perished in the incident, leaving no legal will. With no succession plan, no heir apparent, the future of the property remained in limbo. Mr. Smart-Ass had been right.

On a whim, she typed in 'quicksand' to find out more about its composition and where it would be likely to occur. She found that what Ernesto said was true; sand particles, infused with enough water, separated to the point where friction no longer existed between them to compact and create a solid surface. It would suddenly give way to external pressure ,and objects exerting that pressure--like a person stepping on it-- would sink fast. Hence the term 'quick'.

Even more interesting was the good deal of folklore written about it—how it appeared profusely in stories and movies for a period of time then became cliché and not used. In addition, the chances of people or animals sinking slowly to their deaths in quicksand appeared to be extremely unlikely, as the quick area was rarely very deep. A red flag raised in Zara's mind. This could mean the bones they found were not the remains of some unlucky person stepping in the wrong place at the wrong time. They could be, as Dave suggested, a kind of decoy to confuse and deter anyone from discovering the real answers.

She printed off this information then turned her attention to the older photographs of the Andalusian coastline. In black and white, the familiar structure of El Mirador appeared clearly in the distance, while period-costumed beachgoers cavorted in the foreground. The facade of the building screamed 1960s with its diamond-shaped exterior panels. Concrete balconies protruded outward from the windows, staggered from one floor to the next, The topmost floor appeared to be all glass. Instead of a typical mid-century commercial flat roof, the glass walls extended upward in a pyramidal shape, resembling a glass birdcage. The peak converged into a tall spire, with something like a beacon at the top.

Overall, an attractive building. Not everyone appreciated the mid-century vogue in architecture. In fact, all over the world great examples of the horizontal and symmetrical stylings of this period had been torn down in favor of new construction. A shame really. Zara believed all period styles were worth preserving. Like people, buildings were a product of their time.

Like people. She decided to research something else. She browsed the news sites using keywords 'Flynn' and 'Jakarta, Indonesia.' Narrowing the results to August of this year, a dozen or so references appeared and she clicked on them one by one. Nothing much new presented itself—the date, the time, the names. The repetitive journalistic accounts of the incident gnawed at her heart as she read, feeling her dad die again each time the story was retold. All of the reports established the sudden collapse of the partially completed complex and most hinted at faulty materials, worker carelessness or unheeded safety measures. Her face grew hot with anger. That was not possible for a project with the Flynn name on it.

Going down the list, the results became more fragmented, less relevant to the hard news listings above. The Spanish excerpts slowed her reading, but one entry stuck out. A local free press publication had a different view, stating in no uncertain terms that the project had been sabotaged as an act of terrorism. The pattern of destruction was consistent with explosive demolition methods. It made special mention of Tristan Benjamin Flynn, CEO of Flynn Enterprises International, stating that Mr. Flynn had been on site due to a personnel shortage which had put the project behind schedule. Crews were working overtime when the accident occurred at approximately 7:00 p.m. local time.

A soft knock sounded on her open office door. Jorge stood there, smiling. "It's five o'clock, Miss. You wish to go back to the hotel now?"

She exhaled, realizing she'd just spent her first full day on the job. *"Si,* Jorge. It's quitting time," she said, placing her printouts in a neat pile on her desk.

She stood up and surveyed the room before leaving. Yes, she really could feel at home here. A big step, leaving Montreal behind and embracing the European lifestyle. It wasn't what she'd planned. She'd pictured herself back in her Westmount condo by Christmas. She would talk with her mother about it when she came. Picking up her bag, she followed Jorge out into the reception area.

Everyone else had left. She cast a thoughtful look down the hall where she'd seen Dave go into his office. "Uh, can you wait just a minute, Jorge?" She went to his door and knocked. No answer. She tried the doorknob and peeked in. Loads of books were stacked in neat piles on his drawing table and in orderly rows on shelves. Clean desk except for his laptop, a phone, an inbox, daytimer and pens. Neat freak, she concluded.

In one corner of the office—Zara did a double take—lay several dumbbells of varying weights and a guitar resting in a stand. His framed diplomas hung on the wall next to a Ted Harrison painting. She resisted the urge to check if it was an original or a limited edition. An iconic set of deer antlers were mounted on an adjacent wall and cradled across them, a beat-up hockey stick. Clearly a multi-faceted individual, this Mr. Parker. More intrigued than ever, she closed the door and went down to the cool relaxing space of the Mercedes.

"Did you get bored waiting for me?" she asked Jorge as they pulled out into traffic. She had been at work the entire day and felt badly having him wait around all that time.

"De nada, Miss. I can always find something to do, but I look forward to driving you anywhere you please most of all." She remembered he'd driven Dave back to the office after the site visit yesterday.

"I hope you didn't mind driving Mr. Parker yesterday? I

thought it was the least we could do. He missed a day of work to come with us."

"Not at all, Miss. He is a nice boy, very polite." He paused, then added, *"Tu le gustas,* he likes you, you know."

"Verdad? Really. And how do you know this?" she asked, sounding unconvinced. If she didn't know him so well she'd swear Jorge planned to meddle in her personal affairs.

"Lo sé, " he said. "I know. The way I know about cars, like this Mercedes. She's a good one."

Zara thought about this. Jorge had never been interested in the men in her life before, aside from her father. He'd been like an uncle to her, a familiar comfortable figure that she'd always known. If what Jorge said was true, how did she feel about Dave? She couldn't deny he was attractive with his dimpled, boyish good looks and casual style. His six-foot-plus frame moved with an easy grace she found sexy. *But that smart mouth of his.*

He'd invited her out two times now; first for a drink, then to take a ride with him to Gibraltar. If nothing else, he was persistent. She also thought about Miguel and their crazy rendezvous Tuesday night. The Hispanic Hunk had gotten her mojo going and she didn't seem able to shut it off. She regretted her careless behavior on that occasion, but secretly wished she could see him again without passing out like a drunken sailor.

Since the chances of that were remote, why not get to know Mr. CET, B.Sc., aka Smart-Ass, a little better? Accept his offer? They did have quite a bit in common. But she'd made plans with the Ridleys and didn't want to duck out on them. Perhaps she could find a way to meet him 'accidentally' in Gibraltar. She would talk to Bette and Diggy tonight. Having dinner with them had become a bit of a routine; she enjoyed their company.

"He does seem like a very trustworthy person," Zara said,

not wanting to give Jorge any further ideas about playing matchmaker. They drove back to Marbella in silence. When they arrived at the Club, Zara saw one of the desk clerks, a girl with huge boobs, waving at her and beckoning her to the desk. Thinking there must be a message from the Ridleys, she walked over.

"Miss Flynn, I have message for you!" she said with excitement.

"Yes?"

"The manager wants to give you a complimentary gift, for the inconvenience of changing rooms. We are sorry you were unhappy with the first one."

"That's quite all right. Marta took care of the switch. There's no need for a gift."

"Gracias, Miss. But we want our guests to be very, *very* happy with our resort, so this is for you." She handed Zara an envelope. She opened it and withdrew a gift certificate—a cable car tour of Gibraltar and a one-night stay at a place called the Aragon Pub and Hotel. What a coincidence! The tour was for up to four people. She could treat Bette and Diggy in appreciation for being so nice to her.

"Gracias," she said to Delores. "Is it valid on the weekend?"

Delores' smile wavered a little. "It is only good for Friday, tomorrow," she said. "I hope that is satisfactory. Can I call and make the reservation for you?"

"Um, I would like to invite some friends. Let me check with them first," Zara said.

"No problema, Miss. Please call the front desk when you are ready. I will be here all evening," Delores said.

Zara smiled and nodded, holding up the envelope. "Thank you again," she said.

When Zara got to 514, she dialed the Ridley's room. Bette answered. "Hi Bette, it's Zara."

"Oh, Zara dear, so nice to hear from you. Did you have a nice day at the office?"

"I did," she said. "The people are so nice and I got to work on some projects right away. I think I'm going to like it there."

"Aww, that's terrific, luv. Are you up for dinner tonight? Dig and me is craving seafood. You fancy lobster or sommat, dear?"

"Sounds great, Bette. And I have some good news. You still want to go to Gib this weekend?"

"Of course, luv. It's one of our favorite places, just like back home. Can you come with us?"

"I'll do better than that. I have a gift certificate for a tour and overnight stay tomorrow. Would that work for you?"

"Brilliant!" Bette said. "Dig, we've got a tour and an overnight in Gib," Zara heard her say off-line to Diggy. "Tomorrow's fine, luv. Can you tear yourself away from work? We should make a day of it. You'll love it there."

"I think I can swing that," Zara said with a laugh. "I'm the boss, after all."

Bette giggled. "Smashing, dear. We'll talk about it over dinner. Meet you downstairs in an hour?"

"I'll be there," Zara said.

Chapter Fifteen

Miguel Montana, international superstar and Latin singing sensation, lay soaking in a bubble bath in the penthouse suite of Club Marbella. His own music played loudly throughout the room as he laid his head back on the little bath pillow with his eyes closed, listening intently to his performance on the recording. He had one more show to do here Saturday night, so he reviewed the last show's sound files as he always did, noting the crowd reaction, backup band sound and other elements in order to make changes or improvements.

Whatever else he might be, Miguel was a consummate performer, devoting himself fully to his art, his music. He thanked God for his life and livelihood. He loved nothing better than to sing, except perhaps to compose new music. These talents were gifts and being raised Spanish Catholic, he of course knew these things came from God. He was aware that many called him "Mickey Mountain," the literal English translation of his name, which seemed to amuse the Brits. It inferred him being built as big as a mountain in certain places. But he never gave much thought as to whether he was large, small, or average in that department, content in his belief that he was exactly as God intended him to be.

A simple wooden crucifix hung above the tub. After bathing he would say a prayer, give thanks for his last show, and ask a blessing for success with the next one. He listened to the closing number, smiling at the sound of his last note and the screaming of the crowd in approval. Not a thing he would change, he concluded. One of his best performances. He 'd been inspired when he saw the beautiful lady he had met in the elevator sitting in the crowd. Normally the stage lights were too bright to see the audience, but at that moment he happened to be standing at just the right mark between the spotlight's crossbeam to see her.

Miguel took this as a sign that she was someone special and that he should select her as the one to share himself with that night. If he loved anything as much as his music, it was love itself. He loved everything about his life and he viewed it as a personal tribute to his gifts, to make love to someone each night of his touring engagements as the ultimate expression of thanks for his talent and good fortune. However, his interpretation of his faith's concept of universal love extended to more than just women. He loved all people, men and women, and celebrated this idea of interconnectedness by swinging both ways in his desires.

Miss Red Dress, as he'd first dubbed her, was as sweet and fresh as he'd imagined when Luis and Raoul, his personal bodyguards, had brought her to the penthouse. Already drunk, she carried herself with aplomb nevertheless. He thought speaking French a nice touch. It made him feel like he'd taken them both to a special, private place for just the two of them to share an intimate connection.

He didn't know she would react badly to the tranquilizer in her water. A mild substance, he often used it to cloud his partner's memory a little. That way, most of them didn't remember enough to make an issue of it to the police or their lawyers, or anyone else. It all seemed like a pleasantly erotic dream. Occasionally though, he took lovers of both sexes. Typically these were people of use to him who helped him acquire other, more transient partners in his travels. The lovely Miss Zara Flynn for example. She'd been procured by faithful Delores, his main contact here at the Club Marbella where he toured once or twice a year. In exchange for her services, Miguel would often 'service' her just the way she liked it.

Delores had a thing for role-playing and costumes. She loved being someone else and would delight Miguel with a new guise each time they met in secret. And oh, those magnificent, cantaloupe-sized breasts! He licked his lips just picturing them in his mind, stroking their round firmness, feeling the weight of them in his hands. The places they met were arousing too—the hidden storage room, in particular— provided a wicked, forbidden atmosphere of secrecy that Miguel found amusing. Thankfully, Delores had been kind enough to help Miss Flynn into bed after she'd passed out. But as much as he appreciated Delores, he didn't feel guilty in the least about standing her up. He'd received a better offer.

It didn't matter as long as he delivered his gift of lovemaking while he was on the road, and Delores would come running back to him another time as she always did. He didn't often get to experience the kind of scenario he had last night. He smiled thinking about it. The element of danger and decadence his *Ángel Oscuro* offered, his Dark Angel, was irresistible. He accepted it as a challenge to his expression of universal love, to mix male and female when presented with the opportunity and so he opted to be with Ángel instead of Delores. Ángel wanted to see him again on Friday, and for the moment, he'd agreed.

He also hoped to resume his meeting with Zara before the tour ended. He remembered cupping her smooth buttocks in his hand, preparing to give her such pleasure when she'd slumped to the floor, unconscious. Luis knocked at the bathroom door.

"Message coming in from the front desk. Friday night, 9:00 o'clock, in 1004. I should accept?"

Miguel smoothed the fragrant bathwater over his face with both hands, the wet curls of his hair sticking to his handsome face. *"Por supuesto,* Luis. Of course," he said, wiggling his toes beneath the bubbles. Ángel would just have to understand. Mickey Mountain would have his second chance at Miss Red Dress.

*

Ignacio sat in the hospital waiting room cradling a cold, bitter-tasting coffee between his hands. He'd been here more than twenty-four hours since Carmella had collapsed in their kitchen yesterday. He didn't know what to do. His sister had taken the girls to her house for a few days, the poor things. They were upset and frightened.

Why must Carmella always be so critical of him? He made a good living, had given her a home and family, and now when on the verge of success with his new company, she lay in this place, fighting for her life and blaming him for everything. It wasn't fair. He deserved better than this. He almost hoped she might not pull through, thus ending his misery in trying to please her and impress his father-in-law.

He shook his head to cast the thought from his mind. That would leave his girls without a mother. How could he entertain such an idea? Her inheritance would pass down to Daniela and Ericka in that case. They would be set for life.

If he could just get Vistamar Holdings to pay off as big as he hoped he could buy himself a completely new life, including a new wife. The country had no shortage of gold-digging, self-centered women who wanted nothing more than to lie on the beach and have a rich husband support them. The crazy idea swirled and formed in his mind until he felt dizzy, almost nauseous.

He realized he hadn't eaten since lunchtime yesterday, but couldn't bring himself to take a meal. Surely not hospital food in any case. His cell phone began to vibrate—such devices weren't to be switched on while in hospital, so he'd set it on silent. He fished it out of his shirt pocket and read the screen. Cruz was calling. This brought him back to reality and to the problem of El Mirador.

"Si," he answered.

"How is your wife?" came the response.

"I'm not sure," he confided to his assistant. "The doctors, they don't tell me much. Just that she is under observation."

"I'm sorry to hear that. You are under a lot of strain. Are you going to be all right?"

"Bernardo, I'm not sure about anything right now. Are you at the office?"

"No. I've let them know I'll be there in the morning. I took the afternoon to...move forward with Vistamar." Ignacio brightened.

"What is the status?" he asked.

"The fire is in the hole," Bernardo replied. "I can pull the trigger at any time. Since you are indisposed, I felt we should move ahead sooner rather than later. I might not have time to watch Flynn's movements and cover for you at the office as well. There's no reason to wait."

"Very well. When will you do it?"

"This weekend. I'll let you know. Stay with your wife, it will make a good alibi."

Ignacio nodded in agreement. "Bernardo, I don't believe I have thanked you for your services," Verrera said, emotionally and physically drained.

Bernardo paused, as if uncertain how to react to this statement. *"De nada,* Señor Verrera. It is what you pay me for."

"You are assuming great risk. You will be fairly compensated, believe me. Like you were in Indonesia."

"That was incidental and in the past. I look to the future, as should you," Bernardo said, changing the subject. He evidently didn't want to review that event.

"Por supuesto. Of course, Bernardo. Keep me appraised." He disconnected. He could tell Cruz did not want to talk about Indonesia. His work there had taken a different twist than intended, but what was done was done.

When Tristan Flynn's purchase trumped Vistamar's bid for the El Mirador site, Verrera had nearly lost his mind. He sent Cruz to Indonesia, the site of Flynn's new build in central Java. Before he knew it, Flynn was dead, caught in the explosion of his own project. He'd intended only to destroy the building, to make Flynn reconsider his purchase of El Mirador and divert funds to the Indonesian venture. But the man had been where he shouldn't have and suffered the consequences. This led to his daughters' presence here and a new obstacle to his plans.

He tried not to think about the dark turn his new company had taken. Soon, it would be over and Vistamar would emerge as brightly as the sun, fueling his new destiny. He tossed his half-empty cup into a nearby wastebasket. *I must talk to the doctors,* he thought. *It has been too long without information.* He needed to know whether his wife would be part of his future or not. He started down the hall to the nurse's station.

Chapter Sixteen

David Justin Parker recalled that, as an ordinary Canadian kid, he'd had no idea what he wanted to be when he grew up. He'd spent his youth in typical fashion, loving the outdoors, going to the lake on summer vacations with his family, and partying with his high school friends. He bought his first car at seventeen, saving up money from part-time jobs. While working at a building supply center, he'd discovered a love of the construction trades. Math and Science came easily to him and he had no difficulty gaining entrance to Lakehead University in Thunder Bay. After two years there he applied to the prestigious Massachusetts Institute of Technology and was accepted. After graduation he scored his job with Flynn Enterprises in Boston. At the age of twenty-seven he now lived in Spain, supervising construction projects all over the Andalusian coast.

He thought he'd done pretty well for himself, and his family back in Thunder Bay took great pride in him. He pounded up the steps from the waterfront to the bike path on the causeway. Only a few blocks from his apartment now, he'd nearly finished his usual three kilometer morning run. He passed the familiar office towers and commercial buildings of downtown Malaga. He could still glimpse the sea beyond their concrete and glass silhouettes.

What a view. He felt lucky to have ridden his career to this beautiful place in life. The Costa del Sol teemed with exciting nightlife, great cuisine, stunning beaches, and even more stunning women. In the three years he'd been here, he'd met dozens, dated several and slept with one or two. In fact, he'd recently broken it off with a certain auburn-haired esthetician whose painful obsession with looks took on literal meaning when she'd insisted on waxing him within an inch of his life. The rest were equally superficial. He couldn't say he'd been in love with any of them. He'd certainly never spoken the words.

Now this Montrealer had breezed into his life and made him realize something. That he missed home and the kind of girlfriends he'd known in his youth. The kind who made the volleyball team, weren't afraid to dive off the dock, bait a hook, or chug a beer. More than that, she made his heart ache with a nagging question. How would she feel if she knew her father went to Indonesia because of him?

He checked his watch. 7:45 a.m. He'd told her to call by eight if she was interested in coming along to Gibraltar today. He found himself feeling anxious, knowing he'd be disappointed if she didn't call. God, she turned him on.

He'd kept his cell phone clipped to his shorts while he ran, just in case. He slowed his pace as he reached the steps to his apartment building and went inside. Opening the door to his third-floor apartment he took out his cell phone and looked for missed calls. Nothing. *Did I offend her that much?* She puzzled him. Normally people flocked to him, not eyed him up and down as if he were the village bum. He wasn't used to being…*rejected?* Huh. That word didn't exist in his lexicon.

He set the phone down and stripped, heading for the shower. His voicemail would pick up any new messages, and he wouldn't feel like he was waiting on her call if he just got on with things. If she did call, he'd have her number and an excuse to call back.

Showered, dressed and ready by 8:15, his cell phone sat where he'd left it on the coffee table, undisturbed and unblinking. He shoved it in his pocket, grabbed his file box of work orders, and left the apartment. *Just another lonely day in paradise.*

*

Ernesto's cell phone rang. When he picked up, he heard Zara's voice on the other end. *"Buenas días,* my dear. *Como esta?"*

"Good morning, Ernesto. *Muy bien, gracias.* I was wondering. Mr. Parker mentioned he might go to Gibraltar today. Do you know what suppliers he planned to visit?"

Ernesto thought for a moment. "Well, he normally visits the shipping office at the harbor. I think he also had some safety supply orders coming in, that would be at Prof International, in downtown Gibraltar. Why do you ask?"

"I planned to come in to the office again today, but an opportunity's come up to treat some friends of mine to a tour in Gibraltar. I thought if Mr. Parker would be there, I might invite him to dinner with us, to thank him for his help. It *is* Friday, so…"

"That's very thoughtful of you, Zara," Ernesto said. "I'm sure he'd love to join you. Why don't I give you his cell number, you can catch up with him between appointments."

"That's okay, Ernie. I have his card. I want to surprise him. Thanks. See you Monday!"

Alvarez hung up the phone and smiled. It seemed he wouldn't have to work that hard to interest these two young people in each other after all. He'd purposely chosen Dave to lead the site visit and wanted to keep him and Zara working together. He hadn't been entirely truthful when he'd told Zara he had no insight into her father's thoughts. The last time they'd seen each other, Tristan said to him, *"Ernie, I have a lovely, talented, strong-willed daughter who needs to find more than just a career. If she would just come and work for me, she could have this office, spend weekends on the beach, and have a little romance for a change. I don't know what it would take to make her change her mind."*

Ernesto thought of Zara. She *was* lovely. She *was* talented. He found it difficult to look at her without seeing Marlena. But she had a career and now the responsibilities of Flynn Enterprises as well. For a girl like her, the only way to grant Tristan's wish was to provide work and romance in the same place. That's where David came in.

Aside from the fact that he liked him, Ernesto knew that Dave was single, a truly good man and an attractive one, according to some of the office girls. They called him *'El semental Canadiense'* behind his back. The Canadian stud. Certain that Dave had no idea he was being 'fixed up,' Ernesto wanted to keep it that way. His smile grew a little wider. Tristan would have been pleased.

*

The rising sun turned up the heat on the beaches of the Costa del Sol. Zara felt totally carefree today, racing down the coastal highway with Jorge at the wheel of the Mercedes and her 'foster' parents Bette and Digbert Ridley in the back seat. It really seemed like a vacation now, with nothing more pressing on her schedule than sightseeing and shopping.

"Well, first we've got to take the cable car up the Rock," Bette said. "Did you know there was monkeys living up in them cliffs there? It's true! Then we'll have a right nice lunch and hit the shops for the afternoon. We'll watch the sunset from the harbor and have a slap-up night in the pub." Bette seemed to have everything under control, as usual. Diggy sat silent, humoring her and enjoying the view out the car window.

Even on this bright day, Zara felt anxiety building as they neared the turn off at El Mirador, but this time she could drive right by it and not concern herself with it. There was no other route to Gibraltar. But the problem remained in the back of her mind. It would be a huge undertaking. Would it be worth it? She remembered the photographs she'd collected. Perhaps she shouldn't try and resurrect the dead; leave its memory be. But left unrestored it would have to be taken down. It presented an ecological hazard. And still, there must be a reason her father had given it to her. There was more to the story, she could feel it.

But she didn't want to solve mysteries today. Today she would enjoy with her new friends and if luck prevailed, a certain special friend. The hills to the north began to flatten and soon their route passed through a plain-like region, creating a wide horizon before them. Out of the haze to the west, the Rock began to reveal itself. Even in the distance, the distinctive shape of Gibraltar was awe-inspiring. It looked exactly like every photo or drawing ever made of it and it grew larger and more solid with each passing kilometer.

Jorge reminded them they would require their passports to cross La Linea, the border between Spain and Great Britain. When they arrived at the crossing, the Rock of Gibraltar's imposing silhouette seemed to fill the sky. They entered the territory on foot. A car wasn't necessary and Jorge had other plans for the day. His cousin and her children were meeting him at Bermuda Beach, a few miles east of La Linea. He would return for them tomorrow.

They bid him goodbye at the base, Gibraltar being home to a major British military installation. Its airport formed a kind of 'no man's land' between the two countries. The path from the parking lot to the border station ran alongside outbuildings, barracks, and parked aircraft belonging to the British Navy. With the temperature rising and no shade to speak of while traversing the base, Zara worried about Bette and Diggy walking that distance in the hot sun. Bette assured her they were quite used to this trip, having been here many times.

With their passports stamped at the entry point, they continued down Winston Churchill Avenue into the town of Gibraltar. They found the cable car station, bought their tickets, and went across the street to a charming coffee shop done up in a faux Tudor front before taking the seven-minute ride to the top. They bought their coffees and selected a table by the leaded-glass front windows to sit and chat. Bette and Diggy seemed right at home in the little English-style room. Bette identified the rustic country print on the tablecloths as a 'toile' pattern. They sipped hot coffee and talked about life in England. The Ridleys loved their vacations but always looked forward to returning to the gray skies and changing seasons of the British Isles.

"We was born there, and we'll be planted there," Diggy stated firmly.

They took turns asking Zara questions about her personal life. Did she have a boyfriend back home? Would she stay in Spain for a while or return to life in Montreal? And what about children, did she like children? "Wait a minute. What's with the interrogation?" Zara asked. "I've told you most everything about me, why so many questions?"

"We's just interested, dear. Our Jamie's long grown now, moved off to Scotland raising his prize piglets on a farm there. Don't suppose he'll ever get married, he's happy enough on his own. And what lass would be interested in pig farming eh, I ask you?" Bette continued.

"Dibbs out," Zara said.

Bette shook her curly hair and laughed. "Oh, no dear. You're hardly Jamie's type," she said, taking a sip of her coffee. "But you must have plans for a family someday? Pity Mickey Mountain's not available eh…he'd make good breeding stock and all!" she added with a wink.

Zara clapped a hand to her forehead. "Puh-lease, Bette, enough of Mickey Mountain! It's embarrassing enough as it is. And I haven't seen his henchmen lurking around anywhere, so I think I'm safe. Let's drop it."

Bette eased up, set her cup down on its saucer, and peered out the window to watch the cable car loading and unloading at the base station. "Like they say, the right guy will come along. I'm in no hurry," Zara said. "And I do like children, to answer your question."

Diggy patted her arm. "And a great mam you'll make someday, too. No need rushing things now is there?"

They finished their coffee and moments later were rising up the slope of The Rock. The views of the Mediterranean were incredible and to the west, the Alborean Sea. Beyond that, the open Atlantic beckoned. The interactive tour guide rambled through its spiel, pointing out the flora and fauna along the way with tidbits of history thrown in. There were indeed wild monkeys, called Barbary Apes, in the area as Bette had said. However, none of them seemed amenable to making an appearance today.

They reached the summit and disembarked, everyone gasping "oohs and aahs" and pulling out cameras and binoculars to capture the view. The misty African coast, visible on a clear day like today, took Zara's breath away.

They browsed in the gift shop, shunning most of the touristy trinkets, but Diggy emerged from the shop sporting a baseball cap with "Gibraltar Rocks!" embroidered on the brim. Bette chose a whisky flask shaped like the Rock and Zara found a lovely green chiffon scarf and wrapped it stylishly around her neck. It set off her eyes and went beautifully with the emerald green dress she wore.

She posed with Bette for Diggy to take a photo, the blue sea at their backs and the imposing peak of the Rock looming to one side. They had fun behaving like tourists, snapping photos and strolling through the botanic gardens. Then it was back down the mountain for lunch. Diggy insisted on going to a traditional English-style pub to show Zara what proper fish and chips tasted like.

As they walked down the street near the harbor, Bette and Diggy stopped to look in the window of a pawn shop. Seeing something of interest, they went in to check out the merchandise. Zara followed them, assuming that it probably took one junk shop owner to know another. In the cluttered interior she saw everything from can openers to camo wear, TVs to tumble dryers. It smelled faintly of kerosene and a thin layer of dust covered most everything. Lamps and wind chimes hung from the ceiling. They tinkled unrhythmically as she made her way to the back counter where the Ridleys huddled over something along with the proprietor.

As she came within a few feet of the group, Bette straightened, slinging an antique rifle expertly in her arms, peering through the sight and checking the bolt action of the piece. Zara recoiled on instinct. Bette set the rifle back down on the counter. "It's decent, not sure we need another one of them. How about the Colt, then?" The proprietor showed her a classic handgun next, which Bette picked up and examined in a similar manner to the rifle. "We'll come back later, if we're interested," she said.

She and Diggy turned to leave and saw the dumbstruck Zara standing there. "Oh, Zara dear, I suppose we've given you a fright! You look positively gob-smacked. So sorry, did we mention that's one of our shop specialties back home?"

"Just a hobby line, really," Diggy said. "Collector items mostly, anything related to the Empire's military history."

"Guns?" Zara said, barely managing to speak. "You sell guns in your curiosity shop?"

Bette waved her hand nonchalantly. "Collector pieces," she affirmed. "No ammo."

"Bette's a crack shot though. Get her to the skeet range and look out," Diggy quipped, tapping Bette on the backside as he passed her on his way to the door.

"Oh, give over. I haven't done that in years," she said, following him.

Zara stayed frozen to the spot. When they noticed she wasn't in step with them, they turned around to see the shocked, blank expression on her face.

Bette let out a laugh. "Come along, lass, you look as though you need a stiff drink!"

"We're harmless, really," Diggy added. They linked arms with Zara and led her out of the shop. "Ah, here's the Mucky Duck," he announced after they had walked a few blocks.

The old style pub sign hung out on a wrought-iron frame. 'The Black Swan,' it read in bold curvaceous letters, a dark silhouette of the bird painted beneath them. Zara got the joke. Familiar with Cockney slang which nicknamed things and places with rhyming synonyms, "Mucky" meant Black, and "Duck" instead of Swan. They went inside and settled into a booth nestled under a large window. Lacy curtains trimmed with black pompoms hung above it. Wall sconces flickered with candlelight and dark papered walls sported a traditional Tudor plank molding. Zara found the whole place charming right down to the unvarnished wood floor, scuffed and distressed to perfection.

Diggy ordered pints for all three of them. It felt good to get out of the heat and sip a cool beer in the cozy darkness of the pub. Diggy also insisted on the fish and chips and in no time, a huge platter of steaming hot fillets and newspaper-lined baskets of fried potatoes appeared on their table. Bette doused the chips with vinegar and squeezed lemon wedges over the fish. The mouth-watering aroma overshadowed the fact that the fare was loaded with innumerable amounts of fat and calories. No one could resist the greasy, battery goodness that lay before them. "Tuck in, ladies," Diggy said.

As a second round of pints arrived, Zara looked out the window to admire the view of the harbor. Across the street amid the collection of jewellery shops and camera stores stood the harbor control office, according to the lettering on the door. Suddenly, it swung open. In the back of her mind, she'd hoped to spot him somewhere today and here he was, stepping right in to view.

Dave Parker came out of the harbor office, heading across the road toward the Black Swan, looking like a man with a thirst on. He wore sunglasses, steel-toed work boots, jeans, and white tee underneath an unbuttoned cotton shirt. He looked both ways as he crossed to the pub, his long, lean legs carrying him in a casual but purposeful stride, like an athlete. He stepped up to the door and took off his sunglasses before entering the darkened establishment. A few heads turned to see the newcomer, including Bette's.

She looked Dave up and down then turned back to the table. "Ooh, who's this then?" she said in a sly tone. "He's a right looker, eh?"

Zara smirked, undecided on how long she would let things go before revealing that she knew the handsome stranger. "You think he's good-looking, Bette?" she asked casually, swirling the dregs of her pint around in its mug.

"What, not your type, luv?" Bette asked. "The hot sun must have boiled your brain if you don't think he's a nice bit of stuff." Diggy rolled his eyes in his long-suffering manner.

Dave took a seat at the bar with his back to them. The

landlord saw to his order and began pulling a pint from the tap. *Well, he did offer to buy me a drink the other day. Perhaps I can return the favor,* Zara thought. She excused herself from the table despite Bette's objection that she should get her second pint down her. "I have to make a visit," she whispered, pointing to the washrooms. Instead, she approached Dave's chair from behind. He sat with his elbows on the bar, reading a local newspaper. She took the seat next to him, mimicking his body position. The landlord returned with his pint and Zara spoke up. "I'll get that," she said and slid a fiver of the local currency across to the barkeep.

Dave raised his head, stared straight ahead for a split second then turned toward her. His face displayed a priceless mix of shock and delight. "What are you doing here?" were the first words from his lips.

"You might say thank you," she said, pointing to his foaming pint of beer.

"Thank you," he echoed.

He stared at her for a few seconds then burst into a full-on smile. With his dimples and sparkling white teeth showing, the pub no longer seemed dark. Zara couldn't help but smile back. She watched his eyes travel down the length of her body. Aware of her short skirt, she crossed her legs, a bit á la Sharon Stone, and tilted her ankle up and down. The tiny rhinestones on her sandals glinted in the muted light.

He swallowed hard and reached for his pint, as if suddenly thirstier than he'd realized. "I thought you would call me for a ride. How did you get here?"

Zara cocked her head in the direction of Bette and Diggy. "I told you I had some friends who wanted to take a trip here. That's Mr. and Mrs. Ridley from Liverpool."

Dave turned to look in the direction she indicated. Bette and Diggy stared at them from their table by the window, Diggy smiling broadly and Bette's eyes practically spinning around in her head. Dave nodded and raised his hand in greeting. They waved back absently, appearing confounded at this new turn of events. He turned back to Zara. "They seem a little old for you."

Zara laughed. "They kind of adopted me on my first day here. I wanted to treat them to a day out."

"I see," Dave said. "And how's the day been so far?"

"We've been up the Rock already and took a ton of pictures. After lunch we plan to hit the shops. Any recommendations?"

"I thought shopping wasn't your thing," Dave said, taking a sip of his pint.

Zara looked him straight in the eye. "I lied."

Dave's eyebrows went up as he leaned his head forward in a suspicious nod. "Well, like I said, I mostly hang out in supply yards. But if you just head down Main Street you'll find a lot of designer shops and jewellery stores."

"Thanks for the tip. Care to join me?" she asked.

"Oh, I wouldn't want to tear you away from your adoptive parents," he said.

The barkeep appeared with another pint for Zara. She glanced back to the table by the window. Already making a fast exit, Diggy sent her a mock salute and Bette waved her hands toward her in a 'carry on' motion. "We'll see you at the Aragon, dear. Have fun!" Bette said loudly.

As they bustled out the door, Dave said, "I think you've been booted out of the nest. Time to try your wings."

Zara felt a little guilty ditching them, but inwardly grateful to have some time alone with Dave. The intensity of emotion she felt in his presence surprised her. A fine line existed between wanting to be near him and wanting to take revenge on him for all his snide remarks. They finished their pints and Dave ordered another along with the famous fish and chips. Zara opted for a Margarita.

"Your poison of choice, Tequila?" he asked.

She brushed the salted rim of the glass with her finger and then licked the stray crystals off the tip. "Oh, I think there are worse poisons," she said after a pause. She rubbed the tip of her finger against her tongue and glanced sideways at him. "Like workplace relationships."

Dave pursed his lips in a silent whistle. "Poison indeed. The Devil's water."

He studied her with the concentration deserving of a complicated building tender. Seeing she had his full attention, Zara took an anticipatory first sip of her drink and swallowed appreciatively. "Mmm…yeah." She bobbed her head in a slow nod, tracing her tongue across her upper lip. He'd quoted a song lyric. She recalled the words and spoke them aloud. "The devil's water it ain't so sweet…" She paused. "But you don't have to drink right now." She flashed him a sweet smile.

His eyes glittered while he appeared to assess her words and work out the next line. "But you can dip your feet?" he said.

He'd caught on. Zara nodded. *Good Lord, I'm flirting like a high school girl.* He let out a sharp laugh as if to snap her spell over him, then looked away, focusing on his pint mug and sliding his fingers up and down the wet glass.

"Coming from lake country I've always favored jumping straight in," he said.

"Oh. To get it over with?"

"No, to enjoy the experience as long as possible." He tore a chunk of fish from the steaming fillet on his plate and popped it in his mouth.

"Most people like to know what they're getting into before they jump," Zara said.

He swallowed his fish and washed it down with a gulp of beer before stealing a sidelong glance at her. "I already know what I want to get into."

Zara's mouth dropped open a little. His boldness didn't

seem to have many boundaries. And despite being taken aback, she had to admit this trait held a roguish charm. They lingered at the bar, exchanging double-entendres over a second margarita and two Spanish coffees.

Dave checked his watch. "Uh-oh. It's nearly two. I still have a few stops to make. Do you want me to give you a lift over to Main Street?"

Zara felt pleasantly lubricated. "Not really. Mind if I just tag along with you?"

An enigmatic half-smile crept across Dave's face as he rose from his barstool. He reached for her hand to help her down. "Okay, but I warn you, it might be boring. Are you sure?"

She accepted his hand and slid off the stool. "I'll risk it," she said, looking deeply into his eyes.

Chapter Seventeen

Bernardo squirmed uncomfortably in his office chair. He'd done just about all the paperwork and phone calls he could stand for one day in Verrera's absence and his anxiety level climbed higher by the minute. Business waited to be taken care of in Marbella. And so did Michelle. He had a difficult time keeping his mind off her and the prospect of seeing her again tonight, as they'd planned. But, first things first. He needed to get back to the Club to keep an eye on Miss Flynn and her cohorts. Certain things had to be done that would not be served by sitting here in the Malaga office. He decided to call it a day.

The shadows lengthened in the late afternoon sun and the temperature dropped just enough to make the drive back to the Club enjoyable. Bernardo put the top down on his convertible, feeling the wind swirl around him as he drove faster and faster. The sound system on full, he grooved to a lively salsa track and pushed the accelerator all the way down. Victory dangled almost within reach and he couldn't wait to take it.

Once in his room at the Club, he pulled off his shirt and tie and turned on the shower. As he undressed, he took a long look at himself in the mirror. The reflection of a skinny man with a heavy five o'clock shadow, shaven head, and protruding ears stared back. His best feature, he decided, were his eyes. Deep brown. So dark a shade that his pupils were barely distinguishable from the iris surrounding them. Someone once told him his eyes were like those of a mouse. But he didn't care. He thought the darkness of his eyes made him look worldly and mysterious.

He admired the small tattoo on his chest over his heart. A tiny figure with wings in black ink. The lettering above it read *'Ángel'* and below it, *'Oscuro.'* The Dark Angel. The same winged figure appeared on the back of his left hand. Smiling, he turned and stepped into the shower to get ready for the evening.

*

Friday afternoons were always busy at Club Marbella's front desk. Delores and Marta both worked at top speed to accommodate all the check-ins. Taxis and airport shuttles seemed to arrive every few minutes. As they coded cardkeys and entered information into the reservation system, Delores' shift passed quickly.

She had big plans for this evening, even if her 'date' didn't know it. She'd used the master cardkey earlier that afternoon to make some final touches to room 1004. She ordered roses from the floral shop on the mezzanine and set a bottle of champagne to chill in the bar fridge. An assortment of bath oils and fizzy bombs lay in a tray on the tub ledge and candles of all shapes and sizes filled the room.

Almost ready to leave, Delores quickly tapped her instant messenger. 'Keys at drop location 9pm' she typed, hitting enter to send the message. '9pm confirmed' came the reply. *All set,* she thought, proud of herself and her clever machinations. A stroke of genius, the gift certificate would guarantee the relatively flat-chested Zara Flynn to be out of the picture for the night. Delores would be the one getting all the rewards she deserved in suite 1004 tonight. Excited just thinking about it, she hurried to the staff lounge to change.

*

Ignacio Verrera stood in the hospital ward talking to Dr. Rojas, the cardiologist. "She is very lucky," the doctor said. "Many heart attack victims die from the first onset. But your wife is responding well to treatment and there is no significant damage…this time. The best advice is to reduce stress and follow a healthier diet. I recommend you see the nutritionist before Mrs. Verrera is discharged."

"When will she be able to come home?" Ignacio asked.

"I would like her to stay one more night for observation, so in the morning would be best. We have reduced staff on the weekends, so she may get better rest at home."

"Thank you, doctor," he said as they parted ways, Dr. Rojas returning to the nurse's station down the hall and Ignacio walking the few steps to Carmella's room. He entered quietly and stood by the bedside, watching the rise and fall of her chest, her head turned to one side and hands folded on top of the coverlet. The cardiac monitor beeped and showed a steady readout. Fatigue washed over him.

Tomorrow they would be back home and the girls could return from his sister's. But would things be the same? He thought not. He might have to hire some domestic help for a while, until Carmella recovered. And how would she feel about him now, after the argument they had? He felt sure she would blame him for her heart attack, that her frustration at his inadequacy had caused her condition.

He thought about what Bernardo had said too, that the time for action was now. He must acquire El Mirador as soon as possible and approve the development plans. The sooner it produced valuable fossil fuel, the sooner he'd be a very rich man.

Carmella began to stir. Her fingers twitched and she moved her head from side to side. Ignacio took hold of her hand and stroked her forehead with the other. The tight curly strands of her black hair stuck to her face and he brushed them away gently. *"Cariña."* Her eyes fluttered open and she gaped at him for a short moment, as if not recognizing him. Then her gaze softened and her lips tried to form words. "You don't have to speak," he said gently. "Just rest." Her right hand shook as she placed it overtop of his. Her eyes focused fully on him now, the look in them one of faith and forgiveness. *Perhaps all was not lost.*

*

The quiet streets lay darkened as the sun set behind the great Rock. The couple walked unhurried down the cobblestone lane that led to the Aragon Pub and Hotel. The sound of their steps against the stone echoed in the narrow lane. His arm loosely around her shoulders, hers encircled around his waist. To a passerby, they might have been two people who'd known each other a lifetime, but in truth had only met two days ago.

Against her better judgement, Zara knew she was falling for this man. They'd spent the remainder of the afternoon finishing Dave's errands, then window shopping along Main Street. With no end of interesting buildings in Gibraltar, of different centuries and cultures, they admired and critiqued them with their combined knowledge of architecture and engineering as they walked leisurely through the town.

Mr. Smart-Ass seemed to disappear when he really got into a topic of interest to him. His speech became animated and his voice filled with an infectious enthusiasm as he expounded the virtues of arch construction or cantilevered beams. Sharing their common passions made her feel drawn to him in a way she hadn't experienced with anyone else. They walked the last few blocks along the narrow, steep streets to the Aragon.

"Have you worked up an appetite for dinner yet?" he asked her.

She looked down at their feet stepping slowly in time with each other, his work boots next to her dainty sandals. Even in her heels, he stood at least a head taller and Zara felt safe, locked in his embrace as they walked. "For dinner...not yet," she replied and looked up at him, admiring his handsome face with a trace of beard starting to show.

"A drink, then? My turn to buy," he suggested.

She stopped walking, halting their steps. Dave looked at her with curiosity. Moving closer, she raised her hand to his chin and pulled it toward her. Her heart thumped with a delicious anxiety, each beat pushing caution further from her mind. "In a minute," she whispered. He let his head tilt downward until their noses nearly touched. She moved first, sought and found his lips with hers. They felt warm and soft. He responded to her kiss gently at first, then more urgently—as if to say 'what took you so long.' Her arms went around his neck, and all her doubts evaporated. She wanted him, surely and completely.

He pulled her close with both arms, his hands moving from the small of her back up to her shoulders and down again, as if trying to memorize the curves of her body. Their lips could not get enough of one another. Their tongues met and began a seductive dance, seeking to quench the thirst they each had. Pressed against him, she felt his growing erection through his jeans. He pulled away from her.

"How much further is that hotel?' he asked, his voice rough.

She kissed him again. "Not far."

"Good," he said and took hold of both her hands. "Lead the way." They ran hand in hand the last half block to the Aragon. Almost dark now, they ducked in through the pub entrance to find that Happy Hour had begun and the room crowded with patrons. As they made their way through the tables toward the small lobby, they heard a familiar voice.

"Yoo hoo, over here!" Bette's loud voice called to them from a corner table. They froze like deer in headlights and looked at each other, then over to where Bette and Diggy stood.

"We've hit a check-stop," Zara murmured.

"Looks that way," Dave agreed. "What do you want to do?"

"Uh, beam us up, Scotty?"

Dave laughed. "As convenient as that would be, don't think that's happening. We'd better go talk to them."

"Briefly," Zara emphasized.

"I do owe you a drink," he said. "Might as well be now, we might be a little busy later." He squeezed her hand.

"Yeah, that could be," she affirmed. With a smile and a wave, the two of them joined the Ridley's table.

"Well now, what have you two been up to since we last saw you?" Bette asked.

Diggy stood, pulling out a chair for Zara and nodding to Dave in greeting. "Uh, just walking around," Zara said, unable to think of a better explanation. Realizing they'd not been introduced she added, "Bette and Digbert Ridley, this is David Parker."

"Hello, luv!" Bette said brightly.

"Pleasure," echoed Diggy, shaking Dave's hand. "Call me Diggy."

"I apologize for taking your girl away for the afternoon," Dave said.

"No apologies required, dear boy," Diggy replied, motioning for them both to sit.

"If it were me, I'd be escaping with you and all," Bette

said. "And how do you know each other, then. Our Zara didn't just pick you up in the Mucky Duck, now did she?"

Dave and Zara exchanged looks. "No, Dave is, ah…" Zara began, not sure how to describe their relationship.

"Actually, she's my boss," Dave said. "I work for Flynn Enterprises. Since Miss Flynn took over as CEO that makes her the head honcho."

The Ridleys looked impressed. "That makes a change eh, woman on top?" Bette quipped.

Wincing, Zara looked over at Dave who without missing a beat said, "I certainly hope so." Diggy guffawed and raised his pint to Dave in a salute before taking a long swig. Finally, someone had beaten his wife to the punch line. "Can I buy you folks another drink, Mrs. Ridley?" Dave said, changing the subject before she could react.

Bette paused, looking him over. "Cheeky devil," she said. "Go on, then."

Dave waved to the server. "What can I get you," he asked, pointing to their empty pint glasses.

"I recommend the house dark ale," Diggy said, nodding.

Dave smiled. "House dark, it is." He ordered four.

Elbows on the table, Bette cradled her chin atop interlaced fingers and stared Dave down. "So what do you do then, for a living that is," she said. It sounded more like a command than a question.

"I'm a construction supervisor," he said. "I oversee building projects, handle labor and materials."

Bette raised her chin. "I see. Pays well, does it?"

"Well enough," he said, maintaining eye contact.

Their exchange reminded Zara of a job interview. Bette grilled Dave on his work, his clothes, his eating habits. He took her investigation in stride and seemed to enjoy her attention, but enjoyed outwitting her even more. He adroitly dodged her questions about girlfriends. *Girlfriends?* Zara most definitely didn't want to picture this man with anyone else. The idea made her…good grief…*jealous?* Then she felt Dave's hand touch her knee beneath the table.

Warm fingers roved the surface of her skin then traced circles on the inside of her thigh. Damn, he would drive her crazy if he didn't stop—and she didn't want him to stop.

Chapter Eighteen

The cell phone whirred its soft text signal. Bernardo stood in front of the mirror tying his necktie. He went to check the message. 'Michelle.' Bernardo punched the button, anxious to receive confirmation of his evening. *'lo siento ángel, change of plans, meet saturday instead?'*

Bernardo sat on the edge of the bed. He'd been looking forward to tonight, but what could he say? Something important must have come up. He texted back, 'disappointed but promise saturday, k?' and waited. The phone vibrated in his hand with a reply. 'k ur mi ángel oscuro, will txt time Sat.' Bernardo pressed the return key and set the phone down.

He felt empty now; deflated—despite the use of his secret name, Dark Angel. He decided to go down to the bar, get some dinner, and a scotch. And with some unexpected free time on his hands, he might as well catch up on the doings of Miss Flynn. He chuckled to himself at how easily he'd followed her all day Tuesday, snapping photos at will. Had Verrera enjoyed his artsy nude portrait of her, he wondered? He included it on the USB stick as a bit of a joke to keep Verrera on his toes.

He sat in the terrace bar, ordered some tapas, and polished off a second scotch. He surveyed the bar carefully, but no sign of Flynn or her English cohorts. Hadn't seen them in the dining room either. In any case, he appeared to have plenty of time to wait.

He watched some sports coverage on the TV screens in the bar. He observed guests come and go, on the lookout for his prey. He ordered more scotch. At eight o'clock he left the bar to have a more thorough look around the Club. He went to the café and back through the dining room, winding up in the lobby. He took note of the desk clerk staff; a fat middle-aged man and a thin woman with eyeglasses suspended on a chain around her neck.

Offhand he wondered where one of the more noticeable clerks, the girl with the big breasts, was tonight. He wandered out to the entrance, moving away from the doors and the well-lit steps toward the shrubbery hidden in shadows. He stopped to have a good look around. The fragrance of flowering bushes hung heavily in the cool night air.

A few guests were moving about but no trace of Flynn or the others. Frustrated, he decided to take a more direct approach. Picking up some hotel literature and a local paper on his way through the lobby, he rang for the elevator and got in. Stepping onto the tenth floor he made his way to 1004. A general sweep of the area revealed nothing. Behind its closed door, no obvious sounds came from inside the suite. Miss Flynn appeared to be out.

A settee and a console table situated near the elevators provided a good vantage point. He made himself comfortable and pulled out his newspapers and brochures, making his best effort to look like a nondescript hotel guest.

He noted the big green marble urn set between the elevator doors. The same on every floor, they had made a suitable receptacle for his cardkey a few nights ago—for the convenience of his mystery guest. Wishing he could be entertaining that guest right now instead of posting a stake-out, he sighed and pretended to read his brochures. And waited.

At eight forty-five, he heard someone coming. He kept his head down and watched from behind his papers. The big-chested desk clerk walked up to the elevators, obviously off-shift as she'd dressed in regular street clothes. She pushed the button for the elevator and as Bernardo watched, slipped a cardkey into the green urn. In a few moments she disappeared into the elevator.

Waiting for the closing thud of the doors, Bernardo's mind began to race. Who else knew about this trick? *It could just be coincidence.* It would be a likely place to hide a key. No one but the owner would know which door it opened, unless they tried every door in the hotel. A light switched on in Bernardo's mind and on a hunch, fished the cardkey out of the urn.

Making certain no one watched, he approached the door to 1004 and swiped the card in the lock. Miraculously, the green light went on and he pushed the lever without making a sound. He placed his newspaper in the door jamb and listened for any movement from inside the room. Nothing. He returned the cardkey to the urn and crept inside the suite. He didn't turn on any lights as he ventured deeper into the room.

As his eyes adjusted to the dimness, the room appeared unused since housekeeping had been there. Everything seemed in place, beds made, towels changed and folded. He didn't see any luggage lying around. He smelled the fragrance of flowers from a vase on the coffee table and noted an ice bucket with champagne and glasses set out as if company were expected. Interesting, he thought. It might be very helpful to know whom Miss Flynn planned to entertain.

Bernardo went toward the faint light coming from the windows. Unlatching the shutters, he stepped out onto the balcony. Out of plain view of the other rooms, he felt it safe to wait there. He closed the shutters and adjusted the vanes to allow for sight and sound from inside the room. He settled himself on a patio chair in a corner of the balcony and checked the time. Eight fifty-five.

He inhaled the night air, taking a rare moment to appreciate the fragrance of the surrounding flowers and the faint sounds of faraway traffic. The moment didn't last long however, as some action stirred within the room. He heard the door open and soft footsteps. A switch tripped on and the strip lighting around the bedroom area began to glow. A vague silhouette moved about and he heard the rattle of ice cubes in the champagne bucket. The sound of a struck match and the glow of candles being lit.

The figure moved slowly around the room, arranging things as if preparing for a royal visit. He heard a zipper opening and as he peered through the shutter vanes, made out the shape of a woman. She removed clothing from a bag and began to change. He looked away, scanned the area outside the balcony, checking for other spectators. Too many floors up for people on the ground to see and no visible guests on nearby balconies.

The woman put some music on. The slow exotic sounds of Indian music with plenty of sitar and finger cymbals began to play. She swayed to the music as if performing for a private audience. Bernardo checked his watch again. Nine twenty-five p.m. She stopped dancing and began to pace back and forth. It appeared her guest was running late.

The figure came toward the balcony doors. Bernardo shrank back into his corner. She pushed the shutters open and stepped out onto the dark balcony. She leaned on the railing with her back to him, looking out into the night as if she could wish upon a star for her visitor to arrive. Bernardo hadn't come to 1004 for this purpose, but the opportunity to eliminate one of his obstacles materialized right in front of him.

With the alternative being discovered spying on her, the

decision was easy. He lunged three steps toward her. She began to turn just as he hit her, full force, his elbow and shoulder smashing into her side and toppling her over the railing.

As she fell he could see the gauzy material of her outfit flailing about her and realized with horror it wasn't Zara Flynn.

As if in slow motion, the busty desk clerk landed on the ground ten stories below him. He backed up from the railing, groping for the shutters and clambering back into the hotel room. What was she doing in 1004 and where was Flynn? Panicking, he took a moment to gather his wits, but it cost him.

The security lock clicked open as someone swiped a cardkey in the reader outside. Whirling toward the door, he froze in place as he saw a man in a dark suit holding it open for someone to enter. There, framed in the light from the hallway, stood Michelle.

Bernardo gaped, realizing with agony that Michelle wasn't Michelle tonight. She'd exchanged her costume for her true self--Miguel.

Miguel paused in the doorway staring at Bernardo. Speechless for a moment, he motioned for Luis to follow him in and close the door. *"¿Que haces aqui?"* Miguel said, with quiet accusation in his voice. "Why are you here?"

"I could ask the same question," Bernardo replied. "This was your change of plans? Chasing the skirt of the *puta Canadiense?"* Jealousy rose inside him.

"That's none of your business, Ángel. Answer me, *que has echo? Donde está la Señoritá Flynn?"* Miguel glared at him, stone-faced. The look sent a stab of anguish through Bernardo. How dare he question his choices? With this he'd damaged his relationship with Michelle/Miguel beyond repair, and terror grew in the pit of his stomach over the body lying in the bushes below.

"See for yourself," Bernardo said in a vengeful voice. He found the will to move aside, gesturing to the open balcony doors. Miguel signaled Luis to check them, keeping one eye on Cruz. Only candlelight flickered in the room, and when Miguel looked away, Bernardo bolted for the door.

Chapter Nineteen

The first beams of sunrise cut across the bed from the not-quite-closed curtains. A slight wind fluttered them as it blew through the open window and the calls of seabirds could be heard in the distance. David lay wide awake, feeling the breeze on his skin, listening to the birds, taking in every detail of the moment. The white paneled walls, the cool cotton of the sheets, and most of all, the gorgeous girl sleeping next to him.

He wanted to touch her, kiss her, make love to her again as he had last night and hear her soft moans as he pleasured her. But he didn't dare to wake her just yet. The picture was so perfect, so blissful, he felt suspended in time and feared that if he moved a muscle the scene might burst like a bubble and be only a dream. He breathed deeply to catch the scent of her perfume. He tried to commit to memory the look of her hair cascading across the pillow, her eyelashes, the lightly freckled nose, the silver chain and dolphin pendant nestled at her collarbone.

The white sheet partially covered her nude body. One breast lay exposed, and risking that the dream could shatter, he leaned down and licked the nipple, feeling the bumpy texture of it against his tongue. Christ, he felt hard again already. He loved everything about this woman, wanted to possess her forever. He moved upward with his tongue, tracing a line to her throat, over her chin, and across her lips. Her closed eyes began to twitch and flutter open. She blinked, bringing him into focus. A smile crept across her face as she looked back at him. He almost felt relieved that she recognized him, that it hadn't all been a dream and she was here in the present with him. He smiled down at her. "Good morning, Montreal."

"Hey, Thunder Bay," she replied. "Or should I say, Thunder Boy?" She grinned sleepily.

Dave hoped he hadn't made quite as much noise during their lovemaking as all that, but if he'd made her feel like she'd been caught in a crashing, rollicking Great Lakes thunderstorm and liked it, that pleased him.

She reached up and put her hand on his cheek. "Are you real?"

He turned his face so that her finger slipped between his lips and he bit it gently. "Afraid so, mademoiselle. Anything else you'd like to know?"

She smiled mischievously. "Yeah, are you ready for round two?"

He raised his eyebrows twice in a villainous fashion and leaned down to kiss her. "Ding, ding," he answered, mimicking a ringside bell. He let their lips find each other again as he pulled the sheet away. He laid against her, his stiff cock showing her exactly how ready he was. His hand followed the outer curve of her breast and then circled the edge of her nipple with his fingertips. They stiffened instantly and he could hear her soft sigh even though he kept her lips fully occupied. He broke their kiss in favor of taking the taut, pink-brown berry in his mouth. He swirled his tongue around it and sucked, thinking no food or drink on earth would ever taste this sweet. She groaned and leaned her head back against the pillow. Oh, he could do so much more for her.

Taking more of her breast in his mouth, he sucked harder and slid his hand down to her hip, then across her abdomen. He rubbed her mound gently before sliding a finger into the wetness between her legs. She gasped and arched her back as she moved into his touch. Her slickness made his dick throb with wanting to enter her.

But not yet.

He stroked her sweet hot-button of flesh and heard her breath catch with each pass. He slipped one finger inside her, then two, moving them slowly in and out until she moaned aloud. The pressure of blood in his dick rose to a maddening level. He felt as though he'd break apart if he didn't fuck her right this second, but no, he'd finish her and watch it happen. His mouth left her breasts and he dragged his lips across and down her belly. He heard his own voice whispering her name, "Zara..." Though it sounded ethereal and bodiless as if floating above them. Instinctively she raised her knees and Dave thought he just might die of pleasure as he brought his head between her thighs and tasted her sex, his tongue taking plunging strokes against her clit.

Her hands rested on his head, fingers entwined in his hair as she followed his motion. He looked up and, incredibly, saw her gazing directly back at him as he continued his magic. Their eyes locked while he worked his clever tongue against her until he pushed her over the edge, watching her as she came. He could taste it, smell it, knew he'd reached his goal of bringing her to orgasm. Her eyelids closed as if overwhelmed by the power of it. Her hands trembled as they remained tangled in his hair. Now. He needed her now and moved his body overtop her. She wrapped her arms around his neck and drew her thighs up on either side of him. So hot and wet, he slid easily into her and felt like he'd been granted permission to enter heaven itself.

Joy and lust collided in his soul as he drove deep, without

restraint, again and again. She kissed his face, his neck, rubbed her hands up and down the muscles of his back as she moved in sync with each thrust, accepting him deeply and completely. She held him tight as he climaxed. *Sweet mother of God*. He felt as if caught in an avalanche, tumbling helpless and unthinking in a white storm of sexual release. His mind blanked, aware of nothing but the hammering of his heart in his chest and the hot fluid pumping from him into her. He took in deep, ragged breaths as his heartbeat slowed, recovering. He nuzzled her neck and when he raised his head, saw tears in her eyes.

"Oh, God, I'm sorry," he said in a strained voice. "Have I hurt you, please, tell me–"

She reached up to touch his lips, as if to stop the words from coming out. "Much worse," she said. "You've made me fall in love with you."

He looked into her watery eyes, seeing the truth there. He kissed her fingertips, knowing it was fast, crazy and wonderful all at the same time. Just because it happened fast didn't mean it wasn't right. "Oh dear," he said in a regretful tone. "There's only one cure for that." He stroked the sandy blonde hair falling across her forehead and wiped away the tears from the beautiful green eyes with his thumb. "And that's to love you right back."

*

When he'd finished in the shower, Dave returned to the main room to see Zara sitting in a chair facing the mirror. Wrapped in a hotel bathrobe, she held her cell phone to her ear. He supposed they had to check out soon, but honestly hadn't thought about the time for the last several hours. Several incredible hours.

He'd lost count how many times they'd made love. He hadn't used any protection, but she hadn't asked for any, either.

It wasn't like him to be careless in that regard. Well, maybe once or twice. It seemed they'd both lost their heads a bit. Or perhaps found them. A deep and wordless understanding seemed to exist between them, one that foreshadowed the future. Then it dawned on him how much he wanted that future.

He approached her from behind, leaning down to rest his chin on her shoulder as he gazed at their faces framed in the mirror. Naked, his reflection showed off muscular arms and tanned shoulders as he held her fast in the chair. He hadn't any shaving tools with him, so he sported a Marlboro-Man stubble as he smiled his signature, dimpled smile at her. He hoped she liked the rugged look.

"Jorge," Zara said into her phone. "Buenas días."

"Buenas días, Miss. I am en route now. Esta problema?"

"No hay problema," she replied. "Just wanted to ask, would you mind driving the Ridleys back to the Club? I'm going to drive back separately, stop in at El Mirador."

"Certainly, Miss, but how are you getting there? Have you rented a car?"

"Well, Jorge, I ran into Mr. Parker here in Gib and we're going to drive back together in the company truck." Dave heard Jorge's words coming over her handset and listened with curious amusement to her answers. He squeezed her tight, pretending to pant and lick her face like a rambunctious puppy. She tried not to giggle into the phone and fended him off while she concentrated on her conversation.

"Muy bien, Miss. I will be at the Aragon about noon. Have a safe trip back."

"Gracias, Jorge. I'll meet you at the entrance to say goodbye, adios!" She disconnected the call and tossed the cell phone on the dresser. Trapped in the chair, she reached up and grabbed Dave by his hair with both hands. "Okay, Thunder Boy, that's enough!"

"Ouch." He released her from his grip. Zara rose from the chair, and wagged her forefinger at him.

"Be a good dog, now." She stepped toward him, letting the bathrobe slip to the floor.

He embraced her and revelled in the sensation of their bodies touching from head to toe. "We'd better get moving," he said softly. "Or I'll need another shower, a cold one." As she relaxed against him, he found himself wondering how he could have ever felt truly alive before today. Reluctantly, he let go as she went into the bathroom to put on her makeup and pack her things. When she'd closed the door, he laid down on his stomach on the unmade bed.

They hadn't slept much, but he'd never felt more energized than he did right now. This changed things, his relationship with Zara. Could this work, with them both at the same job, or worse, could it work if she decided not to stay? His plans for moving up in the company might take a sharp turn either way.

Would she feel betrayed if he told her why Tristan had been on the Indonesian job? The question stabbed at his heart like a knife and set the man's words echoing in his ears. *"Get yourself back here. We need your young blood, Youngblood. I'll not have you dying of some poxy jungle fever."*

If he hadn't come back, he'd never have met her. But if Tristan had returned...same result. Sometimes the truth sucked. They were so right for each other and had so much in common. Not only their work and where they'd come from but also a deep loyalty to one person. It was too much coincidence for them to meet here, now, for it not to be fate. *It has to work out*, he decided. *It must work out.*

Right now it felt like he'd die if it didn't.

Chapter Twenty

Zara and Dave walked into the lobby, where Bette and Diggy stood waiting at the checkout desk. Bette spotted them first. "Aww, there you are, you two. It's almost noon, don't tell me you were canoodling right up 'til now?" Bette had a way of telling it straight. You were never left doubting what she meant about anything. It's what Zara liked about her most. And it wasn't really a secret what she and Dave had been up to. It had been pretty obvious in the bar last night what was going on between them.

"Well, the Guinness people were unavailable for comment, but I think we might have broken some sort of record," Zara said.

Bette laughed and patted Diggy on the shoulder saying, "Let's get a move on, Dig."

"Jorge will be here in a few minutes. I hope you don't mind if I send you back to Marbella with him? Dave and I are going to make a stop along the way." Bette eyed her dubiously. "Really, business stuff," Zara reassured her.

"Of course, dearie," Bette said, rolling her eyes. "Two young lovebirds are always stopping to 'take care of business'." Then she turned to Dave, pointing a pink-painted finger at him. "You bring our girl back safe, yeah? I'll never forgive you if you don't."

"Leave the lad alone, luv," Diggy said as he joined them. "I'm sure he's the responsible type, aren't you, mate?" He reached out for a handshake.

Dave returned the handshake and nodded. "I can tell you with complete confidence, Mr. and Mrs. Ridley, she'll be in good hands."

Diggy laughed aloud, shaking his head. "Young lady, this lad's a right scream. You hang on to this one. He'll have you laughing 'til your golden years."

Dave really did have quite a sense of humor. Zara wished she could have appreciated it more on the day they first met. If only she hadn't been so hung over.

"Thank you, dear, for a lovely trip," Bette said, taking Zara's hands in hers. "You take care and we'll see you back at the Club, right?"

"You're welcome, Bette. Thanks for being so understanding." Zara hugged her and the four of them strolled out to the street to meet Jorge.

*

Ignacio pulled up his cobblestone drive. As he got out of the driver's side, the front door of the house burst open. Daniela and Ericka came running out, their aunt following in their wake. She'd brought the girls back to the house to greet their mother home from hospital. "Mami," they called, jumping up and down with excitement. Ignacio helped Carmella out of the car and her girls swarmed to her, putting their arms around her. Carmella smiled and hugged them both.

"Be careful, girls," Ignacio said. "Mama is still very tired from the hospital. Take it easy." He looked at his sister as she hung back on the doorstep. *"Gracias,* Elena. I can't thank you enough for staying with them."

Ignacio guided his wife into the house then returned to collect the rest of her things from the car. Waiting outside, Elena spoke. "You know she's very lucky, Ignacio. Many people don't live through a heart attack. I hope this is a wake-up call for you both."

Ignacio put his arm around her shoulder. "Elena, I think things are going to be very different from now on."

*

Miguel sat on a deck chair on the penthouse balcony staring out to the sea. He tried to compose himself after last night's incident. He had a performance to prepare for. The show must go on.

Delores had broken her neck in the fall off the tenth floor balcony. Not one, but two of his lovers had been compromised in this affair and it pained his soul that anyone had been hurt. His world was about love, not revenge or jealousy.

'Michelle' had been but one of many alter egos he assumed while pursuing his less conventional affairs. In a way, he was like Delores in that he enjoyed 'dressing up,' too. It turned him on, to pretend to be female at times. Sadly Bernardo, his 'dark angel' could no longer be part of the entourage. Miguel could not tolerate such an act of aggression. He didn't know where Cruz had run to. He'd sent Raoul to track him down, but Cruz had managed to slip away. Luis and Miguel saw to the discovery of Delores' body by hotel security without directly revealing themselves. He'd hoped they'd find her still alive, but they had been too late.

Miguel tried to piece together how and why this happened. Why was Bernardo on the tenth floor with Delores in the room? Why would he have killed her? Where was Miss Flynn? Had Bernardo found out about Delores' relationship with the singing star and killed her out of jealousy? Miguel remembered Cruz' words. *'La puta Canadiense'*, the Canadian whore. Was it Miss Flynn he was really after? Perhaps he expected to find her in 1004 just as Miguel had. Poor Delores, she'd wanted to be with Miguel so badly she had unknowingly put herself in harm's way.

Delores always made the room arrangements. She could easily have moved Flynn elsewhere and lain in wait for him in her place. A disquiet gathered over him like gray storm clouds. He needed to find Cruz before he harmed his real target. That meant he had to find Zara.

*

Bernardo had run blindly out of suite 1004 not really sure where to go. He just felt lucky to escape. Knowing Montana's delicate situation, he wouldn't have alerted hotel security or the police. This bought him enough time to find a hiding place. Cramped in the trunk of his car in the hotel parking garage, he'd been here several hours now, thinking and listening. But his bodily functions couldn't be denied much longer.

He felt frightened and desperate. Not only had he failed to take Miss Flynn out of the picture, he'd killed an innocent woman. Worse still, he'd lost Michelle. He would never have that joy ever again and his despair soon gave way to anger. Flynn was in the way. He needed to proceed with the next phase of the plan. He could wait a little longer, until dusk fell. Then he would make his move.

Chapter Twenty-One

Zara converted her red handbag to backpack position. She loved the piece's versatility; large enough to serve as everything from handbag to briefcase to shopping bag. She donned her one change of clothes, a pair of comfortable capris and a white tank top. Her hair seemed to have acclimated itself and she'd given up doing anything but letting it flow loose and free. Dave didn't seem to mind. They'd missed the complimentary breakfast, so they stopped at an outdoor market to buy food and drinks for the road.

As they drove east, El Mirador appeared in the distance. Zara talked about what she'd found online and how none if it revealed the complete story behind its current condition. The closer they came to it, the more anxious Zara felt. So agitated that by the time they drew within a kilometer, she asked Dave to pull over and take a walk.

The mid-afternoon sun scorched the beach. They found a path from the lookout point that led down to the sea. The shimmering white sand spread before them in both directions and they set out barefoot for the water's edge. The waves lapped at their toes as they walked hand in hand. It felt so good.

"You're awfully quiet," Dave said. "What's on your mind?"

Zara tried to sort out her emotions before answering. "It's hard to explain. There just doesn't seem to be a reason for my dad to leave El Mirador to me. I can't figure it out. Restoring it would cost millions. Tearing it down feels like there's no point in having it in the first place. I feel nervous, now. Like I shouldn't be here."

"Yes, you should," Dave said. "Otherwise I wouldn't have met you." They walked a few more steps in silence, then he stopped and turned her to face him. "Everything happens for a reason. You're here. I'm here. We're together for a reason, I'm sure of it. So is El Mirador. The reason will come. Don't think about it so hard."

She tried to do as he asked and clear her mind. Placing one foot in front of the other, she concentrated on the feel of the sand between her toes and the warmth of his hand in hers as they walked on. "Why did Ernesto ask you about explosives?" she finally asked.

Dave looked out over the water for a long minute, chewing his lower lip as though trying out various answers in his mind before speaking. "He's worried about a potential saboteur."

"What? Why?"

"Because of what happened in Java."

She slowed her pace and regarded him suspiciously. The words came rushing back to her. *Sabotage. Explosive demolition. Short-staffed. Overtime.* "So it wasn't an accident. You're telling me for certain that my father died in a deliberate act of destruction," she said, her voice monotone.

Dave took a deep breath in. "We think so, yes."

She wanted to verify what she'd read, see if his answer would corroborate the story. "Ernesto said he went there sooner than he'd planned. Do you know why?"

He hesitated and kept looking straight ahead. "Because I left."

Zara stopped in her tracks. "What do you mean? You were there?" Her mouth dropped open in disbelief. "And you never said anything?"

He pulled her by the hand to face him. "Hold on, I wasn't with him. Yes, I did go there, Tristan asked me if I wanted the foreman's job. We were short of trained workers. I went to check it out and I got sick. They had to fly me back inside of a week. That's when he decided to go there himself."

She felt dizzy. *Dad left. Dave came back.* She didn't like where this thought was going. *I wasn't allowed to have both men. One or the other would have died there. Could fate be that cruel?* Her balance began to waver, and Dave took her in his arms to keep her from falling.

"Hey, you know what," he said, verbally shifting gears. "We haven't eaten anything since yesterday. Let's take a break, crack open that wine. Maybe you'll feel better." They'd been walking toward El Mirador all this time. It stood only a few hundred meters ahead.

"Yeah, okay," she said in surrender, tired of thinking. "But I've got another idea."

The surrounding beach lay studded with rocks and sharp outcroppings. Not much for shade, they found a spot between several boulders that afforded not only protection from the sun, but privacy as well. Zara put down her bag, which held a bottle of wine and a selection of cheeses, olives, and fruit bought at the market in Gibraltar. She surprised Dave when she began to take off her clothes.

"I'm going for a swim," she announced. "How about you?"

"Hell of an idea," Dave said and quickly doffed his shirt and jeans.

Naked, they both ran for the water and dove in. Zara felt completely free, as if the water could wash away all her concerns. She swam underwater for a few strokes, then surfaced, flipping onto her back and just floating. The water and the sun caressed their bodies, entreating them to let go of troublesome thoughts and just exist in the moment. They swam alongside one another then embraced and kissed, weightless in the water.

They made their way back to the boulders, opened the wine, and munched on fruit, cheese, and olives. They didn't bother getting dressed.

"Well, this has to be the first nude picnic I've ever been to," Dave said. "We really must do this more often. Invite the neighbors, y'know?"

More relaxed now, Zara laughed. *Diggy was right,* she thought. He would keep her laughing until they were old and gray.

She felt a sudden surge of bittersweet emotion. She'd fallen in love with him, no help for that now. But what he'd said about her father taking his place struck so deep a chord of irony within her, it made her chest ache. She looked across the short distance between them, her mind a mass of mixed feelings. He had a great body. A smooth, well-muscled chest and flat stomach. Legs that looked like he spent some time running. And she'd been with enough men to know he'd been…gifted…in the size of his penis. In spite of the heat, she shivered with the memory of their lovemaking, which had been both wildly sensual and tender beyond words.

I must be crazy…I barely know this guy…we work together, this can't end well. Yet I know we belong together. Left to dry in the sun, his hair curled up around his face. She set down her wine and went to him, a sense of purpose becoming clear to her as she drew near.

He lay on his back, on top of his t-shirt and jeans with his arms behind his head, gazing up at the sky. He looked like a modern-day Tarzan. She knelt down beside him and catching him off-guard, swung her leg over and straddled him like a horse. She sat upright, looking down on him.

"Whoa now," he managed to say. "Uh, let me guess. Girls from Barrie are sent to equestrian school for summer camp?"

For a change she got the last words in. "No. I went to… *private* school," she said, winking. "You've got your wish, Thunder Boy. Woman on top."

He looked up at her and fell silent. He reached up and cupped her breasts in both hands, brushing the nipples with his thumbs. She felt the sweetly painful tingle as they hardened and stood erect at his touch. She closed her eyes and let him explore as he wished. Then she leaned forward to kiss him. He moved his hands up to her face, stopping her a few inches away.

Looking into her eyes, he mouthed the words, "I love you," then brought her lips to his. Her heart clenched and Zara emptied all the passion she felt into this one kiss. She yearned to pleasure him in ways no one else could. She wanted to forget everything but this moment. If she was allowed only one man, then she would have every square inch, every last drop of this one. She tasted the salt on his lips, explored his mouth with her tongue. She could feel his heartbeat accelerating, his breath rapid. *Good, good…come with me, let me lead where no one else can take you.*

His cock grew hard against her inner thigh as she lay atop him, her legs hugging his hips. She kissed his neck, his Adam's apple, worked her way across his chest, flicking her tongue against his tight, contoured pecs. He groaned. And she smiled.

Just you wait, Thunder Boy…show's not nearly over. She wriggled lower, tickling him mercilessly by brushing her lips against his hard stomach. Something about the area around his navel made her ultra-aroused. She felt her own sexual muscles contract in anticipation. *When did I become this naughty,* she wondered, amazed she could think at all. She reached to take his erection in her hands, her touch as deft as with clay on a potter's wheel. Stroking it, she rubbed the tip with her thumbs, a glistening drop of pre-cum appearing there. She licked the stray fluid from the tip, heard his breath hitch and another groan escape his lips. She swallowed the starchy liquid that tasted faintly like fresh bread. Her mouth closed around the satiny head of his cock, tasting him as thoroughly as he'd tasted her.

She heard a whispered, "oh, babe..." as she held the tip against the roof of her mouth and sucked with a pulsating rhythm. She took all of him in, bore down on him until the head bumped the back of her throat. He groaned helplessly.

Zara eased off, withdrawing him from her mouth like a Popsicle on a hot summer day. She sat up, grinning at the power she wielded over him. She heard far-off calls of birds and smelled the pungent, late afternoon air as it found its way to them in spite of the sheltering rock.

His eyes snapped open as the sudden wisp of breeze touched his wet member. He made quite a sight, fully aroused and the question of 'what next' written across his face. Her grin turned devilish as she rose up on her knees and placed herself upon him, fitting him into her with a calculated slowness. Oh, God yes, he felt so good inside her.

Her next moves took even her by surprise. She rode him like a saddle bronc, satisfying some base, primal need that she didn't realize she possessed until this moment. Her hips rose and fell at a pace and force she alone decided, taking control of her own pleasure, filling herself with him to the max. Dave caught her by her wrists as she flipped her head back and two final grinding pushes sent him past his breaking point. Her warm body encased him, felt his muscle pulsing as she coaxed every drop of seed from him.

His eyes clenched shut and he laughed softly as he surrendered to her. When it subsided, she held him close, bestowing soft butterfly kisses on his face, his neck and the tops of his ears. He belonged to her now. She'd left a mark on him as telling as a scar.

"You are," he said, stroking her hair, "an absolute Goddess. What you do to me…I'm speechless."

Zara giggled. *Mr. Smart-Ass? Speechless?* "It's about time," she said.

"You realize payback will be significant."

"I consider it an investment," she said, laying her head against the moist skin of his chest, her hand exploring its muscular landscape. For a long while they lay entwined together in the sand, serenaded by the hushed sounds of waves cresting and retreating while the sun sank low in the sky.

"If you still want to have a look around El Mirador, we'd better do it now," Dave said. She agreed and they began to dress, brushing sand from themselves and their belongings as they prepared to leave.

"It's only a few hundred meters," Zara said. "Let's just walk."

"You sure?" he asked. Zara nodded. They'd come this far and her earlier foreboding had dissipated. They walked along the beach, seeing the ragged outline of El Mirador loom larger with every step.

*

Bernardo made it out of the parking garage without notice. He drove fast along the highway, the setting sun glaring in the windshield as he went west. He slowed at the exit to El Mirador, parking at the same lookout point as before. Carefully, he took the laptop case from behind the driver's seat and walked down the embankment, out of sight from the road. He sat on a flat rock and peered through binoculars to ensure no potential witnesses were in sight. He scanned the beach, the surrounding area and even out to sea, checking for boaters. Nothing.

He took out the detonator device from the laptop case then visually swept the shore one more time. Something caught his eye. Of all things, two people walked on the beach on a direct course for the scarecrow-ish remains of El Mirador. His binoculars zoomed in on them. Adjusting the focus, Cruz could make out a man and a woman dressed in casual clothing, seemingly doing nothing more than taking a stroll. He zoomed in to maximum and let out a stifled grunt upon realizing what he saw.

Flynn and what looked like one of the men from Wednesday's site visit walked directly toward the abandoned structure. Looking around, touching the pillars, pointing and talking to each other. He blinked, recalling he'd actually seen this man before.

At the airport in Jakarta.

Bernardo closed his eyes. He'd waited this long; he could wait a little longer until they progressed so far into the building they wouldn't escape in time. He trained his binoculars on them, held the device close to his chest, and waited for the right moment.

*

She noticed the smell first. The pigeons cooed and clucked, lying about as she and Dave approached the elevator column. Despite their presence, it occurred to Zara what had bothered her about the previous visit. "Can't you smell it?" she asked. Dave stood still, listened and inhaled. A mélange of many odors wafted around them, not the least of which was pigeon dung. He shook his head, apparently unsure which smell she referred to. They stood at the opening to the elevator well. A good twenty-foot drop stretched down to the basement, as they knew.

"It's oil, crude oil," she said in a quiet voice, prompting him for recognition. He looked at her and nodded. Zara gazed down the black shaft of the concrete well. "There's one way to find out for sure."

"Oh, you're not going down there, no way. We're not even supposed to be here. Ernie would freak if he knew I'd brought you back here, this close. We don't have safety gear and it's twenty feet down, for God's sake. What was I thinking…I'm such an idiot." He grabbed her arm to pull her away and get them both the hell out of there. They started to move away when Zara stopped short. She looked down at her feet then up at Dave.

"What?" Dave asked, grabbing her by both arms. "C'mon babe, we gotta go, it's getting dark." A shudder coursed up her spine, as though she'd stuck her finger in a light socket. She felt rooted to the spot, vibrating. It lasted a split-second, then her eyes went wide as she looked at Dave and choked out one word.

"Run!"

He bolted, half dragging, half lifting her along with him. The sound deafened them and the ground shook beneath their feet. Dust filled the air and she couldn't see him, only feel her arm in his grip. Chunks of concrete rained down like mammoth hailstones and she felt the ground give way. Dave grabbed hold of her around her waist and dropped into a roll, hurling them outward from the building. It was the last thing she remembered.

*

Cruz sat pinned to the rock, still clutching the deadly device in his hand. The building hadn't come completely down. Perhaps he hadn't planted the charges in exactly the right spots. But he'd done enough damage to end anyone's plans of restoring the structure. He waited for the dust to clear, watching through the binoculars for any sign of movement. Soon, darkness shrouded the deadly scene. Satisfied, he put the detonator back in the laptop case and scrambled up the bank.

SPANISH SEDUCTION TRILOGY

Chapter Twenty-Two

Elena prepared to leave her brother's house. She'd stayed long enough to help Carmella get settled and cook dinner for the family, but told Ignacio privately that things must change between him and his wife if he wanted his girls to have a mother beyond the next few years.

"Good advice," he told her. "Good things are coming, Elena. Trust me." While they chatted on the patio, he glanced through the kitchen window and watched Carmella re-organize the cabinets. She disliked strangers in her house. The girls had gone to watch a movie in the playroom after supper. As she rearranged plates and cutlery, Ignacio wondered what Carmella had thought about in the past seventy-two hours. Her health, her marriage, her daughters?

He'd stayed nearly three whole days in hospital, not leaving her side. Surely this would mean something to her and demonstrate his effort to improve. Lucky to be alive this time, what would prevent another heart attack from happening to Carmella? His daughters must be provided for, in the event she wasn't so lucky next time. He should meet with a lawyer as soon as possible to review his will. As he saw Carmella take a broom from the closet, Ignacio turned away from the window and walked Elena to her car.

*

As she swept along the kick plates of the cabinets, something skittered out into the middle of the floor. Carmella bent down to pick it up and blew the dust off it. Examining it for a moment, she slipped it into her pocket and continued sweeping. Outside, she heard Elena's car start and drive away. Ignacio stepped into the kitchen.

"An excellent dinner, my dear," he said. "We could have ordered out you know, you didn't have to cook. You just got home. How do you feel?"

"I feel fine," she said. "But I should probably rest now. Why don't you run the girls their bath and get them ready for bed so I can sit for awhile."

Ignacio nodded. "Of course, dear. You should take things slow. I'll look after them, you relax. Can I make you a coffee before I go?"

"No, the caffeine would be bad for me, you tend to the girls."

"All right." He changed the subject. "Do you remember, I said there were a few projects underway for my new company? Well, I think things will start to happen this week and we could be seeing a profit very soon. I think you will be pleased." She looked back at him, gave him a vaguely supportive smile. She'd never felt confident about his 'projects.' Even he admitted he'd not been much of a success at anything outside of his day job.

"That's nice, Ignacio. I'm happy for you."

He beamed as though he'd just sunk a difficult putt. "Be happy for *us*," he corrected and gave her a kiss on the cheek on his way to the playroom.

Carmella leaned against the kitchen counter while her husband and daughters trooped upstairs. Then she went into Ignacio's office. Except to collect coffee cups and occasionally empty the ashtray after Ignacio had indulged in one of his nasty cigars, she seldom went there. She walked to the computer desk and sat down. The screen was dark but the computer's power light glowed green. She took the memory stick from her pocket and fitted it into one of the ports before switching on the monitor.

*

Ignacio let the girls splash around in the tub while he went to lay out their pajamas. His good mood made him feel like whistling. He felt certain Bernardo would have news for him soon. The bid proposals for the El Mirador property had been drawn up for weeks. It would only be a matter of time until they were accepted; the site would be next to worthless after Bernardo finished with it. Nearly ready for tenants, he expected his two downtown projects to start producing a positive cash flow any time. Vistamar was becoming a reality.

He returned to the bathroom and opened the door just wide enough to tell the girls to get out of the tub and dry off. "Go put on your pajamas and pick out a book, then I'll come read to you." He went down the hall to his own bedroom and searched in the bottom drawer of his nightstand, withdrawing a plain brown envelope. He just couldn't help taking another look at the papers to assure himself that all his dreams would soon be real.

He pulled them from the envelope and scanned over them. The proposal lay on top, outlining the 'clean-up' plans and offer to purchase for an obscenely below market price. The incorporation papers for Vistamar lay beneath that, the name of the principal stakeholder appearing at the bottom. The shadowy Salvatore Rodriguez.

Ignacio chuckled to himself. Bernardo did brilliant work.

No one knew that Vistamar's principal and the regional development officer were the same person.

He shoved the papers back inside. Instead of returning them to the drawer, he decided to keep the documents a little closer at hand. He folded the envelope and stuffed it in his back pocket. He planned to go down to his office as soon as the girls were in bed. He peeked into their room, bade them pick out their storybooks and get under the covers.

"I will be back to read to you in two minutes," he said, holding up two fingers.

"Okay, papa," they said and leaped in unison on top of their twin beds, bouncing up and down. Ignacio shook his head, smiling at their antics. He closed their door and started down the stairs. The sound of smashing glass startled him and he nearly slipped and fell down the steps. A second, muffled crash came from inside his office. Confused, he hurried to his office door and flung it open.

There, in front of his cigar humidor stood Carmella, brandishing an old soccer trophy he kept on one of his bookshelves. She'd broken the glass door of the humidor and boxes of his prized collection lay scattered over the floor, smashed and stomped on. His mouth dropped open in horror at the look on his wife's face. Her eyebrows knitted together over glaring eyes. She didn't speak, but pointed to the computer. He'd forgotten all about what he'd been doing before Carmella had collapsed in the kitchen three days ago. The last picture he'd been viewing displayed on the screen, zoomed in tight. The image of a topless Zara Flynn.

"Vete de aqui!" It sounded more like a growl than a scream. It rose in pitch as she repeated, *"Vete de aqui!* Get Out!" She advanced toward him, the heavy trophy on its wooden base in her hand. Ignacio backed up, stumbled over the threshold of his office door. "Get out, and don't come back!" She raised the trophy higher, as if meaning to strike him with it. Ignacio

turned and ran. The keys still in his pocket he dashed madly to his car and backed out of the driveway, having no idea where he would go.

*

"Have you found her yet?" Miguel asked, as Luis entered the dressing room.

Luis shook his head. "Nor Cruz, either. His car is not on resort property. Señorita Flynn moved to room 514 three days ago but she is currently out. We are looking for Señor and Señora Ridley, the elderly couple she's been seen with during her stay here. Perhaps they'll know something."

Miguel sat in his dressing room chair, elbows on his knees and fingertips pressed together. *"Bien,* Luis. If you find her, please bring her to me as you did before. She needs to know the danger she is in."

"Is there anything else?" Luis asked as he turned to leave, his hand on the doorknob.

Miguel needed mental prep time. Wardrobe and makeup had still to be done before going on stage at 9:00. Miguel shook his head and stared down at the floor. Luis closed the door. No time to think about this now. He had a show to do.

Chapter Twenty-Three

Bette wrung her hands nervously as she and Diggy sat waiting in the Club Marbella lounge. They had tickets for Montana's Saturday night show, which was about to start. But no sign of Zara or Dave.

"Here comes your G and T, luv," Diggy said, as the waiter approached. "Go on, get that down you." He tried his best to remain calm, his years of military service gracing him with a steely surface. Jorge had brought them to the hotel early this afternoon. They didn't really expect Zara back until dinnertime, but when dinner had come and gone, Bette began to worry.

"What if they've broke down on the road, or had an accident, or—oh God, been victims of a drive-by?" she fretted, her imagination escalating her fear.

"They've got cell phones, haven't they? We'd have heard if they was in trouble," Diggy said. "Don't get your knickers in a twist just yet, luv. Drink your drink and let's enjoy the show."

*

The dirt and dust in her mouth made Zara choke as she tried to breathe in. She coughed and spat out mud and saliva. She lay on her side, her cheek flat on the ground. Her face stung as she felt the rough particles rubbing against it. She opened her eyes and tried to raise her hand to wipe the dirt away, but she lay pinned in an awkward position. She tried to gather her whereabouts and squinted to see in the darkness. Studded with a few early evening stars, the sky above the water still held some light. What seemed like a ten-ton weight lay on top of her. She moved her legs and managed to raise her knees a little. Her foot touched an unmoving Dave as he lay behind her, his arm still clutched her around her waist. She began to shake, suddenly feeling very cold. And afraid. *Please be alive,* she thought desperately. She moved her feet again, trying to prompt some movement from him. With painful effort, she lifted his arm enough to break his grip.

This got a response and she sighed with relief. He was okay. At least not dead. He let go and miraculously rolled away from her and sat up. She twisted onto her back, feeling rocks and concrete chunks shift beneath her. They'd made it halfway to the water before the building collapsed. What remained of the structure now lay in a dark heap, its outline barely discernable against the deepening sky. Rubble lay all around. Somehow, they'd managed to get clear of it.

Her left arm hurt like hell. Dave started to cough and she reached for him in the darkness with her right hand. "Jesus," she heard him swear, and then he spoke her name. "Zara…"

Her hand made contact and he grabbed it, turning toward her. She could hear the tumbling of rocks and debris as he moved. "Are you okay?" He coughed some more.

"I think so," she said, surprised to find her voice at all. "You?" She heard him spit aside into the rocks.

"Yeah," came the one-word response, but nothing more.

She had a feeling it wasn't really the truth. She tried sitting up, but her left arm wouldn't cooperate.

"Pull," she said, nudging her right arm against him. He pulled and she sat up. In the moonlight, she could see part of his face. Thank God, they were both still alive. "Are you hurt?"

He didn't answer. "Dave," she prodded. More silence."Dave, answer me," she demanded, raising her voice.

"Huh?" As if he hadn't heard her properly. Something was horribly wrong.

"Are you hurt?" she repeated.

"I don't know." He sat very still.

Damn, her left arm hurt. She would have to try and stand, get them moving if she could. "Can you stand?" she asked. He leaned forward, pulling her with him. She manoeuvred her feet underneath her and pushed with her legs. Together they managed to rise to their feet. She wrapped her right arm around his neck. He steadied her with an arm around her back.

"What happened," he asked. Zara really didn't know but remembered a sensation, like an electric shock, just before the noise. A premonition. As if her brain knew what was coming even if her body didn't.

"It sounded like an explosion. Or maybe an earthquake."

"How did we get here," he asked next.

Worry flooded her brain. He wasn't talking right, his voice sounded muffled. He didn't seem to remember what just happened. Wincing with pain, she reached up to touch his face. It came away slick and wet with blood. She ran her hand up over his forehead and around the back of his head, feeling for a wound. The entire left side of his head felt warm and slippery.

"Ouch." He pushed her hand away.

"Oh God," she said, her voice trailing off. *Something must have hit him in the head. How bad?* "C'mon, let's get to the water." He didn't say anything. They moved toward the water's edge, Zara thankful they could walk. Her mind raced. He seemed disoriented, lethargic. He might have a concussion. The salt water would help stop the bleeding and keep him conscious. At the least, it would wash the blood and dirt away. She remembered him more or less tackling her as they ran out from under the falling concrete. He had probably saved them both. They got to the water and waded in up to Zara's waist.

"What are you doing? he asked, sounding dazed.

She couldn't tell exactly where the blood oozed from. The waves slapped against her ribs. Far enough. She stopped and faced him squarely. "Okay, sweetie, we're going to duck under the water for a sec. On three, okay…one, two, three." She pushed down on his shoulders as best she could with her bad arm and under they went. Her face stung in the salt water. Wherever they were cut, the salt would tell them.

They burst out of the water, Dave yelling in pain, holding his hand to the side of his head. She followed his arm up to the spot and could feel some swelling there.

"What the fuck are you doing," he swore.

"I'm sorry, baby, I'm sorry," she said, knowing he was hurting. "I just need to keep you awake, okay? We can get out of the water now, let's go." They sloshed their way back to shore and sat down out of reach of the waves. She held him tight as she could and felt herself starting to cry. "Okay Thunder Boy, snap out of it, I need your help here."

He was shivering, but reached over and held her head in his hands. "I'm okay, shhhh…stop it now." He stroked her hair, brushing it away from her face. "Shhh, it's okay. I feel better, thanks. Boy, you sure know how to throw cold water on a guy."

She started to shake with relief. Now she knew he was okay.

He was cracking jokes again. She laughed weakly through her tears, holding her aching arm.

"Let's see that arm," he asked.

"It hurts." He felt it up and down. She gasped in pain when he closed his hand around her forearm.

"You may have broken it," he said. She nodded, but there was nothing for it. Neither spoke for a few minutes. Then Dave said, "I don't think it was an earthquake. That felt like a bomb going off."

Zara took a deep breath. "I think someone's just tried to kill us."

"We've got to call somebody. Do you have your cell phone?"

Shit, she thought. *In my bag, but where's the bag?*

"My bag," she said and crawled back toward where they'd fallen, groping around for it. By sheer luck, her hand touched the smooth surface of the red handbag and snatched it up.

Dave came up beside her as she rummaged through it, feeling for the pocket where her phone should have been. It came apart in pieces in her hand. "No…shit, no!" She flung the pieces across the wreckage. "It's toast."

"My phone's in the truck. We'll have to get back there," Dave said.

She knew he was right. They would need water soon, too. She'd stowed some bottled water in the truck. Slowly, they started westward along the dark, deserted shoreline.

Chapter Twenty-Four

Now he had intentionally done murder. This thought weighed heavily on Bernardo. First the woman on the balcony, now the Flynn girl and her partner. The ghosts of his faith began to dance forbiddingly in the back of his mind. Would he be condemned to purgatory? He forced the thoughts away. He should contact Verrera, let him know the trigger had been pulled and that he could present the bid again. With the papers signed, he could do away with Verrera too, and assume the identity of the mysterious Mr. Rodriguez.

Yes, he thought. *That's the answer.* If anyone had seen him, or in any way connected him with the explosion, Bernardo Cruz would be the scapegoat. He must become Rodriguez as soon as possible. He turned the car around and headed east. All the documents and ID were in the office in Malaga. Once there, he could ditch the vehicle and go elsewhere, anywhere, and Cruz would cease to exist. He felt a pang of regret at this but regretted even more that he and Michelle would never be together again.

*

Ignacio felt the tears streaming down his face. Just when he thought things were going right, they had again taken an evil turn. Even if Carmella divorced him, he wouldn't care so much about that as the thought he might lose his children. What to do now, where to go. To Elena's? She'd already warned him to make a change and he had brushed her off. He could think of only one place. His downtown office.

No cars filled the parking lot, no lights illuminated the building. He parked and went to the entry keypad at the main doors. The device buzzed green after he punched the code and went inside. He crossed to the elevators, rubbing his palms together. A cold sweat covered his body. He rode up the seven floors in the Government Building as he had done every day for twenty years. The steps to the Planning & Development Office from the elevator landing were mechanical now. He sometimes never recalled walking the distance between them.

He again input a code into a keypad and entered the outer office. He didn't bother turning any lights on for he knew the way by instinct, moving down the hall from the reception area and into his personal office. He felt for the edge of his desk and slumped into his chair. Breaking down, he laid his head on his desk and blubbered in misery, cursing his luck and his situation.

After awhile, with his emotions spent and his tears dried, he sat with his head down feeling completely empty. He had no concept of how long he stayed like this; it might have been hours or minutes. Then he heard a noise. Someone else was coming into the front office.

How could this be? On a Saturday night, of all days to come here, what were the odds of someone else dropping by? He remained quiet, seated at his desk. The intruder might be a cleaning lady who would be gone as quickly as she'd come. He heard footsteps crossing the reception area, but no lights switched on. No noise to indicate a cleaning cart or other equipment. The steps came to a stop outside his open door. The doorknob across the hall began to turn. Cruz' office. *What the devil is going on? What is Cruz doing here?*

A light flipped on. He could see Bernardo entering his office, dressed in casual clothes. He went to his desk, took a key from his pocket, and opened one of the drawers. The same as Verrera's, the government-issue desk had only one drawer with a lock on it, the bottom left. Did Cruz keep booze in there? Drugs? No, he pulled out some papers and sorted through them.

Ignacio stood up and quietly went to the door to confront him. He'd expected to hear from him by now, anyway. He appeared from the shadows to stand squarely in the entrance of Cruz' office. Bernardo didn't seem to notice him at first, but when he glanced inadvertently to the doorway, he jumped almost a foot in the air. The folders he held slipped from his hand and scattered to the floor.

Cruz stumbled backward in fright, tripping over his chair and losing his balance. Verrera almost felt sorry for him. He hadn't intended to scare the living daylights out of his assistant. But neither of them were exactly in a place they should have been. "Bernardo, what's going on?" Verrera asked. He stooped to pick up the items that had landed nearest him.

Cruz scrambled to get up. *"Mierda,"* he shouted. *"¿Qué coño haces aquí?"*

Verrera crouched down, staring at the documents in his hands. A passport and a driver's license. They bore Cruz' photo and the name Salvatore Rodriguez. He felt frozen to the spot, though his face burned.

He'd been double-crossed.

Cruz would have taken all his hard work, all his careful planning and stolen his future from him. The ungrateful, skinny little *bastardo*! Verrera stayed still but peered at Bernardo from the corner of his eye.

"*¿Qué coño haces aquí?* What the hell are you doing here?" Cruz repeated.

Slowly, Ignacio stood, a murderous look in his eye as he turned his gaze on him. They stared each other down for only a second before Cruz swept all the items from his desktop at Verrera then launched himself over the desk and hurtled through the doorway. A small man, Ignacio could easily have overpowered Bernardo if he'd caught hold of him. As it was, the wiry Cruz ran for the exit leaving Verrera, overweight and ten years older, woefully behind in pursuit.

When Verrera got outside the office, he heard the slamming of the stairwell doors. If no one else entered the building, the elevator should still be stopped on this floor, he reasoned. Ignacio pressed the button and the elevator doors slid open on command. He pressed M, not knowing where or how Cruz might have entered the building. More than one set of doors existed on main. But with only one parking lot, surely Cruz would have seen Verrera's car. Therefore, he hadn't come through the front. He still held the IDs in his hands as the elevator descended.

Did it matter if he caught up with Cruz? He had the evidence right here. He couldn't exactly turn him in. What could he charge him with, committing fraud more cleverly than his boss? Only one course of action presented itself. Despite the unfortunate circumstances, Ignacio found himself smiling as the seed of a new plan took root.

Chapter Twenty-Five

At last, they could see the lightposts marking the viewpoint where they'd parked the truck. It took a lot longer, in the dark and injured, to return to it than it had to walk to El Mirador from it this afternoon. Zara had lost track of time, focusing only on reaching the truck, the cell phone, the bottles of water, and getting back to Marbella. Or a hospital, whichever they passed first.

She felt sure she'd broken her left arm above the wrist, or at least severely sprained it. Dave seemed to be okay but she worried how much blood he might still be losing, or God forbid, if there might be brain injury. "How ya doing?" she asked him, checking the bump on his head to see if the bleeding had stopped. "There's the truck, up there."

"I see it. I'm not worried about me. How's that arm?"

"Hurts," she said. "Broken bones are simple. Brain cells are not. Keep talking to me okay, so I know you're all right."

"It's no big deal, it's not the first time," he said.

"What do you mean?" They walked a few more steps.

"I've had a concussion before."

"When?"

"I used to play hockey for MIT. I've had my bell rung a few times."

"Oh." That explained a lot, especially the deer antlers in his office. They were almost at the path to the viewpoint. Finally, they arrived at the truck and in the lamp light took stock of their condition.

"Oh babe, your face," he said sadly, seeing the skin scraped away across her cheekbone. He cradled her arm in his hands. A blackish-red swelling blossomed from elbow to wrist.

"Let me see," she said, looking for the gash on his head. Hidden by his hair, the bleeding had stopped, but he definitely needed stitches. He pulled the keys from his pocket. "Maybe I should drive?" Zara said.

"If I faint, you have permission to take over," he replied, opening the doors and fishing the cell phone out of the glove compartment. He called the local emergency number to report the explosion and then called Jorge, asking him to meet them at the hospital in Marbella. He started the engine and pulled out onto the highway.

*

The stage lights flashed and the crowd went crazy as the pit band played the intro to the song they'd all come to hear. The screams grew louder as they recognized Montana's current Latin chartbuster, *Una vida por mi*, 'One Life for Me.'

Miguel advanced to center stage, holding his arms high. Girls tried to rush the stage, held back by the beefy security guards surrounding it. Dressed all in white again, he flashed his brilliant smile to the crowd and basked in their adoration. Motioning for the audience to clap to the beat, he waited teasingly. And when sufficiently ramped up, he stepped to the microphone and began to sing:

"Una vida, un amor por mí,
a cantar y ser libre, La canción me sostiene,
Una vida, un amor por mí"

One life, one love for me,
to sing and be free, the song will carry me,
One life, one love for me.

From his tiny vantage point wedged between instrument cases deep in the backstage, Bernardo listened to the words he knew by heart, as he did most of Montana's compositions. He'd topped 150k on the motorway from Malaga. With his future crumbling around him, he felt desperate to be near Michelle no matter the cost, no matter whether she was man or woman tonight. For she was both and neither.

From a loading bay in the rear of the hotel, he'd managed to enter the backstage area undetected. He knew the layout well but sat frozen in his hiding place, feeling alone, afraid, and trapped. Hiding from himself and what might lie ahead. Where was he to go now?

*

Bette sat in her seat, clapping to the rhythm of *Una vida para mi*. Though one of her favorite numbers, she wasn't enjoying it tonight. She worried about Zara. She and Dave had not returned by show time, and at Diggy's insistence, they went ahead into the auditorium to take her mind off them. Forty-five minutes into the performance, Bette couldn't sit still any longer. She told Diggy she would be back in a few minutes and left the theater. She returned to their room, and setting her handbag on the bed, saw the message button flashing on the house phone. She dived for it.

Jorge's voice stated he was leaving immediately to meet Miss Zara and Mr. Parker at the Medicenter in Marbella, that there had been an incident and would explain later. Zara had requested he contact the Ridleys, tell them the situation, and not to worry. They would return to the Club as soon as they could. Knowing they were at the Medicenter did nothing to ease Bette's anxiety. If anything, it made it worse.

She mixed herself a short G and T and sat down to drink it. The gin hit the spot and she visibly relaxed after a few belts. Polishing off the drink, she rose to leave but stopped just short of the door, as though she'd forgotten something. She dug in her suitcase until she found it. Tucking it in her handbag, she left the room.

*

Dave lay face down on the treatment bed as Dr. Mendez, the on-call physician, sutured the lacerated skin on his head. "Do you have a headache now?" Dr. Mendez asked.

"A little. Not bad."

"Can you say your name, last, first, and middle?"

Dave sighed. "Parker, David Justin."

"And can you count backwards from twenty, please?" Dave hesitated. "I apologize if these questions sound foolish," Mendez continued. "It is only a precaution."

"Twenty, nineteen, eighteen, seventeen…"

"*Muy bien,* that's fine," the doctor said, satisfied that Dave was all right for the moment. "If the headache persists, please take an analgesic. If they become severe you should come back and see me, is that clear?"

"Yes."

"I see someone is worried about you," Dr. Mendez commented, as he dabbed the wound with an antiseptic gel. "You can sit up now."

Dave sat up just in time to see the duty nurse parking a wheelchair at the end of the room. In the chair sat Zara, her forearm in a cast and a bandage on her cheek.

"Hey," she said.

"Hey, yourself. What's with the wheels? "

"They just like to be careful. From now on, I'm never going to turn down a free ride."

He gestured to her arm. "Broken?"

"I have a non-displaced linear fracture," she recited. "Pretty minor, considering." She turned to Dr. Mendez. "How many stitches did he need?"

The doctor held up five fingers. "You are both very lucky to have such minor injuries. Mr. Parker has some bruising and two cracked ribs, but the head wound should heal nicely," He glanced from one to the other. "Oh yes, since he has a history of previous concussion, it would be wise to have someone stay the night with him. Can that be arranged?"

"Yes," they said simultaneously. Mendez raised his eyebrows, but said nothing more as he left the room.

Dave stood and went over to kneel beside Zara's chair. "You look a little worse for wear. How do you feel?"

"Tired, mostly. Sore."

Dave nodded and looked into her eyes. It broke his heart to see her in pain, bandaged up like this. He thought about what she'd said earlier. "You said, 'someone just tried to kill us.' Do you still feel that way?" She bit her lip, then nodded. "And are you going to tell the police that?"

"Not yet. It's just a feeling."

"So far, your feelings have been pretty accurate. That look on your face right before we booked it out of there, what were you feeling then?"

She thought about it for a moment. "Electricity," she said. "Like lightning going through my body. As if my brain was receiving the detonator signal and telling me to run."

Dave shook his head slowly from side to side. "Weird. You saved our asses, you know that."

She looked at him steadily. "I wouldn't have made it out fast enough if you hadn't been with me."

He took her hand, kissed it, and stood up, chuckling. "What a team. Lightning Girl and Thunder Boy," he announced.

Zara laughed too, even though it hurt. They turned to leave and saw Jorge in the doorway. "You are both okay?" he asked. They nodded. "It is almost midnight. David, I think it's best you leave the truck here and I will take you both back to the Club. I'm sure we can arrange a room for you. Also, the police say they want to interview you both tomorrow. Shall we go?"

With Dave's arm around her, they made their way out.

Chapter Twenty-Six

The concert ended at 11:30. Bette and Diggy paced nervously in the lobby of Club Marbella, waiting for Zara. They weren't the only ones waiting. Separated by several meters, Luis and Raoul had installed themselves casually about the room dressed in street clothes. The automatic entrance doors slid open and Bette's eyes fixed on the threshold until at last she glimpsed Jorge entering the lobby with Dave and Zara close behind. Dave held Zara, her arm in a sling, as they walked. Bette fairly ran to them, her pink heels clattering across the marble floor.

"Ye Gods, what's happened to the pair of you?" She went to hug Zara, uncertain of how to put her arms about her without disturbing the sling. Diggy stood behind Bette, equally concerned.

"It's a long story," Zara said, reaching out to Bette with the uninjured arm.

Diggy shook Jorge's hand, saying, "Good man, rescuing our kids, thanks for ringing us." He turned to Dave and slapped him on the shoulder. "You're a sight, lad. I knew you'd protect our girl."

"We should have just come back all together," Zara said to Bette. "I'm so sorry we worried you."

Jorge stepped in. "Señor and Señora Ridley, we should let them get some rest now. You can all talk over coffee in the morning."

Diggy held up a hand. "Of course, you're totally right, mate. We's just so happy to see you safe and sound. Sort of," he added, pointing to their bandages. Happy to see the Ridleys too, Zara clung to Bette with her good arm, reassuring her she was all right, when she spotted them over Bette's shoulder.

"What's wrong, dear?" Bette said, feeling Zara stiffen.

"It's double-oh-seven," she whispered.

Bette whirled about. Luis and Raoul approached them swiftly. "Miss Zara Flynn," Luis said in a low voice. Zara stared them down, and as they came within a few feet of her, Dave stepped in front.

"Can I help you, gentlemen," he said, in a most un-friendly tone.

They both sent him a condescending look. "Step aside, *vaquero.* We have information for the lady."

"From whom," Zara said sharply.

"I think you know who," Luis said. Dave looked over his shoulder at Zara. Her face expressionless, Bette stood fast next to her.

Luis relaxed his stance. "Bring *el vaquero* if you wish. *Es importante,* for your safety." Dave scowled at the cowboy reference. He kept his eyes on Zara, seeing what she wanted to do.

"Me and all," Bette said. Luis shrugged and waved them forward. Zara stood still, thinking at light speed. As attractive as the prospect of seeing Miguel again would have been just a few days ago, the situation was very different now. What information could these two possibly have? Why would they be concerned about her safety? They didn't insist she come alone this time. *There must be something else going on*, she decided. However, she refused to go to the penthouse again. Perhaps they'd be willing to meet on neutral ground if the matter was so important. Something told her she should leave Dave behind, too. Not because it might be awkward, but so she could call for backup if anything went wrong.

"Who are these guys and how do they know you?" Dave asked, impatience in his voice.

Zara put her hand on his shoulder, whispered something to him and slipped him her cardkey. Then she spoke to Luis. "Listen, we've had a really long day, we're tired, and we're grouchy. Can we do this somewhere neutral, maybe the lounge?"

Luis considered this. He nodded to Raoul, who turned away and began using his headset. In a moment, he finished his call and said, "We can use the backstage. We'll meet you there." Raoul turned and left.

Luis took over. "This way, please."

Zara took Bette by the hand. "Come with me?" she asked.

"Too right, I will." To Diggy she said, "You stay put, luv." The two women followed Luis toward the theater.

*

As they moved out of view, Dave turned to Jorge. "She wants you to give me your cell phone. We lost hers, but she has mine with her and she'll call your number if there's any trouble. Mr. Ridley, she said you'd explain who those guys were."

Diggy crossed his arms and watched the ladies disappear around the corner. "I'm not exactly sure," he admitted. "But they work for the Latin loverboy, Mickey Mountain." Dave and Jorge looked at him blankly. "Miguel Montana, the singer," Diggy went on. "He's been performing here all week. He took a bit of a shine to our Zara after Tuesday's show. That's when them two blokes turned up."

"She's met this guy before?" Dave asked, his voice hardening.

Diggy uncrossed his arms, patted Dave on the shoulder. "Take it easy now, lad, nothing happened, according to her. She's safe with our Bette playing watchdog. When you've been with a missus as long as I have, you learn when to trust. You'll learn, too."

*

Zara felt too exhausted to be frightened. She just needed to find out what they wanted from her. She and Bette followed Luis through the theater and around to the backstage area. They stepped around electrical cords, light banks and spot stands, packing crates and folded risers. In a clear area, Luis pulled out some stacking chairs and offered them a seat. He put his hand to his headset, listening. "They will just be a few moments," he affirmed.

Bette sat nervously as Zara recounted what had happened since morning. How they'd almost been killed and couldn't shake the feeling that it had all been planned. And that Miguel somehow had related information. She discreetly showed Bette the cell phone in her hand. Bette nodded but looked doubtful that a phone would offer much protection.

Raoul returned. Behind him, dressed in the same plain gray hoodie to hide his face, walked Miguel. As they came closer, Zara recognized the same pleasant scent he'd worn the other night. Miguel fixed his eyes on her, a look of concern on his face when he saw her arm. Bette nearly swooned, catching in her breath as she glimpsed the famous rock star up close and personal.

"Miss Zara, what has happened to you? Are you alright?"

"Your men say you have information for me," Zara said.

Miguel looked from her to Luis to Bette. He spoke in a soft voice filled with regret. "I apologize for this intrusion. It is good you have brought someone who loves you, *Cherie*. Life is nothing without love. There is strength in love."

It seemed a lifetime ago that Zara sat facing him in the penthouse. He appeared even more handsome now, as he exposed this genuine and vulnerable side of himself.

"I think someone is trying to kill me," Zara said. "Do you know anything about this?"

He sat down in the chair opposite her and reached for her good hand. She took it and waited. "You are in danger. I see that he has already tried to reach you," Miguel said, touching her bandaged face. "It is my fault. He is here because of me."

"Who is here?" she asked. "Who?"

Miguel sighed in anguish. "I call him *El Ángel Oscuro,* Dark Angel. But his name is Cruz. Do you know him?"

Zara searched her mind for that name. Then she remembered the skinny man at Monday's meeting. *Why would he be involved?* "I think so. Why am I in danger? What will he do?"

"He came to your room on the tenth floor. But you were not there. He didn't know you had moved. Someone he thought was you fell to her death from the balcony. At his hands. I don't know the reason, but perhaps you do."

Drained, she couldn't sort out anything logical in her mind. She vaguely remembered Cruz, an assistant to the Planning Officer. She clasped Miguel's hand tighter.

"No. I don't. I only met him once." She forced herself to think harder. *It must be to do with El Mirador.* She visualized the quiet, odd sort of man. Kept his hands in his pockets. "How do you know him?"

Miguel displayed an enigmatic smile. "Let us say, I *know* him. He is not pleased with me right now. He is…a jealous person. And he means to kill you. It is only *suerte,* luck, that he didn't succeed the first time," he said, gesturing to her sling. "You will know him by a tattoo on the back of his hand. A tiny angel in black ink. Be warned, I have not seen Ángel since yesterday. He may still be here, or he may not. He is dangerous."

Zara looked at him as though for the last time and leaned toward him. "Thank you. And I apologize for…not being very good company."

Miguel smiled. "*De nada*, Zara Flynn. It is enough that we are friends, yes? I am glad." He looked up at Bette then back to Zara. "You should go now." He stood and held out his hand to Bette. She eagerly placed her hand in his and he kissed it in knightly fashion. "Take care." He turned toward his bodyguards and with a loud snapping sound, the room instantly went black.

*

Bernardo waited by the electrical panel, listening for movement. He'd watched them the entire time, crouched in his hiding spot since the performance. He couldn't believe his eyes. What was she doing still alive, the bitch? He knew their positions, but they didn't know his. He would move straight for Flynn. The others didn't matter. He could escape before they found the light switches.

Luis and Raoul immediately assumed their prime responsibility, seizing Miguel and moving to the exit. Their training made it second nature to have memorized the layout of any area their client entered. This left Bette and Zara unprotected. Bette's chair scraped the floor, as if getting up to run. Deathly tired and with her arm throbbing, Zara didn't want to move at all. Better to wait until someone restored the lights.

In that moment what felt like a bulldozer hit her from the side, knocking her chair over and sending her hard to the floor. Someone dragged her by the arm across the bare wooden surface. She screamed, swung and kicked her legs trying to wrench loose from her attacker. Suddenly her arm jerked free and she rolled away overtop of her cast, mindless of the pain. She fumbled for Dave's cell phone and hit the recall for Jorge's number. She felt a hard kick to her ribs and for a moment thought she might vomit from the pain.

*

After sending food and water up to suite 514, Dave joined Jorge and Diggy in the late night bar. He felt ready to collapse but out of his mind with worry over Zara and Bette. He ran his hands through his matted hair, wincing as he grazed the bump on his head. Diggy ordered beer for all three of them. Dave told them all he could remember about the explosion, how they'd escaped and how Zara felt they were being targeted. They nursed their pints, not particularly enjoying them under the circumstances. The three sat silent for a few minutes until Jorge spoke up.

"You care deeply for Miss Zara, yes?" Dave raised his head to give Jorge a pained look that said it all. Jorge nodded as if confirming a fact he already knew too well. "I could feel it when we talked the other day. I knew you were the right one."

Diggy added his two cents. "Flaming hell, the only one what didn't know that right off was the lass herself. But she's mad for you too, lad. Anyone can see it just by looking at the pair of you."

The three men nearly jumped when the cell phone went off in Dave's pocket. He grabbed for it, flipped it open, and felt his blood run cold at the ungodly noise coming from it. Amid the cacophony of shouts and screams were gunshots. He was across the room before Diggy could shout to the bartender, "Call security!"

*

More shots rang out ahead as he charged into the dark,

cluttered backstage. Fear spiked in Dave's brain. *Dear God, no, no, no, No! Please let her be safe, away from whatever crazed bastard fired that weapon.* He dropped to a crouch at the sound, hoping to find something, anything, to take out the sick son of a bitch. Another gunshot from the opposite direction and then footsteps running, crashing into God knew what in the darkness.

Diggy found the panel and one section of lights came on. A final shot dropped a body to the floor, frighteningly close to where Zara lay curled in a fetal position. The victim, a smallish man, neither of the two from the lobby, sprawled awkwardly barely a meter from her. Only a little farther away and holding it in a curiously expert stance stood Bette, pointing a handgun at the body. Dave blinked at the bizarre scene and felt his stomach start to lurch.

More lights came on as security guards swarmed in and ringed the area where Zara lay. Sick with relief, Dave knelt beside her, unsure if he should try to move her. Despite the maddening chaos, the cavernous room seemed to shrink around him, vacuuming out all sound as it did so. The visual images in front of him grew in intensity and he saw everything in acute detail. Her shuddering body curled up next to him. Jorge huddled over her on the opposite side. The crumpled form of the man felled by a bullet just inches away, his left arm stretched out on the floor and the black mark on the back of his hand oddly conspicuous.

As if seen through a zoom lens the black mark filled Dave's field of vision, enlarging the tiny winged angel to enormous proportions. In a moment of blank clarity, he relived sitting in the airport lounge in Jakarta, waiting for his flight, when the little man in the suede jacket stepped next to him at the bar. His gaze fixed on the unusual design on the back of his hand. His head still foggy from his meds he'd said to him, "Sweet tattoo, man." The image rolled up and away like a window blind and Dave slipped back into the present, hovering over his terrified girl.

He laid his fingers at the side of her throat and exhaled silent thanks at feeling a strong pulse. She opened her eyes, then closed them again and began to tremble and sob uncontrollably. "Take me out of here," she begged in between ragged breaths.

Dave's ears seemed to flood with noise and heard what seemed like hundreds of voices all speaking at once with only a few random words piercing through the muddle. *'Policía, custodia, espere aquí.'*

Then his own voice. "Do what you have to, but I'm taking her." He lifted her in his arms and she clung to him like life itself. She buried her face in his chest and cried like a baby.

Chapter Twenty-Seven

On Sunday, church bells rang throughout Marbella and beyond. Amid their chiming, Zara sat in the local police station giving her account of the previous day's events.

The body removed from the Club Marbella theater had been identified as Bernardo Dominic Cruz. Listed as a public servant for the municipality of Malaga under the supervision of Ignacio Verrera, Cruz had no prior police record. He also appeared on the registered guest list at the Club Marbella. Police were dispatched to El Mirador after receiving Dave's call about the explosion. Evidence supported the use of explosive charges and a search of Cruz' vehicle found a detonator device concealed within an empty laptop case. Verrera would be sought as a person of interest in the case.

"Can Mrs. Ridley be released?" Zara asked.

The detective shuffled papers into a file folder. *"Si,* Miss Flynn. Señora Ridley's firearm had the proper licensing and appears to have been fired in self-defense. She is free to go. We will be in touch if we require more information. *Buenas Días."* Zara rose from her chair with a little help from Dave, and the two of them walked out into the bright daylight.

"You did great in there, babe," he said, his arm around her shoulders. He kissed her bandaged cheek. "How do you feel?"

"Like I need a vacation," she said. "Somehow bombs and gunfire just seem to take it out of me." They laughed together, standing in the police station parking lot. A strong breeze came off the waterfront, blowing Zara's hair across her face. She pulled him to her with her good arm and kissed him lightly on the lips. "I was supposed to be watching over you last night. Instead you rescued me. Again."

Exhausted, they'd spent the rest of the night in Zara's room. They woke up locked in each other's embrace, still fully dressed.

"Well, I'll let it go this time," he said. "But you owe me." They walked to the Flynn truck, retrieved from the Medicenter earlier. "I talked to Ernie," Dave said. "The reports will be in tomorrow."

"Oh, poor Ernesto," Zara said, thinking how bad this all sounded. "He's got a mess on his hands. I'll bet he wasn't pleased with us."

"No. But he's glad we're safe. We'll have some explaining to do when we get back to the office." He held her close and rested his chin on her head. "I need to go home for a while, get cleaned up," he said. "Can I come back for you, have dinner together?"

"Well, like you said, we both need to be at work tomorrow. You needn't drive all the way back for me."

He released her only to grip her by the shoulders and give her an admonishing look. "I don't intend to spend tonight or any other night of my life without you, Lightning Girl. Get used to it. Pick you up at six."

Zara looked at him, drinking in the image of him so she could never forget how he looked at that very moment. She adored him. She didn't want to be apart from him either. Not one minute. Her heart was full. "In that case, why don't I come to your place? I'll talk Jorge into loaning me the Mercedes. What are you cooking tonight?" He tightened his arms around her waist and lifted her into the air, kissing her madly. He seemed to have forgotten his two cracked ribs.

When he dropped her off at the Club, he made sure she had his address and her promise to be there by six or he'd have her arrested. She wanted to say goodbye to the Ridleys and see them off before their four o'clock flight. More than that, she needed to thank Bette for saving her life. Who knew the flamboyant, middle-aged Englishwoman was a practiced sharpshooter? She shook her head at the strange turn of events. As she made her way through the lobby, a man waved to her from his seat on one of the overstuffed couches. It was Mr. Verrera.

"Señorita Flynn, I am sorry to intrude like this." He stood to greet her, holding his briefcase in one hand. He stared at her arm in its cast, and the bandage on her face. "I need to speak with you."

"The police are looking for you," she confided. "I won't tell them I've seen you."

"*Gracias*. It appears my assistant was working against me. And you. He tried to defraud you of your property under a false company name. I am sorry for the trouble he caused. Are you certain you're all right?"

He seemed sincere and truly concerned about her. "*Si*, Señor. Verrera. It looks worse than it is," she said, raising the arm a little. "But I'll be fine. I was lucky. Your assistant, not so much. He's dead." He looked at her and nodded, his expression unreadable. "I'm not sure we'll be able to proceed with the restoration plans you approved," she said. "It may be awhile before any decision or progress is made."

"It is of no importance now, Miss. You see, I will be leaving my job here and going away. I have some other opportunities that have presented themselves. I wanted to make sure you were all right and wish you well in your endeavours. And thank you again for…not seeing me," he said with a slight grin.

"*De nada,*" she replied. He took her good hand and kissed the back of it gallantly.

"*Àdios,* Señorita Flynn. *Buena suerte.*" His cell phone beeped in his pocket. With a nod, he took his leave. Verrera put the phone to his ear. Zara saw him smile as he took the call. "*Si,* this is Rodriguez," he replied.

*

Not large, Dave's apartment had a great open-concept space and a terrific skyline view. The Mediterranean exposed itself intermittently beyond the downtown towers. When Zara arrived, he stopped her at the door and stepped out into the hallway. Carrying her inside, he kicked the door shut and set her down on the couch where a frosty margarita pitcher waited on a side table. They toasted and Zara savored the salty crystals on the rim of her glass.

Her short sundress with skinny spaghetti straps showed off the beginnings of a tan on her neck and shoulders. Dave decided against a shirt altogether, going for comfort in a pair of favorite board shorts. As Zara looked around the place, she noticed two guitars side by side in their stands against one wall; one acoustic and one electric.

"I presume you play," she said.

"Once in awhile, when I can't sleep, sometimes."

"I bet your neighbors appreciate that. Would you play something now?"

"Sure, if you'd like." He picked up the acoustic and sat down on the couch, tuning it before strumming a few introductory chords. He played softly while they sipped their drinks. "You figured it out, didn't you; what's underneath El Mirador," he said. "You were trying to tell me something."

She'd hashed things over in her mind what seemed like a thousand times since yesterday. One thing she felt absolutely certain of. "The smell," she said. "It's very distinctive, raw bitumen. There's a lot of it out west. My class went on an exchange trip one year to the tar sands. When we were at the site on Wednesday, I couldn't place the odor. But the second time, it was unmistakable." She recognized the tune he was playing and guessed the title. "Roundabout?"

He smiled, nodding she was correct. "Maybe your senses weren't as sharp that day," he suggested, alluding to her hangover.

"Ah, no," she admitted. "You weren't exactly catching me at my best. But if there's a bitumen deposit under the foundation of any significance, that means a lot of money to whomever gains mineral rights to the site and can extract it successfully."

"Which right now, happens to be you."

She nodded. "I see now why Dad paid more than market value for it." Dave had switched to a new tune. "Malaguena," she stated, smiling at him. "Did you know I received an offer to buy it?" He shook his head, but grinned in enjoyment of their impromptu game of name-that-tune. "A company called Vistamar Holdings faxed in an offer on Monday. For less than half of the price, stating it was contaminated and an 'eco-hazard.' They lowballed to justify the expense of the alleged cleanup. Now I see they planned to clean up, all right. Monetarily, not environmentally."

"I've heard that name, Vistamar Holdings," Dave said, starting another song. "Ernie gave me their report before we went out on there on Wednesday. They're a small sub company, did surveys for us a few times. I didn't know they were bidding on properties."

Verrera's words began to echo in Zara's mind. *'He tried to defraud you under a false company name'*. "It was Cruz," she said, a light coming on in her brain. "Cruz was Vistamar Holdings." She listened to the guitar again, pausing to think a little harder about this new tune. Then she pointed to the instrument and said, "Sleepwalk."

He stopped playing and set the guitar back in its stand. "You're good," he said, but his face turned serious. "Cruz was also the one who nearly got us killed." Dave frowned in thought. "Did you see the tattoo on his hand?" he asked.

Zara thought about what Miguel had told her. *El Ángel Oscuro.* He had some sort of relationship with him. One she didn't want to think about. The most beautiful flower arrangement waited in her room when she returned from the police station. *'Amour toujours,* Miguel' the card read. "Yes, I saw it."

"I've seen him before. In the Jakarta airport when I flew out. He ordered a drink from the bar and I saw his tattoo." He regarded her carefully.

Her eyes darkened and in a barely audible voice said, "Go on."

Mindful of her arm in its cast, he came and sat close to her. "He might also have been responsible for your father's death," he said, sounding reluctant to speak the words that he knew must be spoken. Zara's throat went dry. Dave's words were logical, but it didn't matter much now. Tristan was gone and she would have to make her peace with that. She nodded in agreement.

"So the only question left is the one you wanted answered most," Dave said. "Why Tristan left El Mirador to you, and what did he expect from you?"

She looked into his eyes. If they had been two cobalt-blue oceans, Zara would have dived in headfirst. "I don't know." Her voice squeaked. "I wish he could tell me." He put his arm around her, kissed her forehead, and stroked her hair. The only comfort he could offer was his presence. For the moment, it was enough. She leaned against him in silence.

After a minute or two he reminded her, "Hey, we haven't eaten yet. Hope you like clam chowder."

This made her smile and brought her back to reality. "Love it. Not in your average guy's culinary repertoire. Where'd you learn to make it?"

He laughed. "Remember, I lived in Boston. It's a criminal offense there if you don't like crab and clams. And beans."

"Go Bruins," she added with a closed-fist salute. "By the way, what did you get sick with in Indonesia?"

He grabbed her hand and pulled her up off the couch. He tilted his face slowly toward her. "Food poisoning. Let's eat." This time her tears were from laughter.

They ate, talked, and drank by candlelight for hours about anything and everything. Particularly interested in the renovations Dave had made to the apartment, she started to ask how he'd managed to alter the joists to achieve the ceiling effect in the room when he cut her off. "Okay, Lightning Girl, that's enough shop talk for today." He took her glass from her and set it down. "We'll have plenty of that in the morning." He snuffed out the candles and took her by the hand. They stood silhouetted against the evening sky, the lighted windows of office towers glittering like stars in the distance.

He led her to the bedroom, his bedroom. She could feel desire rising inside her, as if she'd been apart from him for days instead of mere hours. It felt so right, being here. In his domain, where she belonged. They stood in the darkness and he pulled her close, kissing her long and hard. His fingertips traced up her arms, slipping the thin straps off her shoulders and letting the dress fall to the floor. He slid his hands down her back and around her buttocks. She'd worn nothing at all underneath her dress, as if she'd been waiting for this moment.

She could almost feel him burning inside, sending the heated blood rushing to his loins.

"I liked your playing," she said. "Thank you for sharing it with me."

"No problem," he whispered. "Let me know if you can't sleep. It works like a charm."

"I don't want to sleep." The Velcro closure on his shorts made a ripping sound as she pulled it open, pushing the shorts down over his hips until they, too, fell to the floor. He stepped out of them, grabbed her behind her thighs, and lifted her to him.

"Good," he said.

She wrapped her legs around him as he carried her to the bed, the bolts in its steel frame chattering as he fairly flung her onto it. Caging her with his body, he streaked kisses across her collarbone and over her breasts. Her breathing heightened and her body begged for his touch. "You don't know how much I wanted to get you here," he said. "Get you home." He licked her nipples and tugged gently at them with his lips, making them tense and harden. Zara thrilled to both his words and his hands. "Home safe. Just us. No one else in the world." His whispered words tickled her skin in between kisses.

She wanted him so badly. No, needed him so badly. "No… No one else," she echoed, her voice choked with emotion. He stroked her thighs and they parted, asking for him. He obliged and his fingers connected with the wet, needy flesh between them, insisting, exploring, demanding. Zara felt blinded with arousal. She raised her hips in response to him. She wanted to scream out his name, giving his neighbors more than guitar playing to worry about. Instead it left her lips in a throaty purr, "Oh, Dayy-vid…"

She heard him chuckle softly. "Ah, the Goddess speaks."

She wanted to return the mind-blowing pleasure he was giving her. She rolled them both over so that she was on top.

He sprawled leisurely beneath her, awaiting whatever erotic delight she had in mind. Her tongue licked a path down his abdomen to the base of his marvelously erect member and painted the sides of it with the broad strokes of an artist's brush, working her way up its length. He uttered deep, groaning sighs and he grasped the strands of her hair that swept across his clenched abs. She took him in her mouth and glazed his hard muscle up and down with wet lips.

He accepted her gift. For as long as he could. Suddenly he gripped her shoulders and pulled her upward. In a single swift motion he flipped her to one side, landing her on her stomach. "I see I will have to tame the Goddess of Lightning," he said, his voice raspy yet teasing. "Lest she kill me with her powers."

Goosebumps raised on Zara's skin at the subtle change in his voice. A tingle of anticipation ran through her, something not quite fear, but a feeling she was about to lose all control. Dave pulled her forward, yanking her up onto her knees. She let out a gasp of surprise and reached out, grabbing for the steel rail of the headboard.

He reached around and took hold of her breasts in both hands, his chest tight against her back. He snuggled his chin on her shoulder and whispered in her ear, "Behold, Goddess." Zara trembled with excitement. His male force radiated from him like kryptonite, making her feel weak. He fondled her breasts in a thorough, possessive way and she could feel his groin pressed against her bottom. His erection nestled between her cheeks. She bowed her head in blissful surrender.

His hands slid down her front and touched her inner thighs, nudging them further apart. Every hair on her body stood on end as she waited, barely drawing breath, for what would come next.

Both hands met at her crotch, fingers spreading her and reaching inside her folds. Graceful strokes sent thrills rocketing through her and she cried out in meaningless syllables of an unknown language. His stroking kept on. Mad, incoherent images flashed in her brain. He whispered in her ear again, "Lightning always comes before thunder."

"Ah." She choked out something that resembled a laugh, her breath coming in short, rapid intakes. She leaned forward to brace her right hand against the wall, trying to hold out for just a few more seconds. "There…is no thunder without… light…ning…" He entered her from behind. The dual stimulation made her explode into orgasm. Colors swam behind her closed eyelids, the unspeakable waves of pleasure marauding through her core and extending to every limb.

His hands were on her hips now, steadying her. His first thrust lifted her knees off the surface of the bed. She drew in a shuddering breath. He made a low-pitched sound worthy of a martial-arts move as he pushed into her a second time and then a third. She'd never felt anything so exquisitely powerful, so primeval, making her want to succumb to it and to him for all eternity. She felt him tensing for another thrust and she leaned into him as he plunged forward, taking all of what he had to give her.

His arms wrapped around her waist, pulling her against him as he sank back on his knees. She felt the tremors of his body as he came. He leaned his forehead against the nape of her neck and uttered her name in an almost mournful cry. "Zara…I love you."

Chapter Twenty Eight

"I miss you, Mom. I'll be so glad to see you," Zara said as she sat at her desk at the Flynn offices. "We'll be at the airport to pick you up. Safe trip." She paused, listening to her mother's voice. "What? I guess so, sure. Hold on." She pushed the hold button and looked up at Ernesto standing in her doorway. "My mother will be arriving on Friday," she said. "We'll be taking the weekend to visit family in Zaragoza." Ernesto nodded. "She's asked to talk to you," she said, raising an eyebrow.

Ernesto peered over the top of his eyeglasses and returned the gesture. Smiling, he said, *"Muy bien.* I'll take it in my office. Come as soon as you're ready." He still hadn't made his optometrist appointment.

Zara rose from behind her desk, looking sideways at him. "I'll give you a few minutes." If her mother wanted to talk to him, then who was she to question it? She walked into the reception area. Pilar smiled and nodded to her.

"Como esta, Señorita. Flynn. How is that arm?"

"Muy bien, gracias," she said. "I should have this cast off in a few weeks."

Dave came into the reception area to see the two of them chatting. *"Hola,"* he said. "Am I interrupting anything?"

"Not for me," replied Pilar. She looked back and forth between them then cast a glance toward the other office girls, whose faces held all the disappointment of unchosen puppies.

Oblivious to them, he nodded at Zara. "Ernie's ready for us, shall we?" He reached out for her hand.

They took a seat at the center table in Ernesto's office. Already present, Chavez stared at the cast on Zara's arm. Ernesto swiveled around, still talking on his phone. He spoke softly in Spanish. Zara blushed. Roughly translated he'd said, *"Me too, I can't wait. Hurry back, dear friend."* Was he still talking to her mother?

He hung up and turned his attention to the boardroom table but couldn't hide his delighted smile. Zara sent him a wicked look. Ignoring her, he said, "Chavez, please proceed."

Chavez passed around copies of his analysis. "First off, you should know that the bones we found were not human. Turns out they were bovine, and not even from the same area of the animal. Looks like someone dropped them there by accident or as a joke. At any rate, they are not significant. The core samples however, tell us quite a bit more. They contained a great deal of seawater, which caused the unstable texture of the sand. However, the sand itself is actually bitumen, commonly known as heavy crude oil. Tar sands." He paused and glanced around the table.

Dave grinned at Zara. She'd been right on with her assessment. "Do we know how much is potentially there?" she asked Chavez.

"To determine that would take a more detailed survey. But it's unlikely to be a large deposit. Although fairly common in many countries, only two sites in the world account for ninety percent of reserves and have sufficient upgrader technology to produce usable oil."

"So, it could remain in place, undeveloped," Ernesto said. Chavez nodded.

"And is it hazardous to leave it in place, from an environmental standpoint?" Zara asked, thinking about the Vistamar report.

"It's a natural resource. The problems exist with its extraction, not its presence."

"Why would the original structure have been built over it in the first place?" Dave asked.

Chavez shrugged. "Ignorance, probably. The original building footprint was smaller. An addition came later, and since they couldn't pour footings in the soft bitumen, they simply built around it. Which explains the absence of columns in that area. The exact cause of the fire, though, is still unknown."

Zara shifted in her chair. "I found it on the internet," she said. "The fire occurred nearly forty years ago. Official news makes little mention of it, but social network chatter, blogs, and community news archives paint a more colorful story. It seems the original owner, Sr. Ariel Torres, intended to burn up his cheating mistress while in bed with her lover right in his own hotel. It burned very quickly. No doubt the petroleum deposit beneath it provided a healthy fuel supply. Unfortunately, Mr. Torres lost his own life in the incident."

"About the explosion on the weekend," Ernesto said. Chavez looked at him, taken aback. He hadn't heard this news yet. Ernesto turned to Zara, indicating for her to explain.

"I went back to have another look around. I shouldn't have and I didn't intend to get so close, but…as they say…" She looked at Ernesto again. "We were in the wrong place at the wrong time. Someone planted explosives and set them off. We were nearly killed." She gestured to the cast on her arm and sent Dave a meaningful look.

He held her gaze steadily. "Tell them your theory," he said.

"Vistamar Holdings falsified the survey on the site, trying to devalue it so they could purchase it cheaply," Zara explained. "Then extract the oil and make a profit."

"How was the explosion triggered, and by whom?" asked Chavez.

"I can't prove it, but I believe the person responsible was involved with Vistamar. This same person murdered one of the clerks at my hotel and then came after me. I think he also set off the explosion in Indonesia." She looked directly at Ernesto. "Bernardo Cruz. He's dead now, also."

Ernesto looked shocked. The room fell silent. "What happens to the site now?" asked Chavez.

"That's up to Zara," Ernesto said. "But the structure is, for all intents and purposes, destroyed. It must be removed. Mining the area would be a serious undertaking, but is one option. Or?"

Zara stared down at her hands for a moment and then looked up as an idea occurred to her. "Or, we can let nature restore it. Build something else. An interpretive center, perhaps."

Ernesto smiled. "That's an interesting option."

Zara waved her hand. "I don't know really. The parcel is over one hundred hectares, there's room to build more than one thing. There's no hurry."

With that, they adjourned their meeting, Ernesto tasking Chavez with a more detailed survey on the size of the bitumen field. Dave would start arranging crews for the remaining demolition and removal. He and Zara exchanged knowing glances as they prepared to leave. Ernesto didn't try to hide his satisfied smile as Zara sidled up to him.

"All right, Señor *Misteriosa*, just what are your intentions toward my mother?"

Ernesto blushed in spite of his swarthy complexion. "It is a long story, Zara, but I believe it may yet have a happy ending." He smiled, refusing to say more. She wagged a finger at him but smiled back nonetheless. Her mother would get the third degree from her.

Zara went back to her office. With Marlena arriving by week's end, she'd been thinking about her next move. She would have to decide soon. To return to Montreal, be an arms-length CEO? Maybe. A Flynn office operated there. Her friends were all there, her condo, her car. Or stay, as her heart told her to do.

She thought of Dave's words in the parking lot yesterday. *"I don't intend to spend tonight or any other night of my life without you."* Would he leave here, come back with her? She couldn't ask that of him. What stopped her? Did she miss home? She could always visit. The idea of not being with Dave every day made her feel sick. Then she remembered something. She pulled open the top drawer of her desk, looking for the envelope of Tristan's drawings. As she did so, something slid from the back of the drawer into plain sight.

The small desktop photo frame held a picture of her mother, her arms around a little girl. Herself. It looked like a vacation photo, a smiling Marlena with her dark hair whipping around in the wind. Zara, peering into the camera with the wide eyes of a five-year-old, clutched her mother's arm. She turned the frame over, looking for a date or caption. She pulled away the hinged cover to inspect the reverse side of the print. Jammed between it and the frame backing was a DVD. She teased it out with a fingernail and held it for a moment, realizing with a cold tightening in her stomach that it was meant for her. Sliding it from its paper sleeve, she inserted it into her computer's optical drive.

The auto-play launched a video file. The opening sequence showed an overhead fly-by of open countryside. Flat tundra-like plains furred with boreal groves of spruce, pine, and aspen. The scene transitioned into a panoramic view of a surface mining operation, miles wide, its gigantic transports lifting masses of dark, clay-like clumps to conveyors on their way to steam-assisted processors. This image dissolved into a disturbing aerial shot of a spewing underwater well, the oil an unwelcome passenger on the water's surface that advanced steadily upon an unprotected shore. Then followed the heart-wrenching images of waterfowl coated in the brownish sludge, unable to move.

Shifting again, the scene returned to the open spaces of the original frames, this time showing the transformation of a reclaimed tailings pond—its surface repaired with thick, rich topsoil that fearlessly presented tender new grass shoots and spruce seedlings. Zara knew this place. The great oil sand fields she and her classmates had toured.

The picture changed to a close-up of a pair of gloved hands that gingerly cupped a tiny duckling amid the newly sprouted grass. Panning outwards the crouched, hard-hatted figure holding the creature became visible, lifting his face to the camera and smiling broadly. Freeze frame. Zara stared, immobile, at the familiar craggy features of her father's face. Tufts of his still-thick, graying, blond hair stuck out from under the hardhat. A voice-over began to play.

"To the only women in my life. Marlena, whom I have loved since that wild day in Zaragoza. Remember it was all for you. Little Zara, named for that place, you are not so little now. I know you wanted to make your own way in the world and I will be forever proud of you. Someday you will be my successor, and I have no doubt you will take the torch and hold it high. I pray you have the joy of children in your life and can pass it on to them as well."

"I must place on you a great burden, which I regret. But you are the only answer. El Mirador will become your legacy. It has a dark past and you can bring it to light. Let what lies beneath it be used to teach others about the

sustainability of the earth's resources and what it means to our future. Show them we have the technology to become great stewards of the land. Because of your education you are in the best position to carry out this undertaking, by responsible means, in whatever way you see fit. I know you will make the right decisions. Because it will be yours outright, you might also choose to build a home there. Your future, like the view from El Mirador, will be magnifico."

Zara stared at the screen, fighting waves of both joy and sorrow at seeing these precious last images of her father and hearing his voice, traces of his Welsh lilt still audible. He used the same words she'd uttered a week ago. *Magnifico.* He'd answered her question…the why. Her father had been as much a conservationist as a builder and did not want the beautiful beaches of the Costa del Sol mutilated by uncontrolled mining efforts. He trusted her to do the right thing. She was never more proud to be a Flynn. She knew now what she would build there.

She took the drawing from the portfolio case, went out into the hall and across the reception area. Pilar and two of the office girls immediately stopped talking as she passed by. Curious but too overwhelmed by emotion to ask questions, she continued on to Dave's office. The door stood open but she knocked anyway. "Excuse me, Mr. Parker?"

At his desk, Dave finished a phone call. He hung up and looked at her, bemused. "Why yes, Miss Flynn?"

She closed the door behind her. "My mother is coming on Friday."

"So I heard. Does this mean you've come to a decision?" He meant about staying in Spain.

"Yes." She stood still. Concerned, he moved out from behind his desk and leaned on the desktop, holding out his hand for her. She grasped it and held up the drawing for him to see. Her father's sketch for the villa La Dulce Zara. "This was meant for me, for us. This is what I want to build at El Mirador. A home."

Dave held the sketch along with her. The artist signature in the title block read Tristan B. Flynn. Zara felt her heart begin to swell, as if it had sprouted wings and would take flight from her body at any moment.

I just said 'us'. She'd found her why and it included Dave. His eyes gave him away, their blue color intensifying beneath gathering tears. He brought her close and held her so tight she could barely breathe.

"You're the boss," he said, his voice breaking. Then he kissed her with all the passion that had grown between them. When their lips parted, Zara was out of breath.

"They're going to wonder what we're doing in here," she said with a soft laugh.

"No they won't," he said. "They already know."

Epilogue

March, 1973

Marlena held out the newborn in her arms for Tristan to see. Most people would say that a baby's resemblance to a parent wouldn't be noticeable so soon after birth. Yet he could already recognize the strong features of Ariel Torres in the tiny boy's face.

"My aunt has name him Jorge," she said in her beginner English. "She love him very much." Tristan felt glad the child's mother had accepted him after all and that she herself had not become an outcast. Still a vivid memory, he'd managed to drag the pregnant Juliana from the flames that engulfed El Mirador that night and could recall the sickening smell of burning flesh even now.

At the time, he worried that saving her might be a mistake—and bringing her back to her family in Zaragoza an even bigger mistake. But he learned that fate was a wily companion, for in doing so he had met her niece, Marlena. He couldn't take his eyes off the brunette beauty as she stood there rocking the babe and humming a tune for him. Barely eighteen, she was his reason for coming back all these months later, because whatever his destiny might hold, Tristan knew she would be part of it.

He hadn't been able to save El Mirador. But he did save Ari, as he swore he would. Because he had saved Jorge.

*

The End
EL MIRADOR

Spanish Seduction Book One

EL PRECIO:
The Price of Passion

SPANISH SEDUCTION TRILOGY – BOOK TWO

by Jean Maxwell

DEDICATION

For my boys, who are the true heroes of my world.
May you always follow your passions, as you
have encouraged me to follow mine.

Chapter One

The sound of jet engines aroused her. Zara Flynn's pulse accelerated just watching the 707 taxi to the gate through the viewing windows, its powerful whine audible even through the thick glass.

From behind, a pair of hands fell gently to her hips and pulled her close. The familiar, sexy scent of Lacoste cologne drifted around her in a comforting cloud, announcing his presence. She leaned back against his chest, undecided whether she felt weaker from his male pheromones or the thunderous advance of aluminum hull filling the window.

"Are you getting excited?" he whispered in her ear, his tone suggestive of both the view in front, and other satisfying possibilities. His wet tongue tickled her earlobe.

"David," she said evenly. "This is my mother arriving on this plane, not a shipment of two-by-fours." A knowing smile crossed her lips. Anything to do with construction piqued Dave's interest, in addition to sex. Sex with her, to be precise. Zara inhaled with contentment. In the space of a week, she and David Parker had lived through a harrowing adventure and found themselves as soulmates in the process.

Life for Zara seemed to be riding a fast wave. Becoming

the CEO of Flynn Enterprises, a global construction company, was a curve ball life had thrown her without warning. She deeply mourned the loss of her father, top engineer Tristan Flynn. He'd overshadowed so many elements of her existence, from loving father to career mentor, triggering her decision to become an architect. He'd loved her mother so. And now, he was gone.

Emotions tugged at her heart as the aircraft parked its enormous nose just outside the window, bringing Marlena Sanchez Flynn that much closer.

"I know. I owe your mother a lot, bringing such a beautiful woman into the world as you," Dave said. "I can't wait to meet her."

His arms moved to encircle her upper body in a sensuous hug. Zara hadn't come to Spain to fall in love, but fate had other ideas. David Justin Parker appeared in her life as if ordained by some higher power. An engineer in the Malaga office of Flynn Enterprises, he had stolen her heart bit by bit since the day she arrived. Smart mouth and acerbic humour aside, she adored him. They'd been through life and near-death together.

Zara tried to suppress the flood of desire rushing to her core as Dave touched her. Not now. Time for that later.

The gangway extended into position, allowing the passengers to deplane. She broke from Dave's embrace, to gain a better vantage point. Zara watched the wave of passengers disembarking, and after interminable minutes caught a glimpse of a familiar brunette head coming into view.

Dressed in a white skirt and matching jacket, Marlena Flynn strolled up the entrance ramp, her Dolce & Gabbana valise in tow and her chocolate brown tresses coiffed in a sleek French knot.

Marlena looked up and waved, her perfectly lip-sticked mouth breaking into a broad smile. Tricks of her former modeling career had left its indelible imprint on her personal housekeeping. "Zara," she called above the hum of human traffic.

"Mom!" Zara shouted, raising a hand in reply. They met and embraced amid the stream of bodies pouring into the arrivals area. Marlena laughed merrily while Zara fought back tears. Dave reached to take Marlena's carry-on from her.

"Gracias, young man," Marlena said as she released the bag and gave Zara an extra squeeze. "Querida, how have you been?"

Zara hugged her mother with all her might. She hadn't expected to feel so emotional at her return, and being called 'querida.' The word meant 'beloved' or 'dear one' in Spanish. "Hi, Mom," she sniffed, hugging Marlena's small frame even tighter. Loving hands patted Zara's back.

"It's good to see you," Marlena's voice soothed. "No need for tears, sweetheart. I love you. Smile, querida."

Zara obeyed. "You had a good flight?" she asked, releasing Marlena from her hold.

"Si, little one. No problema," she replied.

Dave dropped his gaze as he stood clutching Marlena's carry-on.

"Who is this fine fellow you've brought with you?" she asked.

"Marlena Flynn, this is David Parker," Zara said, glowing with happiness despite feeling close to tears. Her heart melted at the sight of Dave's shy attendance to her mother.

"A pleasure, ma'am."

Marlena's expression transformed from polite smile to awe-filled recognition. "You are 'Youngblood,' " she said, reaching for his hand. He took it in his palm, squeezing with affirmation. His dimples blossomed in a charming smile.

"That's me." He nodded in admission.

Zara felt a warm, burning sensation in her core. Youngblood?

It struck her that Tristan might have given him this name. Perhaps her father had known even then, there was something special about David. With a shiver, Zara realized she might not be the only one destined to keep Flynn Enterprises alive.

"Jorge is bringing the car around. Let's get out of here," Zara said, tugging on Marlena's arm. They moved through the milling throng of people in the Malaga airport toward the cool comfort of a waiting Mercedes.

Jorge Allesandro stood at the vehicle's side, its doors open and beckoning in the pickup roundabout. Marlena zeroed in on him, her arms wide in welcome. He blushed and bowed his head as she drew near. They embraced, and she whispered heartfelt greetings in Spanish.

They stood this way in silence for a few moments.

Dave grinned as he stowed Marlena's baggage in the trunk. Zara stood nearby, watching the emotional exchange between her mother and her cousin. She'd known Jorge all her life, but recently gained a new appreciation of the deep bonds within her family.

An idea played in her mind lately, that Jorge might also be a big part of the Flynn legacy. She suspected a connection existed between Jorge and El Mirador, the abandoned resort property left to Zara in her father's will. Currently under major reconstruction after the explosion that had nearly killed both her and Dave, the elegant strip of Andalusian coastline where El Mirador stood, had a much darker history.

They piled into the car. Marlena took the front passenger seat, while Dave and Zara entwined themselves together in the back. Marlena twisted around and cast a speculative gaze over the pair of them. "You two look very content. Is there more you want to tell me?"

Zara smiled, but said nothing. Dave, on the other hand, was never lost for words. "Is there more we need to?" he replied, drawing Zara close and stroking her cheek with his forefinger.

Zara had dubbed him 'Mr. Smart-Ass,' for his quick-witted retorts. She marvelled at his ability to speak the right words when she herself felt tongue-tied.

Marlena's mouth pursed in amusement. "Nope," she said as Jorge put the Mercedes in gear and pulled away from the curb. She winked and turned to face front, giving them their privacy. Dave nudged Zara's chin toward him and planted a kiss on her lips. Zara kissed him back, her mouth lingering on his, reluctant to part from him.

She drew back only enough to whisper to him. "What's with 'Youngblood'?" she asked as she felt his fingers tease the hem of her skirt.

"Just a nickname around the office," he said, their lips still partially connected. "Nobody calls me that anymore." His fingertips rubbed insistent circles against the sensitive skin of her inner thigh.

God, the man was insatiable. He'd have her right here in the back seat, if she'd let him; the presence of her mother and second-cousin be damned. "Later, Thunder Boy," Zara murmured in a husky voice. "Don't you dare lose that thought." This time her kiss made her hunger plain as she darted her tongue inside his mouth, then sucked gently on his lower lip before pulling away. Her nipples went hard just gazing into his striking, cobalt-blue eyes.

"Not a chance," he said, matching her stare.

Chapter Two

Ivette Melendez paced to and fro in the physicians waiting room. This couldn't be happening to her, she thought. It would ruin her career. Beauty was her business. She'd spent her life at it, styling hair, giving facials, makeovers, waxing, chemical peels, spa treatments, Brazilian blowouts. Not to mention daily workouts of yoga, pilates, and zumba.

After years of working for others, she finally had her own salon. In addition to sinking her life's savings into it, she'd gone into heavy debt to do it. Now she was afraid. Carlos had encouraged her, almost goaded her into leasing the high-priced studio space downtown.

"You deserve it, sweetheart. Why shouldn't the best and prettiest esthetician in town have the best and prettiest salon? You are the best, aren't you?" he'd said, almost as an accusation. Daring her to disagree with him. Daring her to be as flagrant and self-important as he. She'd signed the lease right then and there without another thought. If she was going to play with the big boys, indeed, marry the biggest boy, Carlos Sabados, she must look the part.

Where was Carlos? Handsome, dashing Senor Sabados? Certainly not here, pacing the doctor's office floor with her.

He'd been so attractive, so suicidally attractive. Ivette couldn't pull herself away from him, like a moth that stupidly kept returning to the flame. He had made big promises. Big, fat, empty promises. Behind all the flash, the money, the clothes and cars, were lies. Where was he now? On his way to jail, possibly. For tax evasion, fraud, loansharking and who knew what else. A price must certainly be on his head.

And his child was in her belly.

Ivette turned on her heel, her thick auburn hair swinging around as she did so. Her figure would be ruined, her health compromised! Her face might break out, or her ankles swell beyond recognition. All this she'd read about; things that happened to pregnant women. How could she work this way? And she must work, if she was to keep up the payments on her new salon space. Above all else, she'd never give Carlos Sabados the satisfaction of seeing her fail. No matter where he might be. The bastardo, telling her he'd had a vasectomy. More of his lies!

Oh yes, she was afraid. More afraid than she'd ever been in her self-gratified life. It might be too late to have an abortion. She felt trapped. She needed money.

She needed a plan.

"Senora Melendez?" the doctor's assistant called out.

Ivette spun to face her. "It's Senorita Melendez," she snapped, annoyed. The other patients in the waiting room glanced up at her sudden outburst. Ivette shrugged a shoulder and marched past the assistant into the examining room.

She waited for the doctor to finish her arcane probing and prodding. She distanced herself by staring at the bland, pale green ceiling, wishing to be anyplace, anywhere, other than this room. The hot sting of tears began to build under her eyeballs. No. She would not cry. It would ruin her makeup.

The doctor pulled the sheet back over Ivette's lower body. "All done. You may sit up now," she said, patting Ivette's arm in a grandmotherly way. Ivette sat up, anxious to dress and get the hell out of there.

"Oh now, take it easy, senorita," cautioned the doctor. Ivette ignored her, casting the sheet aside and reaching for her clothes. "Well?" Ivette asked.

The doctor paused and looked at her from behind unflattering black-rimmed glasses. She picked up her clipboard and scratched a few notes on Ivette's chart. "Well, I was about to say congratulations. You and your husband must be thrilled."

Ivette narrowed her eyes at the doctor before looking away. No reason to be rude. She may need the woman's help in the weeks to come. "I don't have a husband," she said, emotionless.

"I see," the doctor replied quietly. She made another note.

"How far along am I?" Ivette asked.

"I'd say ten weeks. That puts your due date around…" The doctor skimmed her ballpoint pen over a calendar on the wall. "…the fourteenth of June."

Ivette cringed at the thought of not being able to wear a bikini come spring. "I want an abortion," she said, slipping on her high-cut panties.

The doctor frowned, tapping her pen on the clipboard. "That's a bit sudden. You've thought about this decision?"

"There's no other decision possible," replied Ivette. "This will ruin my career."

The doctor regarded her in silence for a moment. "That is your choice, of course. What about the child's father? Does he not have a say?"

Ivette looked her straight in the eyes. "Why should he? He's not here, obviously. How soon can you arrange the procedure?"

"Miss Melendez," the doctor began. Her tiny frame seemed to shrink next to Ivette's tall, slender one. "Abortions are not possible beyond twelve weeks. If this is indeed your decision, it must be made quickly. Are you certain you can't contact the father?"

Ivette flinched at the realization she really could not. She swallowed hard, trying to soothe her throat that had suddenly gone dry.

The doctor made an assumption. "You don't know who it is, do you?" she asked.

Ivette glared at her. "Of course I do," she spat. "He's…" she searched for words that would cover the truth. "Away on business."

The doctor leaned against the desk in the corner of the examining room. "He's married, then," she said with finality. Ivette's anger began to rise. She hadn't thought about that possibility. For all she knew, that could be another of Carlos' lies. He was already married. The thought sparked an idea.

"He's an engineer," she retorted. "He's on a business trip inspecting new building sites." The words seemed to spill out of her, fabricating a story as she went along. "He's out of the country. I can't reach him."

"It's none of my business, Miss Melendez," the doctor interrupted, holding up a hand. "Of course, it would be beneficial to have both parents involved in this decision. But you have only a few days to decide. And we cannot do the procedure here. We would have to arrange a clinic in Germany and that takes time, and travel. You may be beyond twelve weeks by then."

Ivette blinked, the tears threatening for real this time. "Por que? Why? Why can't you do it here?"

"Because of the church. Surely you know that."

Ivette cursed silently. The goddamned church. It would cost money, too, she realized. Something she didn't have right now. She pulled on her blouse and did up the buttons, not looking at the doctor anymore.

"Please, Miss Melendez. Think about your options. There are many families wanting to adopt. Sleep on it, at least," the doctor said, reaching for the doorknob to exit the room. "Don't decide anything today."

Ivette stood motionless between the door and the examining table.

"Please see my receptionist before you leave, and make an appointment by the end of the week, all right?" The doctor interpreted her continued silence as compliance, and left the room, closing the door behind her.

Ivette considered her plan that had begun to form as she'd blurted out her fictitious story to the woman. Not bad. It just might work. But first, she had to find him.

*

"Does it still hurt, querida?" Marlena pointed to the worn-looking plaster bandages on her daughter's left forearm.

Zara turned from the car window to look at her. "This?" she asked, lifting her arm a little. She shook her head. "Not really. I should be able to have it off by the time we get back from Zaragoza." An idea occurred to her. "Why don't you sign it?" Zara reached in her handbag for the purple Sharpie she kept especially for this purpose.

Marlena laughed. "What should I write?" she asked, taking the pen from her.

"Whatever you like. How about something that rhymes?"

Marlena held Zara's arm steady with one hand and put the purple pen tip to the surface of the cast. She tilted her head slightly while scrawling her message in a deliberate, decorative script. When she'd finished, she examined her work with a smile. She replaced the cap on the pen and handed it back to Zara.

Looking down at the elegant penmanship, Zara read: Roses are red, violets are blue. My Zara is brave, and there's nothing she can't do.

Zara laughed and swung the bandaged arm around her in a hug. They sat side by side in the back seat of the Mercedes, an hour or so away from Zaragoza. Jorge, Marlena's cousin and family chauffeur, steered the powerful vehicle down the winding motorway. Zaragoza, the city of Marlena's birth, sat in the north-central Spanish plains. The Pyrenees loomed to the northeast, while desert conditions prevailed to the southwest.

She'd never visited before, but Zara felt permanently connected to the place. She'd been named for it, after all. Her mother's family lived just outside the city proper, but Zara hadn't met many of her relatives. An ancient combination of desert, rolling hills and forest scrolled past the window as they traveled northward.

"Jorge," Marlena said, "your mother is so excited you are coming. When did you see her last?"

Jorge turned his head slightly to the right, without taking his eyes off the road. "Oh, Marly, you know I see her every Semana Santa, at Holy Week. This year was no different."

"Si, but you know she's not well. You must make an effort to be with her more often. You will never get this time back again, Jorge." She fell silent for a beat, the next words seeming to catch in her throat. "You never know how much time you may have left."

Zara caught the emotional stumble in her mother's speech. Despite her calm exterior, she'd just lost her lifemate, and couldn't keep the pain in check forever. Mom set a fine example, but Zara knew how gaping a hole had been left in both their lives by her father's untimely death on a job site in central Java. She grabbed Marlena's hand.

"Mom. It's okay. You can cry, you know. You're only human."

Marlena focused on her daughter. "I've cried enough for both of us, Zara." They sat wordless for a few moments.

"Ernesto is getting more information, you know," Zara

said. She wasn't certain how much Marlena knew about the accident. In the past few weeks, Zara had found out a great deal, enough to convince her of what she felt was the truth. She owed her mom this knowledge. "I haven't told you the whole story behind this," she said, gesturing to the cast on her arm.

Marlena's magnetic brown-eyed gaze told Zara that she desperately wanted to hear it. Okay, here goes. Like Dave said, sometimes you need to jump straight in.

"The Indonesian project was sabotaged." Marlena's brown eyes grew wider. "A despicable little man named Bernardo Cruz went to Jakarta. We have reason to believe he blew the place up, for financial gain." Marlena continued to fix her countenance on her daughter, waiting for more. "He was here, in Marbella, too. Working for the local government, but kept a side business called Vistamar Holdings. They falsified survey reports on real estate, devaluing them so they could be purchased cheaply. He did this to El Mirador."

Marlena swallowed with difficulty. "El Mirador," she echoed in a voice barely above a whisper. Zara squeezed her hand, wanting to say more, but perhaps her mother wasn't ready for it. "Go on," Marlena said.

"Vistamar declared the site unsafe, contaminated." She recalled the outrageous details of the report. "Then they offered to buy it, clean it up, like they were some sort of eco-saviours."

The brown eyes began to narrow. "Quanto. How much?" Marlena's mouth settled in a tight line.

"Two-point-five million. I said no."

Marlena nodded. "Por supuesto," she said. "Of course you said no. Then what?"

"We went to the site. I called you, remember?" Marlena nodded again. "We did a legitimate survey. We thought the building was sitting on quicksand." A trace of a smile tugged at the corner of Zara's mouth. "But it wasn't."

"How did you get injured?" Marlena prodded.

Zara took in a long breath. "Dad knew what lay underneath El Mirador. Not quicksand. Tar sand," she concluded. "Do you know what that is?" Marlena shook her head. "A form of crude oil, called bitumen. It can be refined into usable oil, gasoline, et cetera. Black gold. You can see why someone else would want it."

"Yes," Marlena replied. "The fire," she said, a spark of recognition lighting her words. "That's why it burned so fast."

Zara nodded. Through much research, she'd discovered why El Mirador, an abandoned building on the southern Spanish coast, had burned horrifically more than thirty years ago. Due to legal wrangling over ownership, it had lain untouched for most of this time, until her father bought it and left it to her in his will. The petroleum deposit that lay underneath it fuelled the flames with devastating ferocity, and the original owner, Ariel Torres, appeared to have set it on fire deliberately.

"They wanted me gone, too," Zara continued. "I went back to the site, on my own. Senor Cruz thought he could get rid of me, just like…" She paused, not sure she could choke the next words out. "Just like he did Dad." Marlena squeezed her hand tighter. "I can't explain it exactly, but Dave and I, we went to have another look around, and…I felt something. I knew something bad was going to happen. Then we ran. The place collapsed around us. We managed to get clear of it. He saved me, Mom. He…" Her voice trailed off.

"Youngblood," Marlena said. "You are in love with him, yes?"

Zara faced her mother, her eyes welling with tears. "Yes," she managed. "That's how I broke my arm. We were caught in the explosion. We could have died."

Marlena held her daughter tight. "It's all right. It's over, you're here now. David is a fine young man. I'm glad he was with you."

Zara returned her embrace, squeezing her eyes shut. "Tell me about 'Youngblood'," Zara said. She wasn't aware that her father and Dave had known each other that well, and wanted to know what sort of relationship existed between them. "Where did he get that name?"

Marlena stroked Zara's blond head. "I don't know, but your father referred to him often. He seemed very proud of him, admired his youth and talent. I think he trusted him very much." She paused, taking a steady breath in and out. "He's in love with you, too. Anyone can see that."

Her mother's words were exactly what she wanted to hear, but she needed to hear them from Dave. She had to be sure.

Chapter Three

Dave felt the warm surf wash over them, and tickle their toes as it retreated again to the ocean. Sand particles shifted beneath them, chasing the water back to its source.

Zara lay naked next to him. He had his arm around her neck, and his other hand roved over her wet body. The goddess of lightning had somehow transformed herself into a goddess of the sea, appearing almost mermaid-like, with her sand-speckled skin and wet strands of long hair sticking in waves about her shoulders and chest. Tiny chunks of seaweed lay caught in it, and small beads of something that glittered like diamonds in the hazy sunlight.

The silver dolphin on its chain nestled in the hollow of her collarbone. He wanted to ask about the dolphin; why did she have it around her neck? Who had given it to her? His lips moved, but no sound came forth.

Her green eyes seemed to glow, enticing him nearer. He drew his face close, his lips grazing hers in anticipation of a kiss. He felt himself growing hard. He touched her breasts, so full and round, ran his hand over her smooth stomach, inching his way to the luscious heaven between her thighs. Another wave coursed warm seawater over them, floating the dolphin off its resting place. The dolphin grew larger. It blinked at him with steely eyes and opened its pointed beak to reveal tiny sharp teeth. Its maw gaped wider and wider, until he felt swallowed into the darkness of its insides.

Lightning flashed. She was dead. Her once warm body now lay cold in his arms. The emerald green eyes stared pale and lifeless into the dark sky above. Storm clouds roiled in circles overhead, throwing the landscape into shifting shades of gray. A bitter wind lashed at his back, and another rush of surf flooded ice-cold over them. Thunder rolled menacingly as he screamed into the wind. "No!" Like before, his mouth moved, but seemed incapable of producing sound. "No…" he repeated, the thunder's crescendo drowning his voice in any case.

She began to fade, her face growing so pale he could see through it. Everything went white around him and consumed what remained of her image. His arms clutched at the empty sand where she had lain.

"No." His voice returned to wake him from his nightmare. Dave's eyes shot open and he gasped for air, the sounds of thunder still echoing in his ears. Sweat pooled in the small of his back. Beads of it collected around his neck and trickled down his chest. The terrifying vision receded from his memory as he fought to control his breathing and his fear. It wasn't the first time this dream had come.

But he prayed it would be the last.

He stretched his hand over the empty expanse of bed where she'd slept over the past several days. Her absence seemed to reinforce the sense of loss that pervaded his dream. He could still smell the faintest whisper of her perfume in the sheets. God, he'd give anything just to hold her right now. He told himself she was fine, she was with her mother in Zaragoza. She couldn't be safer. But the words didn't help.

He threw back the covers and sat up. If the nightmare

persisted, he wouldn't last the two weeks she'd be away. He might find himself on a mission to Zaragoza before then. He rubbed his eyes, thinking how foolish that might look to her. She knew how to handle herself; maybe he couldn't say the same about himself. What a dork. I need a shower.

He stepped into the bathroom of his small, renovated apartment. He should get a bigger one, he thought. He'd been here more than two years already; time for a change. Especially if its occupancy might be expanding soon. Technically Zara still resided at the swank Club Marbella, a resort property built by Flynn Enterprises, but she'd stayed with him on a number of nights, and he wanted that to change, too. He wanted her with him every night, every damn night, and he'd told her so from the beginning. I don't intend to spend tonight or any other night of my life without you, Lightning Girl.

He chuckled at how their nicknames for each other had come about. She'd called him Thunder Boy after the first night they'd made love. Partly because he came from Thunder Bay, but mostly because he'd rocked her world so thoroughly she'd felt caught in a thunderstorm. When the two of them had wandered into the crumbling remains of El Mirador, Zara gave them a running start by claiming she'd felt electricity through her body, signalling the building's impending collapse. So they became Lightning Girl and Thunder Boy—a perfect pair. As the water from the shower washed over him, his body became acutely aware that half the pair was missing.

He would have to remedy this soon, before he walked around town with a permanent hard-on for her. But how to convince her? She'd mentioned taking a vacation awhile back, maybe he could whisk her away somewhere and…and what? Propose to her? Jesus, he'd only known her a few weeks. How pathetic would he look if she said no? Why would she say no? Because she can. Because she's stressed out with taking over her father's company. Because, you said it, she's only known you for a few weeks.

A phrase he'd been using often lately, gave him comfort. Just because a thing happens fast, doesn't mean it isn't right. He knew where he would take her. If he hurried, there'd be enough time to stop at the travel agent's on his way in to work.

*

"Let me help you, Tía," Zara said as she picked up the tea tray laden with a silver pot and porcelain cups, and carried it to the garden. She's aged a great deal since I saw her last, Zara thought. Her great-aunt shuffled with difficulty as they walked out of the kitchen. She leaned on a cane now, her gnarled hand pushing down on its handle with each painful step forward. Burn marks and age spots formed a bizarre patchwork on the skin of her knuckles.

Marlena waited for them in the garden by the round metal table that stood in its centre, surrounded by hibiscus shrubs and rosebushes. Zara set the tea tray down and helped her aunt settle into a nearby garden chair. Juliana's once flaming-red hair, now shot through with streaks of gray, hung in a long ponytail that draped over one shoulder. She'd taken the trouble to apply a lovely coral shade of lipstick for the occasion. Her graceful, hooked nose that poised above the coppery-burnished lips spoke of a remembered beauty.

Scars remained etched on the rest of her face. Her aging skin accentuated the damage incurred by a long-ago incident. Frightened by this as a child, Zara never knew how her great-aunt had become so disfigured. She wanted the whole story now.

"Where has Jorge gone?" Juliana asked, annoyed. Zara realized that after arriving at the family villa near Zaragoza, Jorge had greeted his mother only briefly before continuing into town for supplies and groceries.

"I'm sure he won't be long," Marlena said, pouring the

tea. "You said you needed sugar and flour, so he's probably haggling over the price at the market to get you the best deal."

"Tía," Zara said, changing the subject. "You've never told me why you didn't marry Jorge's father. Who was he? Where is he now?"

From beneath hooded eyelids, Juliana looked at her with the fiery glare of a flamenco dancer. Zara flinched inwardly. Others must have melted under that gaze in the past, but she would not. You never know how much time you have left, her mom said. It might really be the last time she would ever see her great-aunt. It was important that she know the truth. Zara cut some slices of spice cake and handed Juliana a piece. Juliana took it with a trembling hand.

"He died, of course," her aunt said, after a moment. "He didn't know about Jorge. Then he was gone." She nibbled on her piece of cake. A long silence followed, the lazy buzzing of insects and scent of late-season flowers hanging in the void.

"It was long ago, Zara," Marlena said. "You needn't ask such questions, they mean nothing now."

Zara shot her mother a look. "If that's so, then what does it matter if I ask the question? This could be important for Jorge," Zara said.

Marlena raised an eyebrow. "For Jorge? Why?"

"Basta," Juliana said. "Stop it. I won't be around much longer. My son—and all of my family—deserve the truth. There's no reason to hide it now." Her niece and great-niece looked at her sharply. "His name…was Ariel Torres."

Chapter Four

"You knew," Zara said as she turned down the covers on the guest room bed. She looked at her mother from the corner of her eye. Marlena stood unpacking her valise and laying items in the dresser drawers.

"Knew what? About Jorge's father?"

Zara fluffed the pillows, her plaster cast imparting a lesser impact than she wanted. "Yes. Why didn't you tell me?" She tossed the pillows in place and faced Marlena.

"You must understand; nobody told anyone anything," Marlena replied. "We didn't speak of it. She was unmarried, and pregnant. She nearly died, Zara. Scarred for life."

Zara sat down on the bed. Poor Aunt Juliana. In those days, in a Catholic country, her situation must have been unthinkable. Her exhaustive research suggested that Senor Torres set El Mirador on fire to take revenge on his cheating lover. Was it Aunt Juliana? This story was getting more and more interesting. "Why would Tía Juliana be with such a man, and not make him marry her?"

Her mother sighed as she laid the last pairs of underwear in a top drawer and slid it closed. Marlena looked out the window, as if searching for something. "Zara, I'm as shocked as you.

Our Tía was…quite wild as a young woman. Promiscuo. My grandmother tried to beat it out of her." A wan smile drifted across Marlena's face as she turned to her daughter. "She was beautiful, though, and she knew it. She wanted to be a famous dancer, so she ran away for a while. She met lots of men like Senor Torres, any one of them could have been the father. She used them to further her dance career. They would fight over her."

"Maybe, kill for her?" Zara asked after a pause.

Marlena's shoulders sagged a bit. "I don't know all of what happened. But if Senor Torres caught her with another man… yes, he was capable of such actions. According to your father, he was very passionate."

"Dad knew him?" What the hell…this just gets better and better.

Marlena nodded. "They were close friends, he said. In fact, your father and I wouldn't have met if not for Ariel Torres."

Zara widened her eyes and gaped at her, clearly waiting for more.

"Tristan," her mother said, his name caressing her lips in adoration, "brought Juliana here, after the fire. He saved her life. And Jorge's." Her smile turned wistful in remembrance. "Fue mi héroe." She looked warmly into Zara's eyes. "He was my hero."

Something twisted in Zara's heart, seeing the naked love for Tristan in her mother's eyes as she spoke. My dad, the hero. What a love story. She'd thought of fate as a cruel jokester, not a hopeless romantic. Now she realized he, or she, could be both.

"You know what this means," Zara said after swallowing the lump in her throat. Marlena regarded her with a tilt of her head. "Jorge is the rightful heir to El Mirador."

*

Dave left the travel agency with e-ticket receipts in hand

and walked the few blocks to the Flynn Enterprises office tower. He'd booked a week's vacation for two, leaving on the 28th of November. That would only be a week after Zara returned from Zaragoza, but enough time to let her catch up on her work and sweet-talk Ernesto into letting her sneak away again. Not that it should matter to Ernesto. He wasn't her boss, after all. He wasn't even Dave's boss, organizationally speaking. Both of them reported directly to Zara, Flynn Enterprises new CEO.

Even so, Operations Manager Ernesto Alvarez remained the lifeblood of Flynn Enterprises EU division in Malaga. He lived and breathed the company, worked at it tirelessly and earned great respect for his dedication. They'd worked together a little over three years now, but Dave had always wondered why Ernie, as he called him, had never married. Had Zara not been appointed to take her father's place, certainly Ernesto would have filled the CEO's chair, with unanimous approval.

Even a month ago Dave would also have applauded that scenario, for it left the Ops Manager seat vacant. He recalled being annoyed that it didn't happen that way, but had no regrets. Flynn's beautiful daughter had flown in and scooped both the CEO's chair and Dave's heart. He couldn't be happier. Except that she wasn't here, and his body ached for her.

It wasn't until a familiar fragrance blasted though an open storefront to assault his nostrils that he realized he'd walked past the Bella Spa. He'd been so lost in his thoughts as to take a route he'd been avoiding for months. The smells of aromatherapy oils and other assorted cosmetics turned his head enough to make him look inside the air-conditioned little shop. Luckily, no shiny auburn head or stiletto heels turned his way. He moved on before they could. The sharp sting of his chest hair being waxed off, flared in his memory, making him walk even faster. It occurred to him he'd been lucky to escape the clutches of that madwoman.

Dave found Ernesto in his office, as usual.

"Hola, David," Ernesto said, looking up from his desk.

"Holy shit, Ernie. You finally got new glasses." Dave smiled at him, thankful he wouldn't have to watch the man peering at him from overtop his old, outdated lenses any more. "Muy bien, amigo!"

Ernesto smiled back. "Gracias. I thought you'd be pleased."

Dave swung into one of the leather chairs facing Ernesto's desk. "They look good…took you long enough, though."A thought struck him. "Hey, wait a minute. You wouldn't be sprucing up for the benefit of a certain senorita, now would you? That would be extraordinary."

Ernesto deflected Dave's commentary with a look of impervious amusement. "I'm a bit too old for that sort of thing, don't you think?"

"Hell, no. You're never too old. Amor makes the world go 'round, buddy," Dave said, kicking his chair into a childish spin with one foot.

Ernesto laughed. "I can see it does for you, David. I'm happy for you and Zara."

Dave stopped his chair in mid-rotation and fixed Ernesto with a solemn look. "Thanks, man." He exhaled in satisfaction, admitting to himself that he really was happy. Really…in love? Shit. That tore it. He was a goner, for sure. "I wish she'd hurry back."

Ernesto stacked file folders in a pile on his desk. "Si. Yo tambien."

Dave considered his colleague for a silent moment. "So, I don't think I've ever asked you. Why isn't there a Senora Alvarez?"

Ernesto stopped shuffling papers and folded his hands together on his desktop. He paused in thought, as if asking himself the same question. "I suppose, as they say, the right girl never came along. Or rather, didn't stick around." He shook his head slightly, as if dismissing the memory. "And anyway, if I'd have gotten married back then I'd probably never have gone to University, never built a career."

Dave picked up the regretful vibe. "Then? When was 'then'?" The verbal slip smacked of more story than Ernesto let on.

Ernesto looked a bit disconcerted. "I meant, when I was young. I worked two or three jobs at a time, to save up for my education. I didn't have time for girls."

Dave nodded, conceding that might have been true. "Okay. But how about now? I still think there's something behind those new glasses you're not telling me."

Finally, Ernesto cracked a full-on smile. "You're a pest," he said. "Get back to work."

"Struck a nerve, did I? There is a lady in your past, then. Come on, tell me about her."

Ernesto rose from behind his desk. "There's nothing to tell, David. The past is the past."

"Bullshit. Who is she? Can you get in touch with her again?"

Ernesto sighed at Dave's persistence and cast him a patronizing glance. He leaned forward with his knuckles on the desk. The corners of his mouth began to curl. "Well, not until she returns from Zaragoza. With her daughter."

Dave's mouth dropped open, speechless for a count of three or better. "You sly dog, Ernie. You're Marlena's ex?"

Chapter Five

Zara's arm itched, and flakes of skin puffed into the air as she scratched. Grateful for the absence of the irritating plaster cast, at the same time she mourned the sickly, atrophied appearance of her left forearm. She smothered it with lotion to ease the dry symptoms.

"It looks horrible," she said to her mom as they rode the elevator to the eighth floor. "I should have worn long sleeves."

Marlena laughed and put her arm around Zara's shoulder. "You look fine, querida. In a few days you won't even notice."

Easy for her to say, Zara thought. Her mother stood next to her, looking totally put together as usual, her body-skimming mauve dress draping perfectly on her slender figure, its lace edges providing that so-right feminine detail at the neckline and hem. She envied her panache.

The elevator slowed to a stop. After their visit to Zaragoza, this Monday morning found her and Marlena about to enter the Flynn offices in Malaga. She hadn't been here for two weeks, and dreaded the thought of how much work had piled up in her inbox. But coming back to work also meant coming back to Dave. She missed his tall, muscular frame moving about her world in its casually graceful style. Oh hell, who was she kidding? She missed his muscles. One in particular. They stepped out onto the eighth floor and entered through the big steel doors bearing the Flynn logo.

The plump woman behind the reception desk leapt to her feet at the sight of them. "Senora Flynn!" she exclaimed, snatching her bejewelled eyeglass frames from her face and leaving them to dangle on the silver chain around her neck. "How good to see you," she said, moving toward them with arms akimbo.

"Hola Pilar, como esta?" Marlena asked, accepting Pilar's embrace. The two women hugged for a brief moment, then Pilar held her at arms length.

"I'm so sorry, senora," Pilar said in a hushed voice. "We are all still in shock. How are you managing? You must miss him terribly, as we all do." Marlena acknowledged her condolences with a nod and a smile. Pilar turned to Zara. "And you, Senorita, we've missed you around here. So many clients have been asking to meet you, I think we need to hire you a publicity agent."

The three women laughed as the reception area began to fill with people. They swarmed around Marlena, their fondness for their beloved CEO's widow evident. Zara stepped back a few paces, gratified at the welcome being accorded her mother. Amid the crowd, Zara caught sight of two figures lingering in the hallway. Ernesto held his hands firmly together in front of his body, as if willing himself to stay fixed in position. Unlike him, Dave moved toward her the moment her eyes fell on him.

She no longer heard the babbling voices in the room. Indeed, all sight and sound faded to black save for his image. Heat rose up in her torso as he drew near and she felt unable to look away from those cobalt-blue eyes and boyishly handsome features as they advanced upon her.

"Welcome back, Lightning Girl," he said with a dimpled

smile, his voice low and raw with emotion. He took her hands in his. She thought her knees might give out as she caught the undisguised need in his gaze. She swallowed hard.

"Hey, Thunder Boy," she said, embarrassed at the squeaky, adolescent voice ensuing from her lips.

"May I escort you to your office?" he asked, casting a sidelong glance at the small crowd surrounding Mrs. Flynn. Zara nodded weakly, feeling incapable of uttering another word. Dave's arm slipped around her shoulders and guided her away from the action and down the long hall.

At last, they reached the cool solitude of the CEO's office, Dave closing the door behind them. They didn't get much farther. He spun her around and braced her against the heavy oak paneling, trapping her between him and the door.

"My God, I missed you," he said, his mouth seeking hers insistently. She barely heard his words above the pounding of her own heart. Her lips trembled as they met his in a searing, all-consuming kiss. If he'd not been holding her so tight, she'd have melted to the floor in a pool of desire. She pulled her hands free and dove them into his tousled locks, dragging her fingers through the soft, collar-length waves of light brown hair.

When they broke their kiss, neither of them breathed lightly. A kiss wasn't nearly enough to quell the urges seething within. Dave leaned his forehead against hers, his eyes closed.

"This is completely unprofessional and inappropriate," he whispered.

"I agree," she said, trying to catch her breath. "What on earth were you thinking, Mr. Parker?"

"Ha." He flashed his signature half-smile as he continued to hyperventilate. "I was thinking, a demonstration might make things more clear, Miss Flynn." He swallowed and brought his respiration rate down to a manageable level. "With your permission?"

"By all means, you have my complete attention, sir."

He pushed away from the door, pulling her with him. He dragged one of the hard-backed visitor chairs over and jammed it up against the doorknob. Walking backwards, he towed her across the room to the oversized drafting table between two massive bookcases. He lifted her to sit on the vinyl-topped surface, wedging his body between her knees. His hands framed her face while he kissed her, hard.

Without conscious thought, Zara's fingers went to his belt, flipping the buckle open and sliding it through the jean loops and onto the floor. She undid the metal button and worked the zipper down in a few tugs. He caught up strands of her hair and massaged them against her cheeks as he deepened his kiss, letting her continue undressing him. She separated the buttons on his soft denim shirt, slipping her hands inside to stroke his muscled chest. Her fingertips found his taut nipples and lingered there, tickling and touching.

He wrenched the rest of the shirt off, then set to work on the front buttons of her sweater, stripping her down to her lacy black bra. His mouth moved to her chest, licking and kissing the mounds of her breasts as he pushed up the hem of her skirt.

With her hormones raging, Zara felt like she might leave a puddle on the tabletop if she didn't get his dock inside her in the next ten seconds. She grasped at the waistband of his jeans and pushed them down past his hips, releasing his swollen member from its bounds. He pulled her roughly to the edge of the table, lifting her enough to free her skirt from around her bum. Her thin panties were no match for Dave's insistent fingers. Not much material to them in any case, they shredded easily in his hands. He slung one arm under her knee and lifted it to his ribs, creating enough clearance to plunge his throbbing penis into her.

Zara sucked in air at the sudden, aggressive entry, surprised at how much the rough play excited her. Her arms went tight around his back, her fingernails digging into his skin, clinging to him like a cat on a scratching post. She relished the pounding rhythm of his cock driving into her. Holy Mother, was this how it would always be between them if they were apart for more than a few days? God, she hoped so.

She took all of what he had to give her, mindless of the blueprints and mechanical pencils scattering to the floor from the rocking tabletop. Without the benefit of much foreplay, Zara still felt the rising tide of orgasm flow toward her center as she matched his thrusts.

It usually didn't work that way for her, the tender tissues between her legs typically requiring a bit more encouragement and…finesse, but…right now…felt good. Jesus, this was her workplace! At least twenty people stood not five meters outside the door. This is crazy!

A burning flush rose up her chest, her breasts tingling and tightening, while her inner thighs quivered on the threshold of surrender. The very idea of making it on an office desk, and that they might be discovered at any moment, brought an unexpected thrill. This is beyond crazy…this is unconscionable…this is…oh, sweet Jesus, Mary and Joseph.

She tumbled into orgasm, and so did he. As Dave was about to let out a satisfactory moan, Zara covered his mouth in a smothering kiss to prevent any telltale noise from exiting the room. His free hand cupped the back of her head. She listened to the sound of his breathing and the soft grunts trapped in his throat as he buried himself in her kiss.

Their lips parted, and he nuzzled her neck and licked her earlobe before speaking in a painful whisper. "I'm sorry…if I rushed you. Did I hurt you? I never want to hurt you. I can do better."

She kissed his cheek. "If you were hurting me, I sure as hell like being hurt," she replied. "And if you did any better, I'd have to fire you. For being so unprofessional. But your, demonstration, was certainly convincing. Remind me to have you make business presentations more often."

"Even when inappropriate?" he asked, still holding her knee to his side.

Her new phone buzzed loudly in their quiet moment, vibrating in the pocket of her skirt that now lay bunched around her waist.

"Speaking of inappropriate..." They laughed at their awkward position. Unravelling themselves from each other, Dave lifted Zara to her feet and tugged her skirt down before hitching up his jeans and zipping them closed. The phone buzzed again.

"You going to answer that?" he asked.

"Not without underwear," she said. "What am I supposed to wear for the rest of the day, Thunder Boy?" She kicked at the torn remains of her panties with one high-heeled foot.

For a change, he had no snappy retort. He held his palms up in the air. "I said I was sorry."

Two loud knocks sounded on the door. Zara flashed him an open-mouthed gesture that said, "For Christ's sake, what now?" She pointed to his shirt, crumpled on the floor and reached for her soft cashmere sweater dangling off the edge of the drafting table.

Hastily doing up buttons and smoothing out wrinkles, Dave removed the chair from under the doorknob. He looked at Zara, and at her nod, opened the door.

"Ah, David," Ernesto said, standing back a few feet into the hallway. "Could you see me in my office, please?"

Dave ran his hand through his hair in an attempt to look presentable. "Sure, Ernie. Now?"

Ernesto cocked his head to one side, his tongue creating a peak on one side of his mouth. "Si. Now," he confirmed, eyeing up the two of them.

Dave turned to Zara. "Will that be all, Miss Flynn?"

Zara coughed into her fist. "Oh, yes. Have those demolition reports on my desk by morning," she said brusquely. She leaned on her desk, crossing her arms and ankles in dismissal.

Dave smiled and turned to follow Ernesto out into the hallway, closing the door behind him. Zara shook her head in disbelief. She'd never done anything so wicked in her life. And she liked it. Her phone buzzed a reminder. She fished it out of her pocket and blinked at a caller's name she hadn't seen in a long time.

Stephane. What the hell did he want?

Chapter Six

"It's wonderful to see you," Ernesto said as the waiter filled Marlena's champagne flute.

"Gracias," she said. The waiter nodded and retreated from their table. She fixed Ernesto with a no-nonsense look. "Y tu, mi amigo."

"Solo amigo?" he asked. "Just friends?"

Marlena smiled. "You know better than that, Ernesto. We will always be more than friends." She sipped her champagne, keeping eye contact over the rim of her glass. He returned her gaze with an intense stare. After a moment, she set her glass down and glanced around the restaurant. "This is lovely."

A Mediterranean vista displayed in the windows surrounding the trendy dining spot on the top floor of a high-rise tower. Soft jazz played in the background. From this vantage point in downtown Malaga, the calming waves of the sea could be seen cresting and receding in the distance, as eternal as the universe.

"Zara said you were receiving more information about… the incident," Marlena continued, looking out upon the water and sand so far below.

"Little by little," he affirmed, finally looking away from

her and fidgeting with the silverware as he spoke. "Most of it you know already. The accident occurred near seven in the evening. Normally the crews would have been finished for the day, but we were behind schedule and working overtime."

"And Tristan was on-site," Marlena said. "That's unusual, isn't it?"

Ernesto compressed his lips in concentration. "Not unheard of, but unusual, yes."

"Have they determined the cause of the collapse?"

"Not officially," Ernesto said. "But I think the evidence will point to a conclusion your daughter has already reached."

"Sabotaged, she said."

Ernesto nodded. "Explosives. I don't think the people responsible intended to kill anyone. The project should have been deserted at that time of day, but it was not the case. The whole thing seems to have been a diversion, to halt progress and drive costs up. To force the sale of El Mirador to finance it."

"Ach," Marlena said, dropping her forehead into her hands. "El Mirador. I'm sick of hearing about it. I almost wish Zara had sold it to those…whoever those people were. It's brought nothing but sorrow to our family."

Ernesto held his hand out on the tabletop, entreating her. She looked up, saw the pain in his eyes, and slipped her hand into his.

"You still have family, mi amor. Maybe new family," Ernesto said, his voice soft with affection. His tone suggested more than one meaning to his words.

"Youngblood?" she asked in amusement, considering the possibility.

Ernesto tipped his head to one side, raising his eyebrows in concession. "That," he said, "and…don't discount yourself. Give yourself another chance at love."

Marlena blushed. "Ernesto," she admonished. "It's too soon."

He squeezed her hand. "Perhaps. But, as Youngblood said to me recently, 'amor makes the world go 'round.' Don't step off the carousel just yet. Please."

Ernesto hoped he looked somewhat dashing in a dark business suit, his steely-gray hair smartly styled and sporting a brand-new pair of designer glasses. Very different from the skinny boy who'd carried her schoolbooks all those years ago.

A slow smile began to spread between Marlena's flushed cheeks. "Okay," she said. "I might ride it once more around."

Ernesto felt relieved that his first pitch hadn't landed outside the catcher's mitt. The next might hit a home run, and pick up the game where he'd left it all those years ago.

He loved her still.

"You know, Tristan saw great promise in David," he said, altering the drift of the conversation. "He called him Youngblood for a reason. He once said, 'Ernie, old dogs like you and me won't be around forever. We need some young blood.' Zara and David are the future of this company." He paused, as if weighing his next words. "I think Tristan knew that. He went to Indonesia to spare him, you know. David took over the foreman's position there, and became very ill soon after. Tristan took his place so he could come home. Your daughter might not have met him otherwise."

Marlena began to look teary-eyed. "Destino," she said. "Fate. He is a wily companion." She placed her other hand on top of Ernesto's, forming a living knot between them. "What about El Mirador? How can we make life from death?"

Ernesto smiled. "The way we always have. Go on living." After a heartbeat, he asked, "Do you want to see it? See what Zara's plans are?"

Marlena nodded. Ernesto waved for the check.

*

Zara wasn't about to call him back. Stephane Vanier could rot in hell for all she cared. He had a lot of nerve contacting her after everything that happened. Granted, her old phone, destroyed in the explosion at El Mirador, would have prevented him from getting through these last few weeks. But the curiosity remained. What could he possibly want?

A corporate lawyer in Montreal, Stephane had worked for the architectural firm from which she'd been laid off last summer. For a while, she'd held him chiefly responsible for the round of layoffs that left her and many others unemployed. The rat. One of those "strategic moves" of corporate restructure that typically did little for company efficiency but left human devastation in its wake. Damned fucking lawyers.

But the layoffs were only part of the reason for her hostility. Prior to that, the oh-so-slick Mr. Vanier had not only been the senior counsel for the firm, he'd been her lover. A flicker of nausea rippled through Zara's stomach at the admission of this fact. She'd been such an easy target for him, young, inexperienced and swept up in her first professional gig.

His good looks, money, and practiced charm were no match for the thin barriers she tried to construct against him. It began with lunches, moved on to dinner dates; gifts and flowers. Soon they were spending weekends at his cottage in Collingwood. What a sucker! Zara felt thankful her mother didn't know about him. As far as Zara was concerned, Stephane Vanier amounted to nothing more than a big, black blip on the wall chart of her life.

The worst part? She'd made the mistake of thinking their relationship held the element of exclusivity. Far too late, she discovered the string of other women from the firm that had fallen victim to his routine. She didn't even want to guess what number might have been on her jersey.

Enough about him. He didn't rate a moments' more conscious thought from her. She'd stewed about it all day as she worked her way through emails, work orders and projects that had piled up in her absence. She took a break at lunchtime and made a quick trip to the nearest centro commerciale to purchase several pairs of underwear.

She sat at her desk and felt a blush rising in her face. Sex on a drafting table was a bit of fantasy come true. She had to laugh inwardly at how the scene would have looked on a movie screen, her and Dave making it like a couple of rabbits in a pile of blueprints. An unbidden thought lasered through her mind and exited just as quickly. She'd succumbed to Dave's charms just as easily as Stephane's. Easier, in fact. Nah. She rejected the idea. That's not true. I'm not some kind of floozy, falling into bed with every man I meet. Far from it. It's just…suerte, coincidence. Fate had brought Dave into her life; and he loved her, she was certain of it. He'd risked his life for her. He made love to her like no one else ever had…like she was the only girl in the world.

Zara winced at that line, straight from Lady GaGa. She tried to discourage the next thought from forming, but it materialized anyway. Maybe she was more naïve than she thought. Ugh. Her stomach squirmed again.

Someone knocked, but didn't wait for a response. She looked up to see Dave's tall, athletic form filling the doorway.

"Excuse me, Miss Flynn. May I come in?"

"You're already in, why bother asking?"

He looked at her sideways, an eyebrow rising in concern. "Something wrong? Que pasa?"

She closed her eyes for a second, reciting a quick mantra. I'm not naïve. He loves me. I love him. I shouldn't doubt my heart so easily.

"Nothing," she said, exhaling. "Just inundated with work, is all. Did you need something?"

He stepped into the room. "Besides you?" he said, smiling.

"Not a thing." He held something in his hand. "Do you think you'll dig your way out by next Saturday?"

Zara rolled her eyes. "Dunno. I hope so. Why?"

He laid an envelope on the desk in front of her. She took it and opened the flap, pulling out the folded contents. A travel itinerary. She scanned the print for details.

"Tenerife?" she said, glancing up to see him grinning in triumph at her.

"Tenerife, babe," he affirmed. "Need a new bikini?"

She shouted a gleeful "woop!" and circled her desk to take him in her arms. He did love her! "Depends," she said. "If you'll give me a chance to even put it on."

"Oh, you'll put it on. If only so I can have the pleasure of taking it off," he said, his voice dropping to a sexy growl. His hands slipped down to squeeze her bum, his fingers sliding over the elastic of her panties. "Hey, new underwear?"

*

Ernesto adjusted the sizing strap on the hardhat before placing it securely on Marlena's head. "There," he said. "That fits properly, now."

Marlena touched the sides of the yellow hat in recognition. "It's been awhile since I've worn one of these," she admitted. "Do I need those loathsome steel things as well?"

Ernesto looked down at her feet, clad in a pair of Nikes. "I think you'll be okay, we're not going that far in," he said. Together they started down the graded slope toward the shovel-bucket machinery clearing away debris and loading it in transports to be hauled away.

Ernesto held her hand in the crook of his elbow as they walked. "After the explosion, we had no choice but to demo everything and begin removal," he explained. "But Zara has this idea about building an interpretive centre. I think it's a great concept."

"An interpretive centre? To interpret what?"

"The natural resources here. How they formed, how they can best be managed. She went into a lot of detail around the technological advances they're making in Western Canada, reducing the carbon footprint and water usage to extract the oil. And their exceptional reclamation procedures. She's very excited about the process."

"That sounds like my querida," Marlena said, nodding. "Such a beautiful spot, though. It would be a good site for a villa. She'll need a proper home, if she plans to stay here."

Ernesto agreed. "I believe she found some sketches that Tristan left behind. She talked of building a house based on one of his designs." His next words were as measured and careful as their steps. "Y tu? Do you plan to stay here?"

Marlena stopped walking to appreciate the view. The mechanical sounds of excavation equipment hummed further down the slope. The soft, saline breeze off the Mediterranean blew strands of her brunette hair about her face as she lost herself in thought for several moments.

"Ernesto," she said, still looking out over the water, "I do believe you are preaching to the converted. I love this land, you know that. It's my birthplace. But my home is in Ontario. I have responsibilities there." She inhaled a hearty breath of sea air then turned to him with a smile. "But, if Zara wants me to stay, I will stay."

Chapter Seven

"Mount Teide, in Spanish 'Pico del Teide,' or 'Teide Peak', is a volcano on Tenerife, Canary Islands. Its 3,718 meter summit is part of the Las Canadas escarpment and the highest point in Spain. It ranks the third highest volcano in the world after Mauna Loa and Mauna Kea in Hawaii," Zara read aloud from her tourist booklet. "Did you know that?" she asked Dave.

A grunt issued from beneath the brim of his baseball cap. "Nah."

Zara looked over to the deck chair on which Dave lay. His relaxed, prone form made Zara exude a longing sigh. His luscious body had so many better purposes than napping. Oh well. She folded up her tourist brochure and tossed it in her trusty red Fendi bag. She and that bag had been through a lot together. Today however, it served as nothing more than a beach tote.

She looked out over the expanse of black, volcanic sand that made up the main beachfront in Puerto de la Cruz. Elaborate sandcastle sculptures lined the two-mile stretch, entries in a competition that took place on this particular weekend. Everything from traditional castles to spiny crocodiles decorated the scene, the details of each creation an astounding testament to their artists. It felt so good to relax and enjoy the simplicity of lying on a beach, soaking up the sun and appreciating the singular talent of those who wrested such beauty from nothing more than buckets of sand.

Zara looked forward to exploring more of Tenerife, the largest island of Las Canarias, the Canary Islands. Her tourist handbooks explained the history behind the name, which had nothing at all to do with small, yellow-feathered birds. 'Canarias' was a mispronunciation of the word 'canaris,' referring to the Latin 'canus,' meaning 'dog.' Early explorers found the island populated with wild dogs, giving rise to the original name.

The Atlantis theory proved far more interesting. The popular train of thought described the Canary Islands, among others in the region, as the last vestiges of the lost continent of Atlantis. The idea that she could be sitting on soil of such legend excited her to say the least.

She turned a lazy eye back to Dave, his tanned body displayed in all its sculpted glory. God, she loved that body. She felt another of the odd twinges in her stomach that she'd been experiencing lately. Bad on her, for not taking precautions. Double bad, she'd not asked him to wear any protection. But deep down, she didn't care. They were meant to be together, and if these feelings meant she could be pregnant, so be it. Fate, as her mother often said, was a wily companion.

"I'm going for a walk, want to come?" Zara said.

Dave nudged up the brim of his cap with his thumb, as he turned his head toward her. "You've got that much energy, I clearly didn't keep you in the bedroom long enough," he replied.

"Is that a yes or a no?"

"Okay, Lightning Girl, let's go explore," he said, swinging his legs over the side of the deck chair. They walked hand in hand past the mighty sand sculptures and the beach vendors hawking their jewelry and paintings. Zara stopped to buy a necklace made of the distinctive blue coral that grew in the region. Dave placed it around her neck and fastened the clasp. The choker-style fit closely around her throat, in contrast to the silver dolphin pendant hanging on a longer chain.

He fingered the little charm for a moment, looking absently at it, as if trying to remember something. Zara cocked her head. "What?" she said with a hint of a smile, placing her hand over his.

"Where did you get this?" he asked.

Zara had to think about it. With a sour twinge, she realized who had given it to her. "A gift. I don't remember when," she said, glossing over the tiny lie. Dave continued staring at it, rubbing its shiny curved surface between his fingers. "Do you like it?" she asked.

"No," he said quietly. "I mean, yes, sure. If you like it," he backpedaled, dropping it to land against her bronzed skin. "It's nice, fine." He reached for her hand to resume walking.

What was that all about? Zara wondered. An avid swimmer, "dolphin" had been her nickname in school, and the pendant a gift from someone whom until a few days ago hadn't crossed her mind.

Stephane.

Suddenly, she felt the urge to rip the silver necklace off. Why did it make Dave uncomfortable? He couldn't know about Stephane. But guessing that it came from an old boyfriend wouldn't be a big stretch of his imagination. It's just a chunk of metal. It means nothing, just like Stephane. Forget it. She hoped no further calls would be coming from him. Come to think of it, why hadn't she changed her number when she got her new phone? What a dumb move. She sighed. One more thing on the to-do list when she returned to Marbella.

She squeezed Dave's hand, grateful and happy to be with

him. They strolled out to the far point of the cove, past the last few hotels, restaurants and beach shacks. The sun began to dip toward the horizon, and the sound of surf grew louder as they moved further away from the populated area.

Then she saw it.

A familiar, cylindrical building with three storeys and a cone-shaped roof. An architectural parody of a lighthouse, it stood alone on a promontory of beach. Narrow, slotted windows perforated its sides and a full-round span of windows made up the top floor. Or they would have, if there'd been any glass left intact.

She stopped short and pointed to it. Dave followed her gesture and let out a whistle. "Holy shit, isn't that one of Tristan's drawings?"

Zara nodded as if in a dream state. Yes, it most certainly looked like her father's sketch.

Los Teides.

Unlike the drawing, however, its exterior stood ravaged with gaping holes and the remnants of a bad paint job. Distinctly ugly. Los Teides. The volcano, El Teide. It made sense. This had to be the same structure as in her father's drawings, but he could never have built something so hideous. Had it been vandalized? Or, were the drawings his plans for restoration?

She thought the latter. An excitement flowed up her spine. She had to buy this thing—finish what Dad had started. "Let's go see," she said, pulling Dave along as she quickened her steps.

"Oh, no you don't. Haven't you learned anything from last time?" Dave said, resisting her tugs and grabbing her arm with both hands to draw her firmly into his embrace. "Safety first, Lightning Girl."

Zara leaned against his bare chest, pressing her hands to his well-developed pectorals. "Well, I'm not likely to find any PPE close by, am I?" she said, looking up at him through her eyelashes. "Come on, we won't go inside. Let's just get a better look. I need to see it."

"Why?"

"You know why. If Dad made a drawing of this place, it was of importance to him. I need to see what he saw, think what he thought. I need to—"

"Be him?" Dave suggested.

Zara blinked, taken aback. That sounded like an insult. "Something wrong with that?" she asked.

Dave's jawline worked a bit, as if biting back a few choice words. "There is when it puts you in danger," he finally said, pulling her close so that his lips brushed her forehead. His voice dropped to a whisper. "I won't risk that again. Ever."

The quiet tension in his voice made Zara's heart skip a beat. The strength of his arms around her sent the simple message of protection. He wanted to protect her above all else and that knowledge made her insides hum. *He does love me.*

"Okay, understood. We'll be careful. Just a little closer, please. I have to know."

He stroked her hair and released her from his hold. "As long as we're clear on that," he said. She smiled and nodded.

As they approached the broken-down structure, more details came into focus. Steps led to a wide entrance way, its doors long gone. Bird nests clung to the sills of broken windows and graffiti lay splattered against its peeling walls. A faded sign dangled from a rusted metal hanger above the doorway, the letters unreadable.

"Now here's a fixer-upper," Dave commented. "I think it's beyond even your magic touch to repair." They stopped about ten metres away. Zara looked it up and down, analyzing it. She peered into the depths of the entrance way, walked a few steps closer.

"It's a restaurant," she said. "Or was. See, there's booth seats

on the top floor, below the window level. That's fascinating."
She looked at the crooked sign above the door. "Pescadore,"
she said, pointing to the faint specks of red paint. "A seafood
place. Right up your alley."

Dave snorted. "I wouldn't be caught stewing barnacles in
this joint," he said. "Have you seen enough? I think we can
find a much better place for dinner."

Zara couldn't take her eyes off the thing. It seemed to call
to her. The urge to possess it grew in the pit of her stomach.
"Let's find an estate agent tomorrow," she said. "I want to
know if it's for sale."

Dave looked at her as though she'd sprouted a second
head. "You can't be serious."

Chapter Eight

The law offices of Coté & Associates occupied the third floor of an office tower on Rue Peel just west of Blvd. Rene Levesque, overlooking Dorchester square. The signage had yet to be changed, but the firm would soon be known as Coté, Vanier & Associates with the recent addition of a new partner.

Traffic noises and mouth-watering aromas from a nearby delicatessen wafted up through the open window. Expecting company, Stephane Vanier grew impatient as the lunch hour drew near. His favorite smoked meat sandwich awaited across the road. He could practically taste the mustard and sauerkraut spilling from between slabs of fresh-baked rye bread. He smoothed his expertly-styled blond hair while he checked his phone messages. As expected, no response would be forthcoming from Zara Flynn. That at least confirmed her position. She did not want to speak to him. No surprise there.

But one way or another, she would listen to him. His next attempt would be a text message with some particularly bad news. His guest knocked on his door.

"Entrez," he said, not moving from his seat by the window. The stocky figure edged its way into the room. "Alain," Stephane said. "You're late." Stephane stowed his cellphone into the breast pocket of his suit jacket. "I'm not a big fan of 'late,' ami. Sit down."

Alain's unkempt black hair appeared to sit at an angle on top of his head. His eyes peered out from beneath heavy dark eyebrows, and a wiry beard and moustache covered the lower half of his face. A checkered flannel shirt and fringed buckskin jacket would have completed the Voyageur ensemble, but instead, Alain wore a black Ed Hardy t-shirt and jeans.

Stephane chuckled. "How does the place look?" he asked.

"I email the pics," Alain replied in his colloquial French accent. "Check your inbox."

Stephane swivelled to his laptop and worked the trackpad for a moment. He scrolled through a half-dozen images, a smile forming on his handsome face. "Excellent," he commented. "Convincing. I trust no one saw you."

Alain shook his head, glancing around the walls of the office. "Non," he grunted, not interested in Stephane's critique of his work. The expensive artwork and furnishings in the room held more fascination. He sized up their value with a thief's practiced eye.

The images showed the interior of a condominium on Avenue Melville in trendy Westmount. The entrance door had been forced, the rooms artfully trashed and significant objects blatantly missing. An empty TV mount lay centered in a conspicuous blank spot above the fireplace.

Stephane reached into one of his desk drawers and withdrew an envelope. He tossed it on the desk in front of Alain. Alain's hairy forearm lifted from the armchair in which he sat to retrieve it. He folded it in half and shoved it in his back jean pocket.

"I'd keep that hidden, ami," Stephane said.

Alain shrugged. "Hide in plain sight," he replied, settling himself back into the cushy chair, in no hurry to leave.

Stephane tapped his foot, annoyed. "I'm going to lunch," he announced. "You can leave now."

"Aren't you buying me lunch, mon ami?"

"I just paid you five grand. You can buy your own lunch. I dine alone." Stephane replied, rising from his desk. "You'd best save some of it for a flight. Now go."

Alain didn't move from his chair. "That only half. Your lady friend may not react the way you hope," he remarked. "What then? I still want the other five grand."

"Piss off. You've got work to do," Stephane said, and left his office. Let the Frenchman stay if he wanted. He had a call to make, but after lunch, he decided. His stomach growled.

*

It seemed to Ivette that the elevator moved at a snail's pace. She tapped the toe of her strappy stiletto shoe in annoyance. At last, it announced its destination with a ding, and she stepped out.

The impressive entrance doors sported a giant metal casting of the company crest. She stood in front of them for a few moments before going in. The business appeared to be doing well. She hoped its engineers were paid proportionately.

She touched the sleek steel handle and pulled. Ivette's Amazonian legs seemed to enter the office before the rest of her did. A stocky woman in a red and black print dress looked up from the reception desk. She adjusted her glitter-rimmed eyeglasses to focus on Ivette, as if tuning in a satellite channel. Accustomed to being stared at, it bothered Ivette not in the least.

The receptionist cleared her throat. "Por favor, may I help you?" she asked.

Ivette flashed a sweet smile. "Si, I'm here to see David Parker."

Under Ivette's stare the woman interlaced her fingers and

placed them squarely on the desk. "Is he expecting you?" she asked in her cultivated, receptionist voice.

"No. Is that required?" she replied, trying her best to intimidate the woman. At five foot ten, Ivette had no difficulty intimidating. She flung a thick auburn thatch of hair over her shoulder in a casual gesture.

The receptionist sat unflinching behind her desk. "No, but I'm afraid you've missed him. He's just left on vacation," she said.

Ivette cursed silently. She could have called him, but needed to achieve maximum impact with her news, and that meant approaching him in person. She lifted her chin and moved back a half step from the desk. "Oh, that's disappointing. I have such good news for him." She reached into her reptile-skin handbag and brought out a pen. "Do you know how I could contact him, then?"

The woman swivelled to one side, producing his business card from a multi-tiered holder and handing it to Ivette. Ivette turned the card over and poised her pen over the blank side, clearly expecting more information. The receptionist seemed to think it over before answering.

"I don't know how you'd reach him, Senora. He's in Tenerife."

Ivette smiled and wrote on the card. "Tenerife," she echoed, remembering a good time there. "Don't worry. I'll find him." She pivoted on her four-inch heels and left.

*

The dolphin spoke. No words came from the tiny saw-toothed mouth, only the chattering squeals typically heard from dolphins. Its snout bobbed up and down, as if trying to articulate a sentence by movement. Dave couldn't make any sense from its gestures. Then it opened its mouth wide, the inky blackness inside swelling to enormous proportions as the creature swallowed him.

Lightning flashed, followed by a deafening crack of thunder. Rain poured down, soaking his shirt and spilling down his collar. In the fleeting brilliance of the lightning he glimpsed her face, empty green eyes staring heavenward. Her swollen lips were parted as if her last breath lay frozen between them. Droplets of rain gathered on her forehead and cheeks. His arms tightened around her cold form. He needed to kiss her, breathe life back into her, before it was too late.

His lips touched hers in a desperate kiss, begging her come alive again. They met with dead flesh that held no warmth, no softness. "No," he cried, pounding his fist against her chest. "No!" He shook her, slapped her face. The wind whipped the rain harder against them and he felt as cold and flat as the wet sand that they lay upon. An icy wave surged up over them and as it receded, began to pull her body away from him.

"No!" he shouted again, clutching at her arms as she slipped relentlessly toward the water.

"No." The sound of his voice forced his eyes open, only to be greeted by the steely metal gaze of the dolphin. It lay inanely against the curve of her breast, fettered by the silver chain fastened around her neck.

Dave recoiled from the sight of it, bringing the rest of the scene into focus. His sweating hands held Zara's arm in a death grip, just as in his dream. Only they weren't on any beach. No rain poured down and no lightning snaked overhead. Her chest rose and fell in a slow rhythm as she slumbered next to him in the snug warmth of their hotel bed.

He exhaled in relief, blood thundering in his ears. He felt out of breath, as if he'd just finished his morning run. Shit. The nightmare had returned. He drew himself as close to her as he could, wrapping his arms around her sleeping form. At least they were together this time and he hadn't woken to the dreadful emptiness that usually followed the horrifying dream. What did it mean, dammit? What did the stupid dolphin signify?

He closed his eyes and concentrated on the feel of her skin touching his. The scent of her perfume reached his nostrils as he slowed his breathing to deep, measurable draughts. As he became hyper-aware of her, his body reacted in typical male fashion. A moment ago, he'd been terrified for her. Now all he could think of was fucking her.

He stroked her stomach for a start, eventually moving his hand up to her breasts. He revelled in their firm, yet yielding texture, his palm caressing the outer curve and fingertips massaging the soft brown nipples.

She began to stir, a low murmur starting in her throat. Dave smiled. His erection grew stiffer as he felt more blood rush south. He moved his knee overtop her leg and could resist the luscious little buds no longer. He swirled his tongue around her nipple and closed his lips around it, sucking gently.

Zara turned her head from side to side, her murmurs elevating to little moans. That's it, Lightning Girl, just go with it…let me take you places in your dreams. Dave's hand slid down between her thighs and pushed her legs farther apart. He reached upward, parting her pussy lips with his fingers to find the needy nub of flesh to entertain.

She inhaled sharply as he did so, and exhaled in a throaty moan. His index finger stroked her clit with the barest touch, triggering the flow of wetness. Her hand withdrew from under the covers, and nestled itself on his head. Her fingers twined around his wavy brown locks and she began to move her hips in sync with his touch.

His lips moved to her other breast, repeating his artful manipulations. He felt overwhelmed by the need to remain physically connected to her, as if that would stop her from being dragged away from him in his dreams. He slid his fingers inside her entrance, moving slowly in and out.

Both her hands were tangled in his hair now as his head lay pressed against her chest, alternately sucking and biting down on her tight, swollen nipples. Contented groans left her throat with each breath. He thought the sound of her rising pleasure alone might drive him over the edge himself, but he would not stop.

He felt a sharp tug on his hair, forcing him to look up. Zara's green eyes glowed like emerald fire as she stared back at him. God, the sight made him want to weep with desire. She drew his face to hers and took his bottom lip gently in her teeth before invading his mouth with her tongue, fueling his desire to an even deeper level. His dick ached with the need to be inside her.

"Roll over," she whispered, pushing on his shoulder. He had no idea what she had in mind, but would refuse her nothing. His hand slipped away from between her thighs and he twisted onto his back. She drew the crisp cotton sheets aside and sat up. For a moment, he worried she would leave the room. Instead, she straddled him facing away, the 'reverse cowgirl' move making his heart skip a beat. He watched in awe as her lovely buttocks hovered over his reddened member.

My God, the girl knows a few things about sex. She had his legs pinned under her. He was at her mercy and he didn't care. The upright head of his cock met with her hot wet pussy as she bore down, past the outer lips with their teasing resistance followed by the blissful rush of his member sliding inward to full penetration.

He laid his hands on the creamy skin of her back, caressing the fine ridges of her shoulder blades beneath her tossing mane of sandy blond hair. Her hands gripped his ankles as her hips rose and fell, gliding up and down the length of his shaft. The little bit of daylight he could see between her ass and his crotch with each stroke she took, nearly drove him mad with lust. He moved his hands to her buttocks, pressing his thumbs into the pale white flesh around her anus while she banged against his rod.

His vision seemed to blur and fill with shifting, kaleidoscopic colors as he lost control and hot fluid exploded from within him. Lost. He felt purely lost each time they were together, and each time told him with increasing certainty that he could never be without her.

The chic décor of their hotel room came into focus as his head cleared and his heart rate returned to normal. Her shoulders still heaved up and down as she too, recovered from their exertion. He gathered her hair in his hands and stroked it downward, hand over hand, feeling its silky length slipping through his fingers.

"Zara," he said, his voice a strained whisper. He tugged on the rope of blond locks he held. Slowly, she separated her body from his and turned to face him. She laid herself across his moist, muscled chest and brushed her lips against his unshaven jaw.

"Did you like that, Thunder Boy?"

He closed his eyes and smiled in wonderment at this unbelievable jewel of a woman that fate had seen fit to place in his path. For maybe the second time in his life, he felt speechless. A coherent sentence refused to form in his mouth.

"Mmmm," he grunted. "Thunder Boy like. A lot."

Chapter Nine

"Condemned?" Zara repeated. "Of course it's condemned. I can see that. I want to know if it's for sale," she explained to the estate agent over the phone. Having found the office closed when they first came by this morning, the agent had returned her call. She and Dave sat at a small open-air table at the edge of the cobbled strand, slurping shaved ice in paper cups from a nearby vendor. The African sun beamed overhead and the blue waves of the Atlantic crested at their backs.

Zara looked out over the rushing surf as she listened to the agent's words. She liked Tenerife. It felt beautiful and exotic; the lifestyle here European, yet not physically connected to Europe. The dark sand beaches added to its wild allure. She glanced over at Dave, lounging comfortably in his chair. She admired his muscles straining through his tight white t-shirt as he leaned back with his face turned upward to the sky. Her Tarzan.

"How much?" she asked, the breeze making the agents words difficult to hear. "What do you mean, you don't know?" She paused, trying to make sense of the explanation. "Well, when would it be passed inspection?" Another pause. "Well then, schedule one." She furrowed her brow, losing patience.

"Fine, what if I brought my own people in? I assure you, I have access to the proper quality control personnel."

Dave looked over at her, appearing to sense things were getting complicated. Zara rolled her eyes as she listened to the agent's voice. "Never mind. I'll call you back tomorrow."

"Problem?" he asked.

Zara shook her head as she pocketed her phone. "Apparently they can't put it on the market until someone coughs up the cash to inspect it," she said with a sigh, then one corner of her mouth curved up in a crafty grin. "Fortunately, I have the cash. And my own QC team." She leaned back and draped her arms over the sides of her chair in a grand gesture. "Sometimes it's good to be the king." She looked at Dave and smiled triumphantly.

He straightened in his chair and leaned his browned arms on the table between them. He returned an odd sort of smile; one she hadn't seen before. He swallowed hard, as if trying to dredge up some long-hidden words from deep in his throat. Her smile faded partway as she tilted her head in puzzlement.

"What?" she asked him.

"You sure ask a lot of questions."

"Yeah? So?"

"How about if someone asks you a question?"

Zara blinked. *Where is this leading?* He seemed to be preparing to ask permission to ask a question. Weird. She'd never seen him trip over words since the day they'd met in the Black Swan over a month ago. A buzzing sensation started in the pit of her stomach. *Oh. My. God. He has. A question.*

His lips parted, and the buzzing became real as her phone vibrated in her pocket. With his mouth still open, his eyes went to the source of the sound. Out of habit, she reached for it.

"M—maybe that's the agent calling back," she stammered. She pulled it out and looked at the screen. *What the hell? A* text message from Coté Vanier Assoc.' Startled, she stabbed at the icon with her fingernail.

Dolphin, since you won't return my calls I'm sorry to have to inform you by text message. Your condo in Westmount has been broken into and your vehicle stolen. As I am now legal counsel for the insurance company with which your property is covered, I thought it best to contact you personally. I sincerely regret this may cut your European visit short, but it is in your best interest to return to Montreal and attend to this matter at your earliest convenience.

P.S. I miss you. Stephane.

Zara felt her whole body begin to shake, uncertain if with anger, fear, indignation or a combination of all three. She looked up at Dave, only to find he wasn't looking at her anymore. The unspoken question in his handsome face had been replaced with a stony visage directed a short distance behind her. She twisted awkwardly to get a view.

A tall, auburn-haired creature stood a few feet from their table. Her long chiffon skirt billowed in the breeze, revealing long, shapely legs in stiletto heels. Looking like an ad from a women's fitness magazine, her bronzed skin glowed with health, her pretty face radiant. Thick auburn locks fell about her shoulders.

"Hola, David," she said, her Spanish accent lush and sexy as she spoke his name. Zara could feel blood pulsing in her ears and her face growing hot as she stared in bewilderment at the mystery woman. She fought back the unsavory thoughts building in her mind. This could be anyone; his dentist, for all she knew. Her thoughts reeled in multiple directions. Dave's unspoken question, Stephane's upsetting news. This, this goddess-statue appearing out of thin air. Nausea buffeted her stomach as she watched Dave rise slowly from his chair.

He touched Zara's hand, as if commanding her to stay put, while he moved toward the woman.

"Aren't you going to say hello?" the woman asked, smiling as he drew near. Dave moved his six-foot-three frame between them, shielding Zara's view. His body language appeared to be enough to make the lady step backward, away from the table.

"What are you doing here, Ivette?" Dave asked, his voice emotionless. Her glossy lips pouted, apparently disappointed at his lack of warmth.

"David, you seem almost hostile," she said. "Am I so hideous you can't greet me civilly?"

"You haven't answered my question," he replied. "What are you doing here?"

"The same as you. Enjoying Tenerife."

"Really. And you just happened to bump into me. I don't believe you."

She smiled and raised a manicured hand to his chest, rubbing it suggestively. "Well then. Believe this. I came looking for you. I have some wonderful news."

He turned his head slightly and narrowed his eyes at her. His silence pressed her to continue. She cleared her throat. "You're going to be a father."

*

Dave didn't react. He stared into her eyes, as if to flush the lie out into the open. She had to be lying. The timing didn't work. He'd broken it off well over three months ago. They'd always used condoms. Shit. Except that one time. In that moment, the tiniest doubt took root. No. She had to be lying. This couldn't be happening, not now. Not when the biggest plans for his future were about to take shape.

"You expect me to believe that," he said, after finding his voice. "I haven't seen you in months. We weren't...together... for weeks before that. Why are you doing this?"

Her smile faded and tears welled up in her eyes as if on cue. "David, why would you think I would lie to you? I love you. I never stopped loving you." She dabbed at her eyes with one knuckle. "It's you who left me, remember? You broke my heart."

"Bullshit. You were too busy waxing and exfoliating to even notice I'd gone. You've no heart to be broken, Ivette. You're an empty shell; an empty, beautiful shell. Some guys like that. I'm not one of them."

"I'm far from empty, David. Your child is inside me."

Hearing these words made his guts turn cold. "Stop it. It's not true. Don't contact me again." He turned away, only to see Zara staring at him. She stood beside the table, clutching her arms about herself as if she were cold. Strands of her hair blew haphazardly around her face and the look in her eyes sent a physical stab of pain through his heart.

She'd heard them.

"Zara," he said, moving toward her. She took a step back, shaking her head in denial. Ivette hadn't left. She stood a few inches behind Dave and put her hand on his shoulder.

"You can't walk away," her contralto voice said. "You have a responsibility, you know. We made this together, David. Please, I want to be with you again. We can be a family."

Dave brushed her hand off him as he turned on her. "Stop saying that. I don't want you, do you get it? And there won't be any 'family' because the kid certainly isn't mine." He began to move away and when he turned back in the direction of the table, Zara was gone.

He couldn't see her anywhere.

He moved up and down the strand, searching in every direction. The milling bodies offered a million opportunities for her to slip away in the crowd. Shit. He re-traced the way they'd come. She didn't know the area and would likely have gone back that way—unless she hopped a cab, or a boat.

Dammit. He dialed her cell phone. It went to voicemail. He disconnected and switched to messenger, thinking of what possible words he could commit. He didn't even know how much of the conversation she'd heard.

Lightning Girl. Ask me anything. I will tell you the truth and the biggest truth right now is that I love you. Tell me where you are, please.

He pressed send.

He looked around, feeling helpless. He started back to the hotel. What a mess, a vacation gone rogue. Ten minutes ago he was about to ask her to marry him, and next she'd done a runner thanks to Ivette's untimely bombshell. Ivette. Where in the hell had she come from with that story? And how had she found him, here of all places. He kicked himself mentally. He knew better. He'd actually met Ivette here; some relative of hers owned a villa on the other side of the island. He felt stupid now, bringing Zara here. Unoriginal. But how did Ivette know his whereabouts?

Of one thing he was certain: no way had he gotten her pregnant. The chances of it were so miniscule as to be laughable. She would have to prove it in any case. And considering her vanity, the idea of growing an enormous belly would have seemed a fate worse than death for the leggy esthetician. Something about it didn't add up.

He shook his head, clearing his mind of her. Consumed with worry over Zara, he didn't want to think about Ivette. He had to find Zara, and fast. He couldn't lose her now, he just couldn't.

Chapter Ten

"Miss, are you certain you want to do this?" Jorge asked patiently.

Zara switched her phone to her left ear and held one hand over her right, to hear better over the noise in the Los Rodeos airport. "Si, Jorge, I'm sure. It's an emergency."

Jorge paused for a long moment. "Miss, at least tell your mother where you are going. She will worry."

Zara rubbed her temples, her head nearly splitting with a headache. "You tell her for me, Jorge. I can't miss this flight. I'll call her when I get home."

Jorge hesitated. "That's a long time for her to wait. I don't think you're being fair, Miss. To anyone, especially yourself."

Zara frowned, unused to hearing such talk from her mild-mannered second cousin. His words showed a deep concern, and she realized how much he must care to express his opinion so openly. She regretted putting him in such a position by her rash decision. She felt awful, but awful didn't even begin to describe how she felt about what had just happened in Tenerife.

"All right, Jorge. I'll call her right now." She disconnected and hit the speed dial for Marlena's number. Zara sighed in relief when her mother's voice mail came on. She explained in a few sentences about the condo and her car and returning to Montreal as soon as possible. She ended the call, but stared at the screen for a moment. Then she reviewed her text messages, re-reading Dave's words.

He said he loved her and that he would tell her the truth about anything she wanted to ask. What should she ask? She overheard only part of his conversation with the strange woman on the strand. But it was plain enough that he'd had a relationship with her, and she wanted him back because she was pregnant. Zara squeezed her eyes shut. She didn't want to think about what might be "the truth."

Her stomach lurched. She wondered if the tall woman felt morning sickness too. Wait. Back up. She had no proof that she herself might be pregnant, any more than the long-legged girl did. Jorge was right—she wasn't being fair to Dave, or her mom, or anyone right now.

But she did have a serious problem in Montreal. As much as she didn't want to see Stephane, she would have to depend on him in order to sort out the insurance and police matters. After that, perhaps she could think straight. Take some time to analyze her life, in the comfort of home. She sniffed and shook her head. She'd begun to think of Marbella as home. Heck, she'd even thought she would build a home, on the site of El Mirador, but could Spain ever really be home?

With Dave, it had seemed possible. Now, who knew? At the moment, she wanted to just curl up into a little ball and cry her eyes out.

*

Dave raced through the terminal, dodging travelers, baggage and airport personnel. Since Zara wouldn't answer his calls he tried the next best thing—Jorge. Fortunately, the little man turned out to be something of a romantic and had no compunctions about telling Dave where he could find her.

When he'd returned to the hotel in Tenerife, Dave discovered that Zara had left without even taking most of her clothes. He booked it to the airport as quickly as possible in hopes of catching her. The departure lounge lay a few hundred feet ahead.

He spotted her staring out the big windows near the gate, just like she'd been a few weeks ago when he'd held her in his arms, waiting for Marlena to arrive. But now, she was the one leaving. He moved swiftly toward her, and spun her around by her shoulder.

"Where do you think you're going?" he asked with more gruffness than he'd meant to express. She looked at him, wide-eyed, with something like fear coloring her delicate, freckled complexion. She took a step back.

"What are you doing here, how did you—" She broke off, looking from side to side, as if searching for an informant that had tipped him off.

"It doesn't matter," he said. "What matters is what the hell you think you're doing taking off without even talking to me, or giving me a chance to explain. Is that what you do to people you trust, people who love you? That doesn't sound like you, defies everything I know about you. Or thought I did."

Zara pursed her lips into an angry pout. "Trust? Look who's talking about trust. Leaving that poor girl, in her condition. Did she trust you, too? Kept that on the DL, didn't you? Didn't trust in me enough to mention it. In fact," she snapped, "you're something of an expert in keeping secrets, aren't you? Like about my father! When did you plan on telling me that he met his death because of you?"

Her words hurt like knives pressing into his flesh. She was being unreasonable, irrational. They'd been over and over the circumstances of Tristan's presence at the Indonesian site. She'd forgiven him long ago, inasmuch as it hadn't really been

Dave's fault. Something else had to be eating at her besides the incident in Tenerife.

"I never intended to keep any secrets from you," he answered. "You know how the accident happened—we're beyond that. As for 'that poor girl', she's lying through her teeth. Okay, sure. I dated her. And yeah, I slept with her. But it was months and months ago. We weren't careless, we weren't in love." He stopped for breath, calculating his next thoughts before they became speech. "We weren't special together, not like you and I."

Dave searched Zara's face for some reaction, some glimmer that his words were getting through. "Can't you see that?" he said, his voice softening. She fell silent, considering it, but still standing apart from him. He desperately wanted to touch her, hold her, make everything right again, but she'd have to come to it on her own terms.

He had another thought. "You can't punish me because I have a past, Zara. I don't expect to know every encounter you've ever had before we met." He held up his hand with an open palm. "Everyone has a past."

The flight attendant's voice announced the boarding for Montreal. Zara looked deeply into Dave's eyes for a long moment. He hoped that moment would turn into a lifetime, that she'd drop her bag and leap into his arms. He waited, willing it to happen, suspended in time for a few glorious ticks of the clock.

"I've got to go," she said, breaking the bubble. "My car's been stolen and my house ransacked. I've been away too long, already."

So that was it. That had been the phone message she received right before all hell broke loose. No wonder she's freaking out, Dave thought. "What about Flynn Enterprises?" he asked. "What about El Mirador and,"—he tried to remember the faded red letters—"Pescadore," he said, tossing out every reason he could think of for her to stay.

Zara shook her head, stepping away from him and toward the boarding queue. "I—I don't know, Dave. I don't know much of anything right now. Except that I need to go home."

Home. How long since he'd been "home"? For three years, Spain had been home. Thunder Bay seemed like centuries ago. He felt like he barely remembered it.

He watched, powerless, as she melted into the throng of departing travelers. And he realized with utter clarity, that his concept of home had changed forever.

Because home could never be anyplace, without Zara.

Chapter Eleven

Ernesto drove fast along the coastal highway that led to Marbella. A misty rain swept along the Costa del Sol as winter descended upon the region. Although one of the sunniest places on earth, the southern Spanish coast did receive some amounts of rainfall, particularly now, with December dawning.

Marlena had sounded distraught on the phone. She feared for Zara after receiving an upsetting voice message. Zara was on her way back to Montreal to address some trouble with her car and condominium. The last Ernesto knew, she and David were vacationing in Tenerife. Next, she was bound for Montreal, barely taking the time to explain, even to her mother.

And David? He hadn't expected either of them back in the office until next week, but he'd yet to hear from Dave. By the sound of things, it didn't seem that he'd accompanied Zara. Perhaps they'd quarreled. Perhaps whatever reared itself in Montreal had stirred up trouble between the couple. That would be a shame, he thought.

He had an inkling that David was about to pop the question to Zara while they were away. Though Ernesto would normally have recommended a long, slow courtship, he could see that these young people didn't operate that way. And he didn't mind. The two were made for each other. In fact, the sooner Zara and David were together permanently, the better for everyone and everything. Like the company succession plan.

With Tristan gone, Ernesto had been prepared to take on the CEO position if called upon. He and Tristan had more or less built the company together. Tristan made no secret of the fact that Ernesto played the part of right-hand man. But in the end, he chose his daughter as his replacement. And David seemed the perfect partner for her. Ernesto saw great things in their future together.

And what of his own future? Retirement loomed not far off. The company would be in good hands, and for the last several weeks, Ernesto sensed that his future lay inextricably linked to his past. A past that waited in her suite at Club Marbella.

Oh, she had been so lovely, that chocolate-haired girl from the edge of the city. He saw her arrive at school on the bus each day, and their friendship grew from carrying her books to joining the drama and citizenship clubs together. They'd worked in the orchards during the summer for extra pay and watched the stars at night.

And then one day, Tristan arrived with Marlena's aunt in tow. It wasn't surprising that he swept her off her feet. Blond, handsome and fearless, Tristan set the whole community on its ear in admiration of him, Ernesto included. He was just that sort of man, the conquering hero who flew into town with his imaginary cape flapping behind him.

When Ernesto left to study engineering at the University in Madrid, Tristan had already been forming Flynn Enterprises and insisted that Ernesto return and work for him upon graduation. The rest, as is often said, is history. He'd never worked for another firm. It was no wonder Ernesto cared for and shepherded the company so stalwartly.

And he'd accepted that Marlena chose to marry Tristan. Life went on, and on. And now, thirty years later, Ernesto found himself driving on a rain-soaked motorway, on his way to her. What was that turn of phrase she liked to use? Oh, yes. Fate is a wily companion.

He parked his car and entered through the grand doors of Club Marbella. His eyes scanned the opulent lobby, with its massive ceiling fans and lush upholstery gracing the huge expanse of marble tile and glittering lights. Marlena stood near the indoor fountain, surrounded by exotic plants, looking like a graceful water bird perched on its stony edge. She caught sight of him, and walked toward him. Ernesto had never seen her look so needful. And perhaps because of this, to him, she never looked more beautiful.

He scooped her into his arms in a protective hug, wishing it were more, yet needing to uphold the position of friendship they'd built over so many years. "Marly," he said, "It's going to be all right, I'm here now."

"I know," she said, returning his squeeze. "I've tried calling her, but she must still be in flight. I've left voice messages. I don't know what's going on."

"Does she have someone to meet her when she lands?" Ernesto asked.

Marlena's head moved side to side. "I imagine she'll take a taxi, but if her condo's been really damaged, or sealed by police, she might not be able to stay there. I'm not sure where she'll go. Barrie is too far from Montreal."

"Well, I'm sure she'll call when she gets there," Ernesto assured her. "Where is Jorge? He might know something."

Marlena nodded. "The Mercedes is gone. He must be out doing errands." She wiped the corner of her eye with one finger, drawing back from Ernesto's embrace. "But where is David? Have you heard from him?"

Ernesto shook his head. "Not yet. It doesn't sound like

he went with her. They weren't due back from Tenerife until Sunday. He might still be there." He had no other words of comfort, but had to do something. "Come, let's get something to eat, a coffee at least," he said, guiding her towards the hotel bar.

She sighed then nodded. She reached for Ernesto's hand as they started across the marble floor together, when she glanced over at the entrance, stopping short. A damp Jorge came walking in, brushing the rain off his jacket. He spotted Marlena, and moved to join them.

"Jorge," Marlena exclaimed, the relief in her voice evident. "Que pasa, como esta Zara y David?"

Jorge took out a handkerchief and wiped the moisture from his face. "She boarded the flight to Montreal safely," he assured them. "She promised to call you. Did you receive her message?"

Marlena nodded. "Si, but she didn't explain much. Who broke into her house? Is someone meeting her in Montreal? What did she say to you? Did David go with her?"

Jorge pocketed his handkerchief. "She got a message from a lawyer with the insurance company. He told her that the apartment had been turned upside down and her car stolen. He advised her to return to Montreal as soon as possible."

Ernesto and Marlena looked at him, their expressions clearly wanting more. "David is not with her," he continued. "He called me. Something happened between them, she left suddenly after receiving the news from the lawyer. He lost sight of her. She had already called me, asking to let you know." He managed an apologetic grin. "I told him where to find her at the airport."

Marlena looked between the two men. "So he might be with her, we don't know," she said. She shook her head and cursed in Spanish. Ernesto raised an eyebrow at her uncharacteristic burst of expletives. Jorge shrugged.

"There's nothing to do but wait. We might as well eat, then," Marlena said, resigned. "Or drink. I think I could use a drink," she decided, nodding. She looked between the two men, who stood before her both gaping in surprise. She waved her hand impatiently. "Vamos, mi muchachos."

 *

"Monsieur Vanier," the hostess said. "This way, please."

Stephane tossed the GQ magazine he'd been reading onto a cocktail table, and rose from his chair to follow the hostess into the treatment area. A massage bed lay waiting for him behind a partition.

Damn, air travel has come a long way, he thought, slipping off his shoes. The airport at Dorval now boasted a drop-in massage studio for the convenience of travellers with long stopovers. The hostess held out her hands for his jacket and tie. This studio didn't offer the kind of full massage he might have preferred, but since he had to wait anyway, he might as well be pampered to the extent a public facility would allow.

He lay face down on the bed while the masseuse worked her magic on his back.

So far, so good. Zara was on her way to Montreal, the flight due within the hour. He would be waiting for her in his polished, lawyer-ish demeanor, ZZegna suit and Nunn Bush footwear. He hoped he hadn't put on too much weight since she'd seen him last. The first impression had to be spot-on.

First, her condo. Alain had rendered it unlivable for the moment, necessitating her accommodations elsewhere. Stephane's house would be generously offered for her use during her stay. In a display of chivalry, he would insist that he himself stay elsewhere, knowing her current dislike for him. But this would change by week's end. Stephane rarely did not achieve what we wanted.

Next, her BMW would miraculously turn up, undamaged, thanks to Stephane's dogged investigation of the theft. Her gratefulness would know no bounds. Until then, he would graciously supply her with whatever transportation she desired.

Then, with a few phony claims papers signed, he would help her shop for new furnishings and hire contractors to redecorate her home in impeccable style. By that time, the holidays would be nearly upon them and his Collingwood cottage, a perfect festive retreat, would beckon for a Christmas getaway.

Somewhere in that mix, he would broach the topic of the Flynn Enterprises Montreal office. The financial reports were a mess. Staff turnover had left the place nearly deserted and project bids had come to a standstill. Or so it would seem. And to the rescue, Stephane Vanier would step in, posted by acclamation to the Board of Directors of Flynn Enterprises North America, and save the day.

He sighed with gratification, as if he'd just watched the whole plan play out on a movie screen. Or perhaps it was the expert manipulations of the masseuse who worked on his lower back, hitting precisely the exact vertebrae that drew satisfied moans from his lips. Perhaps the girl would be looking for a date later on. He turned his head to get a glimpse of her.

A large, East Indian woman bent over him, the muscles in her arms flexing and bulging as she worked. Nope, he thought, observing her heavy black eyebrows with a red dot painted between them. While he wasn't averse to a little brown sugar from time to time, this lady held no appeal for him at all. He turned his face back into the pillow, taking care not to muss his hair.

He pondered the severity of Zara's feelings toward him. Had she softened her attitude at all since her layoff? Bygones were bygones. And though he knew she blamed him for the corporate bloodletting, it wasn't completely his doing.

The firm had financial difficulties. The quickest way to cut the budget was to cut staff. Owners understood this, but employees rarely did. The Montreal operation would be no different, a rational, expedient course of action. He didn't handpick those who were to be let go. It was 'last in, first out' like any other business decision. Zara had simply been there the least amount of time. Well, he smirked, her and a hundred others.

But for one of the first times, his plan hadn't gone exactly his way. She disappeared so quickly she simply hadn't allowed him the opportunity to play the hero, offer her another job, a better job, with a law firm he was soon to partner with.

During the course of their relationship, she'd told him how strongly she felt about not working for her father at Flynn Enterprises. Now, however, it appeared she had accepted the big prize, taking over the European division of the company. Perhaps she'd have a bigger interest in the company now, as a whole, and allow him to proceed with his takeover of the North Am branch.

He checked his watch. The masseuse had finished with him, placing a hot towel over his back and leaving the room. 30 minutes to touchdown. He really did like Zara. She was pretty, and smart. He liked those qualities, although not always a requirement for the ladies in his entourage. But Zara offered something the others did not. Something he wanted, besides sex. He smiled outright, imagining he must look like the Grinch the day before Christmas.

She offered opportunity.

*

Ivette flopped down on a chaise lounge, looking out at the ocean. The terrace of her uncle's villa provided a comfortable refuge from the inner turmoil she felt. Things hadn't gone as well as planned. David had been undeniably displeased at her reappearance in his life.

She almost felt sorry for the little blondish wisp of a girlfriend he'd brought along. He'd have some fast talking to do if he hoped to salvage that relationship. But it made no difference to Ivette. If David had been responsive to her offer, she'd have gladly resumed their affair, even if it meant living a lie. Handsome and funny, she truly did like the man. He'd make a suitable husband, even if he wasn't a big-leaguer like Carlos.

But no matter. All she had to do was push him beyond his guilt threshold and make him pay. He might even feel lucky, to extricate himself from an unfavorable situation merely by parting with a few thousand euro.

There did remain a problem, though. She had no intention of becoming a mother. She found the very idea abhorrent; the ravaging of her perfect body, the existence of a completely needy little being that would consume her every action and thought for years to come. And how difficult to attract another suitor with an infant on the scene? No. This just wouldn't work for her.

The doctor said the procedure couldn't be done after twelve weeks, but Ivette had read otherwise. A therapeutic abortion couldn't be performed, but there were other methods, and other doctors. Both of which cost money. Ivette snorted in frustration, throwing a pebble over the railing of the terrace onto the beach below. Carlos, where are you? she fretted. If only he wasn't running from the law, life could have been so rosy for both of them. Damn him.

She'd have to give Dave one more try. Maybe after he'd had a chance to think about it, acknowledge the possibility he could be the father, he might feel differently. He had a conscience, unlike many men. If that failed, there remained the legal avenue; serve him with papers and a proposal for financial settlement.

She wondered how long she should wait. Her trip to

Holland for medical treatment should be booked as soon as possible, but she had to secure her financial position first. She gave herself two weeks, three at most, to complete everything. With any luck, she'd be serving her first customer in her beautiful new salon, worry-free, by New Years'. That's it, she thought; a New Years' party. A celebration of her new business and her new life would be the hit of the season. The thought made her smile, despite the unpleasantness ahead.

Chapter Twelve

Ernesto returned to the office. By the time he finished lunch with Marlena and driven back to Malaga, the wall clock in the reception area read five fifteen p.m. Pilar and the other staffers had already left. A good thing, anyway. He didn't really want to deal with any people at the moment.

He picked up a stack of mail from his inbox and proceeded to the hallway leading to his office. Treading silently down the carpeted corridor, he heard faint music behind him. He stopped and did an about face. The door to David's office stood open and soft guitar sounds emanated from it. He strode toward it, anxious to see Dave and hear his version of events.

Peering across the threshold, Ernesto spotted Dave reclining in his office chair, the acoustic guitar that normally sat in a stand in the corner resting in his lap. Dave held the instrument in such a way it made Ernesto imagine Zara in its place. Dave's hands caressed it lovingly, gently striking its strings and sliding his fingers along the fret board. His eyes were closed and he seemed to be picking out a tune from memory, losing himself in the melody and whatever personal meaning the song held for him.

Ernesto hung back, appreciating the pensive mood in

the room for a few moments. When the last note sounded, followed by silence, Ernesto cleared his throat to announce his presence. Dave's eyes snapped open and bolted upright in his chair.

"Jesus, Ernie, you could have knocked."

"And you could have called," Ernesto remarked, leaning against the door frame and crossing one foot over the other. He smiled a fatherly smile. "Que pasa, mi hijo?" he asked in a quiet voice. He realized he had actually come to regard Dave as a son, of sorts.

Dave took a deep breath and swung the guitar out of his lap and back onto its stand. "I love this place so much I couldn't stay away."

"I doubt that," Ernesto said. After experiencing Dave's sense of humour all these years, he understood the trait was also the young man's method of coping under stress. "But if that's all you want to say, I understand."

Dave tilted back in his chair again and studied the ceiling, not looking at Ernesto. "I have a lot to say," he began. "But the person that needs to hear it isn't here."

"And why is that?" pressed Ernesto.

"She had personal business in Montreal."

"That much I heard. Why aren't you with her?"

"She's angry with me." He rocked his chair back and forth a few times. "And come to think of it, I'm angry with myself."

Ernesto said nothing, letting Dave get out whatever he was going to get out. Dave turned to face him. "I've let something from my past jeopardize my future." A pointed look from Ernesto made him continue. "Do I have a future here, Ernie? I've put in my time. With a new CEO at the helm, and you still years away from retirement, maybe there's no place for me here anymore. Maybe I should move on."

That spurred Ernesto into action. He stepped into the room and drew up a chair across the desk from Dave. "I won't allow that kind of talk," he said, seating himself. "You and Zara are the future of this company. Tristan as much as said so. What the devil is going on in your head? I can't help you if you won't tell me."

Dave winced as if in almost physical pain. "I'm in love with her, Ernie. That's not a good business plan."

"To use your word, David…bullshit." Dave's eyebrows went up. "It's the perfect business plan," Ernesto continued. "There's no stronger foundation for an organization than family. No one could care more about this company than the two of you. And soon,"—he tapped his index finger on the desk—"there'll be a whole new generation of family to carry it on. I'm sure of it."

At Ernesto's last words, Dave looked as if he were about to choke. He put his hands to his forehead and dropped his face to his desk. "Oh, Ernie," he said. "I've screwed up."

"Why? What are you trying to say?"

"I may already be a father. A surprise visitor turned up in Tenerife; someone I knew…before. She says she's pregnant. She says it's mine."

Ernesto felt Dave's anguish from across the desk. He looked steadily at him, thinking what "fatherly" advice he might offer. No pun intended. "And Zara heard this?" he asked. Dave nodded. "Well." Ernesto said. "Number one, is it possible? Number two, can she prove it? Number three, do you still have feelings for this woman?"

"Yes, maybe and no."

"Go on."

"Yes, it's theoretically possible, but highly unlikely. I've no idea how she'd prove it. Or how I could disprove it, for that matter. And the only feelings I have for her at the moment all start with the letter R. Rage, remorse and repugnance. Not to mention regret."

Ernesto let out a low whistle. "That's a lot of emotions. And what did Zara say?"

"Nothing. She took off. I chased her all the way to the airport before I could get her to talk to me. I told her everything. I didn't want any secrets between us. For a minute, I thought she'd change her mind and stay, but her apartment's been broken into and her car stolen. She got a message from someone right before—" Dave broke off. "She's got a lot on her mind right now. And she's homesick. I had to let her go." He looked out the window.

Ernesto rubbed his chin, thinking. "You're right. She has to make her own decisions. It sounds like she just needs some space."

Dave snorted. "There's a hell of a lot of space between here and Montreal."

Ernesto nodded. "Si, but give her some time, a few days or so. Then I suggest you close that space."

"You think I should go after her?"

Ernesto smiled. "David, for as long as I've known you, you've always gone after what you wanted. Don't stop now."

*

Snow. Pellets of snow whipped past the aircraft windows at an angle, driven by a bitter wind. How long since she'd seen snow? She didn't even have proper clothes for this weather. Zara reached for her Fendi bag stowed under the seat in front of her, preparing to disembark. In a window seat in row thirty-four, she'd be a while yet. She sighed and folded the bag on her lap. Her phone buzzed inside it.

She fished it out and read the screen. Stephane's text message said:

Welcome home, I'm waiting for you at the gate.

Zara's stomach flipped a bit. Had there been some other way to conduct her business here, without having to lay eyes on the man, she'd have done it. But for expediency, she had to take Stephane at his word and accept the help he offered. It would be the quickest way to assess the damage and get the insurance wheels in motion.

She bit her lip, a sick stab of regret striking her insides at the thought of her condo in ruins. Perhaps the damage wouldn't be as bad as Stephane made it sound. Walls were repairable, furniture replaceable, but her car was still missing, and that bothered her even more. Stolen cars were rarely recovered intact. She feared the worst for her poor BMW.

At last, she stood and maneuvered her way into the aisle. She reached into the overhead bin for her carry-on and followed the line of fellow passengers moving ahead. She felt exhaustion about to overtake her. She'd never mastered the art of sleeping on airplanes. She loved flying in them, but could never sleep on them. Stephane said he would arrange her accommodations. Sadly, she could not stay in her own home. She hoped he'd booked a decent hotel. She'd kick his ass if he hadn't. Though fundamentally a cad, the man did have taste. She suspected the hotel would be the least of her worries.

She trudged up the ramp, the grating whine of tiny luggage wheels reverberating in her ears and the bland odor of recirculated air filling her nose. She kept her head down as she entered the arrivals area, her eyes drawn to the fleur-de-lis pattern on the carpet. She felt bone-tired. Suddenly, her luggage was lifted from her grip. Startled into alertness, she followed the vision of the immaculately manicured hand that had caught hold of the handle, then upward past the suit-jacketed arm and the broad shoulders that stooped over her bag.

Stephane's blond head tipped up, bringing his face into full view just inches away from hers. He looked every bit the lawyer she remembered. If anything, an added year or so only increased his attractiveness. He looked...distinguished.

Though her loathing remained undiminished, staring

point-blank into his chiselled features made her recall all too clearly how she'd fallen for the dirtbag in the first place. The alluring aroma of Hugo Boss exuded from him.

"Bonjour, Dolphin," he said in that rumbling baritone she'd stored away in the archives of her memory banks. A bedroom voice. Guaranteed to melt female knees at twenty paces. "Let me get that for you." Stephane straightened to his full height. "You look wonderful," he said. "The Mediterranean lifestyle must agree with you. Bad news, though. It's snowing outside."

Zara looked at him blankly. "Yeah, I noticed."

Stephane smiled. "I've bought you something." He offered out a large Holt-Renfrew shopping bag. Zara looked at him with suspicion, but gingerly lifted the handles of the bag from his outstretched fingers. Rather heavy, she sat it on the floor and withdrew its contents.

She couldn't help but draw in a sudden breath as she handled it, a cape with black fur trim at the collar and hem, the fabric a deep, purple shearling brocade. Its beautiful texture rippled in the fluorescent lighting overhead. It must have cost thousands, Zara thought. As much as she wanted to put it on, it smacked of bribery. "I can't accept this."

"Oh, now, be practical, Dolphin. It's cold out, and I can tell by your luggage you've no winter clothes with you. Put it on. It'll be more beautiful with you wearing it."

Zara's tongue went thick inside her mouth, his flattering words having the same effect as eating a spoonful of honey. He tilted his head and took the elegant garment from her. With a chivalrous swoop, he landed it about her shoulders and snuggled the warm fur collar under her chin.

"There. A Snow Queen," he pronounced.

"I'd like to see my condo, please," Zara said, declining to express thanks.

"Of course. Let's go." Stephane began moving them through the busy terminal. As they stepped outdoors, the bitter wind struck Zara full force. She'd nearly forgotten about winter in her busy few months in Spain, but it made its presence known all too vividly now. She felt grateful for the luxurious cloak around her, though not quite enough to say so.

Stephane's Jaguar sat parked in a VIP zone nearby. Its sleek silver exterior shining even in the snowy gloom. Once upon a time, this car, as well as Stephane's many other toys and luxuries, had impressed her. Now they just came off as pretentious. As he opened the door for her, some long-forgotten words sing-songed in her head.

"Come into my parlor, said the spider to the fly."

Zara hesitated at the curb, staring into the gray interior that threatened to swallow her.

"Something wrong?" Stephane asked.

I'm being silly. It's a car, nothing more. Wheels and an engine. That's it. She shook her head and slid into the leather bound luxury of the passenger seat.

Stephane strode to the drivers side and got behind the wheel. "Buckle up, baby." She'd barely clicked the thing in place before the Jag seemed to throw a couple of G's as he peeled away from the curb.

Chapter Thirteen

The tree-lined street seemed magical, yet foreign in its powder-coating of snow. It didn't look like the neighborhood she remembered, but soon Zara's stately brick four-plex came into view and tripped an unexpected flutter of joy in her heart. She'd come home.

Stephane pulled up at the building's entrance. An arched portico framed the twin front doors, their enamelled red finish gleaming in the wintry light. The caretakers had placed a holly wreath on each one. Everything looked normal from the outside.

Her suite occupied the upper west side of the building. Zara could see her bedroom bay window from the front. She and Stephane walked the stone steps of the veranda to stand before the red doors.

"You have your key," he said, not as a question, but as a statement.

Zara reached into her bag and produced a keychain without comment. The unlocked red doors led into a broad vestibule, decorated in greens and burgundies. An antique mailbox with four compartments stood off to one side, opposite an upholstered slipper chair and round side table. An elegant oval rug covered the floor and a cheery holiday arrangement of cedars and berries topped the little table's polished surface.

"Nice," Stephane commented.

Zara ignored the mailbox and pushed her key into the deadbolt of the inner door. With a twist, the bolt released, and Stephane's hand was upon the handle before Zara could even remove the key. She allowed him to open it for her.

"You won't be happy with what you're about to see," he said, moving close as to put an arm around her. Zara moved forward, away from his reach, and started up the stairs. The sound of her steps on the burnished hardwood treads brought back the memories of a life she'd lived seemingly aeons ago. She dreaded what might await her at the second floor landing.

Turning left at the top of the staircase, her door stood chipped and gouged around the doorknob, where someone had forced their way in. A realtor's lockbox held a temporary latch in place. Stephane had the key for it and removed the heavy padlock. He pushed the door wide for her to enter.

Crossing the threshold, Zara couldn't stifle a gasp as she beheld the dishevelled mess that had been her home. She saw her desk overturned with one leg sheared off, couch cushions ripped and thrown about the room. Not a single piece of electronics remained, the most conspicuous being the flatscreen that no longer occupied the space above the fireplace.

Kitchen drawers lay piled haphazardly atop one another on the floor, their contents strewn across the tiled surface.

Shattered dishes littered the sink, cabinet doors hung open at various angles. She covered her mouth with her hand, feeling her stomach writhe in anguish at the sight. She moved to the bedroom, picking her way across the devastated living space. Her Tiffany floor lamp lay horizontal in her path, its stained-glass shade broken beyond repair. With regret, she stepped over it.

Her bed. Why someone would desecrate her bed in such a way was unfathomable. The mattress lay shoved off the bed frame, and propped against the window. Pillows were thrown to corners of the room and broken items from her nightstand tossed onto the box spring. And covering it all, a mass of feathers from her down comforter that lay torn to shreds at her feet.

Zara began to sob aloud. She felt her life coming apart in two places, first in Tenerife, and now here in Montreal. What had she done to deserve this? Her shoulders slumped beneath the luxurious purple cape, all resistance seeming to have drained from her body. This was too much to bear. She closed her eyes and wished for it all to be a bad dream, and to wake up with Dave's arms around her.

"You're exhausted," Stephane's deep but soft voice said. He stood close behind her, his tall, solid form lending a physical presence that swept over her like a warm breeze. In her despair, she suddenly felt like melting into it, to admit defeat and simply lean on this rock-wall of a man that she despised.

His hands came to rest on her arms, exerting a gentle pressure that Zara felt too despondent to resist. "I think you've seen enough, Dolphin. I'm so sorry. Let me take you out of here and buy you dinner. You must be starving." He tightened his grip and motioned her to turn around. She had no fight left in her. She moved like a zombie, letting him guide her back through the chaos and out the door.

"I'm not hungry," she grumbled.

"I thought you might say something like that. Trust me, you need food."

"I need rest, not food."

"Fine, we'll get you some rest, and then some food. Either way you're going to eat. Just let me take care of you." Keeping his hold on her, they walked to the staircase and began to descend.

Zara had no intention of allowing this callous beast to take care of her. "I can take care of myself," she said, her shoes plonking on each of the treads.

"Sure you can. But for once, let someone else do it. Just this time, okay? I'd never forgive myself if I left you alone in such a state."

Zara snorted a laugh. That did it. She really was tired now, a state of delirious giggling about to set in. Never forgive himself? What a joke. The man had not a shred of conscience in his soul. Why not take advantage of him? It would serve him right. She could ride in his Jag and make him buy clothes and dinners for her, what the hell? He'd get nothing in return.

As she landed on the second-last step, her stomach wobbled again and stars formed in her field of vision. A tingling began somewhere deep in her chest and crept upward, both hot and cold sensations filling her. I'm going to faint, she realized. No, not here. Not with him around! She grabbed the banister and tucked her head down to stop it from happening,

Stephane's arms went around her waist, too tight for Zara's liking, but she hadn't much choice in the matter. Oh, God. Her body spoke to her. Stop. Rest. Get strong. Someone needs you.

"Hey, there," Stephane said, holding her close against him. "You're not well, are you? I should have seen that." He shook his head in admonition. "I'm taking you straight home."

Zara's vision cleared, and straightened her posture. What the hell did he mean? "This is home," she said weakly. "What are you talking about? Didn't you book me a hotel?"

"Are you okay to go on?" he asked. She nodded, and he began to move them both toward the exit. "No, I thought you deserved better. You'll see when we get there."

Once inside the Jag, Stephane pulled out a bottle of San

Pellegrino from behind the passenger seat and handed it to Zara. She knew she must look pale. She felt pale. Worse than pale, she felt like a ghost. She took the bottle from him and twisted it open, taking a swig of the refreshing liquid.

They drove north and, after a few turns onto treed boulevards and through swank communities, Stephane slowed in front of a stunning, Arthur Erickson-style creation that stood at the crest of a hill. Zara eyes panned its frontage, taking in the sleek, modern lines of stone and glass that formed a very impressive façade.

"Where are we?" Zara asked.

Stephane smiled. "You need a home, don't you? Temporarily anyway, so I thought I'd give you mine." Zara swiveled her head and fixed him with a look of utter disbelief. Was the man crazy? "Relax," he said in response to her withering stare. "I'm staying at the suites in my office building for now. The place is all yours." He parked the Jag and turned off the engine. "Look, I know you how feel about me, but I do care about you, Dolphin. I'm just trying to make you as comfortable as possible while we sort this mess out." He turned to look at her with his warm, hazel-eyed gaze. "Friends?"

Zara looked away, the sheer perfection of the mid-century residence drawing her full attention, mesmerizing her. She didn't remember Stephane owning this property. A week or so in his company seemed not a bad trade-off in exchange for losing herself inside this architectural thing of beauty.

"I wouldn't friend you on Facebook, Stephane. But in this case, I'll call a truce."

"Well, that's a start. The kitchen's all stocked up. Let's go in." He pulled the keys from the ignition and got out. As he moved to the passenger side, Zara opened her own door. She refused to act helpless in his presence. Before she could step out, he pulled the door all the way open and reached for her hand. With his big body blocking the way, her only way out was to take it. Resigned, she let him help her out of the Jag.

The home's interior was no less impressive than the outside. The open floor plan boasted gleaming walnut hardwood stretching from wall to wall. Fading daylight streamed from the multiple skylights spread across the room's steep-pitched roof line. Two cream-leather sofas flanked the room's main feature: a breathtaking, fieldstone fireplace.

Stephane aimed a remote at the hearth and, flames roared to life with the touch of a button. Zara stepped closer to it, the warmth drawing her in, begging her to sit before it. A plush area rug beckoned to her. She sank down on its soft surface in front of the fire and drew the cape around herself. She felt ready to sleep in the flames' radiant embrace. Her eyelids began to close.

The tinkle of plates and silverware jolted them open again. Stephane stood behind the counter of a galley kitchen on the far side of the room, pulling out dishes and utensils and reaching in and out of the stainless steel refrigerator. He'd removed his suit jacket, and Zara could see his broad chest and shoulders advertising themselves beneath the stylish silk dress shirt.

A burning sensation flowed to her cheeks. She blamed it on the fire, but knew better. The scene felt familiar, Stephane fussing in the kitchen while she watched. The Collingwood cottage. Oh yes, she'd tasted many of his dishes there, not all of them food. The man did love his food. Had he put on a little weight? Yes, she thought so.

Zara closed her eyes again. Nothing. Nothing would compare to a bowl of clam chowder right now. The memory of that first meal she and Dave had shared in his apartment seemed to fill her brain, blocking out everything else. The rich texture of it, how delicious it smelled, her recollection so vivid she swore she could taste it on her tongue. David. He'd done so much more than quelled her appetite. He fed her soul.

Her stomach growled and she felt desperately hungry, but not for food. She reached for the cellphone in her bag. Withdrawing it, she prayed for Dave's name to appear on its screen. Whether he'd fathered a child with another woman or not, didn't change the truth. She loved him.

Three missed calls. Mom. Mom. Mom. No surprise there. Tears began to sting her eyes. No word from him since she'd left Tenerife.

"Hey, don't fall asleep, I've got something special for you."

Zara put the phone away and looked up to see Stephane carrying a tray toward her. He set it down on a leather ottoman that served as a coffee table. Hesitating for a moment, he decided to fold his imposing frame and sit cross-legged on the floor next to her.

"Okay, picnic it is," he said, lifting a plate from the tray and offering it to her. She let the fur-trimmed cape slip from her shoulders as she took it from him. Under the circumstances she should have devoured every morsel. Red globe grapes, wedges of brie and cheddar, bruschetta piled high with olives and chunks of red onion. Thick slices of tomato layered with little orbs of bocconcini and drizzled in a balsamic glaze. A neat square of paté rounded out the display, nestled on a bed of arugula.

Zara stared at the artistic presentation in her lap. For the first time since she'd landed, she felt gratitude toward Stephane. "Merci." The word issued from her lips barely above a whisper. Somehow she couldn't find the will to eat anything.

He reached over and lifted a cheese wedge off the plate, and held it up to her mouth. "Come on, Dolphin, you need your strength."

Reluctantly, she opened her mouth and accepted his

offering. The smooth texture of the brie mixed with the tart rind made a delicious pairing on her tongue. She chewed slowly, savoring it, and realized just how long it had been since she'd eaten. No wonder she'd nearly fainted in the stairwell.

But when she swallowed, her stomach had different ideas. It seemed to reject the rich little tidbit, and gave a sickening twist. Her face must have registered her discomfort, for Stephane quickly handed her a water goblet. She took a few swallows and set it back on the tray.

"I think I'm going to have to do this slowly," Zara said.

Stephane smiled a catlike grin and nodded. "Oui. Both of us."

Chapter Fourteen

This time the dolphin actually laughed. It spread its beakish jaws and cackled shrilly while bobbing its head up and down. Dave wanted to catch it, wrap his hands around its slippery throat and squeeze the life from it. Enough. Time to put an end to its relentless taunting. But it kept eluding him, each lunge he made for it causing it to move that much further out of reach.

It breached and dove, its tail smacking the surface of the water like a slap to his face. He dove along with it, determined to silence the obnoxious beast once and for all. Dave opened his eyes underwater, searching for it, but no luck. The trail of bubbles led him downward, down and down until his lungs felt like bursting.

Then he saw her.

Zara's nude body floated below him, suspended in middepth, neither rising nor sinking. Her long hair trailed upward with the current, her arms dangling adrift. He descended further, managing to reach her and put his arms around her. As he struggled to the surface, he stared into her open eyes, their green color paling in the underwater gloom.

Rising foot by foot, their ascent seemed to take forever.

His lungs burned from lack of oxygen, felt himself starting to black out. He seemed unable to hold on to her, her body slipping from his grasp before he could reach the surface. Her limbs slid from his hands, the dark depths below sucking her downward just inches away from his goal. Dave's head broke the surface of the water and he inhaled precious air in massive gulps.

He awoke, gasping for breath as he opened his eyes and jerked his head off the flat surface it lay upon. Papers shifted position on the table and pencils rolled off its edge onto the floor. Jesus, he'd fallen asleep at his desk. Again.

And the dream had manifested itself, again.

Only now it took a darker, more ominous path. The feeling it left behind had somehow switched from helpless to hopeless. The damned dolphin. He wished he could crush it with his bare hands.

He rubbed his eyes as he straightened, the stiffness in his neck making him wince in pain. Cold sweat stuck the material of his shirt to his back. He blinked and glanced toward the windows, morning light streaming into the room. God, he couldn't keep going like this and still be sane by the time he got to Montreal. But the drawings wouldn't finish themselves. So he pushed on. They had to be ready for her when she came back. If she came back. No, he'd banished that kind of thinking from his mind. When he brought her back.

He'd been at it for nearly three days straight, the blueprints for La Dulce Zara. Based on sketches she'd found in her father's office, this villa would be the home that Zara wanted to build. On the site of El Mirador.

And Dave was determined to make it a reality.

He'd sent extra crews to clear the site, removing the fallen remains of the old building and shoring up the foundation. The tar sand field would be zoned off, and an interpretive center built around it, just like she'd wanted. The plans for that structure lay in Chico's workstation, having handed that part of the project over to the talented draftsman, who'd shown a creative flair for design that went quite beyond just running the CADD station and plotter.

The design for the villa Dave took on himself, wanting to see to every detail. He needed to show Zara that he'd invested his whole being into its design and construction, and more than that, invested his very heart and soul into their relationship, their future. Because he couldn't imagine it any other way.

He rose from his chair, tired muscles protesting after languishing behind his desk for God knew how many hours. His shirt wrinkled and sticky with sweat, and his jeans in need of a wash, he felt grimy beyond words and proceeded to peel the t-shirt off his body.

Two succinct knocks sounded outside his closed door, but the caller did not wait for a response. The girl entered the room at full speed, obviously expecting his office to be vacant since no one had seen him arrive.

Her name was Franca, an administrative assistant. She'd been pulling files on various topics for the project and held a stack of exactly that in one hand as she moved forward, looking at the papers and not where she was walking.

When she finally glanced up, she flinched at the sight of Dave's shirtless torso just a few feet ahead of her. A snowstorm of papers dropped to the carpet in her surprise.

"Oh, lo siento, Senor Parker," she stammered. "I didn't know you were here…ah…perdoneme…" She blushed furiously, but didn't seem able to look away. He watched her eyes move across his upper body and her face grow redder before she stooped to pick up the fallen documents. "Por favor," she mumbled. "I didn't see you come in…"

Dave tossed the shirt over one shoulder, seeing no point in covering up.

"It's okay, Frankie," he said. "Nobody saw me come in. I

just…never went home. Thanks for those files." He decided that more explanation wouldn't bring down the awkward meter a whole lot, so he just stood there, waiting, while she reconstructed her paper pile and placed it in his inbox.

She turned and hurried from the room, neglecting to close the door in her haste. She nearly bumped into Ernesto as he crossed the hallway toward the reception area. Her panicked movements made him look in the direction from which she'd come. Dave skulked about in his office at the end of the hall, zipping a jacket closed over his bare chest.

Ernesto made a beeline for him.

"What's going on in here?" Ernesto asked. "It's a good thing there aren't any clients in the office this morning."

Dave looked up, and ran his hand through his hair. "Oh. Sorry, Ern, ah…nothing." He stared blankly at Ernesto for a second. "I feel like shit," he announced. "I'm going to run home for a shower then I'll be back."

Ernesto worked his facial muscles for a moment then gave a single nod. "Si. You look like shit, too." He cocked his head to one side. "Franca seemed rather high-energy though. Care to explain?"

Dave blinked and snapped out of his momentary hypnosis. He shoved his hands in his jacket pockets and gave a bewildered shake of his head. "What? I've been here all night. She came busting into my office without warning. I can't help what she saw, or what she's thinking," he said. "Or what you're thinking," he added. A tense silence hung in the air. "You know me better than that."

Ernesto smiled. "Of course I do. Franca on the other hand, does not. And I'm sure she'd like to. Keep it zipped, Youngblood." Dave raised his eyebrows and shot him a warning glance. Ernesto sobered. "And look after yourself. You'll be no good to Zara, or any of us, if you work yourself to death."

Dave nodded and moved toward the door. "Message received. May I go now?"

Ernesto adjusted his stance and reached into his inside breast pocket. He withdrew a folded paper. "Sí, puede. All the way to Quebec," he said, flipping the flight itinerary toward him between his thumb and first knuckle.

Dave's shoulders relaxed as he exhaled. "Thanks, man," he said, taking the paper from him. "I'll be back. Got a few things to finish first."

*

He found the energy to take the stairs to his apartment two at a time. A quick shower and he'd be good as new. The thought of taking off for Montreal spurred him forward. The flight left tomorrow morning and a million things remained to do before then. He reached the third floor landing and pulled the key from his pocket. As he pushed it into the deadbolt, the door clicked open without the benefit of turning the key. Dave froze.

Had he been that out of it that he'd left his apartment unlocked since yesterday? He couldn't remember. He knew he needed sleep, but it wasn't like him to be that careless. Another possibility sprung to mind. An intruder had been, or still remained, inside. He pushed it open without a sound.

Nothing appeared out of place. No movement came from inside. Everything looked the same, smelled the same. He slipped further into the room. He checked the living area, the kitchen. Nothing unusual. Sadly, the dirty dishes hadn't washed themselves since he last looked. He walked noiselessly past the bathroom, to the bedroom, and did a double-take.

Curled comfortably asleep on his steel-frame bed, lay Ivette.

"Oh, for Christ's sake." The words escaped his lips in a tired groan, but loud enough to wake the sleeping beauty. Her head jerked away from where it had lain against her hands, folded prayer-like to one side. She turned her face toward him, and drew her arms slowly down to her sides. Her shapely body squirmed seductively on the bed's surface, her firm, tanned thighs visible through her high-slitted skirt.

He felt like someone had just rewound his life six months.

"What the fuck are you doing here? How—" Dave's voice broke off. He stared in stunned silence for a moment, his tired brain unable to react in any useful way. He ground his teeth at the sight of her, appearing completely comfortable in her languid pose upon his rumpled bed. What felt like a growl built in his throat. How dare she invade his private space. "How the hell did you get in here?"

In no hurry to get up, Ivette smoothed a lock of her thick, dark hair away from her face as she fixed her brown eyes on him. "Don't be angry, please. Don't you remember Samir? The caretaker?"

Dave shrugged, not caring who the hell Samir was. "No. Answer my question, dammit."

"Well," Ivette went on. "He remembered me. When I was more of a...regular visitor here." She cast him a coquettish smile. "He let me in."

So much for building security. He vaguely remembered the dark-complexioned caretaker. He would kick his Moroccan ass for this.

"Well, you can let yourself right back out, lady. You're not welcome here."

She twisted her body into a semi-upright position, leaning on one elbow. He watched her full breasts shift beneath her scoop-necked blouse as she did so, the pose accentuating her pronounced cleavage. No. He did not want to notice that. He wished she would disappear altogether. In fact, he should call the cops. She was trespassing after all. These thoughts lit up in his mind like elevator buttons, but he acted on none of them.

Her mouth seemed to tremble, her brown eyes glistened beneath what Dave thought must surely be crocodile tears.

"I never thought you to be this cruel, David," she said, her voice bordering on a whimper. "The mother of your child, unwelcome? You're not so heartless as that. I know you're not."

Her pleading voice made his head start to hurt. He pinched the bridge of his nose with a thumb and forefinger. Lack of sleep wasn't helping the situation.

"Stop saying that, I'm warning you." His words crawled out from between gritted teeth. "Save yourself a whole lot of trouble because I'll fight you on this. You've got no proof."

"Proof?" She began crying for real. "Do you think proof will change anything? Would it make you love me again?" She hid her face in her hands. "No. I can see that you hate me." Her sobs grew painful to hear. He wished she would stop. Resisting a crying female was difficult under the best of circumstances. Damn, he felt tired. He had no time for this.

"I don't hate you." The words came out on reflex without meaning attached to them. "But please stop this. You and I are not happening, ever. So stop with the lies, stop with the stalking," he said, his voice rising in angry desperation. "And tell me the goddamned truth! Why are you doing this?"

Startled, she dropped her hands and looked at him with fear in her eyes. "I'm pregnant. It's not a lie." Tears streaked shiny tracks down her cheeks. "I'm in trouble." She wiped at her face with the back of one hand. "You were so kind, before. I thought…you wouldn't abandon me. I thought you might be pleased." She snorted a lonely little laugh. "But I'm a fool. I can't afford to raise a child on my own. That's why I'm doing this."

Dave closed his eyes. I can't deal with this. Not now. "So it's money you're after?"

Ivette continued to dry her tears, sniffing. "If it has to come to that, if you want no part of me, or this child."

Dave exhaled, feeling like he might deflate with fatigue. He needed sleep. He needed to get back to the office. He didn't need this extra problem, but didn't see a quick way out if she wouldn't admit he wasn't the father. He hadn't time to argue. "Look. I have to be somewhere in a few hours. Please leave and we'll deal with this when I get back."

She gazed up at him, faint hope glimmering. "You'll help me?"

Dave shook his head, non-committal. "I'm not promising anything, Ivette. But I don't want to see you...suffer. I'm not that much of a bastard."

"I know. I've always known." She sat up and pushed herself off the bed. "You look so weary," she said, her voice softer than ever. She moved in close to him. "You should come to bed. Lie down, I'll see myself out." She reached out and touched his chest, her hands smoothing the material of his jacket. When he didn't move, she took hold of his arms and pulled him in the direction of the bed. A slight nudge, and he collapsed onto it.

It felt good to lie down. *Ernie told me to get some rest. Couldn't think straight. He should get her out, lock the door behind her. Shit. His eyes felt so heavy, just keeping them open seemed too much of an effort.*

He heard his front door slam shut, and he fell asleep without another thought.

Chapter Fifteen

"Yes, everything's under control, Mom," Zara said. "I'm staying with a friend until I get the insurance settled." She took a sip of her coffee as she held the phone to her ear. "I can have the furniture replaced, get some contractors working on the repairs, then I'll come back for awhile." Through the window of the little bistro Zara saw her friend approach the doors and waved to her.

"Sólo por un tiempo?" Marlena asked. "Then what? What shall I tell David? He's worried sick about you."

Zara frowned. "He's got enough to worry about." She watched the dark-haired girl enter the shop, and decided on one last thing to say. "When I come back, I want to sign over the El Mirador property to Jorge. Can you have Ernesto draw up the papers?"

Marlena's silence made Zara wince inwardly. "I'll speak to him about it, sweetheart. But I'm sure he'll want to wait until you return before doing anything."

"Okay, whatever you think. I've got to go, I'll call you again tonight, okay? Bye." She hung up, and the dark-haired girl squealed in delight as she trotted toward Zara, her arms wide for a hug. "Pammy!"

"Zara, Zara, Zaarah!" Parminder Singh threw her arms around her friend, her smile one of unconcealed joy.

Zara returned the hug. "Pam, it's so great to see you!" Both women giggled hysterically, then stepped back to get a good look at each other. "You look great, Pammy. Thanks for coming."

"Are you freaking kidding me, Z? We thought you'd fallen off the earth when you left…of course I came to see you! How is Spain? You've got a tan, you witch! Lots of time to lay on the beach, huh?" Pam's lips formed an 'o' and her chestnut eyes went wide. "Or, maybe a little lay on the beach, hey… hey?" She gave a backhand tap to Zara's sleeve and laughed at her own naughty joke.

Zara blushed a little, thinking how close to the truth her friend's words had landed. "Hey, I worked hard the last two months, wasn't all fun and games, you know," she replied in mock indignation.

Pam laughed, sweeping her sleek black bangs away from her face with one hand. Her teeth shone bright white in contrast to her cocoa-colored skin. "Okay, okay. So what's it like being the CEO of the company? I kept imagining you with your feet up on a big desk, smoking a cigar, or something. Is it fabulous?" She seated herself on a tall stool opposite Zara and began to peel off the scarf and plaid woollen coat she wore.

Zara snorted at Pam's vision of her. "It's hard work, is what! You can't imagine the number of decisions that need to be made in a day. The people are really great, though."

Pam ordered a latte. "That's awesome. I'm so happy for you, you must miss your dad though," she said. "How come you didn't work for the company here? Spain seems like a long way to go."

"Well," Zara shrugged. "He left me some property there, and I guess he thought I needed a break from cold winters."

She sighed and took another sip of coffee. "I'm not so sure I belong there."

Pam stirred her drink and regarded Zara with a friends' knowing gaze. "Z. Something's bothering you, c'mon. Out with it. You jet off to Spain, take over the family business, inherit property, now you're back looking glum as a lost dog. What's up?"

Zara swallowed the last of her coffee. In that moment, she realized she probably shouldn't even be drinking coffee, if what she suspected were true. She needed to confide in somebody, and she trusted Parminder, her old roommate from university. Though they'd chosen very different career paths, Pam a nurse, and Zara an architect, they'd remained best friends.

"I got a call." She looked Pam in the eyes. "My condo's been trashed."

Pam's dark eyes went wide with concern.

"And my car stolen." Zara went on.

"No…not the Beamer…" Pam gasped.

Zara nodded. "My place is ruined, but insurance will take care of that. My car, not so sure. It's still missing."

"Oh, Z, I'm so sorry. What are you going to do? Where are you staying? Why didn't you call me earlier and come stay with me?"

Zara smiled and reached out to touch Pam's arm, glad she had such a friend. "Thanks, Pammy. But it's all arranged. All I have to do is sign a few papers, and go shopping for new stuff. How bad can that be, huh?"

Pam returned her smile, but didn't stop there. "You didn't answer my question."

Zara waved it off. "It doesn't matter. I…have something else I need to ask you." Pam tilted her brown-skinned face toward her in curiosity. Zara took a deep breath. "Do you have the number for that doctor you used to work for, Dr. Klein?"

Pam looked at her steadily. "The obstetrician?" Zara nodded. "I think so. What are you saying, Z?"

"You know what I'm saying. I need to make sure."

Pam scrambled for her cell phone in her purse. "I'll text it to you. Oh, Z, what's going on? Please tell me."

Zara looked away, out the front windows of the shop, and felt the familiar sting of tears start to build. "I can't tell you the whole story, yet. But I will, as soon as I know."

The silver Jaguar pulled up at the curb outside the bistro. "I've got to go, but promise you won't breathe a word to anybody. Please?"

Pam's eyes followed Zara's glance. She felt sure Pam recognized the vehicle. "Oh, Z, you have to be joking. Not that shit-head lawyer."

"Good God, no. It's not what it looks like, Pam, I…" Zara's words trailed off. She motioned to her with her thumb and pinky extended as she moved toward the exit. "I'll call you."

Stephane bounded to the curb to open the Jaguar's door for her, his blond hair shining in the morning sunlight. The temperature had dropped overnight, and a pebbled shell of ice covered the sidewalk. He clutched Zara's elbow as he guided her into the passenger seat. As she watched him return to his place behind the wheel, she noticed he'd exchanged his standard two-piece suit for a plain black turtleneck and wool blazer. His wardrobe choice made his shoulders appear even broader than usual, and a pair of Diesel jeans fitted snugly over his powerful thighs. A big man, any way she looked at him.

He swung into the driver's seat and a waft of Hugo Boss mingled with the crisp outdoor air as he closed the door. "Did you sleep well?" he asked. "I have the insurance documents at my office. After we take care of those, how does shopping grab you?" He smiled in something approaching delight, looking like a kid skipping school to head for the mall.

"For furniture," Zara said stiffly. She found his enthusiasm unsettling. This wasn't a damn field trip. She just wanted to get her place fixed up and be done with it.

"And? C'mon, Dolphin, you have no warm clothes to wear. Let me treat you to a few other things."

"I have things, at the condo, if you'll let me get them. You can drop the sugar daddy act, anytime."

His expression bordered on hurt. "That's uncalled for. I'm just trying to be nice. Have it your way." He started the ignition, but remained in park. "Speaking of Daddy," he continued. "There's something else I need to discuss with you."

Zara eyed him warily. "And what might that be?"

"Your office here. Flynn Enterprises, I mean. I'm afraid it's not doing very well."

Her comfort level dropped several notches. What the hell would he know about Flynn Enterprises? "What do you mean?"

"There's been a big staff turnover. The RFPs have dropped off severely. There's no work for those who are left. It needs a change in management, the board structure. It may be in danger of shutting down."

Zara stared at him, incredulous. How did he know things about the company that she didn't? "How do you know this, Stephane? It's news to me, and I'm the CEO. Explain."

Stephane leaned back, the charcoal-grey leather of the headrest giving a characteristic squeak while releasing its musky scent. The air inside the vehicle seemed filled with masculine intent. He turned his face toward her, and pushed up his mirror-lensed Vuarnet shades with one finger.

"I'm a businessman, sweetie. I read the stock reports. It's not exactly insider knowledge. Besides, it concerns you. I follow everything that concerns you. Is that so much of a shock?"

"Am I supposed to be flattered? I'm way past that, Stephane. I don't succumb to your attentions anymore. You're snooping. Why?"

Stephane shook his head in exasperation. "Snooping," he scoffed. "Public knowledge is not snooping. But if you think I have a personal interest in the affairs of your company, you're right. As for why, I should think that would be obvious. We were a couple once, Zara. I want to see you do well. Why do you think I'm handling these insurance issues? I could have had any number of agents contact you, but I didn't. I chose to look after you personally. Doesn't that tell you something? I believe in you, despite your feelings for me. Or lack thereof." He leaned in a little closer. "I'd like to change that, if you'll let me."

Zara worked her tongue inside her mouth, not believing him for a second. She'd been taken in by his flattery before. As for the company, she needed to see this for herself. "Far too late for that, Stephane. Go cast your spell on someone else. When we're done with the insurance stuff, take me to the Flynn office. You can start by proving you're not the liar I remember."

*

"He's not answering his phone," Ernesto said, disconnecting the call and stuffing his smartphone into his chest pocket. "But, I suspect he's taken my advice and is trying to get some rest."

"When does his flight leave?" Marlena asked.

"Seven a.m. tomorrow. Does she know he's coming?"

Marlena shook her head. "I almost told her, but I know my daughter. She wants to do everything herself. She said she wants to sign over El Mirador to Jorge."

Ernesto sighed and looked out over the water. Sunset cast luminous threads of gold and rose across its choppy surface. "She is…muy independiente. Como su madre."

Marlena gave him a sharp glare then laughed. "No, Ernesto. I've never been independent. Not like Zara." She began to pick up the remains of their dinner. They sat on a park bench along the waterfront, take-out containers and napkins spread between them. "But you know, I guess I never had to be. I had my family, then I had Tristan."

Ernesto stood and tossed the rubbish into a nearby bin. Marlena drew her pashmina tighter about her shoulders against the December breeze. He turned to face her and held out his hand.

"And you had me," he said, his voice tinged with regret. "You didn't seem to notice."

She met his gaze with honest eyes. A look so free of guile or deceit it made his heart ache. A truer, more genuine person he could not imagine in all the world. She would speak the truth, and he hoped it would be what he desperately wanted to hear.

She slipped her hand silently into his. "I noticed. Soy afortunada. I am lucky."

They remained that way for several seconds, he standing and she seated on the bench. All the years putting aside his feelings, forcing them out of his memory just to function and get on with his life, seemed to boil up in his chest and drive his next action like a locomotive. He pulled her, almost harshly, off the bench and into his arms. Her slim body landed against his chest and he held her there, firm and in control. He would not miss his chance again.

His hand slipped under her chin, fitting it into the V between his thumb and fingers and tilting her face toward him. "Marly," he said, his voice low and needful. "Don't let luck slip away. Be with me now." Her brown eyes widened. He felt he could see straight in to her soul, and yes, a flicker of desire dwelt deep within.

He kissed her, his decades of longing converging in that

moment. A moment of passion, of hope, and of promise. Her lips melted soft and moist against his without hesitation or resistance. Thank the moon and stars, he thought. She was kissing him back.

Chapter Sixteen

Yes. That felt good. His dick hardened with each gentle stroke of her hand, arousing him. His mind floated toward consciousness, stringing bits of reality together like a jigsaw puzzle forming a finished scene. *It's all been a bad dream. Zara lay here with him, urging him to wakefulness and carnal pleasures, just as it should be.* Her warm lips nuzzled the back of his neck and graced it with tiny kisses.

Dave inhaled in slow satisfaction, a smile playing at the corners of his mouth. The jigsaw puzzle began to fracture and fall away piece by piece. His eyes snapped open in alarm. *Not real. I'm alone in my apartment, Zara is thousands of miles away…Oh, God.*

He didn't know how long he'd been asleep. The bedroom lay dark, but the warm presence snuggled against his back assured him he was definitely not alone.

And someone's hand was on his cock.

He jerked away, nearly falling off the edge of his bed. What the hell time was it? Christ, he had a plane to catch! He pushed himself apart from the body lying next to him and rolled away, dropping to his knees on the floor. He scrambled for the lamp on the night table. He switched it on, the sudden brightness making him blink and squint in the direction of the bed. Holy Christ, I thought she'd left.

Ivette's long, smooth body lay on her side, her dark eyes moist and beckoning. She wore next to nothing, a lacy pushup bra and matching thong in a color he couldn't begin to describe. She was a damn sexy sight, and his dick agreed. If this were another time, another place, he knew his next move would have been something less than gentlemanly.

"I told you to get out. What the hell do you think you're doing?" he asked, his voice loud but still rough with sleep. He glanced down to discover his fly wide open, with his cock exposed and inconveniently alert.

She didn't move, save for the tantalizing rise and fall of her breasts as she breathed. "I tried. I meant to leave," she whispered. "But I couldn't. I wanted…our baby to be with his father, even for this little while."

This had gone too far. He felt like strangling her and fucking her at the same time. Enough. He had to get out of here. He spotted his cell phone on the nightstand and grabbed for it. She'd turned it off, damn her. When the screen came to life, it read 5:10 a.m. Message notifications began buzzing in steady succession.

"Shit!" he yelled aloud. "Get dressed. I don't care what you thought, or what you wanted. Just get out!"

He made the bathroom in two lunging steps and slammed the door. He'd barely make it to the airport now, never mind finishing the drawings at the office. Taxis were unreliable at best, and there was no time to lose. He punched one of the missed numbers on his cell, of the only person that could help him now.

*

Alain Labelle leaned against a lamppost on Rue Peel, sizing up the building before him. Its plain brick front sported no balconies or fire escapes, its security system nothing special; easily bypassed. The inside he'd already studied during his meeting with Vanier. Business hours ended at four p.m. and as he peered through the dusk, no night patrols seemed to be engaged. Morceau de gateau, he mused. A piece of cake.

His cell phone vibrated in the pocket of his baggy overcoat. He reached for the device while still staring at the building frontage. When he diverted his gaze to its screen, he considered it for a moment before punching the button.

"Necesito su ayuda, mi amigo," came a rasping voice.

Alain clucked his tongue in response. Well, well. So the Spaniard needed help, did he. "¿Es la verdad? Por que?"

"Your Spanish es terriblé, ami."

Alain shrugged. "Si, and your French sucks. Anglais then, eh? What you want, spic?"

A dangerous silence followed. "Watch your big mouth, frog. Your English isn't much better. I need a place to disappear for a while."

"For how long? The safe house, she is…occupado."

The voice grew rougher. "A few weeks. Maybe a month. Get rid of whoever's in there."

"Oh, I no can do that, ami." Alain played coy on purpose. He hated the Spaniard for a deal gone wrong a few years back, resulting in the death of a friend by drug overdose. Alain avoided jail only by sheer luck that time, and for some unfathomable reason, the Spaniard kept in touch.

"You'd better start thinking you can, friend. If you know what's good for you. I'm in town, so empty it, quick."

Alain glanced again at the brick building. "Perhaps another place, eh? Give me some time."

"Make it fast, frog. I'll be waiting." The line dropped.

Alain slipped the phone back into his pocket. An unexpected turn of events. The bigshot wanted the little Frenchman's help. Now here was an opportunity too good to miss. He just might need a temporary partner. Glancing at the building once more, he nodded in agreement with himself. A partner in crime.

Alain loped away from his spot where Rue Peel and Boulevard Rene Levesque intersected. He had some business yet to attend to and, after a walking a few blocks, fished a key from his coat pocket.

The BMW sat where he'd parked it in an alley, the engine still warm. It had been a pleasure to retrieve it from the storage locker where it had hidden for the past week. He'd liked to have driven it around for awhile after stealing it from the Westmount neighborhood, but Vanier said no. He wanted it taken to the outskirts of the city tonight and dumped, so that's where it would go. But he never said exactly when. He got in and turned on the ignition. A nice night for a joyride.

*

Zara stood in the middle of her bedroom, making what order she could from the mass of clothes, bedding and furniture that lay strewn from wall to wall. At least she could salvage some of her wardrobe. Although Stephane had been correct about her needing warm clothes, she refused to take any more charity from him. The fur cape had been bad enough, and she'd only worn it because of the snow. She had no intention of ever touching it again.

Glad to be alone after a long, depressing day, she had time to think while picking out some sweaters, jeans and shoes. After filing the insurance claim, they'd visited several furniture stores and ordered the needed replacements. Stephane had already booked contractors for the cleanup and repairs, but they wouldn't be here for a few days. This gave her time to go through things.

By far the worst part of the day came after lunch. A visit to the Montreal office of Flynn Enterprises added yet another layer of problems Zara didn't need. She hadn't realized how much the current economic situation had affected the North-Am operations, and she felt a twinge of embarrassment that Monsieur know-it-all Vanier had this information before she did.

They were unable to meet with Rejean Houle, the ops manager, when they arrived. A technician informed them he'd been called to a meeting with the only major client contract they had left, one they couldn't afford to lose. Rejean himself had only taken the ops position recently, after several senior staff had left to pursue other opportunities, leaving him, a relatively inexperienced project manager, in charge.

Several seats on the board of directors were vacant as well. Strategic direction was imperative, but Zara knew that she herself was in no position to provide it. For more reasons than one.

However, the more they discussed the situation, Zara became grudgingly aware of one person who could. As much as she hated the idea, Stephane Vanier could very well fit the role of Board President of Flynn Enterprises. Smart, successful and connected, Stephane had undeniable business sense, and killer instincts to match. The thought of him taking a piece of her company the same way he'd taken a piece of her heart made her want to puke.

The condo seemed cold, and too quiet all of a sudden. She shoved aside some of the mess to find her iPod dock and speakers that used to sit on her nightstand. Somehow it had escaped the thief's notice and she plugged it in, connected the iPod and set it to shuffle.

It seemed ages since she'd listened to music, and remembered with sadness the sounds of Dave's guitar as he'd played for her what seemed like so long ago. What was he doing now? Mending his relationship with the she-goddess, accepting his responsibility as a father? The mental picture sent a stab of pain through her very soul. She loved him in spite of all of it. What they'd had together couldn't have been wrong. There had to be some mistake.

She would see Dr. Klein tomorrow, but she couldn't let Stephane know this, and needed a way to get to her appointment. As she debated what to do, she tried to gain some calm and let the music infuse her. The lyrics drifted to her ears.

There she was just a girl,
She expected the world.
But it flew away from her reach,
So she ran away in her sleep.
And dreamed of paradise…

She closed her eyes and let the tears flow uninterrupted.

Chapter Seventeen

"Ernie?" His voice sounded strained and desperate. "Sorry I missed your calls. I fell asleep. I hate to have to ask you this, but can you get me to the airport?"

Ernesto inhaled and shifted position to talk more clearly into his cell phone. "Of course, David. I've been trying to reach you. I'll be right there." He disconnected and set the phone down. He gently pulled his other arm out from beneath Marlena's shoulders as the two of them lay intertwined on the couch. She stirred, and her eyes fluttered open.

"What's going on?" she murmured.

Ernesto had waited for this moment for so long, he felt reluctant to move. He and Marlena had driven to Ernesto's modest, but comfortable, house on the outskirts of Malaga after their dinner on the waterfront. They'd spent the evening watching TV and sharing a fine bottle of Sangiovese. A perfect ending to a perfect day, as if they'd been together all those missing years. Though he knew better than to believe it could become anything serious. She was still in love with her late husband.

"It's David. He overslept. I need to get him to the airport," Ernesto whispered, planting a gentle kiss on her cheek. He rubbed her arm up and down in a reassuring caress. "Wait for me here?"

Marlena brushed a hand across her forehead, pushing a lock of hair aside. "I'll wait," she said. "What time is it?"

Ernesto sat forward, slipping on his watch that he'd left on the coffee table. "Five fifteen. I've got to hurry."

"Adelante. Don't let him miss that flight." Marlena straightened also, leaning her chin on his shoulder and rubbing his back. "Tell him Vaya con Dios."

Ernesto smiled, and wished he could remain here in the dark with her. The early hours of morning always brought him a feeling of suspended solitude, where time stood still and the pressures of his workaday life seemed miles away. "Sí, lo haré." He slipped an arm around her waist and squeezed. "Just be here when I get back."

With difficulty, he pulled himself from her embrace and headed for the door.

*

The December evening held little light save for the street lamps. Parminder hoisted her duffel bag over her shoulder as she left the gym and stepped out onto the darkened street. At the end of her long day, she could not get her visit with Zara out of her mind. She worried that her friend was in trouble, and keeping secrets from her. She'd seemed very stressed, untalkative, and apparently keeping company again with the douchebag lawyer that had broken her heart once already. Worse, the suggestion that Zara might be pregnant made Pam heartsick for her dearest college buddy.

She breathed in the chill night air, and exhaled in a frosty cloud. Her muscles felt tired, but good after her workout. She felt the urge for a cigarette, but forced it to the back of her mind. No sense ruining the benefits of a good workout on a habit she'd worked hard to break. Health professionals should set an example, she thought, and as a nurse, she refused to be seen smoking. She trudged down the block toward the bus stop across the street. A little farther from home than she would have preferred, the inexpensive rates of this gym on the outskirts of town made up for it. An extra bus ride wasn't that big a deal.

She came to the corner and pushed the walk button. Waiting under a street lamp, she wondered if she actually still had any cigarettes in her purse, and decided to take a look while standing in the light. She unzipped her handbag and reached in. The walk light chirped its birdlike signal, and Parminder stepped one foot onto the pavement.

A sudden whine came from her left and a fast-moving vehicle sped around the corner. It headed straight for her, its headlights off. Parminder stopped, paralysed in mid-stride as the car screeched to a halt, missing her by scarcely a meter. She retreated to the sidewalk and stared wild-eyed at the driver.

A man, his own eyes staring back in equal horror to hers, leaned forward against the wheel in response to his pounding on the brakes. Through the windshield, she could see his scruffy beard and unruly shock of dark hair that stuck out to one side. She could feel her heart beating fiercely, puffs of steaming breath escaping her lips in rapid bursts. Neither of them moved for a frozen minute, then the driver seemed to regain his wits and hit the gas.

Parminder swung her gym bag at the offending vehicle, and it grazed the rear panel with a harmless thud as it moved swiftly out of range. Maniac, she thought angrily, and took a good look at the car to make a mental note of the license plate.

With a shock, Pam realized she knew that plate number. And more--she knew that car. A champagne-gold BMW that belonged to her best friend, Zara Flynn.

*

When Stephane arrived at the condo, Zara's eyes felt like a pair of boiled onions from crying. She'd filled two shopping bags worth of her belongings, and he stooped to collect them as she took a last look around the place.

"Dolphin?" he asked quietly. "Are you okay?"

For such a heartless bastard, he put on a pretty good act of concern, but she wasn't buying it. She trained her red-rimmed eyes on him. "What do you think? Would you be okay in my situation?" She waved her arm across the dishevelled room then pulled a wad of Kleenex from her purse to blow her nose. "You're such an asshole."

Stephane stayed silent for a moment then shrugged. "If it makes you feel better, I'm willing to be called an asshole. I can take it."

Having no place to toss out the tissue, she stuffed it in her coat pocket. Noticing that he made no further comment, she eyed him curiously. He actually seemed at a loss as to what to say, and suddenly wished she could take her words back. Being confrontational would solve nothing.

"I'm sorry." The words slipped out of her mouth before she realized it. They stood there staring at each other, until Zara broke eye contact. "Let's get out of here."

"Sure," he said, and they made their way outside with her packages in tow. They drove to his house in silence.

When they pulled into the driveway, Zara spoke. "I need a car for tomorrow."

"Oh? You don't like the way I drive?"

She shook her head. "No, that's not it. I have some things I'd like to do…alone." She looked away from him as he put the Jag in park. "And, you have work. You've already missed a day, and I don't need a babysitter."

"I know that. But I don't mind, really."

In her peripheral vision, she caught his shy smile. It

reminded her of Dave, and a ripple of pain shuddered through her. "It's not necessary. Can you get me a rental?"

He elbowed the driver's door open, his smile widening. "I can do better than that. C'mon."

Unsure what he meant by that, Zara got out and followed him into the house. Setting her bags down, he crossed the foyer and reached into the shallow drawer of a console table that stood against one wall. He tossed something into the air toward her and Zara caught it with one hand. A set of keys jingled in her palm and she shot him a questioning glance.

He gestured toward the connecting door to his garage, and opened it. She peered in, and saw a familiar sight. The little red MG they'd driven on some of their weekend trips to Collingwood, sat parked inside. Damn, she'd loved that car. And he'd let her have it, carte blanche? Huh. The guy presented one surprise after another, and Zara didn't like it. Or the smug look on his face. He must be up to something.

"Does it have gas?' she asked.

Stephane laughed. "Jesus, you really don't trust me, do you? Yes, it has gas."

Zara stepped back, her arms folded in front of her chest. "Okay then, I'll take it."

He shut the door and stood facing her, his jaw dropping a little. He gave his head a slight shake and took a step toward her. "What do I have to do to make you trust me?" he said, his voice slipping into the bedroom version she remembered very well.

Zara stood her ground. He moved closer still.

"I know I hurt you." His eyes searched hers with an honesty that Zara didn't expect. "And that's the biggest regret of my life right now." He reached out the short distance between them and took her by the shoulders. "I really am an asshole. To lose your trust, and let you get away."

His nearness made her both uneasy and a little dizzy.

Maybe it was Hugo Boss, or perhaps some weird pheromone he was giving off. Either way, she felt hypnotized, like prey frozen in the sights of a deadly snake. "I trusted you once. Didn't turn out so well," she replied, her voice cracking. "And once an asshole, always an—"

"I can change," he interrupted. "I want to change," he whispered, so close now his lips hovered mere inches away from hers. "I'd do anything for you." His hands moved up to frame her ears, his hazel gaze so intense it made Zara afraid. "I want you…"

As he moved to kiss her, anger broke the spell and she thrust her hands between them, pushing forcibly against his chest.

"Life's full of disappointments, isn't it?" She shoved him away with all her might. "Have you checked your watch? Your nine o'clock girlfriend must be waiting."

He looked stunned, as if resistance was something new to him. He opened his mouth to speak when his iPhone went off in his jacket pocket. With relief, Zara watched him break eye contact and reach for the phone. He glanced at the screen and tilted his head back, his expression changing from one of annoyance, to astonishment. He thumbed the screen and answered it.

"Oui, c'est Vanier," he said curtly. He turned away, as though the conversation wasn't meant for Zara's ears. "Oui." A pause. "Non! "Où est-ce ?" Another pause. "Sérieusement?' He turned back to Zara with a smile of incredulousness. "C'est fantastique. Oui, merci." He lowered the phone and looked straight at her.

"It's the police. They've found your car."

*

Having completed his task with the BMW, Alain disconnected the call. Vanier certainly had an acting career to fall back on, he thought. And he might need one, too, once this little venture blew up in Vanier's face. The conversation sounded convincing. He assumed that the young lady had been in the same room, and listening. He stood outside the rear entrance to the brick building on Rue Peel, waiting. When another man approached, he moved under the overhang and bypassed the security code with ease. The man, wearing a black jacket, followed him and they both passed over the threshold. Once inside, they moved together down a darkened hallway to a service elevator.

"You're sure it's safe," the man commented.

"Oui, safe as one can be when hiding from the law. What have you done this time, Spic? Alain yanked open the safety gates.

"None of your business, frog. I'll be gone in a week or two, and it will be as if I was never here, comprender?" the man said, with sinister emphasis on the last word.

Alain sniggered. "You should be nice to me, amigo. Remember, you help me, and I help you. That simple. Tell me why you here."

Carlos gave him a cold stare. "Some stash found its way to the polizia in Cadiz. It mustn't be connected to me, see? As soon as someone takes the fall for it, I can go back." He took a step toward Alain as the lift platform clattered to a stop. "And I intend to go back."

Alain shrugged. "I hope you do, for both our sakes."

"I didn't want to leave. I had no choice. I have a good thing going in Malaga. I just hope she's still there when I return."

"She?" Alain asked with sarcasm in his voice. "Elle?" he repeated in French. His manner turned comedic as he snorted a curt laugh. "Elle has been the undoing of many a man such as you. You're better off without elle, mon ami."

"What do you know," Carlos sneered as he stepped off the

platform. "You've probably not had any real pussy in your whole miserable life."

Alain followed after closing the safety gate and sending the platform back to the main floor. "I know I won't ever be compromised by a piece of ass. Can't say the same for you, eh?" He led his visitor to another door with a keypad. He entered his stolen code and the light glowed green. He pulled the latch open and peered through the crack. He pressed his finger to his lips and drew the opening wider.

They stepped in to what resembled a hotel suite with a table and two chairs, a mini-kitchen and a queen-sized bed. "I hope you no have luggage," Alain said. "Don't want the place to look lived-in."

Carlos tossed a pack of cigarillos on the table. "Just these," he said. "Got a light?"

Alain clucked his tongue. "No fumar, estupid! Maybe you just wanna walk to the police station down the street and save time."

Flipping up his collar, Carlos hunkered down into the warmth of his jacket. "Fucking cold here. Need something to keep warm."

"Don't worry," Alain said. "I hear it's plenty warm in hell. You'll be there soon, unless you play nice."

Carlos scowled. "What do you want me to do?"

"See this wall?" Alain pointed. "On the other side are some very pretty things. And you're going to help me steal them."

*

The white-haired head moved through the crowd, edging to the front of the group that waited for the arriving passengers. Dave recognized the familiar loping gait as the older man stepped into view. Having nothing more than a backpack for luggage, Dave slung it firmly over one shoulder and walked toward him.

Bruce Parker smiled at the sight of him and stood still as Dave approached. The old man watched him with the look of an artist admiring his own work. In a way, Dave supposed, it was the truth. "Hey, Dad. Good of you to come all this way."

Bruce put his arm around his son's shoulders. A few inches shorter, Bruce had to reach up a bit to make the gesture. "No problem, bud. How was your flight?"

Dave yawned. "Long and uncomfortable, actually. But I'm here. How's Mom?"

Bruce gave him a few swats on the back before releasing Dave from his hold. "Fine, fine. She's sorry to have missed you, but she's out in the Okanagan with your sister for the holidays. I'm going out there myself the week before Christmas. You look great, son. Tired, but great. C'mon, I've brought something for you." He pointed to the exits and began moving them forward.

"Brought something? Like what? You've already gone out of your way just to meet me here."

"No, no, a stroke of luck, really. I was coming up for an auction in Drummondville this weekend anyway. No sweat."

They walked to the parking garage and Dave's eyes brightened as he spotted the familiar vehicle. His '03 Mustang sat between two concrete columns, its slick paint job and chrome detail shining even in the dim light.

Dave smiled. "You've been looking after her, I see." To say that Bruce Parker was a bit of a car nut would be an understatement. A mechanic for most of his working career, he'd been fixing, buying, selling and tinkering with cars for as long as Dave could remember. The Mustang appeared in top condition thanks to Bruce's tender care. "Hey, you weren't planning to auction her off, were you?" Dave asked, mock suspicion in his voice.

Bruce laughed. "Don't give me any ideas. Drive it away before I change my mind."

Dave looked at his father with a newfound admiration. "Thanks." It dawned on him all the things fatherhood meant. He'd do well to be half the dad Bruce had been. Someday, he thought resolutely. "How are you getting back to Drummondville?"

Bruce shrugged. "I've got a buddy meeting me downtown who's headed for the auction too. Thought we'd grab a bite to eat, then you can drop me off with him."

Dave nodded. "Okay. And how are you getting back to Thunder Bay?"

"It's an auction, Dave," he deadpanned. "When have you known me not to come away with at least one set of wheels at an auction?"

At that moment, Dave realized he'd come by his comedic tendencies honestly. He mirrored his Dad's sense of humor perfectly. With a chuckle and a vague notion about an apple and a tree, he strode over to the Mustang's driver side. "Right. Where to, then?"

Bruce moved to the passenger side. "Where else? Schwarz Deli."

With a grin, Dave tossed his backpack in the rear seat and slid behind the wheel. She felt, and smelled, as good as he remembered, with her hip-hugging bucket seat and soft-grip stick shift. The familiar scent of leather and patchouli pervaded the cabin; a man's space. Bruce handed him the keys, and the Mustang roared to life.

"So, tell me about this girl that's brought you all the way back across an ocean," Bruce said.

Dave sighed. He threw the stick into gear and told his father everything.

Chapter Eighteen

Zara awoke in the white-walled bedroom of Stephane's house with a headache. In addition to the intermittent bouts of nausea, headaches seemed to be plaguing her lately. Another symptom, or just stress? Yeah. Stress. I'm going with stress.

Despite this, she managed to smile, remembering the good news from the night before. Her BMW had been found in an industrial area of the city, apparently unscathed; as if someone had simply borrowed it for an errand. Stephane said the police were towing it to the local impound and they could pick it up later today. A bright spot in an otherwise painful trip.

But until then, she'd have to drive the little MG to her appointment. She hoped she remembered how to drive a stick. It had been awhile. Nursing the pain behind her eyes, she sat up in bed, deciding whether to have a shower or a nice warm bath to ease the headache and get ready for the day.

As she glanced around the room, a stray thought wandered into her head. What would it be like to wake up in this room every day? Beautiful in its simplicity and elegance, the walls sported a subtle tone-on-tone paint finish. Exposed dark timbers accentuated the high ceiling. The carved-wood sleigh bed she'd slept in offered exquisite luxury, piled high with a down comforter and plump, heaven-soft pillows. A spectacular chandelier hung above the bed, a unique, swirling tempest of metal branches studded with almond-shaped bulbs. When lit, it resembled a galaxy of stars descending into the room.

My brain must be going soft. The undeniable charm, looks and taste of the womanizing Stephane Vanier were beginning to work their magic upon her once again.

No. She would not allow that. She clambered from the dreamy bed and padded across the plush carpet to the ensuite. She flicked the light switch, and the gold-veined marble of the tub enclosure and double vanity gleamed in the soft light of the wall sconces. Again, she could not deny the man had taste.

She filled the tub and checked the medicine cabinet for Tylenol. Nada. The vanity drawers yielded none either, so she donned a short robe that she'd brought from the condo, and went to try her luck the kitchen. Reaching the end of the hall that connected to the main living area, Zara stopped short.

Fussing with the coffee machine, and wearing nothing but a pair of workout pants, stood Stephane. What the hell? Had he spent the night? The rat! He'd promised to stay at his downtown suite. She made a scoffing noise. When could she ever believe a word this snake-in-the-grass said?

He turned to look in her direction at the sound. His eyes raked her up and down. Zara clutched the thin robe tighter around herself, knowing it didn't hide much. She found her voice before he did. "I heard you leave last night. What are you doing here?"

Stephane stopped fiddling with the machine, but continued to stare at her. A smile began twitching at the corners of his mouth. "I did leave. Then I remembered some papers I needed from my home office, and came back. I ended up reading through them for hours and, well. Forgive me. I just crashed in the den."

Her eyes narrowed as she listened to his plausible, yet underhanded story.

"I'll make you coffee–" he offered.

"I can't drink coffee." She cursed silently at her verbal slip. "I have a headache, and coffee makes it worse," she said, to add some credibility to the statement. "Do you have any Tylenol?"

"Yeah, sure," he said lightly, as if grateful she'd changed the subject. He turned and opened a cabinet next to the fridge. Facing away, his brawny shoulders were in full view, the curve of his spine creating a pleasant line down his back. Looking past him, Zara could see a quite a collection of bottles within, vitamins and protein supplements and more. From among them he produced a familiar red-lidded container and tapped a few e-Z tabs into his hand.

Zara stood in place at the edge of the hallway, not moving. "And some water," she said. From the fridge he grabbed a bottle of Evian and brought both the water and the medicine over to where she stood. "Thanks," she said, taking it from him. "Now if you wouldn't mind, could you go sleep somewhere else, like you promised?"

She found herself looking directly at his naked chest to avoid eye contact. He may have bulked up a bit since she'd seen him last, but his powerful musculature remained undiminished, and difficult to ignore. Dark chest hair feathered out across his pectorals, and continued in a line down the middle of his torso, ending just above his navel. Yikes. His navel. Her private muscles convulsed in an unbidden reaction. She started to back away when he suddenly reached out and caught hold of the silver dolphin that still hung round her neck.

"Hey, I remember this," he said. "I didn't know you still wore it." He fingered it for a moment then closed his hand around it. He tipped her chin upward with his other hand. "That tells me something."

She had no choice but to look into those hazel eyes, and listen to the dangerously soft and sexy voice. Warning bells rang in Zara's head, bringing the already present pain to a fever pitch. *Why did I wear this stupid thing? I meant to take it off so many times…* She jerked away and the chain broke, leaving Stephane clutching the pendant in his fist, the silver strands dangling in the air.

"Hey," he called, as she turned and bolted for the bathroom. His footsteps lagged behind her only a pace or two, as she raced down the hall. Too late. Stephane closed the distance easily, catching hold of her and sandwiching her with his heavy body against he bathroom door.

His breath blew warm across her shoulders as he spoke. "What's wrong, babe? Talk to me…I'm not the enemy. Please let me help you."

"Let me go," she begged. "I don't feel well…please." Zara could feel his chest moving in and out, as well as the rest of his bumps and bulges pressing in tight against her back. She didn't stand a chance if he decided to use brute force. He took a few more deep breaths, and when she felt a momentary relax of his muscles, lunged forward into the bathroom, slamming and locking the door behind her.

She heard his fist thumping against it. She clapped the red tablets onto her tongue and gulped down the water. "Leave me alone," she called out.

His voice bordered on desperation. "Zara, I don't understand. I've said I'm sorry, I hate myself for having hurt you. I've loved taking care of you these past few days. I love seeing you in my house. I…I've pictured it a thousand times since you left. You have no idea."

As she pulled off her robe and stepped into the tub, it occurred to her it wasn't the only hot water she'd be getting into. Zara shivered even while surrounded by the warm water. It struck her with alarming certainty that Stephane had planned this from the beginning. He wanted her back. He practically held her captive. And she'd let it happen.

Her head felt near exploding with pain. "Fuck off," she yelled. "I have stuff to do. Just go get my car back, and after that, I'm leaving. Now do you understand?"

He landed a final, echoing punch against the door. Then silence. Zara lowered herself deeper into the water, her chin dipping below the surface. She curled her arms around her knees, and waited. A minute passed and when no further sound came from beyond the door, she relaxed and stretched out in the luxurious tub. I guess he took the hint. Things were taking a lot of weird turns she hadn't expected. Time to get a game plan.

First, Dr. Klein. Then she'd call Pam, ask her advice. Pay another visit to the Flynn office; sign the work order for the contractors; go get the Beamer.

And get the hell out of here.

*

Jorge steered the Mercedes through traffic in downtown Malaga, heading for Ernesto's house on the north side of town where Marlena waited to be picked up. Though an unusual place for her to be, Jorge would never question the decisions or behavior of his employer, cousin or no. Marly had her own life, and entitled to live it how she wanted. The entire Sanchez clan knew that Ernesto held a torch for her, and it seemed right, natural, for them to be drawn together again. They all missed Tristan, but life must go on.

He stopped at a traffic light. As he drummed his fingertips on the wheel to the rhythm of a song on the radio, he scanned the streetscape. Pedestrians crossed the intersection, a mix of people old and young, men and women, dogs on leashes. He looked left, then right, and something caught his eye.

On a concrete bench under the awning of an office tower

entrance, sat a woman. She leaned forward with her elbows on her knees and her chin perched atop her clenched fists, looking lost in thought. Her brow wrinkled a little, but in no way detracted from her pretty features. Her long, shapely legs stretched to the ground, terminating in deadly four-inch stilettos.

On impulse, Jorge turned the corner and pulled over. He parked in front of a convenience store that sold cigarettes, candy and sodas. He went to the counter and bought two limonadas, then walked to the front of the tall building. The solemn beauty still rested on the bench, and with two drinks in his hands, he strode up to her.

"Perdoneme, Senorita," he said. "You seem thirsty. Can I offer you something cool to drink?"

At the sound of his voice, she lifted her chin off her hands and swivelled her face toward him, as if being offered drinks from strangers happened every day of her life. She looked him up and down. "No, gracias," she replied, and turned away again.

Jorge edged closer. "Por favor, it's quite warm today. I would not want to see you become dehydrated. That would be a shame." He held out the lemonade within arm's reach.

She gave him a second glance. Apparently deciding he looked harmless and genuine enough, she took the proffered bottle. She exhaled and sat back against the bench. "Gracias, you are very kind."

"May I?" he asked, indicating the empty spot next to her.

The woman shrugged. "Por supuesto. I don't own the bench."

"Life is funny, isn't it?" he said, sitting down, but leaving an appropriate distance between them. "When it gives you lemons, you must make lemonade."

She took a sip of the tart, yet sweet, soda and flashed a grim smile. "How do you know I have lemons?"

"I don't. But I know that I do. And I make the best from what I'm given."

"What's your name?" she asked.

"Jorge Allesandro," he replied with a nod.

She took a second sip as she seemed to size him up then extended her hand. "Ivette Melendez."

"Pleasure to meet you, Senorita Melendez. So what troubles you?"

"My business," she replied after a long pause. "I've made a commitment I won't be able to honor. I could lose everything."

Jorge frowned and nodded. "That's too bad. But you know what I've heard?" He sipped his own drink and looked off in the distance for a moment before continuing. "That you haven't truly lost everything until you lose your sense of humor."

Ivette eyed him curiously then burst out laughing.

"See?" Jorge said. "You haven't lost everything."

When Ivette's laughter calmed down, she took another swallow from her bottle. "And what about you? What lemons do you have?"

Jorge sighed, considering the question. "I have a good life. A comfortable life," he said. "But even comfort can become… boring. You say to yourself, is that all there is? Is there no greater purpose for me?" He shook his head. "Perhaps there isn't."

"Don't say that." Ivette looked at him with a serious countenance. "Perhaps you weren't meant to see it just yet. Perhaps you must make your own purpose."

"Ah." Jorge tipped his lemonade bottle toward her. "Good advice. Perhaps you should take it."

The long-legged lady pursed her glossy lips into an ironic grin. "You are an interesting person, Jorge Allesandro. Have you always been such a filósofo… a philosopher?"

"Philosopher?" He chuckled and shook his head. "No.

An optimist, si. What is stopping you from honoring your business commitment?"

"My partner…disappeared. And so did the money."

Jorge waited for her to continue, but she sat silent for a long minute. "And something else?" he prodded.

"Yes. But I can't talk about it."

"Where is your business?" he asked.

Ivette looked skyward, and thumbed toward the building behind them. "Here. Top floor. Or at least it will be, when I get the money."

"I see. A building like this, rent must be expensive. What kind of business, if I may ask?" When she seemed to hesitate, Jorge added, "Escucha, Listen. I know you've never seen me before. You have no reason to tell me anything. But sometimes you just need to say things out loud. And I have no one to tell. So don't be afraid."

She swallowed the last of her lemonade with finality, as though downing a shot to steel herself. She reached into her purse for a business card from her current shop, and handed one to Jorge. "A salon. I quit my old job to open my own salon and spa. I signed the lease, and I owe money. I have to find him."

Jorge took the card and nodded. "Him? Your partner?"

"More than a partner. He—"—she stopped mid-sentence and looked down at her feet—"we were going to be married." She threw her empty soda bottle into the rubbish bin next to the bench. The gesture seemed to illustrate her feelings on the matter. She turned to look squarely at Jorge. "Pathetic, isn't it? I've been dumped. The party's over, and I'm stuck with la cuenta." Ivette stood to leave. "Thank you for the drink. And for listening."

Jorge rose also. "Don't give up on your dreams. Perhaps the party's just starting."

She smiled at him and reached out for a businesslike handshake. "Good advice. Perhaps you should take it."

Chapter Nineteen

Stephane cursed as he shifted the Jag into fourth and accelerated far beyond the speed limit. Zara didn't seem to be working with the plan he'd laid out. She hated him still. The realization made him wince. But while the crowning jewel to the whole affair would be having Zara back as his mate, for lack of a better word, it didn't have to be a deal-breaker. He could still come out on top. He sensed he'd convinced her of his capability to run the Board of Flynn Enterprises, and also that she had no interest, or time, to do so herself. This worked to his advantage.

Perhaps the BMW would be the clincher. Returning it to her, undamaged, might be enough to sway her back on track and seal the deal. The Frenchman better have that car ready, waiting, and in the condition he promised by the time he got there. Or his other five grand wouldn't be forthcoming.

As he turned onto the isolated street in the warehouse district, he saw the tow truck waiting behind the champagne-gold vehicle. Good, he thought. At least something appeared to be going right today. He pulled up ahead of both vehicles and parked. He gave the tow truck driver an address and instructed him to hook up. Before leaving, Stephane reached under the front wheel well of the BMW and retrieved the magnetic lock box that held the keys. Wouldn't look right if the thief hadn't had to work hard. He threw the box into his glove compartment and drove away.

*

A sweet, middle-aged man, Dr. Klein wished Zara well and bid goodbye. She thanked him for his kindness and for fitting her appointment into his tight schedule. Many doctors didn't take new patients, especially not on such short notice. She had Pam to thank for that, and after re-dressing in her black leggings, tunic sweater and knee-high boots, she returned to the waiting room where Parminder sat flipping through a magazine. She looked up as Zara approached, and sprang to her feet. Zara smiled, and motioned for them to exit.

They walked side by side to the elevators in silence, and as they descended twelve floors to the lobby, Pam couldn't rein in her curiosity any longer. "Come on Z, I can't stand the suspense. What's the verdict?"

Zara looked at her friend, feeling a strange mix of anxiety and serenity. "It's time to tell you everything. Come on, let's go sit down somewhere."

A coffee shop on the ground floor sufficed and they chose a table by a window that overlooked the bustling downtown.

"Damn straight, it's time," Pam said. "All of it."

Zara told her about El Mirador, about the explosion, about Cruz, and Miguel the rock star. But mostly she talked about Dave. "I met someone wonderful. We have so much in common; he's all I've ever wanted in a guy. He's smart, he's funny…" She held out her cell phone, showing Pam a picture of him taken in Tenerife.

"He's gorgeous," Pam said, finishing Zara's sentence.

Zara nodded. "I wanted to give him all of me, too.

Everything. And in a way, I guess I have." She looked at Pam with a sort of Mona Lisa smile.

Knowing intuitively what she meant, the way only a best friend could, Pam's eyes began to fill with tears. "Oh, Z. I'm so thrilled, and scared for you. Where is this guy?"

Zara pocketed her phone. "In Spain. But you know what's funny? He's from here. From Thunder Bay."

"Does he love you? Is he waiting for you?"

Zara looked out the window, as if peering across the Atlantic, asking the same question. "I believe he loves me," she finally said with a certainty that her face didn't quite convey. "But someone else is waiting for him." She shook her head as if trying to jar the little fact loose from her brain and replace it with a new truth. No matter what happened, Zara now knew that she held a tiny piece of Dave inside her, and no auburn-haired Amazon could take that away. Zara explained about the incident in Tenerife and the calls from Stephane.

"Stephane's been helpful, Pam. I thought he'd changed. But he scared the shit out of me this morning. He stayed the night when he promised to keep his distance, and he's trying to win me back for some reason. The sad part is that he's the logical choice of Board President. Would I be crazy to allow it, or crazy not to?"

Pam began to look uncomfortable. "Z, I have something to tell you. I saw your car last night."

Zara blinked. "You mean, where they found it? In some industrial area, I heard."

Pam shook her head, her raven-black hair swinging across her cheeks. "No, I saw someone driving it. He nearly ran me over. About eight o'clock. What time did you hear from the police?"

Zara chewed her lip. "About nine. Or rather, Stephane did."

"You didn't take the call yourself?"

"No."

"You don't think there's something fishy about that?"

The two women stared at each other. "Were the car keys in your condo? Were they missing?" Pam asked.

Zara's brow wrinkled. "I'm not sure. Everything was a mess. Hard to say what was missing besides the obvious stuff."

"Z, think about this. You left everything in good order. Were any other units in your building B & E'd?"

Zara hesitated. "I don't know. Go on," she said.

Pam counted on her fingers. "You get a call from a guy you know to be a conniving, self-serving liar, who has money and connections. Not from the police, or your insurance company, but him."

She tapped a second finger. "Your car is gone, apparently with the keys. And it turns up unharmed? Come on. That never happens."

Third finger. "Now, all of a sudden, the Montreal office is in a shambles, and who's there to save the day? Stephane freaking Vanier." She swallowed hard. "Forgive me if I don't exactly like the man. He hurt you, big time. And he's an opportunist, if he's anything."

Zara fixed her gaze off in the distance. With a determined pull, she drew the straps of her trusty red handbag over her shoulder. Next to Pam, it felt like her closest friend right now. "Pam. I need you to do something. She pushed a ring of keys toward her across the tabletop. "Take the MG. Go to my condo. There's a brown envelope behind the garburetor under the kitchen sink. Bring it to me at the Flynn office. Do you know the way there?"

Pam nodded yes, and closed her hand over the key ring. Zara covered it with her own hand. "Gracias, amiga."

*

Bruce Parker left his son with some profound thoughts.

"Parenthood is an experience not to be missed. Look forward to it. Embrace it. Cherish it."

Dave considered these as he cruised down Rue Sherbrooke, following the GPS readout to the address that Zara's mother had given him. A satellite radio station played a song that seemed to narrate his purpose for being here.

All or nothing, love is war;
Take everything, you want some more.
All or nothing, love is war;
Remember who you're fighting for.

These words resonated within him as he slowed to his destination. He whistled at the attractive exterior of the converted brick building on Avenue Melville. It fit her exactly. Classic and beautiful.

He parked the Mustang and strode up the walkway to the red-doored entrance. Inside the vestibule, he noticed the mail slot with her name on it. He toyed with the idea of leaving her a note, but dismissed it, not knowing when, or if, she would come here. He'd wait awhile then try calling her. He hoped to hell she would answer. His whole body ached. Whether with fatigue, sadness or raw desire, he could not tell. Perhaps all three. It felt like an eternity since he'd held her, made love to her. And he swore it wouldn't be the last. The longer they were apart, the more certain he became that their lives were inextricably bound together. One couldn't survive without the other.

He returned to the car and watched the building for several more minutes. He noted everything he saw, including the movements of anything and anyone along the street. Checking his side mirror, he saw a red sports car pull up several meters behind his Mustang. A brown-skinned girl, maybe five feet tall with long black hair, got out of the car and paced up the walkway to Zara's building.

Dave sat up straight, his fingers on the door handle. When

the girl went inside, he leapt from behind the wheel and followed. He bounded up the steps and wrenched open the outer door. At the sudden movement, the girl whirled to face him, the key still in her hand. She stared at him then blinked hard.

"You're Dave," she said, in a voice that expressed both surprise and certainty.

Dave stopped in his tracks. "Yeah. Who are you?"

"I'm Pam, Zara's friend. She showed me your picture."

He exhaled a tense breath. "How is she?" he asked, his fists clenching and unclenching.

Pam's mouth twitched. "You'd better ask her yourself. I'm going to meet her as soon as I'm done here."

Dave gestured to the inner door that Pam hadn't yet unlocked. "I'm coming with you."

"Okay," she said, twisting the key and yanking open the door. "Are you sure you're up to it? You look beat."

Dave grabbed the edge of the door with one hand and held it open. "I'll risk it."

*

Zara arrived at the Montreal office of Flynn Enterprises just after 3:00 p.m. She pondered the idea of coming to work here. Her father had suggested it more than once. It made sense, especially now with the branch in trouble and no one officially at the helm. If not for his sudden death, Zara realized her destiny might well have landed her exactly here.

This time, however, she stood here alone, without Stephane spelling out every step and procedure for her. She felt a fool, placing her trust in the one person who deserved none. Well, all that was about to change. She pushed open the steel and glass door and stepped into the room in confidence.

As she approached his office, Rejean Houle looked up

from his desk. "Monsieur Houle?" Zara asked. He nodded. "Je m'appelle Zara Flynn. Pleasure to meet you."

Rejean catapulted from his chair. "Mademoiselle Flynn," he said, a genuine smile illuminating his features. He reached to shake her hand, which Zara accepted heartily. "S'il vous plait, sit down. Likewise, a pleasure to meet you. I'm sorry I missed you on your previous visit."

"Oui, moi aussi." She took off her coat and sat down opposite him. She took a business card from her handbag and placed it on one of the few clear areas of his cluttered desk.

"My condolences about your father. I hadn't met him personally, but I know he was well respected in the industry."

"Merci," Zara replied. "But business, just as life, must go on, oui?" She smiled at the red-haired man, who wore wire-rimmed glasses and seemed to have a challenge keeping the same reddish facial hair in check. Zara couldn't help but like him. He exuded simple honesty and an obvious enthusiasm for his work. It appeared that recent developments had the man swamped, documents and notebooks taking up most of his desktop.

"How are things going?" she asked.

Rejean sighed. "We're managing. The project with PCL is keeping us afloat."

"Yes, I heard. Why has business dropped off? I'd like to hear it from you."

Rejean sank into his chair. "A number of things happened. First, three board members resigned on the same day. Then, we heard that two of our RFPs, Requests For Proposals, were rejected. It came as some surprise, as we fully expected those contracts to move ahead." He shrugged.

Zara nodded, her brain working hard as she assessed the facts. "When did that happen?" she asked.

Rejean scratched his head. "As I recall, it occurred the day after the board fiasco. Everyone here was in shock." He fell silent and folded his hands across his stomach as he leaned back in his chair. "Fortunately, Monsieur Vanier came forward and offered his help."

Zara's ears prickled. "Monsieur Vanier? What kind of help?"

"He offered to serve as interim Board President, and to look into the RFP responses."

"And? What did he find?"

"Nothing yet. But just after that, several employees quit, and we had just enough staff to get by on the remaining contracts."

"And do you know why they quit?"

Rejean nodded. "They all received offers from other companies. Better salaries, benefits."

"What other companies?"

"Strangely enough, not engineering companies, but a law firm. Coté and Associates."

Zara stiffened. "A law firm? Interesting, don't you think?"

"Oui. I thought so."

"Did you realize that Coté & Associates has recently become Coté, Vanier & Associates?"

Houle sat motionless. "Are you sure?"

Zara nodded. The pieces fell into place. The Flynn office had been methodically taken apart. She had no doubt the missing employees and board members would reappear the moment Stephane was in charge.

"Monsieur Houle, I intend to remedy this situation. Now."

As if on cue, the front office doors opened. Stephane walked in, looking around the vacant reception area and continuing on toward Houle's office. He stopped short at the sight of Zara.

"Babe, I'm so glad you're here. I was so worried. I had your car towed to Grant's Auto on Maison Boulevard. Not a scratch on it. But I booked it in for inspection, just in case."

"Thanks," she said, breaking the icy silence that descended over the room. Stephane seemed to sense the cool reception.

"What's wrong?" he asked.

Zara stood. "Nothing more than the last time we visited. Monsieur Houle,"—she gestured to Rejean—"has confirmed everything we heard earlier."

Stephane nodded. "Oui. It's a difficult situation, but not an irreversible one. With the right direction from the board, we can turn this around. In fact, I have several colleagues who are willing to let their names stand for election. We'll need to call an extraordinary meeting, of course. You need to be part of that, Zara. So close to the holidays though, we might have to postpone it until the New Year."

As he flashed his signature, oh-so-charming smile, it became utterly clear to Zara that he'd gotten very, very far in the world on his good looks. He seemed to brighten further as a new thought struck him.

"In that case, we could go up to the cottage for Christmas. It'll be wonderful, just like old times." He sent a deep and meaningful look into Zara's eyes. "We could re-start."

Rejean coughed and rose from his chair. "Excusez-moi, perhaps you should finish this conversation alone," he said as he moved past them toward the door. "Please, use my office." He gave Zara a nod before leaving that signalled he'd be available nearby if she needed him.

"What do you say, sweetheart?" Stephane asked, moving close to her and brushing his hands up and down her arms. "I'm sorry about this morning. I'm moving too fast for you, I see that now. Let's get away for awhile, over the holidays. Just what we need, both of us work too hard."

Zara decided to play along. To catch a thief, you must first become a thief. She placed her hands against his thick chest and pretended to study the lapels of his suit jacket. "I'm the CEO. I have no choice but to work hard." She inhaled the full effect of Hugo Boss, and stroked the fine material beneath her fingertips.

Stephane leaned his head down to rest his chin on her head. His hands left her arms and snaked neatly behind her back. He exhaled with what seemed like relief and Zara sensed the tension leaving him in a peculiar way. *He thinks he's won.*

"All that can be behind you now, babe. I'm here, I'll take care of everything. I'll take care of you."

She winced at his use of Dave's pet name for her. Babe. "What if I don't want to be taken care of? I have to work, Stephane. It's my company." She lowered her voice to a teasing tone, hoping to draw him further into his false sense of triumph.

He seemed to rock gently back and forth, holding her in his arms. "Technically, yes. You're the CEO of the European division, but not the North-Am. You'd have to be appointed by the Board. It's a heavy load, babe. You don't need the extra stress. You've enough to carry back in Spain."

Gears shunted and clicked in Zara's head. *He wants to be Board President. The board names the CEO. He could cut me out of the management here with a single vote. How did he think I'd react to that? Smile and play house with him in Collingwood for the rest of my career?* God, she hoped Pam would get here soon.

"Don't call me babe," she said quietly.

Chapter Twenty

"Turn here," Pam said as the Mustang raced along Rue Berri toward Sainte Catherine Street. "You can park underground." She pointed to the underground parking entrance on the south side of the building. Dave cruised down the ramp and pulled into a vacant stall. Deciding to take only one vehicle from Zara's neighborhood, he and Pam hurried to the elevators, their mismatched steps echoing in the cavern of concrete. Dave punched 8 on the panel.

"How'd you know the office was on eight?" Pam asked.

Dave blinked hard "I didn't. Just habit. The Malaga office is on the eighth floor. I pressed it without thinking."

They reached their destination and pushed through the double glass doors in unison. A red-headed man stood in the reception area, startled by their dramatic entrance. "Bonjour, may I help you?" he asked, adjusting his glasses in a way that reminded Dave of Ernesto.

"Dave Parker, from the EU office in Malaga," Dave said, quickly extending a hand to him. "Is Miss Flynn here?"

"Bienvenue, Monsieur Parker. Je suis Rejean Houle, acting Operations Manager." He shook Dave's hand. "I recall your name from the corporate organization charts. Oui, she is in my office with Monsieur Vanier."

Pam made a noise. "Oh, no. What's that rat doing here?"

Dave shot her a look. "Who the fuck is Vanier?"

"Someone you won't like. We'd better get in there."

As they moved toward the closed door, Rejean touched Pam on the arm. "Perhaps you should knock first," he advised.

Pam and Dave exchanged glances. "Like hell," Pam said. "Bust it down."

Dave threw open the door. There, in the greenish glow of fluorescent lighting stood a blond giant of a man with his arms locked around Zara. They both looked toward the door in alarm.

Dave felt blood rising in his neck. Who the hell is this ape with his arms around my girl? He focused in on her face, the face that meant everything to him. The one he'd crossed an ocean to find again.

"Dave," she said, her voice sounding faint and far away. She returned his penetrating stare, her green eyes growing wide and dark like those of a trapped animal. He moved without thinking.

"Get your hands off her," he growled, gripping the man's beefy shoulder and shoving him aside.

"Hey," the ape shouted, raising his arm to deflect the blow. "Who do you think you are?"

"You first, asshole." Dave replied.

"Z, are you okay?" Pam's frightened voice cut through the male hostility that permeated the room.

Zara stepped back, unable to take her eyes off Dave. "Never better."

The blond man looked them up and down. "This is a private meeting."

"Answer the question." Dave said. "Who the hell are you?"

The man continued to glare at him, clearly considering himself above such interrogation.

"Pam," Zara interrupted. "Did you bring what I asked?"

"Yup. Right here." She handed Zara an elastic-bound portfolio.

Zara took it and handled its smooth brown surface thoughtfully for a moment. "Some social etiquette is in order," she said. "Stephane Vanier, may I introduce Mr. David Parker and Miss Parminder Singh."

Stephane remained standing near Zara in a protective manner, appearing unimpressed with either of the newcomers. "Friends of yours?" he asked. "Frankly, my dear, I'd have expected better."

Zara's face blushed hot pink as her temper rose. "Is that so?" she retorted. "Well frankly, Stephane, I expected nothing better from you, you lying bastard."

Stephane gaped at her. "What are you talking about, babe? I thought we had this all worked out. When have I lied to you? What are these people doing here?"

Dave took a step forward. "I'm warning you, step away from her. And if you value your balls, buddy, don't call her babe." He sized up the man in front of him. Although of similar height, Dave figured the guy had at least fifty pounds on him, and showed no sign of being intimidated.

"Spare me the cowboy antics," Stephane said.

"You lied to me from the beginning," Zara interjected. "My condo wasn't broken into by chance. You arranged it. And you sent my car on a little vacation with a friend of yours. Pam saw him driving it around the night it turned up. How else did you find it so easily and without any damage? A smokescreen, all of it, to lure me back here and trick me into naming you to the Board of Directors."

"The company's in trouble, Zara. I'm offering it a way out. I have no other motive than that."

"Sounds like bullshit to me," Dave said, his eyes narrowing.

Stephane relaxed his stance, and moved back a pace. He raised both hands in a halting gesture. "This is ridiculous. You can't come in here, uttering threats. You'd better leave, or I'll have security remove you both."

"There's only one person leaving, Stephane. And that's you," Zara said. She opened the portfolio and withdrew a sheaf of papers. "You say I'm not the CEO of this division, but this document clearly says otherwise. My father's will. You don't seem to have read it thoroughly."

"I've read it," Stephane said darkly. "And it makes you subject to the Board's decisions like any other CEO."

"True. But the terms of succession give me the ability, in extenuating circumstances, to supercede any Board decision, worldwide. Even as President, I could quash any motion you present. In short, you have no power without me. Now get out."

Stephane bristled, anger settling over his countenance like a shroud. He fixed them all with a haughty stare, and tilted his chin toward Dave. "You think I don't know who you are? I've made it my business to know all of the company personnel. You're an over-achieving science major from Buttfuck, Ontario who lucked out getting a job with an international construction giant. Ambitious. Looking to move up in the company." His face twisted into an evil grin. "What better way to climb the corporate ladder than to screw the heiress after its CEO drops dead?" He swung his glance to Zara. "You didn't see it coming, did you, sweetheart? At least I'm trying to pilot the company with my brains and not my dick."

Zara paled at Stephane's crude words. A curtain of red passed over Dave's eyes. He'd only met the man a few minutes ago, yet already hated him with every fibre of his soul. He wanted nothing more at this moment than to get his hands around Stephane's throat. His fingers twitched at the prospect.

"I said get out," Zara repeated, her voice betraying the tears filling her eyes.

"You can't tell me what to do. I'm already serving on the board," Stephane said.

"You'll never be sworn on as President," Zara said coldly. Her hands shook as she tried to shove the papers back into the portfolio.

Stephane cocked his head to one side. "And who is going to stop me? The Lone Ranger here?" he pointed at Dave. "And Tonto?" His gaze slipped over Pam.

That's it. This ape is going down. Stephane stood about a foot away from the wall, his attention directed toward Pam. Perfect. Dave lined him up in his sights, imagining the wall behind Stephane as a rinkboard. With a lunging stride, he nailed him in a crushing bodycheck.

Stephane's head whipped back and banged into the wall with a sickening crack. Pam let out a shriek. Dave saw Stephane's eyes roll back as his heavy frame slid downward. He gave him an extra shove to land him in a heap at the baseboards.

"Not the Lone Ranger." Dave said. "More like a New York Ranger."

Pam screamed again. She rushed forward and crouched down next to Zara, who lay on the floor, unconscious. Dave stepped over Stephane's motionless form to join them.

"She fainted," Pam said, placing her fingers to Zara's throat in search of her pulse. "She's not well. We have to get her out of here."

Dave needed no further urging. In a heartbeat, he scooped Zara's body from the carpet. He murmured the same words she'd said to him on the darkened shores of the Mediterranean what felt like aeons ago. "Okay, Lightning Girl, snap out of it, need your help here."

Pam opened the door to see Rejean rushing toward his

office at the sound of the commotion within. He stood aside as Dave carried Zara into the hallway and laid her on a couch in the reception area. "Get some water."

"I'm on it," Pam said, sprinting to the water cooler at the far end of the room.

"C'mon, babe. Wake up," Dave whispered, brushing her hair from her forehead.

Pam returned with a paper cup and held it to Zara's lips. "Z, drink this," she urged. Zara's head began to move and she opened her mouth to accept the water. She managed a small sip before it ran down the sides of her jaw. Her eyes opened partway and focused on Dave's face hovering over her. The tip of her tongue slipped out to lick the beads of moisture from her white-rimmed lips.

"Thunder Boy," she said weakly. "Are you really here?"

Dave exhaled in relief, an anxious smile quirking one side of his mouth. "Afraid so, mademoiselle. And I'm not leaving."

Zara closed her eyes again. "Good."

"Here's her coat and bag," Pam said, placing the shiny red tote on the floor next to the couch. "I'll hang on to the documents, for safekeeping. Take her home now, she needs rest. Tell her I'll call her later." She stood to leave. "Nice hit, by the way. Defenceman, huh?"

Dave regarded her curiously. "Once upon a time. Where are you going? Aren't you coming with us?"

Pam shook her head, and tossed him the keys Zara had given her. "Nuh-uh. You two have a lot of talking to do. And I don't wanna be here when Shit-head wakes up." She thumbed toward the hallway leading to Houle's office. "I suggest you do the same." She turned on her heel and left, her raven hair swishing behind her.

Dave stared after her for a second, until Zara began to stir. "It's not true, is it?" she said, her voice barely above a whisper. "Screwing your way to the top?" Her eyes looked glazed.

"You know it's not," he scolded her. "Hang on to me." He'd have to let Houle deal with Shit-head. Dave lifted her from the couch and curled her body tight against his chest. She felt so light, weighing almost nothing in his arms. He wondered what Pam meant by "she's not well." He cursed himself for not getting here sooner. He moved her carefully out of the office, into the elevator and down to the parking level, setting her on her feet as they reached the Mustang.

"Nice wheels, Thunder Boy." She spoke as if in a dream state, and it worried him.

"Glad you like it. Let's get you inside." He opened the passenger door and folded her delicate frame into the front seat. The air temperature in the parking garage seemed even colder than the outdoors. Dave draped her coat over her before climbing into the drivers' side.

"Mmm, comfy," she murmured. She looked on the verge of sleep. Something told him this wasn't a good sign, and decided he should keep her talking.

He leaned over and tucked the coat close around her. Damn, she looked beautiful. Every inch of his body ached with wanting to hold her. Hell, he wanted much more than that. "Are you okay?" were all the words he could muster.

Zara opened her eyes fully and looked at him as if seeing him for the first time. A pale hand reached out from under the coat and grabbed his shirt, pulling him closer. "Okay? Okay?" Her hand moved to slip behind his neck. "If that's all you've got, Mr. Smart-Ass, shut up and kiss me."

She pulled his head forward until their lips met in a kiss so hungry it caught him off-guard. Emotions he'd been holding back for so many days surfaced in a sizzling rush. His every limb felt made of molten lava as he enveloped her in a fiery embrace. She seemed to mold herself to his body as he did so, her kisses more and more urgent. He felt his erection pressing painfully against his jean zipper, and knew he wouldn't be able to contain himself for very long. Her reaction to him didn't help. She hoisted herself higher on the seat, climbing over the console between them and wedging herself in his lap.

The cabin of the Mustang didn't offer much room, but it mattered not. Their surroundings seemed to fall away, leaving nothing but their desire for one another to fill the space. He hadn't pictured their reunion in quite this way.

"Zara," he started, in between her fervent kisses. "Babe." Another kiss. He chuckled in delight at her attentions. "This isn't exactly a good place—"

She smothered his words with another kiss. "I said, shut up. It's perfect. We're alone where no one will find us. Like a lunar capsule in space." She undid the buttons on his shirt and roved her hands over the taut skin of his chest.

God. His dick grew harder as she continued to kiss him. Her body rubbed against the bulge in his jeans making it worse. "Hello to you, too," he said, when she finally drew back for breath.

"Hello," she whispered. Her eyes glistened with tears that threatened to spill down her cheeks. "I'm so sorry. About everything. I had no right to judge you, and I don't care about your past. I love you. And you came for me, so you must love me, too. I need to hear you say it."

She was right. He'd never openly spoken those words to her. The closest he came was in a text message, and once in the blinding moments of fucking the daylights out of her. How incredibly lame. She deserved so much better. He brought his hands to either side of her face and held her head steady so that she had no choice but to look into his eyes when he said it this time. "Zara Flynn, listen carefully. I…love…you, do you hear? I love you. And I'm never going to let you go."

He barely got the sentence out before she was kissing him again, her tongue seeking his, as if to suck the words from his mouth and swallow them, to keep them inside her forever. He reached down to ease the seat back and provide more room. The windows had already begun to fog up. A parking lot fuck? What the hell, he felt crazy as a teenager right now, his loins on fire. Her fingers were undoing his jeans and pulling on the zipper.

"Babe, are you sure you want to do this? Pam said you weren't well. I said I wouldn't ever hurt you, and..."—he swallowed hard—"I don't have any protection with me."

She smiled, and pushed his jeans down lower, releasing his throbbing cock. "It doesn't matter." She took hold of his shaft, stroking it. His pre-cum oozed down over her fingers. "I want you to hurt me," she said, her voice taking on a surreal, purring tone. "Hurt me good."

Rational thought left Dave's mind completely. He slipped his fingers under the waistband of her leggings and pushed the form-fitting material down over her hips, his palms gliding over her round buttocks. She flexed like a cat to slide her tall boots off, allowing him to push her bottoms past her knees and onto the floor. He felt dizzy as her earthy scent filled his nostrils. Jesus, he had to get inside her or he'd lose his mind.

Her breasts pressed against him as she raised up on her knees, straddling him. He slipped his hands around the back of her thighs and stroked the soft skin, feeling it prickle into goosebumps. His touch slid upward to her crotch, dipping his fingers into the soft lips of flesh around her entrance that were wet and hot for him. The sensation drove his arousal even higher.

Zara moaned and shuddered as his fingertips touched her clit, sliding forward and back again, pressing, squeezing and tapping in succession. The slippery tissue seemed to swell and writhe between his fingers and, by her rapid little cries, knew he'd found her magic spot. He rubbed the head of his dick back and forth against her well-primed slit a few times before pushing in. Her cries descended into a low groan as she let herself down upon him, matching his upward thrusts.

He lost himself inside her, his hands gripping her buttocks as they bounced up and down, smacking the tops of his thighs with each stroke. The scents of patchouli and sex swirled in his consciousness until oblivion beckoned, and he surged into climax with her body pounding against his. He let everything go.

"Give it to me, Thunder Boy…hurt me, fuck me raw. You belong to me."

The sound of his own heaving breath clouded his hearing. Did she speak those words or did he just imagine it? He liked the sound of them either way. Several moments passed as their bodies stilled, and heartbeats decelerated. Condensation ran in miniature rivers down the inside of the window glass.

"We can't stay here much longer." Dave said. "Let me take you somewhere. Anywhere."

Zara clung to him with her arms around his neck and her chin resting on top of his tousled head. "I'd like that. Take me home."

Chapter Twenty-One

Stephane eased himself out of his Jag, his knees stiff and his right shoulder bruised and throbbing. He dared not move his head left or right, the pain in his neck so intense. He pressed a button on his key fob and heard the familiar double chime of the alarm system activating. In the gathering dusk, he moved stiffly toward the back entrance of his office building. The fair-sized goose egg on his head pulsed miserably with each step, reminding him what a total fuck-up his day had turned out to be.

Options. He needed options now that Zara's personal cavalry had arrived. He still held the cards as far as staffing and project contracts went. Even if he wasn't elected to the Board, the fact remained that, thanks to him, Flynn Enterprises North America had no upcoming work, and no staff to execute it if there were. And it would remain that way until he got what he wanted: control of the company. One way or another.

His head hurt like hell, thanks to the punk-ass engineer. He wondered what sort of charm he could possibly have cast over Zara that would make a girl like her look at him twice. Stephane punched the security code on the keypad and entered the building. He'd have preferred to sleep in his own house, but for the moment, the executive suite attached to his office would have to suffice. He ignored the service lift in favour of the secure elevator to which he had the only key. The doors opened on command and he stepped in. The lift went straight to the top floor, and he limped painfully to the suite's entrance.

A few hours sleep, and he'd be able to think this thing out, like he always did. He entered a second key code and the light turned green. He twisted the lever and pushed the heavy door open, his shoulder protesting in pain. He lurched across the threshold and, balancing most of his weight on one foot, let it fall shut behind him.

He sniffed the air inside the dark room. It smelled funny. Like someone had smoked a cigar recently. He'd just been in here two days ago, what the fuck? Before his instincts could kick in, he felt a heavy blow to his shins that dropped him to his knees. Then another against his back, sending him face down on the carpet. He vaguely heard footsteps shuffling near him and a few words of muttered French, before he blacked out.

*

"Now what do we do with him?" Carlos asked, the wooden lamp base he'd struck the intruder with, still in his hand. He and Alain stood over Stephane's crumpled bulk in the darkened room.

"Stupide! Finish him off or run like hell. Either way you're in shit, ami. No place for you to go, now."

"There has to be someplace. You must know every dive in this frozen town."

"Merde!" Alain cursed. "I not your babysitter. We just robbed his office, can't hang around for your sake. Hit him again. Vamos."

Carlos bit his lip, and shifted the lamp from his right hand to his left. "I've never killed anyone before."

Alain snorted in disgust. "You mean, not by your own hand. The stuff you peddle kills plenty, Monsieur Bigshot. Do it, and I get you out of here." He moved toward the door as if to leave Carlos behind.

Carlos tightened both hands on the lamp, braced his footing, and swung. The wood splintered as it connected with Stephane's head. Carlos let the pieces fall to the floor then rushed out the door after Alain.

The two men took the stairs, bolting down flight after flight until they reached the ground floor and the exit. Darkness shielded them as they stepped outside.

"Where to now?" Carlos asked.

"Not together. You go first, cross that alley, turn right, onto the next street. I be right behind you." As Carlos hurried toward the alley, Alain slipped his cell phone from his pocket and took a photo of Carlos' retreating backside. Alain followed a few moments later, meeting up with him behind a city bus shelter on the next block. Dim light filtered through the shelter's grimy plexiglass panels. Any emotion Carlos felt remained hidden behind the man's olive complexion and Van-Dyke style beard.

"I give you an address," Alain said. "Don't go there until I tell you." Again he used his cell phone, and thumbed the keypad as though searching though his contacts. "Go to Café Paris, on Sainte-Catherine and Crescent. Wait there."

"How long will you be?"

"I have to arrange things with a friend first. Could be an hour, could be five minutes. Have an espresso. You need it. Go that way,"—Alain pointed—"turn left and take Sainte-Catherine to Crescent. On the corner, can't miss it."

Carlos nodded and turned to follow his instructions. Alain pressed the capture button once more then walked in the opposite direction. The image looked a bit motion-blurred, but recognizable as a man on the run. He grunted in satisfaction and put the phone away.

*

A single candle lit the bay window facing Avenue Melville. The table next to the window had been set with what unbroken dishes Zara could find, mismatched silverware, and brandy snifters that would have to double as wine glasses for the evening. The original wood-burning fireplace, retrofitted for natural gas, supplied a romantic, flickering glow at the flip of a switch.

"Are you sure you want to stay here tonight?" Dave asked. "We could get a hotel, you know. Get a massage, have a bubble bath, order room service? Pam said you needed rest."

Zara filled a saucepan of water from her kitchen sink, surrounded by the mess left behind by the break-in. "No way," she answered. "I owe you a dinner. You're not the only one who can cook." She turned to face him as he wrapped his arms around her.

"I'd hardly call spaghetti and meat sauce 'cooking'," he said. "But after a day like today, even peanut butter and jam would sound like a gourmet meal."

"Good. Because it might be all that's left in the cupboard after the spaghetti's gone."

"Seriously, babe." He lifted her to sit on the counter, and pressed her thighs open with his hips. The rough denim brushed against her skin. "Are you sick? Tell me what the hell's been going on."

Zara looked into those cobalt-blue eyes she adored, wishing she could drown in them. She ran her fingers through his wavy hair, grown longer than she'd ever seen it. He'd obviously had other things on his mind lately than visiting his hairstylist. As thrilled as she was that he'd come after her, burning questions filled her mind.

"You heard most of it already. Stephane Vanier is a self-centered, manipulative bastard. You could be in trouble. He's a lawyer and could have you up on assault charges after today. He's the one who contacted me when we were in Tenerife. I didn't know that it was all a set-up, to get me back here and trick me into giving him control of the Montreal office."

"Why would you listen to him? Why did you let him… touch you that way." His lips tightened and the blue eyes closed as if trying to block out the memory of the scene he'd stumbled upon in the Flynn office.

Zara put her arms around his neck and held him close. "Please. It wasn't what it looked like, you have to believe me. I hate him. I was trying to trap him, catch him in his lies."

"By seducing him? That's a pretty old trick." Dave's voice hardened. "I wouldn't have expected that from you."

Zara winced. He doesn't believe me. Her heart constricted at the thought she might lose him over all this, at a time when she'd realized beyond all doubt how she felt about him. She took a deep breath in.

"You said it yourself. Everyone has a past. Unfortunately, Stephane was part of mine. You were right, we can't punish each other for the past. We can only change the future." She rested her forehead against his. "So I need to know. Is…that woman…in your future?" Her throat went dry as she chose her next words. Her voice cracked, and tears stung her eyes as she spoke them. "Are you the father of her child?"

There. She'd let the words out, where they floated in the air like weighted balloons. She felt his body quiver in her embrace.

"Oh, Zara," he said, his voice almost a sob. He breathed in and out a few times, to regain his composure. "I can tell you that I believe, with all my heart and soul, that I am not. And that I will take any measures to prove it. And that it will not change my feelings, or my intentions, toward you. You are with me, in my heart, in my mind, in my soul. As I hope I am in yours."

His words ripped through her like a hot knife. There could be no mistake now, they were bonded to each other in every way that mattered. Zara felt something release within her, and tears streamed down her face. Her insides seemed to twist and buck in a mixture of joy and fear. "You are in me, my love," she said. "More than you know."

Water spilled over from the pot she'd set to boil for the pasta. The hissing noise startled them both, and they jerked away from each other. Zara reached for the controls and switched the burner off. "Are you still hungry?" she asked.

Dave appeared shaken as he stood back from her and the stove. The steam rose in a cloud between them, as he looked at her with an almost frightening intensity. "Yeah. But not for spaghetti."

"It can wait," Zara said. She sat on the counter top, her bare feet dangling like a lost girl in a playground. His arms went around her again, and lifted her off the granite surface. Her legs wrapped around his back as he carried her to the adjoining room. They tumbled onto the floor in front of the fireplace, atop scattered magazines, books and cushions.

The warmth of the flames caressed their already heated bodies. "We're going to starve to death, aren't we?" he said. "In a city full of great restaurants."

"But what a way to go," she answered, and they both began to laugh. As they lay together in the flickering light of the fire, he stroked her hair and gazed into her face, seeming to struggle for any further words. Zara spoke first. "I'm done here. I miss the sun, and the sea. Let's go home tomorrow."

Dave's hands stopped moving. "I thought this was your home. You said so when you left me at the airport."

Her lips retracted into a thin line, then relaxed again. "I was wrong. The longer I stay here, the more I realize what I really came here to do. Close a door. This place represents…a life I no longer live."

They fell silent for several moments, the meaning of her words sinking in. "So what happens to this apartment?" he asked.

"I'll sell it. My car, too. Montreal means nothing to me, anymore."

"What about the Flynn operations here?"

Zara shook her head. "I'm not sure. But I'll figure it out, somehow."

Dave smiled, and placed his hand behind her head, pulling her into his chest. "That's the Lightning Girl I know. Invincible." She clung to him, willing her body to meld with his, become one. "I have a surprise for you," he whispered. "When we get back."

Zara squeezed him tighter, alerting her senses to his every muscle and curve. A rush of heat swept through her, settling between her legs. "I have a surprise for you, too. And I don't think it can wait until we get back."

He pulled his head back, enough to look into her eyes. "What?"

It was all or nothing, now. She inhaled a steady breath.

"I'm pregnant."

Chapter Twenty-Two

Alain counted the cash from the envelope Vanier had given him the week before. Five thousand, in older bills. Better than nothing, but only half of what Vanier promised. Poor dumb shit. Would have been better if he'd died. However, dead or alive, the situation had two redeeming factors. He came away with a very nice cache of stolen goods, and he could still sink Sabados. He headed for the public library. The computers there wouldn't leave a trail, and he could upload his photos and forward his anonymous news tip from there. He thought about the Spaniard waiting for his call, and couldn't decide who was dumber, the Spaniard or the Lawyer.

*

It bit him. The dolphin's pointed jaws closed around his hand in a swift lunging attack, then released it and swam off, giving an insolent flip of its tail. He expected his hand to bleed and sting, yet it remained whole and unmarked. The dolphin's body disappeared into the dark depths below, leaving a sinuous trail of bubbles. Dave swam upward, toward the light; the nearer he got, the more difficult it seemed to break the surface. Something held him back. He clawed at the circle of bright water, unable to send even a fingertip into the air above. He panicked. He felt something slick swipe across his foot, and looking down, saw the dolphin gliding below him, circling and brushing up against him. Its black eyes glinted in the murky abyss. He tried for the water's surface again, when he suddenly felt lifted from below. The damn thing had swum underneath him, forcing him to ride its back like an aquarium trainer.

It rose higher, bringing him closer to the precious circle of light that meant salvation. They surfaced, and sped toward the shore in a spray of water and waves. He pitched forward, landing face-first while the dolphin slipped away with the receding surf. He lay prone on the hard, wet beach, struggling for air as he spat out seawater and grains of sand that filled his mouth.

He coughed, and opened his eyes to reality. Alone in a bed, in a room he didn't recognize. Blood thundered in his ears like remnants of the ocean from his dream. He growled in anger, wondering when in holy hell the vile creature would leave his dreams in peace. As his breathing slowed, his surroundings became clear—Zara's condo on Avenue Melville. But he lay there alone.

He righted himself off the mattress, his eyes searching the room for her. Her words echoed in his brain. I'm pregnant. A thousand emotions ran through him; happiness, fear, anticipation, awe. He wanted this with her, yet somehow felt he'd cheated, robbed her of the joy of her announcement. Where had she gone? He heard water running, and his panic eased. Rubbing the sleep from his eyes, he rose and crept to the bathroom.

*

Bubble-clouds danced on the surface of the bath water as

Zara stretched out in the tub. She closed her eyes and inhaled the delicious fragrances of melon and coconut that rose from them. She heard footsteps approaching, and the familiar creak of her wooden bathroom door. She opened her eyes to see Dave standing there in the nude, all tanned skin and sculpted muscle on display. No tattoos marred his arms or shoulders. Nothing to obscure the view of his youthful, athletic body, from the muscled calves to the tight cords of his neck. And in between, his smooth chest, well-defined abs, and unreasonably cute belly button called out for attention. Her eyes followed the feathery field of hair that began just below his navel and thickened into a soft forest surrounding his impressive cock. Although not a new sight, it still made her insides go hot just looking at him.

"Hi," he said. "Everything okay?"

Zara doused the lusty thoughts forming in her brain. She nodded, the sound of his voice making her smile. "Oui, Monsieur. Care to join me?"

His slow advance toward her, stark naked and in full daylight, was possibly the sexiest thing she'd ever seen. She raised her eyes to his face, and he tilted his head as if questioning her stare. A swath of hair fell across his forehead and over one eye as he did so, making him seem charmingly boyish. The slow-burning smile that she'd come to know so well began its progress across his lips, his adorable dimples forming along with it. They creased his angular jaw, accentuating the day's worth of beard that covered it in just the right places. God, she could eat him up.

Zara leaned forward and wrapped her arms around her knees, making room for him to step into the bath behind her. The water level rose as he slipped down into the water, leaning his chest in tight against her back, and drawing his knees around either side of her. The sloshing water licked at them, leaving daubs of bubbles sticking to their skin. He pulled her wet hair aside and kissed the nape of her neck. His cock pressed against her bottom. She shivered.

He said nothing, but reached for the shower puff and tube of gel on the tub ledge. Squeezing a few drops onto the puff, he stroked it across the wet skin of her back. Down, then up, across and down, up in a circle around her shoulder blades, over the little bump on the back of her neck. She reveled in his touch, and the fact that even this simple motion could get her aroused as hell. No matter that they'd been making love all night, she felt ready for him all over again. She hoped that wouldn't stop in the months to come.

"Will you still rub my back like this when I'm big and fat?" she asked.

He kept scrubbing in the same steady motion. "Nope. I'll do it even better."

Zara giggled. "I'll hold you to that." She concentrated on the gentle passes of the shower puff, enjoying every second of it. Dave hadn't seemed shocked when she broke the news to him. Quite the opposite. The look of pure joy and unabashed tears in his luscious blue eyes when she told him made her breathe a silent prayer of thanks. But, at the moment, this uncharacteristic absence of words disturbed her.

The puff plopped down in front of her. He began smoothing handfuls of bath water over her to rinse off the suds. Even this innocent contact sent bolts of desire through her, and her breathing elevated. When he touched the back of her neck, his motion stopped.

"Where's your necklace?" he asked.

Zara thought for a second. "The coral one?"

"No, the silver one."

She recalled the morning at Stephane's house. "The chain broke. I lost it." Why did he want to know?

At his continued silence, the bath water began to feel chill, quelling her body's rising need for him. "We have a big day, we should get going."

He cupped her breasts. "Not yet. Breakfast first."

"We'll have to get out of the tub for that."

"Not for this kind of breakfast." He rolled her nipples between his thumb and forefingers.

She tilted her head back, trying to ignore the urgent tingling in her breasts. No good. They hardened into little pebbles and she sighed in surrender. "Don't forget, I'm eating for two, then."

His hands slid down around her thighs and in between her legs, nudging them apart. "I like the sound of that," he said, fingertips sliding toward her center beneath the sweet-smelling bubbles.

The red handbag lay on the floor in the empty bedroom, and the repeated buzzing of Zara's phone inside it went unheeded.

*

Zara prepared to say goodbye to the apartment on Avenue Melville as she packed a few last belongings. She felt no regret at leaving now, convinced that her true future lay elsewhere. Montreal had never been kind to her. The more she considered this, the faster she seemed to move. Suddenly nothing seemed as important as getting away from this place.

She went for her phone to see what flights they could book. Between them, she and Dave had decided to return to Tenerife and pick up their interrupted vacation where they left off. She plucked the phone from her bag, and swore aloud. "Shit. I forgot to charge this. Dead as nails." She dug for her charger in another bag, and plugged in.

Dave joined her in the living room with his knapsack slung over one shoulder. "Que pasa?" he asked as she scrolled through the list of calls.

"The Flynn office," she said, casting him an ominous glance. She punched the reply, and got Houle on the line.

"Mademoiselle Flynn, are you all right? I've been trying to reach you."

"Tres bien, thank you for your concern. Please let me apologize for causing such an unpleasant incident yesterday. I do plan to resolve the situation."

"I'm sure you will, Miss." Houle paused. "But I'm afraid I have some bad news." He cleared his throat before continuing. "Monsieur Vanier's office called. There's been a robbery, and he didn't show up for his appointments this morning. They found him in the executive suites, unconscious. He's been attacked, and they've taken him to the hospital."

Zara felt the room start to shrink around her. "Oh, my God." Her throat tightened, unable to respond further. Dave looked over in concern.

"The last they heard from him, he was on his way to our office yesterday. That's why they called. I told them he left here around four o'clock, but didn't go into detail. I'm afraid the situation won't look good for Mr. Parker if the police start to investigate. I don't mean to suggest anything, but can you tell me where you and Mr. Parker went last night after you left?"

Zara swallowed, summoning enough moisture in her mouth to speak. "We went to my apartment. On Avenue Melville. We're still here, in fact." She ran her tongue over her dry lips. I need to know. "What is his…Mr. Vanier's, condition? Is he all right?" Dave shot her a 'what the hell?' look.

Rejean took a breath. "Critical, I'm afraid. Trauma to the head, I'm told. But, I assure you, he left here under his own power. A little bruised, perhaps. Mostly his ego, I think. What happened in there? I'd like to…as you said…hear it from you."

"I have reason to believe Mr. Vanier is seeking control of

the Board for his own gain. He also made some disparaging remarks, racial slurs toward my friend. Mr. Parker took offense to these actions and…became physical. He defended us." She paused, thinking about the situation she'd left Houle in. "If the police do question you, Rejean, please be truthful. We have nothing to hide. I'll keep in touch." She disconnected and set the phone down to continue charging. "Stephane's in hospital."

Dave lifted one eyebrow. "He deserves it."

Zara shook her head. "No, not like that. Someone attacked him in his office last night, during a robbery. He's in critical condition."

Chapter Twenty-Three

Zara and Dave stopped at Grant's Auto and paid for the inspection of the BMW before heading to the airport. Dave insisted that Zara eat, so they met Pam for brunch, where Zara handed her a key and a folded pink paper.

"What's this?" Pam asked, her eyes widening in query.

"Got a loonie on you?" Zara asked.

"A loonie? Why?"

"Because I've signed the registration as sold to you for a dollar. The Beamer's yours. You can keep it, or sell it. Consider it your commission for listing my condo."

Pam looked at her silently. "Z, that's too much. I can't take your Beamer."

Zara closed her hands around Pam's as she clutched the keychain. "You can, and you will. I insist."

Pam's lips formed a stubborn pout. "I'll do it only because you've asked me to. But it feels so final. Am I ever going to see you again?"

Zara smiled at her friend. "Of course you will. In fact, why don't' you come and see me, next time? In Spain. I'll book your ticket whenever you say."

"How about when baby is born?" Pam winked at both of them.

Dave rubbed Zara's back at these words. "Consider it done," he answered for her.

"I'm on shift at the hospital tonight," Pam said. "I can check on, you know who. I feel terrible calling him Shit-head now. Sounds like he's hurt bad."

"They might question you about yesterday afternoon. You're an eyewitness."

Pam nodded solemnly. "Well, I can only tell them what I saw."

*

Just after five p.m., Ivette folded towels and stacked them at all the wash stations on her last day at the Bella Spa. She refilled all the product bottles in the back, and stocked all the retail shelves in the front. She'd volunteered to close up the shop for the day, so she wouldn't have to face everyone's long good-byes.

The other stylists congratulated her on her new business, asked her keep in touch. She couldn't tell any of them that her plans had changed, or indeed, may never even happen. She'd kept a straight face, too self-centered to admit defeat in public, but her determination and optimism of a few weeks ago had weakened, along with her resolve to book her medical visit to Amsterdam. Her pocketbook just wasn't looking that good.

She turned on the wall-mounted TV in the customer lounge for some background noise. At this hour, the international news channel sprang to life, but having no intention of watching, she began to turn away when a familiar face flashed on the screen. Ivette froze. She focused on the Spanish captioning that translated the English voiceover.

"…identified as Juan Carlos Sabados, wanted for trafficking crimes in Europe. Apprehended at a Montreal coffee house, an anonymous tip placed Sabados at the scene of the robbery, and is also a suspect in the assault on prominent local lawyer, Stephane Vanier, found critically injured in the adjoining executive suite. After the hearing, Sabados is expected to be extradited to his home country within a few days to face charges…"

Carlos would be coming home…alive. Headed straight for jail, most likely, but alive. Ivette exhaled a breath she didn't realize she was holding. Her heart seemed divided into two halves, one horrified at the bad news, and the other rising in crazy hope that she'd be with him again soon. That he'd return to witness the birth of his child.

Ivette straightened. That this thought had entered her mind took her aback. She hadn't planned to give birth at all, let alone assume she and Carlos might continue life together as a family. She looked around the empty salon, her senses racing. Her life would feel just as empty if she didn't try to make a success of herself, with or without Carlos. And even emptier if she ignored this chance to have a child. Perhaps she'd never be able to have another.

If she could just get the money, she could still open her new business, pregnant or not. Lots of women did. Just then it struck her as a challenge, to run a successful business and raise a child at the same time. Ivette never backed away from a challenge. Now, her course seemed clear. She would get the money somehow.

The door chime sounded. With a sigh of frustration, Ivette realized she hadn't yet locked the entrance. She turned away from the TV, about to shout "estamos cerrados," when her mouth froze open.

The last person she ever expected to see again stood there in the doorway. She blinked in surprise, and felt a smile spread over her face. "Well, if it isn't El Filósofo," she said. "What a surprise."

Jorge grinned, looking quite uncomfortable. Ivette thought it amusing. She hadn't met anyone so utterly unaware of his own charm. She tilted her head questioningly. "What are you doing here?"

Jorge cleared his throat. "I decided I needed a haircut. You do that here, si?"

Ivette nodded. "And you just happened to come across this shop?"

He stood with his grin stuck in place for a few awkward seconds. "You gave me your card, remember?"

Ivette raised her eyebrows. "That's right, I did." She stepped toward one of the stylists chairs and patted the headrest, indicating for him to sit.

Jorge cleared his throat. "I was thinking about you a lot, your situación, I mean. I thought, I might be of some help, so I…"

As his voice faded off, she patted the chair again, and he obediently sat down. She pivoted the chair toward the mirror, both their faces reflected in it as she stood behind him. The more she looked, the more she found attractive about him. He had a well-shaped face, symmetrical. Squarish chin, not too wide nor pointed. An aquiline, almost regal, sort of nose. His ginger-brown eyes held a brightness that said he had seen much in his lifetime. How old…35, 45? She couldn't guess.

She reached for a comb and set to work on his hair. Thick and curly, there were no signs of gray in it. "You hardly know me. Why should you help me? And anyway, you already know I need a lot of money. "

Facing the mirror seemed to lessen Jorge's nervousness. He had no difficulty maintaining eye contact this way, and Ivette found his gaze remarkably intense.

"Lo se. How much do you need?" he asked without blinking.

*

The big jet touched down at Los Rodeos airport on Tenerife's north coast. The jolting rumble of the flaps meeting the runway lifted Zara's head off Dave's shoulder. For the first time, she'd slept almost an entire flight, and smiled at awakening not only to sunny skies, but the comforting scents of leather, denim and Lacoste cologne that he wore.

As the aircraft came to a stop, Zara switched on her phone. A number of calls began to download on the screen, mostly from Marlena. She hit the reply button and waited for her mother to answer.

After three rings, Marlena picked up. Longer than usual.

"Hola?" came the response, in a somewhat sleepy tone.

"Mom?" Zara asked, puzzled.

"Oh, Zara darling. Where are you?"

"I've just landed in Tenerife. We're going to finish our vacation. What are you up to? Did I wake you?"

"No, querida." Marlena's voice vibrated in a tender chuckle. "I'm quite all right. I take it David is with you?"

"Yes. Everything's fine. We'll be home at the end of the week. We…need some time alone." She grabbed Dave's hand as they walked through the pedway into the arrivals area. "How are you doing? I've been thinking, we can't stay at the Club forever. We need to find a more permanent home. And Jorge, too."

Marlena laughed aloud. "Si, I agree. Why don't you build one?"

"My thoughts exactly." Zara smiled, grateful for the intuitiveness she and her mother shared. "There's room enough to build two villas. So, tell Ernesto to hurry up with prepping the El Mirador site. When you see him next."

"Si. I'll do that. Call me with your flight details, so I can send Jorge to get you."

The phone signaled another call waiting. "Thanks, Mom.

Adios." They'd reached the baggage carousel, and Zara threw Dave an exasperated look as she pressed the call answer.

"Hola, Senorita Flynn? This is Roberta Diaz, the estate agent in Puerto de la Cruz. We spoke last week?"

"Si, I remember you, Senora Diaz." How could she forget the obstinate woman who had no answers to her questions about the old restaurant building? "What can I do for you?"

"Well, if you are still interested, there may be something I can do for you."

"Oh? What's that?"

"The port authority has changed the inspection clause on the property you inquired about. I've been trying to reach you. They are willing to waive the inspection if you can make an offer in the next 48 hours. Unfortunately that was yesterday and you're down to 12 hours now."

Zara's heart leapt. An omen, that she'd made the right decision in returning to Spain. Everything seemed to be falling in place. "I'm interested. But I'll want to see the place, close-up. We weren't able to go inside before. Can someone meet us there, and take us to your office to close the deal if all goes well?"

"I'll make some calls. We close at eight, but I can make some after-hours arrangements."

"Muy bien. I'll go there now, and look around while I wait." They were almost at the exit, and Zara thrust her arms into the air in triumph.

"Oh, Jesus," said Dave as they passed through the revolving glass doors. "Here we go again."

"Sorry, Thunder Boy. I have to meet this lady before eight o'clock. Go check us in, and I'll be there as soon as I'm done, okay?"

Dave shook his head in surrender. "Okay, but I warn you. Acquire any more derelict properties, and I'll have to tie you up."

Zara's eyes lit up. "Promises, promises." She sidled up behind him and stroked his tight, jean-clad butt, pressing her body against his. "If I don't swing this deal, I deserve to be tied up. Do I get to choose? Leather, or handcuffs?"

Dave's mouth quirked as if visualizing the alternatives, and weighing the merits of each. "Gentleman's choice."

The humidity outdoors struck Zara in the chest like a hammer. The usual sunny skies had turned hazy and reflected a sick, yellowish glow.

"Weird," Dave said. "Seems like a storm brewing."

*

"My querida is coming home," Marlena said as she tucked her cell phone into her purse and rolled over on the blanket. She propped her head up on one elbow.

Picnic dinners had become a habit of late, and the unusually warm December day sent a pleasant breeze across the park. She looked over at Ernesto, reclining on the blanket in a similar position. He wore a casual pair of slacks and a short sleeved cotton shirt. Several of the upper buttons were left undone, revealing more skin than he'd exposed in quite some time.

"Esta bien," Ernesto replied. "That will make you happy, I know. And I'll be happy to have David back."

Marlena giggled. "Si. She asked me to tell you something next time I see you. She has no idea I've seen you every day since they left."

"Tell me what?"

"To get busy with the site preparation of El Mirador. She wants to start building."

Ernesto smiled. "She's in for a surprise, then. I take it David didn't let on what he's accomplished."

Marlena shook her head and sat up. "Do you want to go for a walk?"

"Good idea." Ernesto began gathering the picnic things, but out of the corner of his eye, followed the movement of Marlena's lithe body as she stood and brushed a few stray crumbs off her skirt. When she leaned over to fold up the blanket, he took a long gulp from his unfinished bottle of Perrier before looking away.

"This way?" he asked, pointing in the direction of the park's central fountain.

"Okay." They strolled together up the cobbled path, despite the falling dusk.

Neither spoke until they reached a grove of trees that arched overhead. "Marly, what will this mean for you, when El Mirador is transformed? Have you decided whether you want to stay?" Ernesto asked.

Marlena slowed to a stop. "I haven't. If Zara needs me, I will stay. But there are things to be done back home. Bills to be paid, appointments to keep. I have guests invited for Christmas."

Damn. He felt no closer to gaining a commitment from her either way. He thought the time they'd spent together recently had made her consider certain possibilities. It seemed so obvious. Stay here, start a renewed chapter in her life. With him. "I understand. And after that?"

She looked at him with an expression of frustration. "I don't know. What is it you want me to say?"

Ernesto felt steel forming in his spine. If she wouldn't speak her mind now, she never would. It was up to him. Is that how Tristan captured her? Being forceful and controlling? Worth a try. He moved in close, placing his hands on her shoulders. He maneuvered her toward the sturdy trunk of a black oak. Her back met the rough bark, and he held her firm against it, moving one hand down to her waist, and placing the other flat against the tree, framing her in.

"Say you'll stay." His lips came within millimeters of hers, their noses brushing. "Say you'll marry me." He held her eyes captive, not allowing her to look away. They seemed to expand, become luminous. So beautiful, he thought his heart might burst if they broke contact. So he refused let it happen. He consumed her mouth with his own, his skin rough and hot against hers cool and tender. He slid his hand up to her breast, his thumb grazing the nipple through the sheer fabric of her blouse.

Marlena twitched and stiffened, trapped between him and the tree trunk. A soft grunt echoed from her throat. He kissed her harder, unrelenting, until he felt her acquiesce. He pressed his whole body against hers, making her acknowledge his need, then pulled his lips away just enough to whisper. "Say it, Marly. You know this is right."

The sight of her pert bosoms moving up and down with each anxious breath she took nearly drove him mad. "Ernesto," she gasped. "Make love to me…please."

Chapter Twenty-Four

Dave opened the doors to the balcony of their hotel suite. The air conditioning seemed to have failed, leaving the room in a tight, stuffy state. He stepped out, hoping for a cleansing breeze to alleviate the stifling atmosphere. No luck. The yellow-tinged clouds hunkered overhead, sucking the very life from the streets of Puerto de la Cruz.

In the courtyard below, the swimming pool offered a blue oasis amid the gloom. He watched some children splashing about in it, riding colorful foam noodles and tossing beach balls across its surface. Their parents lounged on padded deck chairs nearby. He pictured himself among them, stealing vigilant glances at the little ones from behind magazine pages, ever watchful. The hubbub of delighted squeals and carefree laughter floated up to him, making him smile. A new and different kind of life lay ahead of him. He couldn't wait to show Zara the progress on the El Mirador site.

Turning back inside the room, he decided to take a shower while he waited for her return. He reached for the house phone to make a dinner reservation for later, one he planned would be the most romantic and extravagant in history.

*

Zara gathered her hair behind her head with both hands. The wind had picked up enormous velocity and seemed to come from all directions at once. She tied it in a makeshift knot to keep at least the longest strands out of her face. She checked her watch, and re-set it to local time. Nearly seven o'clock. The estate agent had better show up soon, or the deal might be lost. Los Tiedes, as she decided to call it, stood resolute on its scrap of beach just ahead, ugly and desolate as before. Its conical roof jutted into the gray sky, the light passing through its missing windows forming rectangular eyes that seemed to glow dully at her.

"You will be fantastic!" she shouted at the abandoned walls. "My father said so." That constituted an anointment, of sorts, one Zara swore to uphold. A drop of rain struck her face. She looked upward, noting the heavy clouds had sunk lower and taken on a darker, more menacing hue. She clutched her sweater about herself, and stepped closer to the building. The roof seemed more or less intact. If it did start to rain, it looked safe enough to stand under.

It took only moments for the fat, random raindrops to accelerate into a steady patter. A low rumble reverberated from the temperamental sky, and Zara found herself at the entrance to the structure, hiding under its shallow overhang. At least a hundred meters of open sand stretched between Los Tiedes and the nearest building.

The rain increased to a pelting onslaught, driving sideways so that even the roof overhang afforded no shelter. Zara turned her back to it, and faced the open maw of the old restaurant. The sign with its faded red letters swung loose in the wind. When her shoulders were soaked through with wetness, she stepped inside.

The place smelled of rotting wood, mingled with the

scent of new rain pushing in from outside. The floorboards were missing in several places. She stepped carefully around the open holes to a stable area near one wall. A dull flash of lightning illuminated the windows for a split-second then went dark again. The rain drummed a frantic rhythm on the roof. She told herself it would pass in a few minutes, and she might as well make herself comfortable. She dropped her red handbag onto the weathered planks and sat down cross-legged next to it.

And waited.

Lightning flashed again. She counted, like she did as a child, the number of seconds between the lightning and the thunderclap, each second equaling one mile distant. One-one thousand, Two-one thousand…Crack! Rumble, rumble. Two miles.

The wind howled through the openings, dropping the temperature, but failing to ease the cloying humidity. She hugged her knees and put her head down, condensing herself into a tight ball.

Another flash. One-one thousand, Crack! Way louder this time. The wall she leaned against shook and buckled, and she heard a tinkling remnant of glass falling from the windowpanes on the upper floor. Shit. Not a good place to be. Darkness set in at a rapid pace, her surroundings taking on a surreal and sinister cast. She bit her lip, willing the storm to abate.

She began to hyperventilate, inhaling and exhaling in short, frequent bursts. Considering its sudden arrival, perhaps the storm would depart just as quickly. She clung to this thought, rocking back and forth on her rump on the rough wooden floor.

Another brilliant flash illuminated the space, the millisecond of light throwing sharp shadows off the irregular, crumbling interior. Zara closed her eyes, the vestigial image of broken wall panels leaving a ghostly face to linger in her mind. Crack! The deafening thunderclap made her jump. Not even a count of one. The storm hovered directly overhead.

Her nostrils tingled. The musty air became overcharged with a sharper, stranger odor. On reflex, she shot to her feet, and propelled herself to the doorway. The arched entrance lit up with the next bolt of lightning before she could get even one foot across it. The teetering wooden sign broke free and blew away with the wind. She tumbled out onto the surrounding beach, her ears filled with the hideous sound and smell of splintering, burning wood. She crawled and scrambled toward the water, when something whacked across the back of her neck and made her see stars. She felt about to vomit before her vision faded to black.

*

His text messages went unanswered. Nearly two hours had passed since they'd parted ways at the airport, and the skies roiled and sparked with the oncoming storm. Dave couldn't wait any longer. He laced up his running shoes and left the hotel, striking out along the Playa toward the site of El Pescadore, or whatever she called it.

He passed the bars and restaurants, souvenir shops and market stalls, away from the lighted, paved walkways. No vendors lined the strand hawking their paintings and jewelry at this time of night. He picked up his pace, running almost full out into the darkness beyond. Lightning ripped the sky in jagged scratches. He hadn't seen this kind of storm since he'd left Thunder Bay, and knew better than to be out in the open in such weather activity. But it didn't stop him. Zara might be out there in the dark.

After about ten minutes, he could make out the shape of the old building in the distance with the help of intermittent lightning blasts. Rain pelted down, hitting him in the face and shoulders. The sand squelched beneath his feet, making running more difficult. Thunder rumbled in the wake of the lightning, the wind pushing the rain nearly horizontal against him. He closed the distance between himself and the cylindrical structure, to within about 100 meters, when a horrific bolt of lightning reached down its blinding-white tentacles and struck its conical spire.

Along with an earthshaking roll of thunder came a screeching sound unlike anything he'd heard before. Smoke began to rise from the roof of the building, and Dave flattened himself on the wet sand, waiting for the next strike. He kept an eye on the roof line, while gaining a sense of which direction the storm might be traveling before getting up again. It appeared to be moving to the south, and he took off at a dead sprint toward the smoldering shack.

Like a bad movie, the distance between him and his destination seemed to stretch and expand the faster he ran. Fifty meters, forty, thirty. When he reached the ten meter mark, he could see torn wooden boards hanging over the empty entrance at crazy angles. The whole affair seemed to be self-destructing, loose siding hanging from its walls as if it were shedding its skin. Sparks flared from the roof and sputtered in the drenching rain. The smell of singed wood carried across the beach on wisps of smoke.

He saw no other motion on the near side of the thing, so as he slowed his pace, he veered left to circle the building and scan its perimeter. He could see the angry surf crashing against the sand on the seaward side, the breakers reflecting what dull light remained. The beach appeared as an indistinct band of grey. A flash of lighting, dimmed by cloud cover, spread a temporary brightness over the area. Enough to reveal a rounded shape plastered to the sand by the driving rain.

A body.

Dave blocked all the thoughts that clamored for attention in his brain, refusing to let an irrational conclusion spring forward from the din. He let all sound drop from his consciousness, focusing on accelerating his strides to reach the sodden form. He almost didn't want to know, willing it to be some unknown person who'd fallen down drunk in the storm. The body lay on its side, and he dropped to his knees beside it.

He recognized the material of Zara's sweater.

Oh, God, no!

He gritted his teeth, and placing his shaking hands on her shoulder, rolled her onto her back across his lap. Her left arm flopped toward him. Soaking wet strands of hair stuck to her face, covering the bridge of her nose and the tip of her chin. Her eyes were closed, and he felt something leave his body in a baleful howl. His nightmare had just become reality. Worse than that, because there were two lives at stake now.

A chilling gush of water swept over them as she lay unmoving in his arms, soaking them to the skin before fleeing back from whence it came. Bits of seaweed clung to her hair, and he brushed it away from her face while shielding her from the pelting rain.

"Zara!" he shouted over the cacophony of breaking surf, hammering raindrops, and rumbling thunder. "Zara!" He stroked her forehead, her cheeks, her chin. In his dream, she'd always been alive before the lightning flash. Then afterward, her eyes would freeze open and she would slip away from him somehow. And always, the dolphin mocked him. Then he realized that none of these conditions were present. In fact, they were the opposite. Her eyes lay closed, he held her tight in his grasp and no ghastly metal creature hung around her neck. The outcome could be changed.

He hoisted her upward, and over one shoulder, intending to haul her away bodily. As he pushed to his feet, she coughed and spat water. Dave's heart did a joyous flip.

"Damn you, must you always scare the living hell out of me?" he shouted. Her feet kicked weakly, and he slid her down to land on her toes, keeping her tight against him. He framed her face with both hands, and looked into her green eyes that sparkled with life, not pale death. "Now, you literally are Lightning Girl. When will you ever listen to me?"

Zara's lips trembled as the rain splattered her face. "When will you ever stop rescuing me?" Her voice sounded choked and thin. She licked away the drops that kept rolling into her mouth. "I—I guess you'll have to tie me up."

"Yeah, I'll tie you up, all right," he said, pressing her face to his chest and cradling the back of her head. They had to get out of the rain and the ruined Pescadore offered the only shelter available. Dave herded them both under its ripped and sagging roof.

As the storm moved off, the rain settled to a calmer, steady drumming overhead. Dave moved to the driest part of the interior, and sat them both down on the wooden floor. The red bag lay on its side nearby, its contents partially spilled.

"I can't take much more of this, babe. No more abandoned buildings, okay!" His voice came off angrier than he'd meant. "Are you hurt? And don't say 'I'm fine.' Because you're going to a hospital either way." He removed his shirt, using it to wipe away the wet and sand from her arms and face as he examined her. No cuts or wounds were visible in the inadequate light. "Wasn't someone meeting you here? What the hell happened?"

Zara coughed. "The estate agent was supposed to..." She spotted her cellphone amid the pile of junk from her purse. "My phone," she said, pointing. Dave leaned over to retrieve it.

She took it from him with wobbly hands and thumbed its keypad.

"No signal. They couldn't even call me." She dropped her hands in her lap. "No one showed."

Dave sighed. "Well, we have to get you out of here. I want

you checked over. No arguments," he said, and began scooping up the littered bits into her red bag. "This damn thing," he said, tugging on the shoulder strap, "Is the luckiest piece of shit ever. I think it would survive a nuclear meltdown."

Zara started to laugh, then sucked air in rapid breaths. She seemed paler than the thin moonlight that had begun to emerge from behind the clouds. Instinct told Dave that something was horribly wrong. He scrambled over to her, just as they heard shouts from outside and footsteps on the wet sand. Narrow beams of light began to flash and undulate toward them.

"Senorita Flynn?" a woman's voice called. "It's Roberta, are you in there?"

Zara bowed her head, as if in total fatigue. "Hurts…" she said, before tilting sideways and slumping toward the floor. Dave grabbed her.

"In here!" he shouted as the bouncing flashlight found the opening to the place. Roberta and another man stood in the entrance. "Call an ambulance," Dave said as he slipped an arm under Zara's legs and eased her flat onto the floor.

"Call 911," Roberta said to the man accompanying her. She turned to the pair huddled inside. "I'm Roberta Diaz, from Isla Real Estate. I'm so sorry, the storm came up without warning. Is she all right?"

"I don't think so," Dave said. In the beam of Roberta's flashlight, he saw his arm coated with blood.

Chapter Twenty-Five

Zara smiled as she watched the carousel spin and spin. The summer air seemed to sparkle and shimmer all around. Excited carnival sounds reverberated in her ears, the sounds of children's laughter and calliopes, bells and firecrackers.

The pretty, painted horses cantered up and down on their metal poles as the carousel turned, their faces frozen in pony-grimaces. But where were the children? Not a single one rode on their bejeweled backs. She stopped smiling. There were no children, no people at all, at this carnival. The carousel slowed, and the music seemed to bend and fall out of tune.

The scene faded to white, leaving only the echoes of the disjointed melody in her head. She opened her eyes to a room equally white. Boring, standard ceiling panels connected to pale walls devoid of any decoration. Moving her head, she took in more of the scenery, which consisted of a TV, a radiator, a window, an IV stand and small night table. Turning the other way brought a better view. A sleeping Dave sat in an armchair next to her bed, one arm draped over the side and the other propping his head up with his fist. His brown hair fell across his face in street-gang fashion.

He'd said he would take her to a hospital, but this seemed

excessive. Her gaze fell on the thin plastic tubing running from the hanging IV bag, and followed it to where it connected. *Good Lord. I'm hooked up.* Her foot kicked out from under the sheet and bumped the metal stand. The noise woke Dave up. He raised his head, and inhaled a long breath. Then he jerked upright, tossed the hair out of his eyes, and stared at her.

"Babe," he said. "Thank God…you're back. How are you feeling?" He rose from the chair and leaned his hands on the edge of the bed. He looked tired, dark hollows forming beneath his eyes. "I was so worried."

Zara blinked a few times. "You worry too much, Thunder Boy. How long have I been here?" she asked.

"Since last night. Do you remember anything?"

She thought about it. "I remember the storm. I remember you and I sitting inside…Los Tiedes." She gulped in disappointment. The building she'd hoped to buy was beyond salvaging at any cost, now.

"Los Tiedes?" Dave questioned. "I thought it was 'Pescadore' ".

"That's what Dad called his drawing," she said, frowning. "What's the deal? Did I break something?" She checked under the covers. No broken leg, not even a bandage.

Dave bit his lip. "You lost a lot of blood."

"I did? I don't see—" She broke off upon seeing his expression. His handsome face twisted oddly, his dimples contorting as he looked away, struggling to fight back his emotions. More memories coalesced in her mind. Pain. Blurred images of flashing red lights. A medical crest on the sleeve of someone bent over her.

"My baby," she whispered hoarsely.

He turned his face back to her, his cobalt-blue eyes drowning in tears. He shook his head. "No. Not any more."

*

Jorge panned the good-sized studio, noting the placement of light fixtures and electrical outlets. Once the fittings were installed and the décor staged, it would make a very chic salon. A good investment. At least, Ivette hoped he would think so.

She hadn't imagined taking on a business partner. With Carlos' backing, she wouldn't have seen it as a partnership in the commercial sense. At least she knew what Carlos would have expected from the deal. Not knowing him from Adam, she wasn't entirely sure what Jorge had in mind, but he'd insisted on seeing the space.

He toured around the large loft one more time, checking the windows and doors. Finally he stood with his hands in his pockets, nodding. "It's a good location. You should get many high-end clients. And you could market yourself in the building. Offer specials to employees."

Ivette wrinkled her brow. He sounded as if dictating a business plan. She hadn't asked for that. Suddenly she worried what else he might want in return for helping her out, but he didn't seem the type for blackmail.

"Senor Allesandro," she said. "I don't need any help running the business. I know my trade. And I'm flattered that you want to help me. Shocked, in fact." She paused, and cleared her throat. "But there must be something you want out of this. You should tell me now, so that we…understand each other."

Jorge tilted his head. "Understand each other? I think you give me too much credit. It's not complicado. And call me Jorge."

Ivette spread her hands wide. "Well then, Jorge. What is it? I think you're a nice person, but nice people don't go around offering money to strangers."

Jorge looked up at the ceiling. "I expect…" He paused in thought. "I expect, haircuts for life. And one spa treatment per week for my mother."

Ivette's eyebrows raised. "That can't be all. How do I pay back the front money?"

"You don't. It's a gift. You see, I recently discovered I own a bit of property myself. I won't need much to live on, and I have no children." He turned his face back to her. "Do you have children?" he said suddenly, as if embarrassed he hadn't asked the question before.

Ivette smiled. There truly were good people on this earth, and at that moment, she realized something. That she couldn't continue to hurt an equally good person. He deserved better. She shook her head in reply. "Not quite yet."

*

Pam hesitated at the door to Vanier's room. She really had no business on this ward, but promised Zara she'd monitor his condition. And as much as she couldn't explain it, she felt something around this guy. Guilt? No. He'd called her 'Tonto', for God's sake. Satisfaction? At seeing him punished for his arrogance and for the way he'd hurt Zara? Maybe a little. Or something else? She pushed the door open.

He lay there dozing, the white hospital sheet in disarray overtop him. One foot hung out over the edge of the bed, and his chest lay exposed. His bare, hairy, perfect chest. Whoa, where did that thought come from? Mr. Arrogant apparently did not deign to wear a gown. His nurses probably wouldn't complain though if what she saw so far was any indication of what else might be hidden under that rumpled cotton. She stepped closer to the bed.

Here lay an impressive specimen. The telltale bulges and curves of his body couldn't be missed by even the most casual observer. He'd looked good in a suit, but lying here in the raw…holy shit. Pam whistled.

He moved his wounded head a little at the sound. Pam clapped a hand to her mouth. Waking up patients with head injuries wasn't smart. She prayed he'd fall back asleep. With his hair partly shorn away, she could appreciate the classic lines of his face. He looked a bit like Robert Redford, she thought. In his day.

He stopped moving, but his eyelids lifted to reveal a pair of hazel irises, their tone clear and rich, like vintage scotch whiskey. They stared at her for quite some time, making Pam's feet feel rooted to the floor in a tingling paralysis. His mouth began to twitch as if he wanted to speak. As he slowly licked the dry, cracked skin of his lips, something did a quick dance in Pam's stomach. A helpless, bandaged man in a hospital bed had no right to look that sexy. She scolded herself internally.

"Well, look who's here. Aren't we in a pickle now?" he said, his voice thick.

Pam swivelled her head and gave him a sideways glance. She raised her fingers in the air, mimicking two pistols. "What do you mean, 'we,' paleface?"

His parched lips curled into a smile, and issued a short, tortured laugh. He raised his hands to his chest. "Ooh, got me."

Her hands returned to the pockets of her scrubs. "Serves you right."

"What are you doing here?"

"I work here."

He turned his head away and looked up at the ceiling. "My luck."

"Yeah, you are lucky. You could be dead. But you seem not much worse for wear. What does your doctor say?"

Stephane sighed. "The consensus seems to be, if I weren't such a big, thick-headed brute I'd be in a lot worse shape."

"Mmm." Pam nodded. "So there's no truth to the 'bigger they are, harder they fall,' axiom?"

He turned to look at her again. "You're funny." The hazel eyes moved up and down her five-foot-nothing frame. "How much do they pay you here?"

She folded her arms across her chest. "What the union tells them they must. Why?"

"I hate hospitals. I'm going to need some full-time home care for a while. I'll pay you double what you make here. What do you say?"

Pam's eyes nearly popped. "Are you nuts? What makes you think I'd work for you?"

He licked his lips again. "I'm sorry I called you Tonto. Horribly inaccurate and racist of me. It won't happen again. Now what do you say?"

Pam's mouth hung open, wrestling with how to respond to such an absurd proposition.

"Yes would be a good answer," he prompted.

She caught a glimpse of a powerful, hairy leg peeking out from beneath the sheet. She found herself wanting to snatch the material away and have a good look at what else he had to offer. Before she realized it, a word fell from her lips.

"Yes."

Chapter Twenty-Six

Dear David:

I hope this letter finds you well, and that you will accept my deepest apologies for my behavior toward you in the past weeks. You are a wonderful person and I will always have warm feelings for you. I want to thank you for your kindness and am sorry for the trouble I have caused you.

I must tell you that you are not the father of my child and that you have no legal or moral obligation to him or her, or myself in the future. I acted out of selfishness and fear, and regret involving you so unfairly. I hope you can forgive me.

Sincerely, Ivette.

The letter had arrived at Dave's office a few days ago. Zara folded the notepaper after reading through and mentally translating the lines of Spanish for at least the tenth time. It didn't seem to help.

After losing her baby, depression hung over Zara like a cloud since their return from Tenerife. She'd stayed away from work for more than a week, sequestering herself at Club Marbella, resting, reading, or just staring out to sea. The letter's contents should have elated her, but instead seemed to deepen the sense of loss.

At her mother's urging, she agreed to come to the El Mirador site and find out just what sort of "surprise" Dave had alluded to ever since they'd left Montreal. Jorge pulled the Mercedes into the temporary parking lot created for the construction crews. At the far end of the lot, overlooking the build site, stood a trailer that served as a field office. Dressed in his usual jeans and work boots, Dave leaned against the wall of the trailer, awaiting her arrival.

The warm day found him wearing only his reflective yellow and orange safety vest on his upper body, revealing his muscled shoulders. In spite of the unfashionable attire, to Zara, he couldn't have looked more sexy.

He smiled as he approached the vehicle and opened the door for her. "Good morning, Lightning Girl," he said, reaching for her hand. "Glad you decided to come. Feeling better?"

Zara took his hand and stepped out of the car. "Yes. Now that I see you." They stared at each other for a few moments before he pulled her in for a kiss. She reveled in the sweet taste and texture of his lips and the sureness of feelings they communicated. God, she loved this man, and felt a renewed wave of sorrow wash over her that she no longer nurtured his seed inside her.

"Close your eyes," he said, breaking their kiss and tightening his grip on her hand. He led her to the trailer, guiding her blind steps across the distance and over the threshold. He maneuvered her into position in front of the windows. "Okay, open."

She opened her eyes, and beheld the wondrous vista below. Re-designed foundations ringed the oil sand field, their myriad tines of rebar thrusting upward, waiting to join the next sections of concrete. To the west, she could see footings and piles lodged into the hillside, waiting for additional structures to take shape upon them. Men, materials and equipment moved about in a symphony of activity, and beyond, the shimmering sea drummed its ancient, steady beat in time to it.

Zara's breath caught as she took in the scene. So much, in so short a time. They must have worked day and night to make this kind of progress. She felt like she'd been away from Spain forever and, at this moment, knew she never wanted to leave again.

"Oh, Mr. Parker, what have you been up to?"

"Mmm, look this way, boss." He turned her to the right, pointing her toward the full-color rendering of the finished villa and interpretive centre that hung on the wall.

Zara put a hand to her throat. She'd seen a lot of architectural drawings in her time, and none of them were as complete, as breathtaking, as clearly drawn from the heart as this one. She recognized the sweeping lines of her father's sketch, amplified with an inspired interpretation that transformed it from wistful concept to stunning reality. La Dulce Zara. She swore her own heart stopped beating at the sight of it.

"Do you like it, Lightning Girl?"

She spun around to face him, words and thoughts and feelings reeling about in her head. She nodded, her eyes searching his as if wishing to communicate the tumble of emotions telepathically. "Lightning Girl like. You drew this?"

Dave smiled his usual half-grin. "Didn't know I had it in me?"

Zara exhaled and shook her head lightly. "I do now. You're amazing." Without warning, she felt her eyes filling with tears. "Amazing," she repeated. "How can I…" Dave seemed to sense her imminent emotional meltdown and quickly pulled her to him. He kissed her with an intensity that seemed to draw the strength right out of her body. She wrapped her arms around his neck to keep from falling, and matched his heat. The rest of the world melted away.

A sharp rapping on the window brought reality crashing back. Ernesto stood there, wearing an amused smile and wagging a finger at them. They laughed, but obeyed his gesture that they should follow him outside.

The warmth of the Spanish sun welcomed them as they stepped out of the trailer and caught up to Ernesto. December on the Costa del Sol sure beat the hell out of Montreal. Marlena waited under a portable canopy a little further down the slope, and Zara giggled at the sight of her elegant, slender mother in a hardhat and steel-toed hikers.

"What's so funny?" Marlena asked as the three of them approached.

"Nothing, Mom." Zara waved off her laughter, but noted a small table under the canopy set with a bottle of champagne and four glasses. The edges of its white tablecloth flapped in the breeze. "What's up, Ernesto?"

Ernesto moved next to Marlena, and exchanged a knowing look with her. "A toast." He poured the champagne and passed around the glasses.

Zara's radar went up, and she glanced between them, looking for a clue. "To what?" Zara asked, accepting her champagne, but exasperated at the suspense.

"To the future. Your mother and I have some announcements." Ernesto put his arm around Marlena's shoulders and their champagne flutes clinked together. "First, I'm going to be away for awhile. So we'll be needing a new Operations Manager." He lifted his glass toward Dave. "David, are you willing to take on the job?"

Dave's eyebrows went up. "Uh, yeah," he said, turning to look at Zara. "Of course." He shrugged as if to say he was as surprised as she. "Hadn't you better ask the boss?"

Ernesto smiled. "I'm sure she'll agree."

Zara's radar zipped higher up the scale. "I do, but, this is awfully sudden. Where are you going?"

Ernesto looked at Marlena. "We're going back to Canada, together."

Zara stood as if frozen, her glass in her hand. "Together? You and Mom? What do you mean?"

Dave chuckled. "Like, together, permanently," he said, looking straight at Ernesto. "That's great, Ernie. Well done." He raised his glass, then tipped his other hand under Zara's wrist, pushing her glass into the air. "It's a toast, babe."

Zara's expression turned from dumbfounded to joyous. "I knew it! I knew there was something going on between you two. Oh, Mom, I'm so happy for you." She set down her glass and rushed over to Marlena, giving her a big hug. Then one for Ernesto. "Are you going to get married? Where will you live?"

"We won't decide any of that until the New Year," Ernesto said. "Your mother has obligations back home over Christmas. And, of course, the business won't run itself." He smiled. "We have all this to do." He waved his hand across the panorama of El Mirador.

Zara looked out once more on the busy site. She hadn't thought about how much extra work this put on Ernesto. The project would mean a lot of extra time; time he couldn't spend with her mother. As Operations Manager, Dave could take on the general foreman's role, especially since he'd masterminded the design. Ernesto deserved a bit of relaxation. A crazy thought leapt into her head. Hmm. Maybe not so crazy. "Ernesto," she said, "how's your French?"

Ernesto turned to her. "C'est bon, mademoiselle. Why do you ask?"

Zara took a deep breath in. "Well, there's an opening for President of the Board at the Montreal office. And I know this great condo in Westmount. Fully furnished."

Marlena and Ernesto looked at each other. Marlena's eyes did a humorous roll. "This day is full of surprises," she said.

"And it's not over yet." Dave took his cue to change the subject. "You haven't seen the best part." He set his glass down on the table, and took Zara by the hand. "Excuse us. We'll leave you two lovebirds alone."

"What now?' Zara asked as Dave led her further into the construction zone, stopping to pick up extra gear at one of the tool cribs.

"You have yet to see the best view of El Mirador." He fitted the bright reflective safety vest over her shoulders as they continued on to where a new crane had just been installed. Dave slid open the door to the man lift that would carry the crane operator up to the control platform. He bid her enter with a chivalrous swoop of his hand. "Entrada, senorita."

"Gracias, senor." She stepped into the lift's tiny cab, and Dave followed, closing the door and reaching for the controls.

"Hold on," he said as the hydraulics kicked in and the lift began to move. Zara grabbed a handrail and braced her booted feet. The scene took on an entirely different perspective as they gained altitude. The grand design of the whole site revealed itself, not just buildings, but pools and plantings, pathways and landscaping.

Dave stood close behind her, his arms around her waist and his chin on her shoulder. Rising meter by meter, the scope of the project changed and grew, and soon, some dark stonework became visible just beyond the site's perimeter.

"What's that?" she asked, pressing a finger against the glass.

"You'll see," he answered.

In a few seconds, more of the dark stone appeared, forming a pattern in the sand. It reminded Zara of a giant SOS on a desert island. But the thought stopped dead, when letters became legible from the pile of rocks and spelled out something else entirely.

MARRY ME, ZARA!

Her emotions got the better of her as they continued to ascend, and she began to cry. "Hey," Dave said, squeezing his arms tighter around her. "Is my spelling that bad?"

She made a choking noise. Sometimes his sense of humor made her laugh and cry at the same time, but this was no laughing matter. She desperately wanted to say yes, but her mouth seemed to have other ideas. "I can't."

He loosened his grip on her. "What do you mean, can't? Like, not today?"

She pressed her hands to the glass, staring at the stone letters becoming smaller as they rose higher. "No. I can't make you marry me out of pity. Or because you think you must after what happened."

"Why would you think that?"

Zara pounded on the glass. "Because I failed. Failed at the most basic thing."

Dave seemed at a loss to understand her. "What are you talking about?"

"I graduated at the top of my class. I made my own way in the world. I designed buildings, and tore them down again. I flew halfway around the world to take control of a corporation, and fought off those who wanted to destroy it." She bowed her head and her shoulders began to shake. "And I couldn't do this one simple thing. I couldn't carry your child. I'm so sorry."

He turned her around and gripped her arms with both hands, squeezing hard. She kept on crying, gasping for breath in between sobs. She clutched the mesh of his safety vest and twisted it in her fists, her anguish uncontrollable. He slammed the button to halt the lift, and they jolted to a stop nearly 100 feet in the air.

"That's it," he said roughly, next to tears himself. "We're going to get a few things straight between you and me. Right now." He put his hand under her chin and tilted her tear-streaked face toward him. "You are never to feel sorry about that, ever, got it?" She continued to sniff and blubber. "You are your father's daughter. But you are not him, got it?" She gave a tiny bob of her head. "Everybody can do something. But nobody can do everything, understand?" A tear dripped off the end of her nose as she nodded again. "We are going to build this place together. You told me, this was meant for us, remember?"

"I remember." She looked into his eyes, losing herself in their blue depths.

"So, you are going to marry me, got it?" Was she hearing correctly? "Got it?" he repeated. Her chin bobbed up and down one more time. "And we're going to fill this place with more children, as many as you want. Okay?"

Her tears stopped flowing. Every word rang like a bell in her head, each one louder than the next, until it sounded like the entire cathedral at Notre Dame.

He shook her gently. "Okay?" he said again.

"Okay."

He nodded, lowering his voice. "Okay. Have I made myself clear?"

"Very."

He cocked his head to one side. "I'm not so sure. I think I may have to make another business presentation." He leaned in close, brushing her cheek with his nose. Then with the tip of his tongue, began to lick the salty tears away from under her eyes. The unexpected move made Zara's body react in unholy fashion.

"Up here?" she questioned, her voice shaky. "Sounds risky."

"Safety first," he said, stepping back and positioning her body in the center of the lift's cab. "If nobody moves, nobody gets hurt." He reached into the pile of safety gear and pulled something out. "This should do the trick." Between his hands stretched a standard, construction safety harness. Under normal circumstances, it would be used to tether the crane operator when walking the boom.

Zara had a feeling these were not normal circumstances. She felt a hot blush rising under skin. Not just on her face, but on her belly, her thighs…everywhere, as she eyed the woven nylon straps and metal rings of the harness. The blue of his eyes turned a glittering sapphire, reflecting the same excitement already growing inside her. She'd enjoyed the drafting table incident, but this explored new territory altogether. "Is this standard safety procedure?" she asked, swallowing hard.

"It is now. Take your pants off."

Her jaw dropped in mock protest. "Hey, I thought I was the boss."

"Only on the ground, babe. Only on the ground. Now get 'em off before I rip them off."

Zara's hands went to the waistband of her work jeans and slowly did as requested. First the button, then the zipper. When she'd pushed the denim and panties past her hips and down to her ankles, she realized her boots were in the way. She straightened and looked at him, her lips in a pout and naked from the waist down. "Untie my shoes, Thunder Boy?"

He crouched down and removed her boots, tossing them over his shoulder. He pulled off the jeans, then lifted each of her feet in turn, slipping them into the loops of the harness. He pulled the contraption upward until the loops snugged around her bare thighs, then put each of her arms into the upper straps. Their eyes locked as he tightened the padded strips of nylon over her shoulders.

He fingered the buttons on her shirt. "These will have to go," he said, popping them one by one. "Safety hazard."

"Whatever you say." she replied, close to breathless. "You're the boss now." The shirt fell open, and he pushed the fabric aside to reveal her pink bra. Her chest heaved up and down with each breath, and her whole body tingled with anticipation. This dominant side of him intrigued her, drew her into a new arena of pleasure in which she found herself a more than willing participant. She would do anything he asked, and the knowledge that they were suspended high above the ground added to the thrill.

He traced the outline of her bra with one finger, examining it as if it were something foreign to him. "This is well-constructed. I see it has a breakaway, in case it gets…"—he pulled sharply on the front clasp until it snapped apart—"caught on something."

Zara flinched as the bra released, her breasts tumbling out with nothing to restrain them. Her nipples budded in the sudden rush of cool air. He tilted his head from side to side, an amused smile on his face, as if pondering his next move. Then he fastened the chest straps of the harness across her bosom, snapping the parachute clip in place with a click. The pressure of the strap compressed her breasts into two tight mounds. It seemed vaguely medieval, and it made Zara giggle.

From a toolbox, Dave brought out three large carabiners. He fastened two onto the rescue rings that protruded from each shoulder strap, the reached around her to clip one to the main ring in the center back of the harness. She felt him connect this one to something on the wall of the cab behind her, and realized she could no longer move forward or back. He attached two steel cables from the roof of the enclosure to the shoulder rings. Effectively immobilized in the tiny cab of the man lift, goosebumps rose on her flesh and her knees began to shake. It felt obscene, and delicious.

He stepped back and stood with his hands on his hips. He looked her up and down, as if admiring his work, then nodded in satisfaction. "I think that will do."

Zara wanted to speak, but found no words to describe her feelings at that moment. The sight of this man, about to do with her as he wanted, made her tremble with excitement. She could feel the blood pulsing between her legs, begging him to come nearer, touch her, ravage her. He moved toward her with aching slowness. She wanted him bad.

At last, he came close enough to take her face in his hands and tilt it upward to meet his. The look in his eyes yielded a seething mix of desire, love and pain. They belonged to each other now, physically and spiritually.

"The purpose of this demonstration," he said, "is to prove to you that I'm a man of my word. I said I would never hurt you, so I intend to bring you pleasure, in every way imaginable. Starting now. Deal?"

"Deal," she answered, hear voice little more than a squeak.

"I also said that I would never let you go, and that I would never risk putting you in danger ever again, agreed?"

"Agreed." God, would he ever quit talking and make love to her? The nearness of his body, his rough vest brushing against her bare skin while she stood here in semi-bondage was enough to make her howl with want.

"And that I vowed to tie you up to prevent that, if necessary, correct?"

She nodded within the confines of his hands around her jaw.

"Good. This concludes the audio portion of my presentation."

"Thank G—" she began when her words were smothered by his kiss. Strong and insistent, his lips conquered hers and eradicated all desire to speak. His tongue searched her mouth, leaving no corner undiscovered. Then he withdrew his tongue and moved his kisses down the outside of her throat and to the hollow of her neck. Zara threw her head back in abandon.

Her arms still free, she tangled her fingers in his hair as he worked his way down her torso. Pain and pleasure mingled together as tongue and lips and hands explored her tight breasts, her nipples straining beneath the harness strap. He continued his path down her tummy, pausing to entertain her navel with slow, circular swaths of his tongue.

She convulsed in spasms of ticklishness, the pull of the harness underscoring her powerlessness. When he reached her abdomen, he simply kissed the skin there and pressed his cheek to it for a moment, as if in silent mourning for their lost child. She wept in concert with him.

On his knees before her, he then lifted each of her legs and placed them over his shoulders, suspending her in midair with her pussy spread wide. She quivered in the sensation of helplessness, and the anticipation of his lips nuzzling her in that most sacred place. She crossed her ankles behind his neck and hung there, resigned to his will.

Dave raised his hands and pressed both thumbs to her crotch, spreading the outer lips and exposing her wet and ready sex. He massaged the swollen bud, nurturing that magic spot he'd found before, until she arched her back and cried for mercy.

"Please," she moaned. "Please…don't torture me. I want you, now."

"Patience," he said as he plunged both thumbs into her depths. His tongue stroked the throbbing tissues of her clit, bringing her to orgasm almost instantly. Pleasure filled her mind and body. Wave upon wave of ecstasy washed over her as if it would never stop, yet she wanted more, wanted his cock inside her.

His tongue pressed against her,until the tiny contractions ceased. He lapped up the remaining juices from her quaking flesh and gently lowered her feet to the floor. Only the harness prevented her from falling, her knees seeming to have lost all capacity to support her.

Dave stood, sliding his hands up her legs and caressing her bare bottom as he rose. He released the metal carabiners that held her in place, and she collapsed against him. He whispered into her ear as she lay her head on his shoulder.

"Have I made my point?" he asked.

She wiggled her head in what passed for a nod. "You are…a man of your word."

He stroked her hair with one hand, and held her firmly around the waist with the other. "Have I done everything I promised?"

"No."

"No? What's left?"

"We need to fill this place with children. Starting now."

"You think you're the boss again, do you?"

"Yes." Zara tugged at his belt. "Time to get your pants off, boss man."

Epilogue

Fourteen Months Later

Marlena held the newborn in her arms, her expression positively radiating grandmotherly pride. "Justin Flynn Parker," she said, rocking the sleeping babe while gazing into his tiny face. "I'll bet you can't wait to swing a hammer."

Zara laughed. "Did you say the same thing when I was born, Mom?" She watched her mother fawning over the infant. The fine blond hairs on his head shone in the sunlight.

"No." She smiled in reply, not lifting her eyes from the child. "I didn't have to. I already knew."

Both women laughed. Dave moved across the wide deck of the boat toward them, working his way through the crowd of friends and relatives that had come to help celebrate the birth of their son. "What's so funny? Are you worried he's going to be too much like me?"

"He's like both of you," Marlena replied. "El nino Hermosa." A beautiful child.

Dave sat down next to Zara and watched Marlena cuddle the baby. "One down, how many to go?" he asked her.

Zara threw him a worried glance. "I'm not a building

supply store, honey. You can't just requisition a yard full of children."

"Who says?" he asked, putting his arm around her and kissing her behind her ear. "I'll place them on back-order, then." Zara rolled her eyes.

"Well, I wouldn't mind," Marlena said. "I can't wait to have more grandchildren, but Justin would be enough for me." She looked down at the little boy's face again and touched his perfect, pink nose with her index finger. His eyelids twitched in response, but he continued to slumber in his grandmother's arms. "I wish Tristan could meet him."

"Somehow, I think he already has," Zara said, placing a hand on her mother's shoulder. The deck listed sideways as the boat caught a swell. With the demands of the project and no permanent place to live, a yacht had been the perfect solution for Dave and Zara to begin their new life together. Moored just offshore, they could access the build site in minutes and admire its daily progress each night as the sun set. The boat afforded a different view of a reconstructed El Mirador, but it remained, as Zara's father had said, magnifico.

Jorge came to join them. "Miran," he announced, pointing out to sea. "Un delfín!" They turned to look in the direction he indicated, just in time to see the shining, gray body of the dolphin breach into the air then disappear beneath the waves. Gleeful shouts came from several guests who'd caught sight of the animal. "It's late in the season," Jorge said. "Most have swam north by now. This one must have wanted to stay for the party."

Dave's eyes narrowed as he rose from his seat to get a better look. He strode across the deck toward where the animal had appeared.

"Jorge," Zara said. "Aunt Juliana looks so well. The spa treatments seem to be working wonders. When are we going to meet your mysterious business partner?"

Jorge crossed his arms and smiled. "Someday. But today is Justin's day. Go," he said, pointing after Dave. "Show him the dolphin. Show him the world."

Zara took Justin from her mother, and gave Jorge a wry grin before turning away. She carried her newborn son in the crook of her arm as she joined Dave standing near the bow. He looked out to sea with a worried expression.

"What's wrong, Thunder Boy?" she asked, sensing his agitation. The new family of three stood together in the warm spring splendor of the Mediterranean, watching the dancing waves. Dave bit his lip, not answering. Suddenly the dolphin surfaced one more time, its glistening head bobbing and pointed beak open in a chattered greeting. It flipped and thrust its tail in the air, wagging it up and down in a symbolic goodbye gesture. Then it vanished.

Dave watched for a few moments more then exhaled a lungful of air. It seemed to have departed for good. "Not a thing, babe. Everything's exactly right."

- The End -

EL PRECIO

Spanish Seduction Book Two

INCENDIO
The Flames of Passion

SPANISH SEDUCTION – BOOK THREE

by Jean Maxwell

Prologue

July 1972

The dented little pickup truck ambled and bounced its way down the dirt track that passed for a road. With each bump of the chassis, Tristan Flynn felt the body weight of his passenger lift and crash down again in the rusted bed of the truck box. He winced in sympathy at the pain this must cause her. But he chose to believe that the medication and injections must be making her close to numb anyway.

Jesus, he could smell her burned and infected flesh even from the driver's seat. Appalling, but he felt he could get used to it. Isn't that what they said about the American pioneers on the early wagon trains? To ease the noise of the wooden wheels grinding against their axles as they crossed the endless prairies, they used rodent entrails as a lubricant. Though atrocious, the smell was far easier to become accustomed to than the sound.

Juliana's body lay wrapped in sheets and towels, concealed under a tarp spread over the truck box. The shattered rear glass of the truck's cab made one less barrier between them.

Her presence weighed on his soul, as did the absence of Ariel Torres, Juliana's lover and Tristan's friend.

"Get out of here, now!" were Ari's last words to him two nights ago, before he ignited the carbon gases trapped beneath El Mirador. The hotel had gone up in a firebomb of destruction, leaving little time to save anything. Including Ari.

His friend had sacrificed everything; his life, his business and nearly the life of the innocent woman who now lay in critical condition in the back of his truck. Tristan held little hope for the unborn child she carried. Her reputation aside, no human being deserved to die by another's jealous rage. When Ari had discovered Juliana in bed with another man, right in the penthouse suite of his own hotel, he went insane.

The result lay scarred and bleeding not three feet away from him, and as he drove on, their destination rose from the dusty horizon. Zaragoza. What would her family say when her broken body was returned to them by an outsider; a blond gringo from Wales whom they didn't know from Adam?

It didn't matter. He would take her home nevertheless. He owed Ari this. The child might still be saved.

As he neared the city limits, Tristan noted the olive grove he'd been told to watch for. The road leading to the Sanchez villa lay just beyond it. He made the turn as carefully as he could, the steering column protesting with a gut-wrenching grind. Even so, he couldn't avoid the deep pothole directly ahead and his front wheels landed in it unceremoniously. He felt his cargo roll to one side of the box and come to rest against the wheel well.

He grimaced, and stopped the truck to check on her condition. The merciless sun beat down on him as he peeled one corner of the tarp away. A swath of her red-gold hair fell across the bandages covering her forehead. With a sharp intake of breath at the severity of her injuries, Tristan recalled that same red hair swinging in the air as she'd danced in the Madrid cantina the first night he'd seen her.

Ari had seen her too, and liked what he saw, because he had continued to ogle and grab at her throughout the night, leading to a bar fight in which Tristan had saved Ari from coming out on the losing end. Two months later, the fickle Juliana turned up at El Mirador, Ari's luxury resort on the Costa del Sol, looking for work.

The magnanimous Ariel Torres had given it to her, adding her as a central attraction to his floorshow. By this time, Tristan had hung around Ari long enough to know his generous side. A destitute student just graduated from the school of engineering at Cardiff University, Tristan had accepted Ari's offer to train him in the resort and casino business rather than continue his pointless backpacking trek across Europe.

He soaked a cloth with water from his canteen and dabbed her face gently. Poor reckless thing. She'd wanted to be a famous dancer. Now she'd be lucky to even walk again. If any good would come of this, it would be her deliverance of a healthy child.

Ari's child.

Despite her promiscuity, Tristan felt with unshakeable certainty that the baby was Torres' and no other. He settled Juliana on her back and placed the cloth on her forehead. It had to be Ari's. Only that would give the horrible turn of events any meaning. He closed the tarp and turned away.

Leaning on the side of the truck, he drank from the canteen. What lay ahead for him now? With his mentor dead, the hospitality business seemed distinctly unpalatable. He'd graduated with top marks in engineering, yet had no vision of what he might do with this skill. He hoped some divine intervention would make his path clear to him now.

He started up the truck and gunned the engine. The vehicle jerked itself out of the rain-filled pothole and shot forward.

*

"Basta!" Marlena yelled. Lupé stopped barking, but continued to wag his tail and jump excitedly with the other dogs. As a group, the canines all galloped down the lane toward the main road.

Marlena Sanchez brushed her dark hair aside and her gaze followed the animal's path. Their behaviour could only mean that a vehicle approached. But in midsummer there were typically few visitors, and Marlena could not hazard a guess as to who or what might be driving into her family's villa on a torrid Wednesday afternoon. She clipped the last cotton sheet to the clothesline and picked up the empty basket.

The dogs leapt and lunged at the beat-up truck as it inched its way up the drive. Marlena did not recognize the vehicle at all. She sensed trouble.

"Mama," she called toward the open windows of the house. "Someone's coming. I don't know who it is."

Bianca Sanchez Allesandro poked her head out of the window at Marlena's call, and squinted in the direction of the truck. The vehicle bore no resemblance to anyone's they knew. "Ernesto was supposed to bring the lumber today," she ventured. "Maybe he borrowed someone's truck."

Marlena wagged her chin back and forth. "I don't think so." The truck slowed to a stop about five meters from the house. She moved forward to shoo the dogs away and let whomever the driver might be get out and announce themselves. Lupé and the rest scattered at Marlena's behest, and she stood facing the truck with her hands clasped in front of her. The dented door creaked open.

A long, jean-clad leg stepped out from the cab, followed by a lion-ish shock of blond hair on the driver's head. This visitor was not from around here, Marlena concluded. He stretched and stood to his full height, nudging his aviator-style sunglasses up the bridge of his nose with one finger as he moved aside to close the truck door. He nodded at her.

"Senorita," he said. "Mi nombre est Tristan Flynn. Buenos dias. Esta casa de Sanchez?"

Marlena eyed the man up and down. He seemed young, though older than her own eighteen years. "Si. Que pasa?"

The blond stranger swiped his chin with the back of his hand. "Habla Engles?" he queried. Marlena nodded. "I've brought someone with me. I believe she is one of your family."

Marlena blinked. "Who is it?"

"Is there someone who can help carry her? She's in the back." He motioned to the rear of the truck with his thumb. Marlena drew in a sharp breath. Injured? Drunk? Who could he mean?

"Mama!" she called. In a flash, Bianca appeared in the doorway. "Get help, get José, or one of the other boys."

Bianca turned and shouted in the direction of the barns. Marlena moved toward the blond man. Though his eyes remained hidden, she noted the strong line of his chin and jaw, covered with a fine stubble that indicated he'd been away from any amenities for awhile. She'd never seen hair quite that color before, and so much of it. Its wavy curls stuck out in all directions, and she felt an inexplicable desire to run her fingers through it.

"Show me," she said.

Tristan walked to the rear of the truck, and began to unlace the tarp covering the box. "I'm sorry," he said. "But I got her here as quickly as I could." He lowered the tailgate and threw back the tarp. "Her name is Juliana. Is she one of your family?"

Marlena gaped at the crumpled form laying there, wrapped in layers of bloodied, sodden material. Running footsteps grew louder. José and Marco were nearing the truck at top speed. Marlena's eyes teared up at the sorry sight. How would her mother react? Juliana. Her beautiful and vivacious aunt Juliana lay before her in the back of a broken-down pickup truck. This is how it ended, the fearful nights worrying about her whereabouts, and the company she'd been keeping. Marlena's stomach heaved.

"José," Marlena said, as his running figure lurched to a stop beside the truck. "Get her inside."

Chapter One

March 1973

Tristan wiped the sweat from his brow and hung up his hardhat for the last time. The roadway from Zaragoza to Huesca lay complete after months of construction during the Spanish winter. His crew moved about loading the last of the barriers and temporary signage into transport trucks for return to the company yard.

With no money and no real plans after the El Mirador disaster, Tristan had taken a job with a local construction company in Zaragoza. At least it was one way, he thought, to begin using his education and add something, no matter how menial, to his virtually blank resume.

Road construction hadn't been his thing, though, and with an appreciation for those who had no choice but to do backbreaking labor, made a decision. He looked around the nearby landscape; while the traditional economies of the region remained strong, the tourist industry had even more potential. A relaxed atmosphere had settled over the country, with the aging Franco's declining grip on national affairs.

Tristan could envision what was possible for the future, and he was going to build it.

Long, arduous months on the job left him lean and well-muscled. Lonely tedious nights left him frustrated just as the relentless heat made him thirsty. For more than just water. As much as he'd tried, he could not rid his brain of a particular pretty brunette.

He'd learned her name was Marlena. Her delicate frame yet determined countenance as she stood facing him in the driveway at her villa stuck in his memory. A juxtaposition of softness, strength, youth and maturity radiated from her. This seemed an unusual and fascinating combination of traits in such a young woman.

And it turned him on.

He supposed this fact was what kept him both in the Zaragoza area and at a measured distance away. If she was underage, the girl would be absolutely off-limits. At twenty-two, Tristan thought she might even consider him too old to even look at.

But time would change things. It had been eight months since they met. He guessed she might at least be eighteen by now. But he knew little about the social culture here, and how relationships were pursued within the traditional confines. He had a feeling they remained strict. Perhaps they still applied arranged marriages. Perhaps being a non-Catholic disqualified him. Perhaps just being an outsider was enough to bar him from even calling on her.

He finished packing his tools and hoisted himself into the open box of one of the trucks that were headed back to the company yard. Five other crewmembers rode along in the open vehicle with him. As the truck jerked uncomfortably down the highway, the vibrations made Tristan's cock grow hard in frustration, exacerbating his unholy desires toward the girl that haunted his dreams.

Marlena. He pictured her standing there in the road in her white cotton dress carrying that laundry basket. The breeze lifted her skirt a bit, and he wondered what would be revealed if the wind were just a little stronger. He imagined marching toward her, yanking the basket from her hands and tossing it into the ditch. His little fantasy alternated between ripping open the buttoned front of her dress to take her pert little nipples in his mouth, and backing her up against one of the trees that lined the driveway. This version continued with him slinging his arms under her knees, pushing her legs up and apart, the rough bark scraping her back as she begged him to thrust into her fresh little pussy.

"Oy, Flynn!" One of his co-workers yelled. "Ride's over, man. Get your ass off the truck and go home." Jostled back to reality, Tristan saw they'd arrived at the yard.

Home? He didn't have a home, just the temporary lodgings the company had arranged. But he did have a purpose, now. And if he didn't have a home, he would build one. Perhaps one big enough for a whole brood of little brunette beauties like their mother.

*

"Marlena!" Bianca called. "It's nearly time. Get fresh towels and take them to Juliana's room. If you need more, tear up some of the older bedsheets. Make sure the water pitcher is filled and bring some ice."

"Mama!" Marlena called back. "I know what needs doing. I've been doing it for weeks now, looking after Tía. You don't need to explain it every time." Marlena dressed quickly, making sure to tuck a well-worn magazine under her mattress before rushing to her mother's summons. It wouldn't do for mama, Consuelo or anybody else to discover it, as none of them would approve of its content.

She'd flipped through its pages countless times, but none

drew her attention more than the center fold, it's glossy surface dulled and smudged from thousands of fingerprints laid upon it even before she'd found it in the trash bin outside the farmacia. If what she saw was what the modeling industry expected of its stars, Marlena must not be afraid to imitate it.

She dreamed of being a model someday; but that dream would have to wait, at least for today. Juliana's baby was expected any time now, and as much as she cared for her aunt, Marlena really didn't want to miss classes for the event. Final exams were only weeks away, her passage of which would secure her entrance eligibility into University. Though she'd dreamed of nothing else but a modeling career her whole life, a degree would at least provide her with a choice of other vocations to pursue. Perhaps Aunt Juliana might give birth in the next 30 minutes; then Marlena could be on her way to school as though nothing had happened.

Ernesto would be waiting for her at the bus stop as always. Ernesto Alvarez lived nearby and attended the same school as Marlena. In fact, they'd attended all the same schools together growing up. She couldn't recall a time when she hadn't known Ernesto. Tall and slim, he'd grown into what many of her class mates considered a very handsome boy. With his curly dark hair and penetrating brown eyes, she noted that he turned a lot of girls' heads.

But Marlena didn't see him that way. To her, he would always be just Ernesto, the boy who'd been her playmate and confidante for as long as she could remember.

Sweeping her long hair into a ponytail, Marlena hurried to her aunt Juliana's room to check on supplies as her mother had asked. Her poor tía. She lay on her side, holding her very pregnant belly with both hands. Her chest rose and fell as she breathed, working through another contraction. Was it as painful as it looked, Marlena wondered? If so, her tía never seemed to let on; but then, pain had been her constant companion since the awful accident. Perhaps she just didn't react to it anymore.

Juliana had spent nearly her entire pregnancy healing from the burns she'd sustained in some sort of hotel fire on the coast. Her scars were still red and raw, but she looked much better than the day she'd been brought home.

Marlena considered that day, and recalled the bushy blond-haired boy driving the truck that carried her aunt home. She'd never seen him before or since, yet found those fleeting minutes in his presence inexplicably memorable. His strange accent threw her off; she'd heard British people speak, as there were a fair number of them that vacationed in Spain now that the government had opened the gates to more travelers. But his voice sounded distinctly different, and the time had not been right to interrogate him further, given the urgency of his visit.

In fact, she wasn't certain she remembered his name, though he must have spoken it. Flint, or something. His Spanish certainly wasn't fluent. In any case, they owed him a debt of gratitude for bringing Juliana home, and he'd disappeared so quickly. She liked to think he'd turn up to check on his passenger one day, and they could all thank him accordingly.

Juliana let out a low groan, and Marlena moved quickly to the head of the bed. "Tía, is it time?" she asked. "Shall I get mama and the doula?"

Her aunt made a sharper noise and her scarred faced puckered into a wretched grimace. She nodded in a short, jerking motion. Marlena ran from the room.

"Mama! Tía said to send for the doula!" She rushed down the hall to find her mother Bianca, nearly crashing into her at the intersection of the hallway and kitchen.

Bianca grabbed her daughter by the shoulders. "I've already sent for her," Bianca said. "I'm afraid you'll have to stay home today." Marlena sighed and nodded. Bianca tipped her daughter's chin upward and looked into her eyes. "I need you here to help. We'll call the school later, si?" She smiled in that way that only mothers can, making their child both disappointed yet hopeful in the same instant. "Bien," she said, and dismissed her with a reassuring tap on the arm. "Go shoo the boys out of the house and tell them not to come back until we say."

Marlena ducked into the kitchen where José stood pulling cookies from a jar for his lunch. "José! Hands off the cookies. You have to leave now, my tía is having her baby."

José dropped the last cookie from his hand back into the jar and looked at Marlena wide-eyed. "Mierda!" he swore, but failed to move from his spot.

"Vamos!" Marlena shouted, waving him away with both hands. José turned and bolted out the back door. "Take the boys with you…and don't come back until we say." She followed him out into the courtyard and saw Marco, another of their workers, join him from one of the adjacent outbuildings. The pair of them headed toward the barn.

Marlena continued through the house, scattering any members of the hired help that weren't essential to the birthing process. José, Marco and about ten others worked for the family inside the villa, on either a full or part time basis. The traditional home of the Sanchez family, the colonial-style villa had stood on this land for a hundred years. Only by favor of the Nationalist government had they been able to retain it. Many country people had fled to other parts of Europe to make a living. While pervasive and ingrained in her daily life, tradition held little interest for Marlena. She'd just as soon leave this old-fashioned lifestyle behind for the big city at her first opportunity. I'm eighteen now, she reminded herself. I want to see and do things no one in this place has ever seen. She wanted to be a model, and models belonged in the modeling school in Madrid. Not the dusty farmyards of central Spain. She had already made her application to the school, but heard nothing. For today, though, she would be missing her regular high school classes to tend to her aunt and the coming baby.

Facing the main window of the home's entrance, Marlena saw Ángelina, the doula, approaching the house. A doula was another part of "tradition." Similar to a midwife, the doula was a birthing assistant, though not hands-on with the actual delivery. The doula coached and saw to it that the birthing mother's wishes were carried out, such as no drugs, who was allowed to be present, and the naming of the child.

Marlena snorted. Her aunt should be in a hospital, receiving professional medical care, not left to the back-room ministrations of folk healers. It was the seventies, not the seventeen hundreds, and Marlena considered herself a very modern young woman. Capable and deserving of a life of her own, unbound by the ubiquitous "tradition" that stifled society, and women particularly, under the Francoist regime she'd known all her life.

Besides, the hospitals may have been able to perform skin grafts, and preserve at least some of her aunt's youthful beauty. In this regard too, tradition reared its depressing head. Being pregnant and unmarried, Juliana had brought shame to the family and therefore had been kept hidden away here on the farm, and her scars accepted as a fitting punishment for her sins. And what of the child? How would he or she be treated by the family and society?

As Ángelina stepped onto the verandah, Marlena made a promise to herself. Her newborn cousin would not be shunned. She would make certain of it, take the child under her own wing if necessary. If she could become successful, earn a good living as a model, she would always provide comfort and support for this new little person that waited to be born, despite the odds against it, in the next room.

Chapter Two

"So, it's a boy, then?" Ernesto asked. He pushed back and forth with his foot, swaying the porch swing on which they sat side by side. Dusk shrouded the courtyard, and would soon dissolve into night.

Marlena nodded. "Si, a boy. A perfect little boy. She named him Jorge." Her eyes began to fill with tears.

"What?" Ernesto said. "Why does that make you sad? What could be happier than a healthy little baby?" He cocked his curly head to one side, his eyes searching hers from behind his wireframed eyeglasses.

Marlena's lips twitched in frustration. "It's because he's perfect, and the world isn't."

Ernesto laughed. "Well, that's nothing new. Come on, why are you being so emotional?"

Marlena turned to Ernesto, her friend, her playmate, her keeper of secrets. "I want to get out of here. We're going to graduate in less than a month. Let's move away together. I want to go to University or modeling school in Madrid, and I want to give Jorge a better life than he'll get here, staying hidden from the world in the shadow of his mother's sins. It's not fair. Will you help me?"

Ernesto looked taken aback at her outpouring of words. He blinked his bright brown eyes and swallowed hard. "That's a big step, Marly."

"I know that. But you have to take big steps to do big things. Don't you want something more, something better?

Ernesto paused, then shrugged. "I don't know. I hadn't thought about it like that. I thought I'd just see what comes… you know. Like we do every summer."

Marlena's lips pursed into a pout. "That's not good enough anymore." She looked off into the distance. "I don't want to pick fruit, or mind children, or stitch hems for rich old ladies. I don't want to be like a slave, like a peasant, like…" She stopped there, biting her lip.

"Like me?" Ernesto finished.

Marlena turned and looked directly at him. His expression turned dour, pensive. "I didn't say that."

"But you thought it."

"No. I asked you if you wanted to move away with me. Become something different," Marlena said. "You didn't answer."

Ernesto adjusted his glasses, and moved them higher up the bridge of his nose. "I…" he began, then stopped with a release of breath. "I want whatever you want, Marly. I always have. But moving away from here…I can't see us doing that."

Marlena's eyes narrowed. "Then what do you see?" she asked. "Carrying on, working menial jobs, growing old with nothing to show for it?"

Ernesto regarded her carefully. Their eyes locked for a long moment, then he moved deliberately closer to her on the swing seat. Their thighs brushed against each other's. His arm slid casually around her shoulders. "I want you, Marly."

As he leaned in for a kiss, Marlena seemed to snap out of a trance and pull away. "Hey…" she said, halting his advance. "What are you doing?"

Ernesto blinked in surprise. "I was trying to kiss you, if you didn't notice."

Marlena exhaled a fuming breath. "I noticed. Why? You've never tried to kiss me before. I thought…" she broke off.

Ernesto sat with his body awkwardly perched over hers. "What? That I only saw you as a friend? That I wouldn't notice how pretty you are?"

Marlena drew back and looked at him with her eyes wide. She shook her head side to side. "No. I guess I didn't. I didn't think you could see me that way…we…oh no." A realization seemed to sink into her soul. "Now we can't be friends anymore."

*

The familiar olive grove lay just ahead. Only this time Tristan approached it on foot. He didn't know what to expect when he reached the Sanchez villa; but knew he had to stop there. Bringing the woman home was only part of the story. He had to know if the child lived. He or she would be the only link to his late friend Ariel Torres.

Dressed in the best clothes he had, which were few to begin with, he trudged on toward the gates. Jeans and a rugby shirt would have to suffice as presentable. Spring blooms on the vines covering the gateposts exuded their airy scent as he passed through them. He walked past the trees lining the drive that had figured so prominently in his private fantasy and shivered involuntarily despite the warm day.

Get those thoughts out of your head, Flynn. Or you'll do something stupid. He could hear the pack of dogs starting to bark as he approached. Would the brunette angel appear and shoo them away as she did before? They came now, from around the side of the adobe structure, yipping and yelping, nearly stumbling over each other as they jockeyed for position in the group, running straight for him.

Tristan stopped walking, unsure of his next move should the dogs reach him before someone called them off. He stepped to the side, ducking into a breezeway that divided two sections of the house. Flattening against the plaster wall, he ran a hand through his unruly mane of blond hair, allowing the shaded air to cool his forehead. The dogs seemed to have become confused at his disappearance, their fading barks indicating the animals veering off in different directions. He remained a few moments longer in the shadows, taking a look around.

Shade grasses and wildflowers grew between the flagstone slabs under his feet. His eyes moved upward to an adjacent wing of the house, and noticed an arched window with its shutters wide open on the upper floor. He caught some movement inside; what? Could it be…yes! The very girl that fueled his nightly fantasies passed by the window. She wore only a white bra as she stopped directly in the center of the opening. She leaned over the sash, catching rays of sunlight on her face, her perfect, round breasts in full view.

Tristan blinked, but felt unable to turn his gaze, or move in any direction he was so entranced by what he saw. He knew he should look away…but too late. She spotted him first. A split second passed where they did nothing but stare at each other, then the girl made a noise and drew back, pulling the shutters closed.

Tristan snapped to and bolted around the corner, resuming his approach to the main entrance of the house. It wouldn't do for the girl to sound the alarm at his arrival, alert everyone to the presence of a peeping Tom before he had a chance to announce himself and his purpose here. He lunged up the verandah steps and rapped the iron doorknocker. He stepped back a pace, breathing hard.

In a few moments, a middle-aged woman opened the paneled wooden door. "Si?" she said, her harsh voice barely above a whisper.

"Hola, I am Tristan Flynn, a friend of Senorita Juliana. I've come to ask about her welfare after the accident. May I see her?"

The woman, dressed in black except for a white maid's apron, trained her steely eyes on him. Did she speak English? He didn't quite have the vocabulary to explain why he had come. "Wait here," she said in English, after appraising him from head to toe.

Tristan waited.

A few minutes passed before another woman appeared at the door. Younger than the maid, but mature, and well-dressed. He recalled seeing her the day he'd brought Juliana. She had shouted orders to the farmhands. La dama de la casa, he assumed. Attractive too, now that he saw her close up. Dark hair swept up in a large knot and bangs combed at an angle across her forehead, a la Audrey Hepburn. The resemblance struck him a moment later. An older version of the very girl he'd just glimpsed in the window. Marlena.

"May I help you?" she asked, a polite smile lifting the corners of her mouth.

"Buenos dias, senora. My name is Tristan. I brought Miss Juliana here last summer. Is she well?"

The woman's smile grew genuine. "Si. I remember you. How kind of you to call. Please come in." She stepped back from the doorway and gestured for him to enter. "My sister is recovering well. We are most grateful to you for her return."

"Gracias. I apologize for not visiting sooner. I was concerned for her, but work kept me away. I..." Tristan stopped talking, uncertain of what to say next. He felt like an intruder. "Is her...did she...?"

"Have her baby?" The woman finished for him. "Si. A boy." She reached a hand out to him. "I'm Bianca." Tristan shook her offered hand. "Would you like to see him?"

"Yes, please." Tristan answered. "And Miss Juliana. She

was in my prayers," he added, thinking the comment might buy him some brownie points with what he assumed was a traditional Catholic family.

Bianca gazed warmly at him. "We are grateful. Thank you." She moved further aside to allow Tristan inside the foyer. He noted the polished stone of the flooring, and the finely plastered walls. Dark wood beams supported the vaulted ceiling overhead. Very Spanish, very grand. His engineer's brain began firing as he catalogued the structural features. "Please," Bianca continued, leading him forward to an interior courtyard. Here the ceiling opened to the outdoors, pouring muted daylight over the space. "Sit, have something to drink. Juliana does not wish to receive visitors, but I will bring the baby."

Bianca nodded off to the side, and Tristan followed her glance to see the same maid, or whatever she was called here, standing on the far side of the courtyard, waiting for instructions. He found her voyeuristic presence, pinched expression and piercing stare a tad spooky. At Bianca's signal, she moved off to fulfil her mistress' request.

Tristan sat down on a wooden bench. He liked this courtyard concept; potted plants strategically placed to fit with greenery that grew right out of the ground. Squares of wooden flooring alternated with squares of white sand, giving the space a calming, indoor/outdoor feel.

He gazed up at the sky. He twiddled his thumbs. He shuffled his feet, noting the scuffed and worn appearance of the hiking boots he wore. He wished he had more money. Then he let out a regretful chuckle. Money. Ariel had given him money, plenty of it, and shown him how to make even more money at the casino tables. But what good had it done? Ari was dead, the fool; and the money long gone.

A soft sound from behind shook him from his reverie. He turned toward it, and rose slowly from the bench. Marlena stood there, holding the baby in her arms. God, she looked beautiful. Her long hair cascaded over her shoulders. Beneath perfectly arched eyebrows, lush brown eyes that sparked with emotion locked with his. They telegraphed her indignation at his Peeping Tom act of earlier. How could he explain it was only accidental? In spite of this, he felt his body drawing nearer to her, without having to even move his feet.

"My aunt has named him Jorge," she said in only lightly-accented English. "She loves him very much."

Marlena held out the newborn for Tristan to see. He could already recognize the distinctive features of Ariel Torres in the tiny boy's face, and felt some measure of restitution. He hadn't been able to save El Mirador. But he did save Ari, as he swore he would. Because he had saved Ari's child.

Jorge.

His gaze returned to Marlena, unable to take his eyes off the brunette beauty as she stood there, cradling the babe and humming a tune for him. In that moment, Tristan knew his true reason for returning. Knew with crystalline certainty, that whatever his destiny might hold, she would be part of it.

Chapter Three

Dinner stretched on interminably. Marlena could barely keep herself still at the table, her meal long finished. She set her nervous energy to work at smoothing the corners of her napkin into the flattest fold possible. Her feet swished against the terracotta floor tiles beneath her. Why had her mother asked him to dinner? It was torture sitting here, knowing what he'd seen through the window. It wasn't right; wasn't proper. And why had he come back? It had been months since he'd dumped off Aunt Juliana, like a load of hay, into their care. He could have asked sooner, sent a letter or telegram, if he'd truly cared.

She glanced sidelong at his curly blond head, turned to attention on her mother, appearing to listen with rapture to her words. *Charmer! What are you really after?* Her face felt hot, and an odd sensation settling between her thighs. This took her by surprise. Her restless movements turned to outright squirming.

Marlena felt a tug on the tablecloth and a sudden movement to her left. Seated next to her, she saw her aunt's head bob downward then snap up again. Marlena grabbed her elbow to prevent her from slipping off her chair as she sometimes did when falling asleep at the dinner table.

The silverware rattled against each other as Marlena tilted her aunt's thin frame upright again. All eyes turned toward the two of them. Marlena placed her arm protectively around her aunt's slumping shoulders. Juliana snapped to attention at her touch and glanced around the circle of peering eyes. "Estas bien, Tía?" Marlena asked. "You want to go to your room now?" She purposely spoke to her aunt in Spanish; not so much for Juliana to understand her better, but so that the lion-haired intruder could not. "Vamonos," she whispered assertively, rising from her chair and pulling her aunt along with her.

"I can get there myself, "Juliana argued. "I'm not a *lisiado,* a cripple."

"Por supuesto no," Marlena answered. "Of course not, I just want to help you." She glanced round to the others at the table. "Please excuse us, goodnight everyone."

Tristan immediately pushed back from the table and stood. "Buenas noches, Senorita. Senora." Although he addressed both women, his blue eyes fixed upon Marlena alone. It gave her shivers, and to Marlena's mind, not in a good way. She ushered her aunt out of the room as quickly as Juliana's limping steps would allow.

Not proper. Not proper at all, his provocative stare. He'd seen enough already, Marlena thought, and hadn't the decency to avert his eyes in a moment of respect. Her mother would have him escorted from the property before the plates were cleared if she'd known what had happened between her daughter and this stranger.

When she'd helped brush her teeth and change into her nightgown, Marlena tucked her aunt into bed. Her last duty was to apply the moisturizing cream to Juliana's burn-scarred limbs and face. As always, Juliana insisted on a coat of her favorite coral-colored lipstick, even before sleep.

"Why do you wear lipstick to bed, Tía?" Marlena sighed. "I'm tired of washing your pillowcases every day."

Her aunt's fiery green eyes flashed a warning that Marlena well knew meant, "don't go there, child." Aloud, Juliana said, "My lips may be burned, but they speak with the color of truth. Day and night," She snapped the lipstick tube closed and handed it to Marlena.

"All right. Have it your way," Marlena replied, placing the tube on the nightstand. "But someday, I'll have someone washing *my* pillowcases."

Juliana chuckled, a rare occurrence. Her gaze softened toward her niece. "Be careful what you wish for," she warned in her throaty voice. "It always comes with consequences. I'm living proof. I wanted to be a dancer, and I became one. But the price of your passions can be high, very high. Are you prepared to pay it for what you want, querida?"

Marlena returned her aunt's crooked, wry smile. "I would pay anything. Brave anything. Even fire."

"Mmh," Juliana grunted. "*Incendio.* That's how you'll end up. Consumed by flame, just like me."

"What a thing to say," Marlena said, wary of her aunt's reply. Her mother had always said Juliana possessed a wildness, an awareness beyond that of average people, and often spoke of visions and foreknowledge. Was this one of those times? "What do you mean by that?" she asked.

"The man who brought me," Juliana said, letting her head fall back on the pillow, but keeping her burning gaze on Marlena as if in warning. "He also brings great change. He knows the price I paid, and will be the reason you pay yours."

Marlena hoped she'd say more, but knew the conversation was closed and that she may never know the full story of her aunt's ordeal, or the newcomer's involvement in it. She stroked Juliana's brow. "Goodnight, Tía."

*

Although she did not speak or acknowledge him in any way, Tristan felt gratified that the woman he'd rescued all those months ago was alive and among her family. He watched Marlena and her aunt exit the room, his attention firmly fixed on Marlena's tight little posterior. He felt more like an intruder than ever, troubled by these unwholesome urges toward her, in addition to his unplanned view of the girl in her brassiere earlier. He wondered if she would tell her mother on him later. Or perhaps she was even too embarrassed to speak of such things. He hoped the latter.

"Senor Flynn," Bianca said, interrupting his thoughts. "Would you care for more wine?" She gestured to the open decanter on a nearby serving table, guarded by the omnipresent maid and her stern countenance.

Surrounded by members of the extended Sanchez family, Tristan glanced around the many faces at the table, unsure what would be considered the most polite response. Accept or decline? "No, gracias, Senora Sanchez. As delicious as it is, I must say no. I need to keep my wits about me for the trip home."

Bianca smiled, and lowered her hands atop one another on the table. "That is most sensible," she said. "Will you have more to eat, then?"

Tristan returned her smile and placed his napkin over his plate. "No, ma'am. Thank you so much for allowing me to dine with you. I can't remember a more wonderful meal. I should be going now. I'm so glad Miss Juliana and her son are well and in the good hands of her family. Thank you again. Goodnight." He rose to leave, deciding that her offers of more wine and food might be her way of asking for his departure.

His hostess also stood, and the beady-eyed server wordlessly disappeared from the room at her movement. "As you wish, Senor Flynn. But it is late. I don't like to allow my guests to travel in the dark. We are outside of the city, and the roads can be quite treacherous at night."

Tristan agreed with her on that point. The route into the villa hadn't been easy to navigate; in the dark would be worse, and quite possibly swarming with wildlife as well. But what choice did he have?

"There may be serpentia," she added, her smile fading. "Please, we always have room for overnight guests. You must stay with us, por favor. For your safety, and our peace of mind."

Snakes. Tristan shivered inside. The others at the table appeared to concur. "Stay, sit and eat," said an older gentleman to his right, possibly an uncle or other close relative. "Have more wine. We make it right here in our villa." Two youngsters at the opposite end of the table clapped their hands and chanted for him to stay. It seemed the Sanchez family wouldn't have it any other way. He couldn't escape the feeling of being inducted into some privileged inner circle. Stay he would.

"I don't know what to say. Such kind hospitality. Thank you." He lowered his eyes in humble acquiescence.

"De nada," Bianca said. "Consuelo's gone to turn down a bed for you. Meanwhile, do have more wine." She reached for the decanter herself and filled his goblet with the rich, red liquid, before refilling her own. She raised it in a toast. "To our honored guest, who has reunited our family. Salud."

"Salud," Tristan echoed, keeping his eyes on Bianca as he emptied his glass. So the maid had a name. Consuelo. He'd make sure to steer clear of her if possible.

"What's going on?" All eyes turned to the new voice. Marlena stood in the archway leading to the dining room in which they sat, the question remaining on her face long after the words had left her lips. "What are you all drinking to?" She seemed curious, yet annoyed. Tristan swallowed the last of his wine with an uncomfortable gulp.

"Marly," Bianca said. "Thank you for taking care of Tía Juliana. Senor Flynn will be staying the night. We were toasting our thanks to him for bringing her back to us."

Marlena took a few slow steps into the room. "Si," she said. "For that we are grateful." She glanced between Tristan and her mother. "May I have a glass, too?"

Bianca's smile faltered, but nodded her permission. "Of course you may, dear, you're eighteen now." She filled the wine goblet at Marlena's place setting.

Marlena took it and downed its contents in one pass. She raised the empty glass in Tristan's direction. "Salud," she said, then turned on her heel to leave the room the way she'd come, leaving all eyes staring after her.

Chapter Four

The reflection off the mirrored disco ball overhead cast white, dancing bubbles spinning across the ballroom walls. Loud flamenco music filled the smoky air. It felt hard to breathe, but Marlena inhaled rapidly as she twirled down the runway. The skirt of her sequined, full-length gown spun like a pinwheel about her legs. She'd made it, made the catwalk as a top model and her smile couldn't have been wider.

She stopped at the end of the runway, striking a pose as the cameras flashed. Breathless, she turned and strode back down the length of the catwalk, her long brown tresses caressing her shoulders as they swung to her practiced sashay.

A man waited for her in the dressing room doorway. He had no name, and his features were indistinct. She knew only that he wanted her, and that it was he who'd made the dream possible.

"Cariña," he whispered, taking her into his arms as she landed exultantly against him. "Tu es brillante." Then he kissed her, as full and beautiful a kiss as she could imagine. Her world spun into a shimmering vortex that enveloped her, then faded to darkness.

Drawing a sharp breath, Marlena opened her eyes. No

glittering ballroom did she behold; only the gray, predictable shapes of her bedroom furniture, dimly outlined by the moonlight filtering in from the window.

A dream. Nothing but a dream. She shifted beneath her bedsheets in frustration at being no closer to it than ever before. The room felt hot and her throat dry. She threw back the covers and got out of bed. The floor tiles cooled her feet as she crossed the room. The heavy oak door swung open at her touch and she slipped noiselessly through the hallway and down the stairs to the kitchen.

She had no need for lights; she knew the villa by heart. A large water cauldron stood in one corner of the kitchen. As she plunged the dipper into the cool liquid, the overhead light snapped to life. Blinking against the sudden brightness, she looked up to see their mysterious houseguest standing before her with his finger on the light switch.

"Lo siento," he said, his voice rough with sleep. "I...I came for some water." He gestured toward her as she stood by the cauldron. "I see you've beaten me to it."

Marlena eyed him up and down. His bushy blond hair framed his face and he looked much younger this way with unkempt curls dipping forward into his eyes. He wore jeans but no shirt. She guessed he had slept in the nude, only donning his pants when he came in search of water. Suddenly she became aware of her own attire. A plain cotton nightgown with ruffles at the neck and a hem that reached barely to her knees. She dropped the water dipper to cover herself with both arms.

Tristan blinked and lowered his eyes. "Lo siento," he said again. "I would still like some water. Do you mind?" He edged nearer to the water cauldron.

Marlena moved aside, but continued to stare at him. He lifted the dipper and offered it to her first. She retrieved two glasses from a nearby shelf and handed one to him. He took it, then motioned to fill her glass first. She held it out with one hand while keeping her other arm folded across her chest. When both glasses were filled, they drank. After a few sips, Marlena licked her lips and watched him empty his glass. Her curiosity rose to the surface, emboldened by the absence of prying eyes. "Why are you here?" she asked.

Tristan finished his drink and regarded her with an unreadable expression. "To inquire about your aunt and her baby. You've taken good care of them. Something I couldn't have done."

Unconvinced, Marlena felt her mouth twitch. "What happened to her? Tell me the truth. Why were you involved? Did you hurt her?" Tristan's eyes opened wider. He seemed surprised by her pointed questions. "Did you rape her? Is Jorge your son? Is that why you came here? To see if he lived and ease your conscience?" She hadn't meant to become angry, but the more she spoke, the more she realized she wanted to know. Know who he was; what he'd done. Uncover his true purpose here, if there was one.

"No," he said, his eyes hardening. "I helped her. I saved her. I never touched her."

"Then who did? She won't say; she is too ashamed. Tell me, or my mother will hear about you spying on me. You'll be sent away before daylight."

Tristan set his glass down. "He was a good man, an honorable man. But he's dead." Marlena winced at this but kept silent, prompting him to say more. "He loved her. I swear that he did." Tristan shook his head. For some reason he felt uncomfortable retelling the story. "He got her a job there as a dancer, at the hotel – El Mirador. It caught fire and was destroyed. Himself along with it. I couldn't save him, but I saved her; and the baby."

"Why?" she persisted. "Were you not in danger, too?"

"He was my friend." Tristan shrugged. "I have no other reason."

Marlena softened her gaze. His words resonated with honesty. He was not a brute. Not the one who hurt Juliana. Perhaps he might be just as he appeared, and somehow this made her glad.

"You don't like me, do you?" he said. His abrupt statement doused her warming thoughts toward him. She had begun to like him, and the idea that he thought otherwise made her uneasy. It wouldn't do to become enemies. He might be useful.

"I did not say that," she answered, lowering her arms to her sides. She hadn't considered whether he liked her or not. It would be better if he did, she realized. Perhaps her thin nightgown was advantageous. He looked at her with a new interest, his eyes traveling up and down her lightly concealed figure. She took a step closer. "Have you ever been to Madrid?" she ventured.

Tristan stood his ground. "Yes."

"Can you take me there?"

"What do you mean?"

"I want to leave here. Go to modeling school in the city. I'll never get there by staying here, living this kind of life. Can you take me?"

"I don't have a car. I hitched a ride most of the way here."

"You drove a truck before. What happened to it?"

"It wasn't mine. I borrowed it."

"You can drive. All we need is a vehicle."

Tristan stepped away, in the direction of the exit. "I think we shouldn't have this conversation. At least not until morning."

Marlena bit her lip. She might lose her nerve by morning. A strange insanity began to fill her brain, born of desperation and the heat of the moment. She raised a hand to slip off one shoulder of her nightgown, and cupped her breast with the other. "Do you like what you see?" she asked, her words a breathy whisper.

Tristan shook his head and backed farther away.

"No?" she asked.

"Yes; I like what I see. I've seen you in my dreams since the day we met. But this is not right. You don't need to do this. Please go back to bed. Goodnight."

She stood alone in the kitchen after he'd left. She felt sick. Sick at what had come over her to expose herself in this way. Sick that he'd rejected what she'd offered…she wasn't sure herself exactly what she was offering. Sick that she'd blown perhaps her only chance to escape her small life. Yet his words hung in the air like a tantalizing fragrance. Since the day we met. He'd been dreaming of her? Had he liked her all along? What did he think of her now, now that she'd debased herself in front of him? If only she hadn't been so impatient. Maybe he would have helped her without such brazen encouragement.

Her mind full of conflicting thoughts, Marlena shut off the light and hurried through the shadowed halls to her room. She sank miserably into bed and covered her face with the sheets, falling into a troubled sleep.

*

She awoke to the sound of Lupé's barking. Slipping from her bed, she crossed to the window to determine what had upset the dogs. She could see nothing from her vantage point, so she dressed quickly and ran downstairs. Someone knocked at the back door. Marlena opened it to find Ernesto standing there.

"Hi Marly," he said, pressing a finger to the bridge of his glasses and pushing them into place as he always did. "Sorry it's so early, but I…"

Marlena cut his sentence short by flinging her arms around him. Suddenly, she had never been so glad to see him. The events of yesterday had made her yearn for the normal, the sane. Ernesto was her anchor.

"Hey," he said. "What's all this? I've just brought the rest of the timber order, like I said I would."

"I know. I know I can always count on you," she said, still hugging him tight. Ernesto relaxed his stance, raising his hands to rest on her back. He neither resisted nor reciprocated. Marly sensed he was still resentful of her rebuff from the other night. "I'm sorry for what I said the other day. We'll always be friends."

"I'm glad, Marly. You were just upset before."

She released him and stepped back. "Can you stay for breakfast? I'm sure Consuelo will have something ready soon, come inside."

"Okay, sure," he said. "How is the baby doing?"

"Fine. Everyone's fine," Marlena said, nodding her head in resignation. "Everything's the same. Like always." She stuck her lip out and turned back to the kitchen.

Ernesto followed. "You don't sound fine. Are you still thinking about Madrid?" They sat down at the oversized kitchen table, its thick wood top scarred with years of service and burnished over with dark wax.

"More than ever," she said, remembering with embarrassment how she'd practically begged Tristan to take her. Where was he now? She didn't want to face him again; perhaps he'd already left. She smoothed her hands over the table's worn surface then looked up at Ernesto. "If you won't go with me, could you at least give me a ride there?"

His face registered disappointment. "Where? To Madrid? Drop you there like a hitchhiker? You wouldn't be safe…I couldn't do that, no." He shook his head as if that settled the matter. "What about school? We have less than two months to go before graduation. Surely you don't want to quit now, that would be foolish."

Marlena felt her frustration growing. "Since when are you the judge of what's foolish or wise? Right or wrong? You're the fool, if you think I'm going to stay here forever. And a bigger fool if you stay here yourself. Didn't you say you wanted to learn things, build things?"

"I can learn things right here," he answered. "Build things, too. There's always carpentry work to do, repairs. What do you think I brought that timber for? I'm going to help build that pig barn your mother wanted."

"Pig barn," Marlena scoffed. "Is that the limit of your talent, your ambition? A pig barn?"

Ernesto's brown eyes darkened. He took a moment before speaking. "Maybe you were right, Marly. Maybe we can't be friends, after all." She felt sorry the moment her words left her lips. She'd hurt him without meaning to. She didn't want to fight with him; she wanted to escape with him. He stood up from the table. "Thanks for offering breakfast, but I think I should go."

"No, wait, please." She went to his side of the table. "I'm sorry. Yes, I'm upset. But I shouldn't take it out on you." She reached for his hands and took them in hers. "And we're more than friends."

He seemed wary, but squeezed her hands in response. "You know I want to be," he said, his voice subdued. She laid her head against his chest. A noise from the hallway startled them both. Marlena looked up to see a figure standing in the kitchen doorway.

"Oh," Tristan said, taking a step back in the direction he'd entered. "Excuse me. Sorry to interrupt."

Marlena's heart fell to her toes. Madre de Dios, she cursed silently. Now this newcomer must think her a flirt, a floozy! The day had barely started and it was already a disaster. She dropped her hands and pushed away from Ernesto.

"Who's that?" Ernesto asked, a tinge of insult in his voice.

"Nobody. Wait here," she said, and followed Tristan's retreat into the hallway. He stood there, looking uncomfortable and glancing around for another exit.

"I was just leaving," he said. "Thank you for your hospitality. I see I'm intruding."

Marlena opened her mouth to speak, but Bianca's cheery voice rung out instead. "Good morning, Senor Flynn." Her mother descended the stairs, flashing a bright smile toward him. She looked sidelong at Marlena. "Marly, dear, you're up early. You must have dressed in a hurry. Go put on something more appropriate."

Marlena knew that disapproving look, and closed her mouth like a clamshell. In her haste she'd thrown on a ratty shirt and jeans that had lain on the floor in her room. She knew better than to be careless with her attire when company was about. But something in her mother's attitude struck her odd. It occurred to Marlena that just a few hours ago she was certain that Bianca would throw Tristan out on his ear for impropriety; now she seemed to be welcoming him with open arms. Hmph! She turned and marched up the stairs without another word, leaving Ernesto behind without so much as an introduction. Marlena lingered at the top of the stairs, out of sight from the trio below, and listened.

"Ernesto," Bianca said. "How good of you to drop by. I'd like you to meet someone. This is Senor Tristan Flynn, from Wales. Senor Flynn, this is Ernesto Alvarez, a dear friend of Marly's."

"Buenos dias," Ernesto's voice grumbled.

"A pleasure," Tristan replied. "Um, thank you again for your hospitality, Senora Sanchez. I want to get an early start, so I should be going now. Adios."

"As you wish, Senor Flynn; it was our pleasure to have you stay with us. However, I wanted to ask you something. Are you currently employed?"

A pause. "I am between jobs at the moment. All the more reason to be on my way, to find my next job."

"Well then, I had a wonderful idea come to me overnight. Don Giorgio, the pastor at our church, is looking for someone to help with repairs. You said you studied to be an engineer, I believe?"

Marlena's breath caught. What? She's offering him, a stranger, a job? And right in front of Ernesto, too, who she knows darn well could do that kind of work! Her heart pulsed an insulted ache for Ernesto. Passed over by two women in less than five minutes. How could she let this happen to her best friend? Aunt Juliana had spoken the truth. This stranger brought change with him; and perhaps not all of it good.

Chapter Five

The room in which he slept barely measured six feet across, its length not even twice that. In fact, it hardly met the criteria to be called a room, as it only had three walls. The fourth was actually the outer wall of a church. It more resembled a shed or a lean-to, if one were to get technical. And engineers were seldom less than technical.

Tristan made the best of it though, and straightened the sheet and blanket that covered his cot. He poured water from a pitcher into a basin that sat on a wooden washstand at the opposite end of the narrow space, and washed his face in it. Such were the limits of his amenities at the Dama de Gracia Immaculata parish church, and he wasn't about to complain. Free lodging and paid work were, irony intended, 'blessings' to a displaced and penniless foreigner.

He could feel the temperature rising inside the shelter already, though it was barely past sunrise. The closeness and heat made him uneasy. It brought back too many memories of El Mirador and that terrifying night he'd lost Ari. Confined spaces would be a problem for him forever now, which didn't bode well for an engineering career. For that reason, he'd been up as early as possible every morning, making repairs to the little church. What began with some minor wall plastering had now extended to mending and refinishing the red-tile roof. Not the most desirable job to undertake in the hot April sun but far better to be out in the open air than indoors. He had no doubt the good pastor would continue to bring other deficiencies in the building to his attention.

This spring seemed especially dry, and therefore hotter than normal. He pushed aside the slatted wooden door and stepped out into the bright Spanish morning. It creaked open on its ancient hinges and then slapped shut behind him, the sound reminiscent of the many roadside outhouses Tristan had the misfortune to visit during his travels on the continent.

Pastor Giorgio greeted him at the rear entrance of the tiny church. "Buenos dias, mi hijo," he said with his usual jovial attitude. Don Giorgio's portly frame filled the doorway, his cassock providing minimal disguise to his protruding belly. Tristan liked the man; his stature and personality reminding him of Santa Claus. He never failed to make Tristan feel welcome and appreciated.

"Buenos dias, Padre," Tristan replied with a slight bow of his head. "I should be finished with the roof today. What else do you need me to start on?"

The pastor smiled and placed a hand on Tristan's shoulder. "You're a fast worker, son. I never expected the roof to be finished so quickly. Come, have something to eat before you continue. You can afford to take the time." He guided Tristan inside the building to the small common area at the back of the church that was used as a kitchen, for meetings and various other purposes that didn't have to do with daily worship. A long table stood in the center of it, laid out with dried fruit, pastries and a pitcher of milk. The pastor gestured for him to sit across from him.

Tristan did so, poured himself a glass of milk and tore into a honey-glazed roll. "Delicioso," he commented, savoring the sweet coating of the bread as it melted in his mouth. "Are these from the bakery down the street?"

Don Giorgio grinned. "Panaderia," he said. "Bakery. And calle means street. You have an interesting accent. Do you know much Spanish?"

Tristan swallowed his bread and gave the pastor a look of apology. "Lo siento, I don't. A few phrases, but not enough for a long conversation."

The pastor interlaced his fingers atop the wooden table. "Do you like it here? Enough to stay for awhile? I know I could keep you busy with repair work. And I know others that could use your help as well. You might consider learning the language."

Tristan nodded. He did indeed plan to stay awhile, but not wholly for the reasons the pastor had just outlined. "You're right, I should. And other things about Spanish life, culture. Can you teach me?"

Don Giorgio wagged his chubby face side-to-side in consideration. "Por supuesto, of course, but there are better teachers, and I have my flock to tend," he answered with a chuckle. "Perhaps one of our Sunday School teachers might do. I will ask this week." He nodded in affirmation of his own solution. "Si, that will do nicely. Now, if you've finished breakfast, I will show you what else needs fixing around here. As an engineer, I'm thinking you need a bit more of a challenge than carpentry."

The pair ventured outside and across an adjacent courtyard to a charming, old-fashioned well that stood in the center of the yard. It looked positively story-bookish, with its circular brick sides and tiny gable roof.

"This well has drawn people from all over the region as a place of reflection and prayer. It is regarded as a holy icon, where religious pilgrims paused for renewal on their journeys to spread the faith. It has stopped giving water, however; and the locals take this as a rather bad sign. I'm afraid we may be heading for a drought this year. I suspect it's either a natural depletion of the water table, or something is blocking it. Do you suppose you could repair it?"

Tristan leaned his hands on the bricks and looked it over. "Was the water used for drinking? Is it safe? Has it been tested? How was the water distributed before?"

Pastor Giorgio laughed aloud. "Now those are engineering questions, if ever I heard any. If the water flow is restored, I'm sure it would need testing in any case. Yes, the people believe that to drink it is to become spiritually renewed; however, to bathe in it would be considered especially significant and life-changing. But that's a lot of water to be hauling by hand."

Tristan gazed thoughtfully at the antique mechanism, then smiled at the good pastor. "Si. Por supuesto. Of course."

"Aieee, you are learning already," Don Giorgio said with an approving smirk.

*

Marlena watched from a distance as Ernesto took another swing with his hammer. He pounded into the wooden frame of the soon-to-be pig barn with such force, she wondered if in his mind each nail might have the face of someone on it. Tristan Flynn? Her mother? Maybe even her own, more likely. Bang—the hammer hit home. Bang—again. Bang! She walked toward him as he stood with his back to her, immersed in his project. As she drew nearer, she could see the nail heads countersunk into the wood from his angry blows. Suddenly she felt as though she didn't know the man at all, his manner so different, or rather indifferent, ever since that morning he'd met Tristan.

A good thing that Tristan had left shortly afterward thanks to her mother's intervention. It had saved her the agony of facing him again. She hadn't spoken much to Bianca since then either, so miffed was she at her discounting Ernesto's obvious suitability for the job over a newcomer. How could she repair their friendship, and more, convince him at last to leave this place and take her with him?

"Ernesto?" she asked tentatively, as he held a nail in place and prepared to drive it home. He raised his arm with the hammer in hand, ready to strike. "Ernesto!" she shouted, before he could swing again.

Startled, Ernesto halted his motion and snapped his head in her direction. He gazed at her for a short moment, then turned back to his work. "What?" he asked, re-gripping the tool in his hand, appearing unwilling to pause for her sake. "I'm busy."

Marlena cleared her throat. "I can see that. Can't you stop and talk to me for a minute?"

He drove the nail into place with a single hit, then slung the hammer into his toolbelt. "About what? What's there to talk about?" he said, looking over the structure.

"You. Me. Our future. Our friendship," she tossed out the options.

Finally, he deigned to look at her. "According to you, I have no future."

Marlena winced. "I never said that! I said there was no future here, on this farm. Why are you angry with me for wanting something better? Not just for myself, but for you, too."

"I like it here," Ernesto said simply. He removed his glasses and brushed them on his shirt front, clearing the sawdust from the lenses. "I like you. I like things the way they are, or were," he emphasized his last word. "Why does anything have to change?" His voice took on a painful note.

"Everything changes," Marlena replied. "You can't stop change. Even El Caudillo, our President, has changed, now that he's an old man. And that is paving the way for us to change our own lives, don't you see? It's our time, our chance. Don't waste it."

Ernesto replaced his eyeglasses and looked at her in earnest. "You know what I think is a waste? You and me wasting time arguing…when we could be together. For real. Not just friends."

There it was, in as plain language as it could be. She didn't want to encourage him exactly, knowing he had romantic intentions that she did not reciprocate. But perhaps dangling some hope could spur him into action. "We could be together in Madrid," she said, biting her lip.

He blinked, and stared at her like a startled rabbit. "Maybe we could," he answered after a moment. "But first I have to finish this barn." He thumbed behind him at the partially-built pen.

Marlena's heart jumped. Had she done it, changed his mind? "Lo se, I know. How long will it take you?"

He turned to view the project. "We still have school, you know. We can't go anywhere until after that."

She nodded, a bit disappointed. If she had her way, they'd be on the road already. But he was right; she couldn't afford to fail her exams and ruin her chances for University, in case her dreams of modeling never came to fruition. But she couldn't think that way. She had to have faith in her own determination.

"Marly!" Bianca called for her from the house, interrupting her complicated thoughts. Marlena and Ernesto both glanced in the direction of the voice. "Come here, I need you," her mother shouted.

Marly wrinkled her nose. "I can't wait to get out of here," she whispered sideways. Ernesto laughed, and she couldn't help but join in. She had her best friend back. "Ya voy, mama; I'm coming!" She turned and sprinted to the house.

Bianca stood in the kitchen with Consuelo, tucking items into a large basket. "What's all this?" Marlena asked, noting the generous amounts of breads, cured meats, cakes and fruit filling the basket.

"José is going into town this afternoon to take care of some business for me. I want you to ride along and deliver this basket to Pastor Giorgio."

"Oh, is the church having a food drive again?"

Bianca covered the basket with sheets of newspaper and tucked in the edges. "No. I wanted to thank him for taking Senor Flynn into his employ. I'm sure he can't pay him much, so at least I can see to it that they both eat well."

"Oh." She didn't expect that answer. Her mother seemed overly interested in Tristan's welfare, but perhaps she was reading too much into it. Running this errand also meant she may have to face the man again herself, and that thought made her nervous. Thinking about Tristan Flynn stirred up multiple feelings in her. Embarrassment, resentment, curiosity; some she couldn't even describe. She knew her stomach fluttered when his name came up in conversation. Perhaps she was reading too much into that, as well. "What time is José leaving?"

A vehicle engine rumbled to life in the yard outside. Bianca looked over her shoulder out the window. "Now, I think. Go get changed. I'll tell him to wait for you."

Marlena did as her mother asked, and changed into a dress suitable for wearing in church, along with a cardigan sweater to cover her shoulders, then went outside to meet José. He smiled at her through the open window of the farm truck and gunned the engine as though preparing for a race. Marlena laughed, and climbed in the passenger side. "Yeah right. As if this pile of rust could outrun anything faster than a mofeta!"

José laughed too. "Mofeta? A skunk? This well-oiled machine?" He put a hand over his heart. "I'm offended."

Marlena shook her head. She liked all the workers on her family's estate. She'd known most of them since childhood.

José was about her age, and got along well with him; he always joked around and made her laugh. He would be one of the only things she would miss when she left. "Vamonos," she chuckled, waving her hand forward.

The old vehicle ground into gear and lurched its way to the gate. Marlena held onto the basket handle to keep its contents steady. As they turned onto the main road that led to the city, the ride smoothed out, and a breeze caught the edges of the newspaper sheets. Marlena grabbed one before it flew out of the windowless truck cab, and printed ad on it caught her eye. She read it, and re-read it, to be certain she understood.

Models wanted immediately.
No experience necessary - free training provided.
To audition apply in person.

It gave an address in Madrid. This wasn't the school she'd applied to. It looked like a private agency. With free training? It seemed too good to be true. Her eyes fixated on the printed words, the tantalizing offer bouncing around in her mind. She might not have to wait until graduation! And it would save the cost of courses, too. She folded the paper and slid it into her handbag.

Chapter Six

Miraculously, a slow trickle emerged from the open end of the pipe. Tristan smiled and exhaled in relief. He wiped his forehead with the back of his hand and eased himself upright from his crouched position over the mechanism. He opened the valve wider, and the flow of clear, sparkling water grew to a steady stream.

"Gracias a Dios," Pastor Giorgio exclaimed as he stood nearby. "Bien hecho, well done!" A small crowd of onlookers gasped and spoke among themselves. The revered well again produced the treasured water, with a simple turn of a handle. The Pastor collected a quantity of water from the pipe into a blue ceramic vessel, then Tristan closed the valve.

Don Giorgio turned to the people watching, and lifted the blue jug with both hands. "Bienvenidos, todos el mundo. He aqui, nombramos esta el Pozo Misericordia," Tristan said, repeating the words Pastor Giorgio had written down for him, in Spanish and English, that he would say when the well was opened. "Welcome everyone. Behold, we name this the Well of Mercy."

After some investigation, Tristan discovered that the water table had lowered over a number of years leaving the drinkable water out of reach by manual means. With materials donated or purchased from local businesses, he'd constructed a simple siphon system. A small pump brought enough water up through a pipe to a higher elevation, initiating a downward flow to a tap at a lower elevation. Once the flow began, the draining action perpetuated as long as the outlet remained lower than the supply. The quality tests revealed no contaminants, just a slightly higher salinity with the added bonus of high magnesium content. The health benefits of this local mineral water were perhaps part of the benevolent mystique surrounding the little well.

While not exactly a miracle, the reaction from the residents made it seem like one. A number of children and their mothers approached the tap with pitchers and buckets, while the Pastor did the honors of opening and closing the valve for each recipient to collect their ration of 'holy' water.

With his mission accomplished, Tristan dusted off his hands and strode back toward the Gracia Immaculata. The sun would set in an hour or so, and he welcomed the coming respite from the day's heat. Tomorrow he would start on the next project Pastor Giorgio had lined up for him, whatever it might be. He heard the sound of running footsteps approaching from behind, then a tug on his sleeve. He stopped and turned around.

"Senor," a young boy of about ten years said breathlessly. "Me nombre es Ángel. Puedes ayudar a mi madre?" He spoke so rapidly, Tristan couldn't grasp any of his words beyond "My name is Ángel," and "mother."

He smiled at the kid, and spread his hands out. "Lo siento, mi Espanol es mal, Hable Inglés?"

"Ahh," the boy said, nodding and waving his hand excitedly. "Sure, I speak Inglés."

In that moment Tristan realized this as an opportunity to learn more Spanish, as he'd wanted. "Say your words again, more slowly," Tristan said. "So I can learn. What about your mother?"

Ángel nodded again. "You talk funny for an Englishman. "Puedes," he repeated, "Can you, ayudar, help, mi madre. She has trouble walking. She thinks the well water will make her legs strong again, but each day it gets harder for her. We can't afford a wheelchair. Can you build one?"

Tristan looked at Ángel. The boy's bright eyes and exuberant energy belied his thin frame and worn clothing. He was probably right about being unable to afford much; just staying alive and with clothes on his back might be a challenge for his family. "No sé, I don't know." he replied with a chuckle. "I'm from Wales, not England. I've never tried to build a wheelchair. Can't you get one from the hospital?"

Ángel shook his head. "No, no hospital. Por favor, come and meet her. She's right over there," he said, pointing at the line-up for the water spout.

Tristan turned and eyed the crowd. "Okay, vamonos," he answered. Ángel led him to a startlingly young-looking woman, leaning on a cane and shuffling forward with her water pail in hand. Blond hair peeked out from under a madras scarf pulled around her chin.

"Mami, esta el Milagro, Él te ayudará. He will help us." The woman looked at Tristan with round, blue eyes that betrayed hidden pain.

"Mi nombre es Tristan Flynn," he said, unsure of what Ángel had said about him.

"Gracias, el Milagro," she said, dipping her head in a polite bow.

"What did she call me?" he asked Ángel.

"El Milagro," Ángel answered matter-of-factly. "The Miracle."

*

Tristan made it back to the church before sundown. After scouring nearby businesses and garbage heaps he'd collected three bike tires, a metal chair frame and some wire. A wheelchair couldn't be that different from a bike, he concluded. Simpler in fact, since there were no pedals or brake mechanisms to construct.

He had to smile at Ángel's enthusiasm and his willingness to approach a stranger on behalf of his mother. While he assumed his name must be a variant of 'Ángelo' or similar Latin name, he liked thinking of the boy as an angel, a messenger. He'd certainly been that for his mother.

Pastor Giorgio had already returned to the Gracia Immaculata. As Tristan approached the back entrance, he could see the man seated at the breakfast table inside. He left his pile of repurposed parts outside the door and stepped across the threshold.

A surprise stood opposite the Pastor. Marlena held her hands gracefully clasped in front of her. She wore the white cotton dress in which he had first seen her. It made his cock jump with the memory of what he'd wanted to do with that skirt, but quickly controlled himself. He was inside a church, after all. "Hola, Senorita Sanchez." Damn, he wished he wasn't so dirty and sweaty in her presence. What was she doing here? Was she alone? Had she come here with the boy he'd caught her in an embrace with the day he'd left her family's villa?

"My mother insisted on sending food," she said, gesturing to an enormous basket on the table. Her expression seemed indifferent, almost cold; as though she felt put-upon to complete this little errand of mercy. Tristan was at a loss to understand this girl. He'd seen first-hand that she could be hot as fire, but now appeared chilled as ice. In any case, given the boyfriend, she might be completely uninterested in him aside from what she felt he could help her attain.

"Por favor, give her my thanks when you return," Tristan said.

Marlena nodded curtly, and curtsied to the Pastor. "Padre," she muttered softly, and turned to take her leave.

"Vaya con Dios, mi nina," Don Giorgio replied.

"Gracias," she said as she disappeared into the rectory and toward the front entrance. Tristan felt an inexplicable surge of panic at her exit. How could she come all this way simply to drop off a load of groceries and depart without a backward glance? Was she still angry at his refusal to continue their late-night discussion of a few weeks ago? He never exactly said no to her. There just hadn't been an opportunity to think the idea through.

"Wait," he called after her. "Excuse me, Padre," he said hastily to Don Giorgio, and hurried to follow her path through the church. She continued walking down the center aisle as though deaf. "Marlena, wait," he called again. She stopped, and he closed the distance between them with a few long strides. "Thank you also, for bringing the food."

Marlena turned, but stood her ground. "De nada, I am simply carrying out my mother`s wishes. Whether you eat or not is none of my concern."

"If you're not concerned, why come all this way? Why not send one of your house staff instead?"

Marlena hesitated, then folded her arms in a gesture of aloofness. "I did. José is with me, but he's busy with other duties in town. Don't think I made a special trip just for you," she said.

Her words stung, and Tristan's heart sank at the same time his irritation rose. He realized that he'd actually hoped—no, believed—that she'd come to him on purpose. Perhaps he'd caused a rift in her relationship with…Ernesto…the boy's name came to him. A stray vision skipped through his brain of this lovely girl spread out on his makeshift cot in the shed attached to the building. Her brown eyes watery and welcoming, and the crisp white skirt hitched up above her waist; the temperature around them so hot that tiny beads of perspiration lay on her upper lip as her mouth opened in anticipation of a kiss; her exposed panties damp with excitement. He forced the thoughts away.

"Very well. I won't keep you from your business, then. I suppose I thought you wanted to see me."

"See you?" Marlena repeated, as if the words were foreign to her mouth. "You've seen enough of me in any case; and that shame lies with me. I would ask that you forget all about that night Senor Flynn, por favor."

"I'm afraid you ask me to forget something that is already burned into my brain forever. Don't feel ashamed. You asked for my help, and I wasn't able to give it to you. I'm sorry."

"You never answered me either way."

"I didn't say no."

"But you didn't say yes."

"I hadn't the means to help you at the time. Why do you want to leave?"

Marlena exhaled impatiently. "I told you. I want to go to school in Madrid. I want a career. More and more girls are doing it now that the government isn't so strict; The universities are filling with young women. I want to be one of them."

Tristan frowned in thought. "Maybe there's a way we can help each other. If I can get a vehicle, will you show me around? Teach me more Spanish? I want to learn about the culture here. Then I could take you wherever you want."

Marlena's right eyebrow raised ever so slightly. "Perhaps," she answered. "What is it you wish to learn?"

"Anything. Everything. I'll tell you about it on the way to Madrid." He winked.

Marlena dropped her arms to her sides, a smile forming on

her face. "Buenas dias, Senor Flynn." She spun on her heel and reached for the metal latch on the great front doors.

"Tristan. You can call me Tristan. Is that a yes?" he asked.

She pulled on the latch and the big doors parted. "Tristan," she repeated.

He didn't want her to leave. He wanted to see her again. An idea sprung into his mind. "Can you bring me something from town?" he asked. "Here," he added, digging into his jean pocket. "I'd like some drawing paper and pencils. And a straightedge, if you can find one." He held out a few paper bills as she turned to look at him again.

"I'll look, she said, taking the money from him. "But I have to start home now, José is waiting for me. If I can find any of those items, I'll bring them another day, is that alright?"

Tristan smiled. "Esta bien, that's good. Gracias."

She nodded somewhat approvingly, and slipped out the doors. He watched her leave, her skirt swishing as she skipped down the steps to the street. Damn, he would find out what treasures lay hidden under that skirt if it was the last thing he'd ever do.

Chapter Seven

"I'm not sure, Marly," Ernesto said with a frown. "I don't have a reason to go into town right now." He dipped his paintbrush into the bucket and smoothed the whitewash onto the finished siding of the pig barn. Even Marlena had to admit he'd done a great job on the little building. Though only meant for animals, the structure was sturdy, roomy and almost graceful in its appearance. Ernesto had a knack for the aesthetic, and his coat of white paint certainly added to the finished product.

"Oh," she said absently, swishing a pattern in the dirt with one sneakered toe. "Does there have to be a reason? Why not just go for fun? See a movie?" She knew the idea of a date might spark his interest, even though she didn't see Ernesto that way. She didn't want to lose his friendship again, and if that meant leading him on just a teeny bit, she'd find a way to make things right again once her goal was accomplished.

She could see Ernesto grinning as he bent over the paint bucket and nudged his glasses further up the bridge of his nose with one knuckle while dipping the brush in. "Are you asking me on a date, Marlena Allesandro Sanchez?"

"Do I have to make a date to see a movie with my best friend?" she answered.

"What's playing?" he asked.

"Do you care?" He looked up at her through his paint-speckled lenses, and she threw him a coquettish smile. "Do you?" she repeated.

"Not really. As long as I get to see it with you."

"Saturday," she said, not as a question. "Now hurry up and paint. Haven't you finished that thing yet?" Ernesto made a move as if to chase her with the loaded brush in hand. She squealed in laughter and dashed away. Marlena skipped across the yard and up the verandah steps before turning to look at him. He did not follow, but went back to his work.

Saturday. The day that might change her life! She bought the things Tristan had asked for, and wanted to deliver them as soon as possible. She was dying to know if he'd found a car yet. Even if not, she could try to help him with his Spanish, and make him even more interested in traveling to Madrid. The museums and libraries there would show him everything he wanted to know about Spain. And she just might short-cut her way into the life she'd always wanted.

*

It didn't look like much. The driver's side had a big dent, and telltale rust showed along the edges of the wheel wells and bumper. Still, it was what he needed; a utility van. Parts wouldn't be too hard to find when needed, and the engine didn't seem in too bad of shape. The dent hadn't actually cracked the powder-blue exterior paint. The vehicle itself would do nicely to haul parts and supplies, and in a pinch, serve as a crash pad on wheels. While he wasn't crazy about the color, the price was right. A friend of the Pastor had agreed to trade the van for some work on his house and garden.

"Test-drive?" Tristan asked the man, gesturing with his hands as though turning a steering wheel.

"Si, si, drive," the man said, handing him the key.

With a bit of protest, the engine turned over and rattled to life. Tristan threw the gear into reverse and backed out of the yard, creating a swath through the tall grass that had grown up around the parked van. The man certainly hadn't driven the thing in a while.

The suspension seemed in good shape, as he negotiated the bumps and rocks in the dusty lane behind the yard. Clearly the van needed an oil change, lube and some cleaning up, but as he rounded a corner to turn onto the main street, he felt satisfied that the vehicle would suit his needs. No sooner had he entered the wider roadway of the main street, calle, he reminded himself, he found his route blocked by a giant tree. It stood directly ahead, planted conspicuously in the middle of a cobblestone square that connected with other streets. He stepped on the brake, but the vehicle didn't slow down. He pumped the brake pedal two more times then leaned his full weight on it before the van lurched to a halt, its grille just inches from the ancient, ribbed tree trunk that measured easily three feet across. Shit, a brake job would cost money, and what the hell was this tree doing in the middle of a bloody intersection?

Its black bark was rough and pitted, pieces of it peeled off and scattered on the ground below. A sagging rope fence laced around the tree, but his wheels had torn the cord in half. The tree's mammoth roots heaved up through the earth surrounding its base, the resulting humps more likely responsible for his stoppage than his brakes. He looked upward, taking in the sight of the entire tree, its leafless branches spreading out in a dark, wiry canopy overhead.

The tree looked dead. Perhaps the Pastor's prediction of a drought was correct. Startled passersby stopped in the middle of whatever daily business they had been going about to rubberneck at the scene. A few ventured forward in concern, children held back in their parent's grasp, while others drew nearer. Tristan got out of the van, knowing he would need to explain himself to the approaching onlookers.

"You okay, senor?" asked one man in farmer's coveralls. He looked at Tristan, but soon turned his eyes to the gigantic tree. He stepped over to it and touched the trunk, as though inspecting it for damage. Tristan worried more about the ruddy van, and crouched to examine the front of the vehicle and the tires. He hadn't struck the tree, thankfully, and the gnarled roots hadn't given him a flat tire.

"Buena suerte you did not hit the tree," the farmer man said.

"Si, muy suerte," Tristan replied, stringing together a few of his newly acquired Spanish words to say 'very lucky'. "The van," he said, pointing to the vehicle. "Bad brakes."

Farmer man nodded. "Mucha suerte. Tu Ingles?"

Tristan stood to his full height. "Si. Lo siento, but what is this tree doing right here?" A small gathering of people shuffled in a semi-ring around the area.

"It is El Guardián," the farmer man replied.

A familiar voice spoke up. "The Guardian of Zaragoza." Tristan turned toward the sound with a smile. Ángel stood in the circle of people, smiling back at Tristan. "It guards the city," he explained. "Been here for a thousand years!"

"Has it now?" Tristan said. "How do you know? Are you a thousand years old?" he teased. Ángel laughed, which in turn caused a titter among the crowd. He turned back to the farmer man. "I'll move the van, please stand back." As the people dispersed, Tristan motioned to Ángel. "Get in, if you want. Do you live close by?"

Ángel needed no urging. He happily trotted over to the

vehicle and climbed in. "You be in big trouble if you hit that tree."

"Why? It looks dead to me," Tristan asked as he climbed in the driver's seat. "It should be dug up and removed."

Ángel looked at him in horror. "No, no, It is El Guardián… it can't die."

"Why doesn't it have leaves, then? It's a hazard, in the middle of the road like that."

"Everyone knows it will live forever! It guards the city, it's older than the city!"

"Who told you that?"

"My mother. She said El Guardián wasn't always in the middle of the road. It's the other way around – the road is in the middle of El Guardián! The city grew around it. It used to mark the entrance to town, before there were houses. Before there were even people!" Ángel exclaimed.

Tristan backed the van away from the tree, the two of them bouncing in their seats as it crawled slowly over the monstrous roots. The van's brakes were weak, but functional if he applied them hard enough. The boy made the tree sound like some prehistoric deity. "You mean like a thousand years ago?" Tristan said with a smirk. "I think people have been here longer than that. Can you count to one thousand?"

Ángel shrugged. "It's a lot, that's all I know."

"Well, the tree still doesn't have any leaves. Why is that?"

"I don't know. Some say it's a bad year." Ángel glanced sideways at Tristan, then out the window. "That something bad will happen. I hope it gets leaves soon." He pointed at a confectionery store as they passed it on the street. "Let me out here."

"Okay," Tristan said and pulled over.

"Senor Milagro, have you built the wheelchair you promised?" Ángel asked as he slid out of the passenger side.

Tristan smiled. His to-do list seemed to be getting longer

and longer. "I'm nearly finished," he lied, making a mental note to give that project priority. "But call me Tristan. I'm no milagro, that's for sure."

"Okay, Tris…Tristran," the boy stumbled over the unusual name. "Think what you want, everyone else calls you El Milagro. Adios!"

Tristan thought about the tree as he drove around the block and back toward the home of the van's owner. With roots like that, surely the specimen could be revived, unless it was simply at the end of its lifespan. Impossible to say without knowing the variety. If drought conditions prevailed, the tree would have the same problem as the well, unable to reach the declining water table. It occurred to him that perhaps he could tap into the well mechanism and divert water to the tree through a pipe system the same way.

He found the van's owner standing in his weedy, grassed yard awaiting his return. "You like?" the man called to him as he pulled up.

"Needs brakes. You fix them?"

The man considered it, then nodded. "Si. I fix. Manana."

"Okay," Tristan said. "I'll bring it back tomorrow." With that, he drove off toward the Gracia Immaculata to show Pastor Giorgio their new acquisition.

Chapter Eight

True to his word, the man had fixed the brakes on his van the next day. Tristan drove it back to the Gracia Immaculata with pride. Once he'd finished running a few errands for Don Giorgio, he'd be free for the day, and could attend the Saturday market. He wanted to get some new clothes, locally handmade, to continue his immersion into Zaragozan community life.

As he pulled up to the church, an unfamiliar vehicle took up most of the available parking space. Annoyed, he maneuvered alongside the 1950s vintage truck and cut the engine. The van rattled and shook with some afterburn before coming to a halt. He clucked his tongue in frustration. It still needed some work. He entered the church from the back as usual, to find Don Giorgio, Marlena and—the boyfriend—seated at the table. What was his name again? Ernesto.

"Good morning, Tristan," Don Giorgio beamed. "We have visitors again, as you can see."

"Good morning," Tristan replied, nodding to Marlena and Ernesto. "What brings you both here?"

Marlena placed a shopping bag on the table. "The items you asked me to buy," she said, a coquettish grin on her face. "I hope I got everything right."

Her expression made him happy, and Tristan returned her smile. If she came here especially on his account, it made him happier still. He was excited to tell her about the new vehicle, and that they could soon go to Madrid as they'd planned. "Gracias," he replied, reaching for the bag to take a look inside. Everything was there; the pencils, the paper and the metal straightedge, just as ordered. He wondered what it had cost. "Did I give you enough money?" he asked Marlena. He certainly didn't want her spending her own money on him.

"Oh yes, more than enough. Your cambio," she replied, digging into her handbag for change.

"Keep it, please. There can't be much left over. A little something for your trouble, at least."

"Gracias," Marlena replied, the shy grin reappearing on her pretty face, framed by her glossy brown locks. Her hair looked particularly shiny today, one side pinned back with a barrette. She'd worn a different dress today too, made of a red floral print fabric. Suddenly, it struck him that she and Ernesto might be on a date, and her mysterious smile was for him, and not Tristan. Something seemed to fall inside him at the notion.

"We're going to the movies," Ernesto piped up.

"What's playing?" Tristan asked, more out of politeness than curiosity.

Ernesto glanced over at Marlena, a look of deep affection in his eyes. It couldn't be missed. He was definitely in love with the girl. But was she in love with him? Tristan wondered. "We don't know," Ernesto laughed, taking her hand. "We're just going."

So, they were on a date after all. Tristan folded his arms in resignation and walked to the other side of the room to grab an orange out of a bowl. His stomach growled. He hadn't eaten yet today. "Why don't you come along, Senor Flynn?" Marlena asked. "If the film has English subtitles, it might be a good way to learn more of our language."

"An excellent idea," Don Giorgio chortled, oblivious to Ernesto's thinly veiled scowl. "You should go, Tristan; enjoy the company of people your own age, instead of a boring el Viejo like myself."

"You're not old, Padre," Marlena objected. "You're wise."

Tristan concentrated on peeling his orange. "Gracias por su invitación," he offered, doing his best to use the language of the land whenever he could. Would it impress Marlena? "But I have plans to go to the market today." He had no intention of becoming a third wheel in their private excursion.

"The market, yes!" Marlena exclaimed, with a clap of her hands. "I'd forgotten. We should go to the market, Ernesto. Instead of the movie."

Ernesto's brows knitted together, turning his face directly toward Marlena. "But it was your idea to see a movie, Marly. We can go to the market any time." Clearly, he was not loving the idea of giving up some alone time with her, or a sudden change of plans.

"I know but, it would be impolite not to show a newcomer around town. I'm proud of our town, aren't you?" Marlena argued.

Ernesto heaved a sigh, and clasped Marlena's hand a little tighter. "Of course, I am. If it's what you'd prefer, we can go to the market. Whatever you want, Marly."

Well, she certainly had Ernesto wrapped around her little finger, Tristan observed. The man was moonstruck, for sure. Marlena seemed eager to include Tristan in their plans. It didn't make sense that she'd make a special trip to see a movie with Ernesto, then brush him off just like that. Unless… it wasn't her intention to go to the movies in the first place. Maybe she wanted something else. He almost began to feel sorry for Ernesto.

Almost.

"Don't change your plans on my account," Tristan said. "I

like roaming around on my own time. Besides, I may need to get some more parts for my new van."

Marlena's brown eyes lit up, and Don Giorgio clapped his hands. "You got the brakes fixed?" he asked. "Muy bien, I could use a ride. I promised some of the rural parishioners a visit today."

"Sure, Padre. We can leave right away, if you like."

"You bought a van?" Marlena asked. "Where is it?"

"Come have a look," Tristan said, motioning outside with a tilt of his head.

Ernesto rose from his seat along with Marlena and followed Tristan outside. The three of them circled the rusty blue van, scrutinizing every ding and chip. "It's pretty old, but the previous owner is a mechanic and repaired all the major stuff. It'll be fine for what we need," Tristan explained. As Ernesto bent down to inspect the tires, Marlena stepped closer to Tristan.

"Is it reliable? For a long trip?" she asked, her voice low.

Tristan shrugged. "I guess we'll find out when we take one. But I think so."

Marlena nodded and stepped back a pace as Ernesto straightened and came toward them. "You may need new tires soon," he said, frowning. "Not much tread left."

"You're probably right. But they'll have to do for awhile," Tristan said. "Well, don't let Don Giorgio and I keep you from your movie. It looks like he's ready to leave." He pointed to the Pastor's portly figure approaching them from the church, his overcoat slung over one arm. "I'll head to the market when we get back. Maybe I'll see you there later."

"Maybe," Ernesto answered for both of them. He reached for Marlena's arm to guide her back to their truck. "If Marly wants to."

"Alright, adios," Tristan said with a casual wave, watching her be led away.

Over her shoulder, Marlena caught Tristan's gaze. Without needing to speak, her thoughts telegraphed one word to him. Madrid.

He nodded and smiled. She returned his smile and soon disappeared into the cab of the old truck. "I'm ready, mi hijo." Don Giorgio said, coming alongside him and interrupting Tristan's thoughts.

"Si, vamos," Tristan answered, opening the passenger door of the van and settling the overweight and aging clergyman in the passenger seat. His mind skipped ahead. He might have time next week to make a trip to Madrid. But there was still one potential obstacle. Ernesto. What exactly did his and Marlena's relationship consist of? Clearly, he was protective of her to the point of being jealous; that was obvious. He was certainly eager to please her. Tristan didn't get the sense that her feelings were reciprocal. What would happen if he got between them?

He started the engine and pulled away from Gracia Immaculata as the Pastor gave directions. Tristan had to remind himself that Marlena hadn't shown any interest in himself either, really. In fact, she'd been downright cold on most occasions, except when she seemed to want something from him. Perhaps this trip to Madrid was no different.

Tristan knew what he wanted; and it wasn't only to learn more about Spanish culture. His intentions weren't entirely that innocent. But what did she want? With growing clarity, he knew that Marlena Sanchez was the kind of girl to whom men would likely give whatever she asked for. And if he wasn't careful, Tristan might become one of them.

At each stop along their journey, Tristan waited patiently for Don Giorgio to conduct his official but informal visits, sitting in the van, drumming his fingers on the steering wheel. When it got too hot, he climbed outside the vehicle to stand or sit in the shade it provided. He felt amazed at each home they stopped at—realizing how the people living in these rural areas really had very little. A few chickens, a goat or cow; some grew gardens, others did not. The houses ranged from small but well-kept adobe structures to hovels that were barely more than shacks. Tristan shook his head. The contrast between this and the fast-paced, vibrant decadence of the cities and tourist places like El Mirador was truly stark. Guilt rippled through him as he thought of his time spent in such cavalier style alongside his flamboyant mentor, ignorant of how the majority of the country lived.

Most of the occupants were women and children, Don Giorgio having explained that a good portion of the men had left to find work in other parts of Europe. Those who had returned brought with them new ideas and continental values, igniting the rumblings of social change among the common populace. Change was always inevitable, and had already begun. He could foresee a sweeping economic and social awakening of this land, a land that until now had been steeped in centuries of history and tradition. Somehow, he knew in his soul he was going to be part of it; that by his past actions he owed it to this country to participate in its transformation.

At last, they returned to Zaragoza and the Gracia Immaculata, where Don Giorgio took his leave of Tristan. "Bless you, mi hijo; you have served God and my flock well today by your patience and kindness. Now, go and enjoy yourself in town."

"Gracias, Padre. I won't be long." The rotund cleric waved his goodbye and waddled into his sanctuary, leaving Tristan to his own devices. They had been a few hours on the road, but perhaps the market was still open. He decided to stretch his legs after the long drive and walk the few blocks there. Lively music and mouth-watering smells drifted toward him as he got nearer, and soon found himself in the middle of the action, the little plaza surrounding the stark presence of El Guardián alive with movement and sound.

Some stalls had closed up, but many others were still in business. He found one selling bright colored satin shirts, bittersweetly reminding him of the flashy attire that Ariel often wore. He moved along to another stall hawking woven serapes, ponchos and leather goods. He wondered if he could pull off the look he'd seen in the recent "spaghetti western" films. The girls in Britain went wild for actor Clint Eastwood, and Tristan wouldn't mind that kind of attention. At the proprietor's hearty insistence, he tried on a poncho and then of course felt obligated to buy it; but since his intention was to live like a local, it seemed a justifiable purchase.

He continued along the ring of stalls sporting his new poncho, picking out some decent jeans and a thick, hand-tooled leather belt. Working outdoors as he often did, a hat was a necessity and found a booth selling various western-style hats. He tried on several before discovering one that looked exactly like Clint Eastwood's. As he put it on his head, the savvy vendor smiled in approval, clearly assuring himself of a sale.

"It doesn't suit you," came a voice from behind. Tristan turned toward it, a smile brewing on his face despite the uncomplimentary words. He was rewarded with a view of the lovely Marlena standing a few feet away, arms crossed and looking him up and down in critique. She leaned to one side, displaying a tantalizing length of shapely leg.

"No?" he asked, tipping the brim down over his eyes. "How about now?"

She pursed her lips and shook her head. "You are no Clint Eastwood."

Tristan's eyebrows rose in surprise that she mentioned the actor. "Says who?"

"The film I just saw. High Plains Drifter."

Tristan chuckled at the coincidence. "Well then, I guess I shouldn't try." He returned the hat to the vendor's pile.

Marlena moved closer and plucked a different hat from the pile. "Try this one." She handed him a woven, tri-cornered number, which Tristan easily recognized. He also recognized the comely girl was teasing him. Was this her way of flirting, or did she hold as much disdain for him as her words intimated?

"Isn't that what bullfighters wear?"

"Matadores," she answered. "Yes. It is called a Montera."

Tristan eyeballed the black cap with its rounded knobs of fabric on either side of the ears. "I don't think my head's quite that big," he answered, declining to take it from her. She tossed it back on the pile.

"Have you ever seen a corrida, Senor?" Seemingly out of nowhere, Ernesto appeared by Marlena's side, a disapproving look on his tanned face. His tone suggested a challenge; a dare.

"A what?"

"A corrida—a bullfight."

"No, I haven't had the misfortune so far," Tristan said.

"Perhaps men from your country are not strong of heart. The sight of blood bothers you?" Ernesto continued, clearly trying to get a rise out of him. He wouldn't succeed.

"No. I just think it is a cruel, barbaric ritual."

"It's part of our culture," Marlena interrupted. "You wished to learn Spanish culture, did you not? Are you not a man of your word?"

Tristan felt his hackles rise, and also his jealousy as Ernesto intertwined his hand with Marlena's. "I assure you that I am," he replied, his voice firm. "There is a…corrida…tomorrow, isn't there?"

"There is one every Sunday," Ernesto nodded.

"Bien. Let's go, then," Tristan said, his gaze locking with Marlena's. "All of us."

Chapter Nine

Marlena wondered if the Zaragoza bullring would impress Tristan. If he was an engineer, as he said, he must have seen many kinds of structures and would no doubt be judging its construction as much as its purpose, considering his opinion of bullfighting. To her, the bullfights were simply another part of the omnipresent 'traditions' she had been surrounded by her whole life, and was slowly growing to despise.

But her feelings on the matter were unlikely to change the spectacle they were about to see. As they took their seats in the circular amphitheater, Tristan sweated visibly, the unrelenting sun bearing down on them. As the day wore on, the angle of sunlight would change and give them some relief, but the permanently shaded seats were reserved only for the highest-paying spectators.

The heat did not bother Marlena so much, knowing from experience to wear a wide-brimmed sunhat to these events. Her mother had always ensured she had one that matched her dress, ever since she was a little girl, and out of habit, did the same today. She clutched the brim as a rare breeze lifted beneath it, and stole glances at the men seated on either side of her.

Tristan, looking uncomfortable as perspiration beaded on his forehead; and Ernesto, gazing off into the distance with a defiant tilt of his chin. Both looked equally reluctant to be here. She knew Ernesto was trying to prove something; expose the foreign-ness, and therefore weakness, of their guest, hoping to demoralize him in Marlena's eyes. She did not relish nor appreciate Ernesto's behavior of late, which had all the signs of jealousy. But she had only herself to blame; it was she who forced contact between the two men, whether planned or unplanned.

Tristan too, had something to prove. That he was not faint of heart, as Ernesto had jeered; but Marlena could not shake the impression he thought very highly of himself—even superior to those around him, especially her childhood friend. Without meaning to, she had created enemies; or at least competitors. But competitors for what? Her attention, perhaps; but she sensed it went deeper than that. A ripple of guilt washed over her at being responsible for this uneasy situation, but trickled away as the sound of trumpet heralds signalled the start of the event.

The bullfighting teams paraded the arena to music, their incredible 'suits of light' on display. The brilliant colors and golden sequins flashed in the sunlight, and an electric excitement built in the air. Ernesto's arm curled surreptitiously about Marlena's shoulder, and she nudged it away. They were not on a 'date'. In fact, Ernesto's displays of affection had begun to irritate her. He'd especially begun doing this since Tristan's arrival. Was that the only time men showed their intentions? When there was competition involved? Did it have anything to do with their real feelings?

With this thought, Marlena struggled to analyze her own feelings. Did she dislike Ernesto's attention because she only saw him as a friend—or that she wanted Tristan's attention more? The truth struck a troublesome chord in her heart. She liked this blond stranger, despite her suspicions and hostility toward him. He was different. He was handsome. And he had the potential to change her life, in a way no one else could. Her pulse quickened. Her Tía was right!

She glanced over at Tristan, his mouth stiffened into a stern line, his muscular arms crossed against his body in a tight, defensive stance as he watched the action below. Did he still dream of her at night, as he said he did? The possibilities he represented were intoxicating. He did not need to stay here, shackled by tradition, as she felt. He dictated his own future, made his own decisions, which was exactly what Marlena wanted, too. It dawned on her that they were more alike than different, and it was a mistake for her to have goaded him and pretended to be so aloof. You catch more flies with honey than with vinegar, the old axiom said. Perhaps it was time to spread the honey, if she was ever to gain what she truly wanted.

*

Tristan's discomfort increased with every passing second, seated in the grandstand amid the press of thousands, the oppressive heat only one of many contributing factors. It made him think of the horrible night he'd last spoken with Ariel; facing each other in the darkened bowels of El Mirador, sweat and terror dripping from his skin in equal measure. He shook off the memory by sheer will, and shifted his thoughts back to the present.

Marlena sat next to him, looking blissfully unbothered by the morbid heat and more beautiful than ever in her pretty blue sundress and matching hat; and on her other side…sat his opponent. Tristan still didn't exactly get their relationship. He only knew he was determined to sever it somehow. With self-satisfied amusement he noted Ernesto's attempt to embrace Marlena's shoulders and her subtle brush-off of the same.

Hiding a smirk, Tristan looked away, focusing on the ominous tableau of color, man and beast in the ring below.

The fervor of the crowd, knowing what they were about to witness, stirred unexpected feelings within him. He did not understand blood sport; but a wicked fascination built in his mind, and a strange taste formed at the base of his tongue at the prospect of seeing it firsthand. He supposed it was some vestige of humanity's primal, savage nature that would never be completely submerged no matter how many centuries passed.

"This is the paseíllo, the parade," Marlena said, leaning slightly toward him. Her lovely floral perfume wafted beneath his nostrils. He'd never been this close to her before, nor even touched her; and now their bodies pressed against each other, creating a different kind of heat. One that built in his loins, and felt hotter than the air around them.

"It's quite a spectacle. When does the killing begin?" Tristan asked, mild disdain in his voice.

Marlena shot him a look, her lovely eyes narrowing. "It is not a simple 'killing'. There is much ritual and skill," she replied. Those men are the cuadrillas, the bullfighting teams. They are highly trained. After they circle the ring, we will see the bulls presented."

"Bulls? There's more than one?"

"Yes. A corrida usually has several bulls in one day, and a different cuadrilla for each."

Tristan wiped his brow with the back of his hand. My God, how can anyone stand to watch this? He hoped they did not have to stay for the entire thing. "A whole team against one animal hardly seems fair."

"If it is too much for you, you are welcome to leave," Ernesto interjected.

"Who said anything about leaving," Tristan shot back, refusing to rise to the bait. He kept his eyes on the ring. One by one, three gigantic fighting bulls entered the arena. The animals were massive, larger than any bovine he'd ever seen in his home country. Obviously bred and raised for a singular purpose, their huge neck and shoulder muscles flexed and rippled as they moved about the ring, sunlight reflecting on the ridges of their smooth, dark coats. They were nothing short of magnificent, and it seemed incomprehensible that by sundown, all would be methodically slaughtered amid thunderous applause.

Rich aromas filled the amphitheater, a feral mix of animals and humans, but also of flowers and fried food from the vendors below; a heavy, bloodthirsty melange that settled over the scene like a shroud. A death shroud. But Tristan wasn't going to turn away. If he were to have any stake in this country, or understand the girl seated next to him, he must observe, and learn.

Marlena explained to him with cool, almost bored detachment each part, or tercio, of the fight as it played out before them. Three men of the cuadrilla, called Banderilleros, thrust their colored capes at the animal, inciting him to charge so that the Matador could judge its ferocity, its strengths or weaknesses. Tristan chose to imagine the cheers of the crowd as praise for its grace and strength rather than the antics of its tormenters.

Then came the Picadores, mounted on horseback and armed with ominous, spear-like poles. The horses wore suits of padded armor, but the riders did not.

"This is Tercio de Vara, the part of lances," Marlena said.

"They're going to stab it?" Tristan asked. "I thought that was the Matador's job."

"It is the Matador who kills the bull," she said. "The Picadores simply weaken it."

Tristan's inner anger and apprehension rose. It was one thing to pit man against beast, but there was no fair play here—the outcome was predetermined and assured by multiple levels of assault on an animal who had no chance to escape. Or did it? "Does a bull ever survive the fight?" he asked.

"I don't know. I've never seen that happen in my lifetime," Marlena stated, but it was Ernesto who answered.

"It can happen. Occasionally a bull may survive the faena, the fight. The presidente may also free the bull if he feels it has given an exceptional performance. But it brings dishonor to the Matador either way."

"So, the odds aren't good in other words."

"No, senor. They are not." Ernesto replied, with a piercing glance through his wire-rimmed eyeglasses, telegraphing his insinuation that neither were Tristan's. Tristan matched his stare for a long minute, then turned away. A silent gauntlet had been thrown. More than Matadors were fighting today. He and Ernesto were in the ring, too, waging an age-old combat for the affections of a woman. Only one could win; and Tristan was bound and determined to be the man who did.

He watched in stony silence as the Picadores drew blood from the animal with blows of their deadly lances. As the bull charged at the armoured horses, lowering its massive head in an attempt to gore and lift them, the riders plunged their long blades into its majestic neck and shoulders. Soon, the bull became visibly damaged, its spilled blood seeping into the sand that covered the floor of the ring and disappearing as if it had never been there. Somewhat mercifully, a trumpet herald signalled the end of this phase of the fight, but also the beginning of the next.

The bull pawed and trotted its way around the ring, appearing disoriented and in distress. The crowd cheered and shouted their praise of the Picadores performance, unconcerned with the animal's alarming condition. But the ordeal was far from over. Marlena explained the next part they would see was the Tercio de Banderillas, where the Matador enters for the first time and attempts to lodge several colorful barbed sticks called banderillas into the bull's mighty shoulders.

With much flashing of colored capes and fanciful maneuvers, the bull was further induced to charge directly at the Matador himself, who would then thrust a banderilla into its flesh as it passed beneath the fluttering cape. Wild, enthusiastic applause followed each pass, and Tristan swallowed his distaste at the sight of the heavy sticks dangling from the animal's back as it spun and readied for another angry charge. The energy of the crowd became difficult to ignore, and worse, easy to be caught up in. His own pulse began to accelerate, the smell of the dying animal's blood carried to him on the suffocating waves of heat. The bull staggered as it tried valiantly to lift its great head for another attack. The scene was gory, surreal; yet he would not tear his eyes away. Soon, he too clamored for the animal's demise, and to his disgust, realized it was not only to end its suffering, but in anticipation of witnessing the final death blow.

The Matador left the arena to insane cheers, only to reappear with a different red cape and a heavy sword. Surely this must be the instrument of death, and the moment near. Noise from the crowd reached a fever pitch as the exhausted bull rallied its last ounces of strength to charge at his opponent several more times, the Matador trailing the red cape across its head and horns with deft and dangerous movements. Then, with animal and man just inches apart, the Matador plunged his sword between its shoulder blades, piercing through the spinal cord and aorta.

The crowd rose to its feet all around him. Tristan stood as well, but his parched throat had no shouts of glory to offer. "I need something to drink," he said, then stepped into the aisle and strode away from the seating area.

*

"Where is he going," Ernesto muttered as he applauded the marvelous estocada, the killing stroke, that the Matador had just executed. It was the best outcome possible, the bull receiving a quick and clean death by a skilful estocada. The animal dropped instantly, the horrendous pool of spilt blood quickly absorbing into the sand beneath its felled carcass. "Told you he couldn't take it."

Marlena threw an annoyed glance at her childhood friend. She'd never seen him behave so badly, or speak so impolitely of another person. She felt certain that Tristan had simply gone to the snack bar, hoping to get ahead of the rush of patrons that would soon follow. "He's thirsty," Marlena snapped. "And so am I." Without waiting for Ernesto, she rose and followed the path Tristan had taken, down the aisle and the stairs that led to the public level and vendor stalls. Dodging the milling people, she found him leaning against a wall that offered some measure of shade, sipping from the familiar pint mug in which beer was served. He looked up as she approached.

"Sorry, I…should have asked…if you wanted a drink, too."

"No, I'm fine, thank you," she said, removing her sun hat and tossing a length of her long hair back over her shoulder. She couldn't quite read his expression, or rather, lack of it. His blue-eyed gaze gave nothing away, and that piqued her interest even further. She wanted to know what lay behind the handsome face. And she couldn't deny it any longer. She found that face very handsome, indeed. "So, what do you think of the corrida?" she asked.

"It's certainly an experience," he said.

"So, you enjoyed it?"

Tristan took a long swallow of beer from his mug before answering. "Not exactly. But it was my idea to come."

"True," Marlena said, slowly fanning herself with her hat. "And did you get what you came for?"

His eyes roved over her, eliciting an unexpected flutter in

her belly. She liked it; and liked the way he looked at her, as a street cat looks into a fish shop window. Desirous and calculating, working out his next move. "What do you mean by that?" he asked.

"As you said, it was your idea." She took a step closer to him.

Tristan set his empty mug on a nearby ledge. "It wasn't the best idea. But I think I did get what I came for."

"And what's that?"

He pushed away from the wall and straightened to his full height, moving within inches of her. "To get you alone."

The flutter in her belly began again. His nearness excited her, in a way it didn't before. Or was it just all the sights and sounds and spectacle of the bullring making it happen? "We're hardly alone," she replied, gesturing to the pressing throng of people all around them.

"I meant, without your boyfriend."

Her boyfriend? Is that what he thought? Ernesto was her boyfriend? With alarm, Marlena realized how it must look; not just to Tristan but many others as well. They weren't children any longer. To be seen with Ernesto so often would make people talk and get the wrong idea. The last thing in the world she wanted was to hurt Ernesto. But it had to stop. "He's just a friend," she said.

Tristan snorted. "Right. I've heard that before."

"It's true," she protested. "I've known him all my life, but that's it. We're just friends."

"If you say so. But does Ernesto know that?"

"Of course."

"Are you sure?"

Marlena bit her lip. She hadn't really done much to discourage Ernesto, in fact, she'd done the opposite, in hopes of getting her own way. But standing here, looking into Tristan's clear blue gaze that telegraphed something much more than friendship, she knew she didn't need to do that anymore. "Yes, I'm sure."

Tristan reached out and brushed her chin with his thumb, sending more shivers up her spine. As he moved closer, her breasts brushed against his hard chest, causing them to tingle. His forefinger slipped under her chin and tilted her face upward. "There's something else I came for," he murmured, and before she knew it, his lips were on hers, warm and soft and insistent. She'd never been kissed before, and never expected it to feel as wonderful as this; the pressure of his mouth against hers, firm and purposeful and without hesitation. It demanded a response, and she gave it to him intuitively. Her lips parted, beckoning him inward. The tip of his tongue slid across her upper lip as she did so, sending yet another quivering thrill rocketing through her body. And she wanted more—more of this dizzy feeling, like standing too close to the edge of a cliff, terrified of falling yet unable to step away.

His arms went around her waist, bringing them closer still. Marlena felt each bump and curve of his muscled body as it fitted against her own soft one. The tingle in her breasts spread downward, lighting up every part of her in its path to the apex between her legs. Her private muscles twitched and her lips moved hungrily against his, liking the lingering flavor of beer in his mouth. She'd never been drunk, but thought this must be what it felt like, her head spinning as though looking down from a great height above the ground—even above the clouds.

"Marly!"

The anguished voice cut through the heady mist of her awakening desires. Abruptly, Tristan released his hold on her and stepped back, breaking the magic kiss. Her head still reeling, she turned to the sound, and felt her heart drop to her toes. "Ernesto…"

"What do you think you're doing," he growled, moving toward them, his dark eyebrows dipping below the rims of his eyeglasses in a murderous scowl. "Get your hands off her!" he demanded, pointing at Tristan, whose hands still rested on her hips.

"Let me go," Marlena whispered.

"Why?" Tristan answered. "Because he wants me to?"

"Because I want you to!"

"Alright," he said, dropping his hands. "But I don't think that's really what you want."

"Marly," Ernesto said, grabbing her arm. "Come on, I'm taking you home."

"I don't want to go home," she argued. "The corrida is not over."

"It is for you and me," he snapped, yanking her toward him. He glared at Tristan. "And for you, senor. Everything's over."

Marlena looked at Ernesto in shock, then back at Tristan, her eyes wide. "I'm sorry," she said, uncertain as to whom she was apologizing; to Tristan? Ernesto? Maybe both. And maybe herself. She closed her eyes against the vision of Tristan standing there staring after them, his silhouette, and her chances, shrinking as Ernesto led her away.

Mierda! What had she done? Now they both hated her, and hated each other even more. With burning hot tears forming behind her eyelids, she realized she hated herself most of all.

Chapter Ten

Marlena shoved open the truck's door and jumped out even before it had come to a standstill in the driveway of her family's villa. "Marly!" Ernesto cried in alarm. "Are you crazy? You could hurt yourself!"

She didn't care. She ran to the house, scampered up the steps and disappeared inside before he could say another word. How dare he treat her like that, as if she were property! He'd embarrassed her and on top of that, been rude to someone he barely knew. More than rude, he'd been downright hostile. Ernesto—hostile! She'd never have believed it of him.

She refused to even speak to him on the ride home. At first he remained angry, demanding to know what she thought she was doing, sneaking around and kissing strangers. But her icy silence soon changed his attitude to one of apology, as he tried to earn her forgiveness. She wouldn't do it. She had a right to do as she pleased, like who she pleased; she didn't plan to hurt her best friend but if changing her future meant doing that, so be it. Ernesto would never change. He'd be stuck on the farm forever.

Flinging herself onto her bed, she re-lived the last moments at the bullring, before Ernesto found them together. Tristan's kiss had awakened something inside her, something deep and powerful and wicked. She liked his strong arms around her, the touch of his lips, and the strange, yet breathtaking sensations he aroused in her own body. The tightening of her nipples and the tingling in her legs and tummy were new and exciting to her, and she wanted more of it. Was that wrong? Was that sinful? Her mother might think so; and there was no way she was going to speak of this to her mother. But she had so many questions, and needed so many answers. Who could she turn to?

Burying her face in her pillow, it came to her. Tía Juliana. She could talk to her aunt; they'd grown a special bond in the months Marlena had taken care of her, and their secret conversations had always been exactly that—secret. Besides, Juliana had been out in the world, chasing her dream, though it had nearly cost her life; and more than that—she knew much about men. Yes, she would talk to her tía.

It would be supper time soon, and her aunt would be awake and waiting to be readied for her meal. Marlena slipped noiselessly down the hall to Juliana's room and knocked softly. Her aunt's low-timbred voice beckoned her to enter. "Pasa." Opening the door, she saw Juliana sitting up in bed, attempting to apply nail polish with her unsteady hands. Baby Jorge slept blissfully in his nearby cradle.

"Let me do that for you, Tía," Marlena said, quickly reaching her aunt's side and sitting on the edge of the bed. She took the bottle of polish and placing Juliana's hand on her lap, took over the job of painting her nails.

"Gracias, cariña."

"You're welcome, Tía; you know that. Anything you need."

Juliana gave a slow nod, her bright eyes fixed on her niece. "And what is it you need, little one?"

Marlena looked up to meet her aunt's gaze. "What makes you think I need something?" Juliana chuckled once more, and it made Marlena happy to see her tía's spirits, and her health, lifting day by day.

"You didn't come to see me just to paint my nails, and it's not yet supper time. You're here for a reason, now what is it?"

Marlena let out a sigh of relief, amazed at her aunt's uncanny insight. She had been right to come to her, seek her advice. "Clever Tía," she said, a warm smile on her face. "You know things about me before I even do." Juliana waited for her to continue speaking. "I need your advice," Marlena began. "I…like someone. Someone I've met. And I kissed him, at the bullfight today."

"Your first kiss?" Juliana asked, although it wasn't really a question. "And what did you think of it?"

Now, there was a question she hadn't expected, but glad for the chance to let all her swirling emotions tumbling out; and she knew she could trust her Tía to keep it between them. Marlena capped the bottle of polish and set it aside. "Oh, Tía…I…I've never felt anything like it…I felt swept away… on top of the world; like nothing else existed but us. There were butterflies in my stomach...and other places." Marlena paused, looking to her aunt for understanding. "Is it wrong to feel like that?"

Juliana shook her head. "No. If it is the right man, it is exactly right. Understand something, cariña; something that your mother nor any other woman in this house will probably ever tell you." She leaned forward. "There is no feeling that compares to being with a man, a man you want. It's not wrong, not shameful. It's wonderful, and it's natural. Remember that."

Marlena nodded, relieved but also surprised by her aunt's revelation. She smiled and felt a blush rise to her cheeks. "I thought it was wonderful too, but now I'm not so sure. I kissed him in front of Ernesto…I didn't mean to, but…suddenly he was just there, watching me. Watching us."

"So?"

"So! They got in a fight, and Ernesto dragged me away like an unruly child. I was so embarrassed. I thought he was my best friend…but it's all going wrong. He's different now. He likes me as more than a friend."

Juliana nodded her understanding. "And you don't feel the same way. But you do for this other person. You don't have to tell me who it is," she added.

"But I want to. I need to."

"No, I meant I already know who it is. It's the Welshman, isn't it? Senor Flynn."

Marlena's mouth dropped open, but she should have known her tía would figure it out. "How did you know that?"

"I told you before, he would bring great change to this house. And there would be a price to pay for it."

"I know, but what did that mean, Tía? You never really said. Tell me now, I need to know. Know what you know; know what I should do."

Juliana lifted her hands to display her burn-scarred skin, her fingernails shining with fresh, copper-red polish. "I'm a poor person to ask about the right thing to do. But I followed my heart, my passions, as everyone should. As you should. No matter the price."

Marlena heaved an exasperated sigh. "But it's not as easy as that, is it? You had to run away to follow your dreams. Are you saying I should do the same?"

"No, child. Things are different now than when I was your age. You have choices. And if you choose to involve Tristan, understand that it is yours alone, and that every choice has consequences."

Marlena's ears alerted. She called him Tristan; not Senor Flynn or The Welshman. She must know more about him than she let on. "Then tell me about him, Tía. Is he a good person? Can I trust him?" She longed to hear the truth of the incident that had been kept locked away all these months.

Juliana drew a long breath and cast a loving gaze over her sleeping baby. A smile tugged at the tight, still-healing skin around her mouth. "I first saw him in a cantina, in Madrid. A tiny, lawless place, but they let me dance, so I worked there for a few pesetas a night, plus whatever the customers gave me in tips." She turned her attention back to her niece. "He was with another man, a loud, brash and arrogant man. Whom I found fascinating. And handsome."

Marlena smiled. "Very handsome?"

"Si, muy handsome. But he became very drunk, shouting and showing off his money. He gave me a big tip to dance at his table."

"And did you?"

"Por supuesto. The cantina owner would have been furious if I didn't. Not good for business. So, I danced. Not a flamenco, like I did for the whole house, but a slow, private dance. A provocative dance." Juliana leaned forward a little, and winked. "I shouldn't tell you this, but I liked doing that kind of dancing. Lifting the ruffles of my skirt, showing off my legs; moving my body to the music in whatever way I wanted. I felt free."

Marlena's eyes widened. "Then what happened?"

"Like most drunken men," she scoffed. "He tried to grab me, touch my behind and pull me into his lap. The thing is, I was attracted to him. I would have sat on his lap willingly if he hadn't been so out of control."

"But you didn't," Marlena concluded. "Did he get angry?"

"He was so drunk I couldn't tell. But I know who was angry. Enzo, the big gypsy man who drank there often. He liked me, and was jealous. I left the dance floor, as the owner told me to do when customers got too friendly. I went outside to get some air, and the drunk man followed me. Enzo was waiting for him, there in the alley. They fought; I watched from the doorway, until Senor Flynn came around from the street and broke it up. Led his friend away."

"That's it?" Marlena asked, disappointed if that was the end of the story. It didn't explain much about Tristan, or the stranger she found so handsome. "But you met them again, yes?"

"Not for a few months. But I didn't want to work at the cantina anymore, because of Enzo. Before all the trouble started, I overheard them talking about a place called El Mirador, on the sea coast, where they were going to make a lot of money. So, one day I went to the coast, and found El Mirador, a fancy hotel. They ran the place. They were hiring dancers, and gave me a job. It was my dream come true, until…" Juliana stopped speaking, and looked again at Jorge, who began to stir and fuss.

"I'll get him," Marlena said, not wanting a crying baby to interrupt the story. She had to hear more. She lifted the squirming bundle from the cradle and brought him to his mother. Juliana took the baby in her arms and held him close. "Until what, Tía?" Marlena prompted.

"Until it burned down," she answered, her throaty voice catching. She looked up with tear-filled eyes. "He saved me you know. And Jorge." She stroked the fine skin of the boy's face with a gentle finger. "By the grace of God my son was spared, allowed to be born, because of Tristan Flynn. He rescued me from the fire, and brought me home; he did not have to do that. That should tell you what kind of man he is."

A man with a conscience, Marlena thought. But that still didn't mean he was conscientious, or trustworthy. It didn't help her to know what to do; and it certainly didn't solve the problem of Ernesto being angry with her. Perhaps Tristan was no longer even interested in her, after what happened today. The thought sent a stab of pain through her heart; a hollow, lost feeling, that he might leave and she'd never see him again. He could go back to his home country and meet another girl. Someone who wasn't bound by tradition or family, who wouldn't act so prissy and immature. Panic rose out of the pain; she didn't want him to leave, and more than anything didn't want him to see him with another woman.

In that moment, she realized she couldn't ignore her feelings for him, sinful or not, and that her future was linked to his. Looking down at her new little cousin also made her remember her promise. That she would provide for him no matter what. Yes, she would follow her heart. And this lion-haired man named Tristan Flynn.

With her mind made up, she helped Juliana dress for supper and change the baby's diapers. But another question remained unasked; and after what Tristan told her that night in the kitchen, Marlena suspected the answer. Was the other man Juliana's lover? Jorge's father? She was dying to know for certain, but couldn't just blurt out such a direct question. Perhaps she could coax it out of her another way. "The drunk man—the handsome one," she asked, as she did up the buttons of her aunt's blouse. "You never said his name. Who was he? Did he at least apologize for his behavior at the cantina?"

"He was not a man who apologized for anything," Juliana said, her voice turning cross. "Especially his actions. Now, don't ask me anymore questions. I am tired and I'm hungry. Let us eat our meal and thank our Lord for the good fortune we have." She raised her palm to Marlena's cheek. "You have the answers you need, child. Act on them."

Chapter Eleven

The blazing sun had nearly disappeared below the horizon as Tristan reached the church yard of the Gracia Immaculata, leaving his clothes dusty and his throat as scorched as the surrounding landscape. It had not been an easy walk from the city's bullring; nor a comfortable one. He did not regret kissing Marlena, in public, in front of hundreds of people. He didn't particularly regret doing so in front of his opponent either; but deeply regretted the scene that followed.

Many eyes turned to them as Ernesto dragged her away through the crowd. While he watched her disappear, Tristan suddenly knew how the mighty bull must have felt when the maddening cape fluttered over his horns. Enraged, and ready to charge; his ego bruised and his temper lost. He could have gone after them, pulled Marlena away and back into his arms, asserting his dominance. But that might have embarrassed her further, and drawn an even bigger circle of onlookers. No, he would choose his battles, and where they would play out; but he had no doubt the battle was looming, and that he would win it.

He already knew the outcome, the moment their lips met. The kiss between he and Marlena had struck fire deep in his belly. The way she opened to him, instinctively and passionately, could not be misinterpreted. He felt the frantic beating of her heart against his chest as he pulled her close, and she brooked no resistance, but—had he overstepped? A young girl feeling her first real pangs of desire might not have had the will to stop herself, or him. He could have exhibited more control; wooed and courted her in what her family probably saw as an appropriate way. But was she really that innocent? Her kiss did not seem tentative or inexperienced. He may be operating from a false assumption. He had no way of knowing what desires, experience or motivations she had, but could not mistake the passion of that kiss. He wanted more, and was determined to have it. Have her.

A surprise greeted him at the back door of the church. The small figure ran to him as he approached. "Ángel," Tristan called out. "What are you doing here? Does Pastor Giorgio know you're here?"

"Si, he knows. He said I could wait for you."

Tristan noted the boy wore the same clothes he had first seen him in. Maybe he had no others. He felt for the kid, never knowing impoverishment himself, but was getting an education in it every day he spent here. "Well, here I am. What's up?"

The boy's brow wrinkled in confusion. "What's…up?"

"Si, uh…que pasa, amigo?" Tristan rephrased in Spanish.

Ángel's eyes lit and a wide smile creased his small, tanned face. "The wheelchair," he said. "Have you finished making it?"

Bloody hell. He'd forgotten all about it. That project still lay in a pile of rubber, spokes and castoff metal parts. "Oh. Ángel, lo siento, I've been a little busy." Ángel's face fell a little, clearly disappointed. He shuffled his bare feet in the dirt. Christ, the kid couldn't even afford shoes. How could Tristan have imagined that building the wheelchair wasn't important, and needed right away? Despite thoughts of Marlena, the blood-soaked bullfight, and the possibility of a trip to Madrid, he vowed to make his promise to Ángel a priority. "But you know, it's almost finished," he lied. "I just need a few more days."

"Can I see it?" Ángel asked, excited.

"Oh…no, not yet. I don't want anyone to see it until it's ready, and until I've tested it for safety."

"Do you think you can be finished by tomorrow?"

"That's a little soon."

"But my mother wants to invite you for dinner tomorrow. You could bring the chair with you."

Tristan felt reluctant to accept the offer of a meal from a family that couldn't even afford footwear. It certainly wouldn't be a lavish spread like he'd had at Casa Sanchez. He didn't quite know what to expect. Did the boy have brothers, sisters? All of them needing to be fed as well? And what about a father—that could be awkward. "Please thank your mother for the invitation," he said. "But Don Giorgio needs me here tomorrow. Perhaps another day."

"Which day?" Ángel pressed.

Tristan laughed and tousled the boy's dark hair. "Why don't you come by on Wednesday. The chair will be ready, I promise."

"Okay," Ángel said, dodging away from his reach. "Miercoles. I'll come back then."

"Miercoles," Tristan repeated, imitating the boy's pronunciation. "That means Wednesday?"

"Don't you know the days of the week? You're not a very fast learner."

"I need a fast teacher. What are the other days then?"

"Lunes, Martes, Miércoles, Jueves, Viernes, Sábado, Domingo," the boy yelled as he dashed away. "Adios, El Milagro!"

The Miracle, Tristan scoffed inwardly. It would take a miracle to construct a wheelchair from old bicycle parts by Wednesday, but he would try. Exhausted, he sighed and stepped inside the building. It might take another miracle for him to see Marlena again. It was a good bet that Ernesto wouldn't be bringing her around; but he couldn't just leave things the way they were. He would have to go to her. See for himself if she cared for him, or was only teasing him to get a rise out of Ernesto. In any case, he'd committed his next few days to the wheelchair project. A visit to the Sanchez villa would have to wait.

*

Despite the magazine being flattened beneath her mattress each time she closed it, its pages naturally fell open to the center, the double page spread unfolding in all its glory and revealing the familiar hazy background and delicious pink satin beneath the beautiful blond woman in the photograph. She lay on her side, leaning up on one elbow, her legs slightly bent and one overlapping the other. Her breasts were large, and her hands cupped them firmly through the thin material of the baby-doll nightgown she wore, thrusting them forward so that the dark circles of her nipples were clearly visible.

Sitting on her bed with the magazine, Marlena's own breasts began to tingle as she gazed at the photo, even though she'd viewed it hundreds of times. Today was different; everything was different, since she'd kissed Tristan at the bullring. Sensations she'd never before experienced flooded her body with frightening speed, though they were not at all frightening in and of themselves. They were exciting, pleasurable, and urgent. Aunt Juliana said it was perfectly natural.

She looked down at her own breasts, disappointed they were not nearly the size of the model's in the magazine. She'd heard there were operations to make them larger, but had no idea how it was done. Dropping the book, her hands went to them, rubbing over her excited nipples, surprised at how they swelled and protruded through the fabric of her shirt the more she touched them, the tingling tightness becoming sweetly painful. She cupped their fullness in her palms and lifted them forward and up, as the woman in the picture did. She closed her eyes and imagined a camera in front of her, tilting her head toward the ceiling so that her long hair trailed down her back. It was one thing in the privacy of her own bedroom, but could she do this in front of a camera man? If she wanted to become a famous model she would have to, she reasoned.

Again, the urgent throbbing in her breasts spread downward, reaching between her legs and causing her private muscles to pulse and twitch. What did that mean? Was that normal, too? When would it stop? What if it didn't? Strangely, her body called to her, begging her to go further, urge the wicked sensations onward. Imagining a camera man watching heightened the urgency, and she could not stop herself.

Rolling over onto her back, she reached below her skirt and placed her hand over her throbbing mound, finding the material of her panties moist. She pressed down, hoping to stem the strange ache, make it go away, but it did not. Instead, it grew in strength, seeming both hot and cold at once, making her feel as if she was sinking into her bed. She applied more pressure, as though to force it back inside her, but her body seemed paralyzed, ceasing to operate in favor of this new thing, this wave of something that now exploded in her core, spilling in every direction like ocean surf cresting against the beach.

It was powerful, unstoppable; a feeling of pleasure and euphoria overtaking her so completely that nothing else mattered, nothing else existed. Indescribable joy cascaded over her, gradually lessening until it stopped altogether. When it was over, Marlena lay quietly, panting for breath, trying to understand what had just happened. Had she been possessed? All the Catholic dogma she'd been taught came rushing into her mind, the evils of sin, of el Diablo and other demons always vying for one's soul. Temptation. It was the tool of such vile entities, and she had succumbed to it, been unable to resist it.

But it had felt so good. How could it be bad? Wouldn't God want everyone want to feel like that? Such ecstasy must surely be as if one were in the presence of God himself. She sat up, retrieving the magazine from where it had fallen on the floor and tucking it safely away again. There were many things still unknown, ideas so confusing and conflicting that Marlena had more questions than ever. But who could she ask now, about this? Even her tía might not want to speak of it in such detail. She had felt these things when Tristan touched her. Were they warnings? Telling her to stay away, or to get closer? There would be a price, Juliana had said. She hoped that price would not be her eternal soul.

She was not even certain she would see Tristan again. Ernesto had as good as insulted him. He had no reason at all to come to her villa now; and she had no way to get to the church on her own, unless she walked. And what of their promised trip to Madrid? Just hours ago it had seemed all but a matter of choosing a day, when Tristan showed her the old van he'd bought. But now, everything might have changed. Besides, her mother would never allow it, her daughter riding off with a foreign stranger, no matter how highly Bianca thought of him. She'd have to sneak away somehow, and soon.

From her bureau drawer she took out the faded, folded scrap of newspaper she'd carefully preserved, and re-read the magical, tantalizing advertisement:

Models wanted immediately.
No experience necessary - free training provided.
To audition apply in person.

SPANISH SEDUCTION TRILOGY

Perhaps the auditions were closed by now—the newspaper being weeks old; but if she didn't try, she would never know, and there was only one way to find out. She'd told her aunt she would brave anything, even fire, to get what she wanted, with or without anyone's help. She would get to Madrid somehow, even if she had to hitch-hike.

Chapter Twelve

"You've been working very hard on this," Don Giorgio said, looking over Tristan's work. "But it seems an unusual thing to build. Wherever did you get the idea, and find the necessary materials?"

Tristan spun the wheels on the chair that sat upturned on a makeshift workbench. They moved freely and without much noise. Satisfied, he set the chair upright and lowered it to the ground. "The idea wasn't mine," he said, "but I like a challenge. And you can find most anything if you know where to look."

"Aieee, es verdad, about much in life," Don Giorgio answered, nodding. "Seek, and ye shall find, no?"

"Si." He smiled at the portly Pastor, then gestured to the chair. "Care to take it for a spin?"

Don Giorgio laughed. "I don't drive."

"Perfect. I'll drive. It needs a road test in any case. Por favor," Tristan said, inviting him to take a seat. "I'll go slow."

With an amused shrug, the clergyman turned and lowered his wide frame into the chair. "Vamonos!"

Tristan grasped the handlebars attached to the chair's back, fashioned from a castoff bicycle, and pushed forward. The man's weight required an extra nudge to get it moving, but move it did, and even better than expected. The wide tires rolled smoothly over the uneven ground of the church yard, their low inflation absorbing the contours of various pebbles, stones and thatches of grass in their path. "Ah, now this is the way to get around," Don Giorgio said. "You may never get me out of this chair, my friend."

"Lo siento, but I'm afraid you will have to, Padre. Here comes my client now." Tristan pointed to the church yard gate as Ángel's slight figure scurried up to it.

"Ha ha, El Milagro! I knew you could do it!" the boy exclaimed with a gleaming, toothy smile. He unlatched the gate and strode in. "My mother is going to love it! She will love you, senor!"

Don Giorgio rose from the chair as they came to a halt, turning a curious eye toward Tristan. "Indeed? It is for Senora Ibanez?"

Tristan never actually heard Ángel's surname, but of course the Pastor would know everyone in town, and especially within his congregation. He nodded in affirmation. "My client is very persuasive and insistent. He held me to a deadline."

"I see. And what price did you agree on?" Don Giorgio asked the boy good-naturedly.

Ángel's smile broadened. "He is coming to our house for supper."

"Muy bien. I'm sure—Senor Milagro—could use a fine meal, cooked by a fine hand, rather than mine," the Pastor concluded. "It's been awhile since she has had company to entertain, being a young widow," he added, clearly for Tristan's ears. "And a fine teacher, as well. You can learn your Spanish from her very quickly. A fine trade for such fine work. I'm proud of you, mi hijo." Tristan frowned at the Pastor's amused expression and thinly veiled hint.

Ángel ran his small brown hand over the chair's frame. "You will make my mother very happy. Can we take it now?"

"You go ahead and take it, Ángel. I have other things to do right now," Tristan said.

"But you have to come with me. Supper's almost ready!" he exclaimed.

Tristan held up his hands. "I didn't say I would come for supper, remember? I only said to come for the chair today." The boy looked nearly heartbroken. As Don Giorgio folded his hands across his ample belly and glanced between the two of them, Tristan began to smell a setup. "I don't want to intrude," he added.

"Oh, I'm sure you wouldn't be intruding," Don Giorgio declared. "If Senora Ibanez is expecting you, it would be rude to turn down the invitation. Besides, a young man like you needs to…" he paused, looking him up and down, a wry grin on his face. "…be nourished, no?"

Tristan did not miss the intimation of what young men needed, and the last thing he wanted to do was to disappoint anyone, least of all his employer; but he wasn't interested in whatever the good pastor thought Ángel's mother could offer. "Alright, Ángel," he sighed, flashing a resigned smile. "Lead the way."

With a goodbye wave to Don Giorgio, Ángel grasped the chair's handles and steered it through the gate and around to the front street. "Let me know when you get tired," Tristan said.

"Oh, I not tired, senor. I not old like you."

"Who are you calling old, pipsqueak," Tristan laughed.

"Pip…skw…" Ángel faltered over the unfamiliar moniker. "That better not be a bad word."

"Not as bad as old. Just how old do you think I am?"

"Old enough."

"For what?"

Ángel grinned sideways at him and moved ahead of Tristan, pushing the chair forward in an extra burst of youthful enthusiasm. Tristan widened his stride in response. "Oh, don't even think it, pipsqueak; I can leg it better than most old men."

The boy laughed and sped up, only to come to a hard stop at the end of the block. When Tristan caught up, he followed Ángel's gaze to the center of the cobbled square that lay just ahead. A ring of townsfolk encircled the massive trunk of El Guardián, its bark now nearly completely stripped, exposing a dry and graying cambium beneath, a sure sign of the tree's declining health.

"What are they doing?" Ángel asked, observing as the group talked among themselves, and some men measured the tree's girth with a tape. "Make them get away from it," he scowled.

"Maybe they're trying to help it," Tristan offered, sensing the boy's anxiety. Flaming hell. Among all the other things he'd forgotten or ignored lately, El Guardián had been one of them. His plan to divert the well water to the tree via underground pipe had gone completely by the wayside in his fixation over a certain pretty brunette and her omnipresent boyfriend. He could do it, he was sure, but it might already be too late, judging not only by the sickly look of the tree, but by the clear intentions of the men around it. They were making preparations to cut it down.

Ironically, that was exactly what he'd thought to do, the day he'd nearly crashed into it. Now, the idea seemed abhorrent and brutal. He had to intervene. "Wait here," Tristan said to a nervous Ángel, and strode across the square. He could hear many voices all speaking at the same time, much too rapidly and jumbled together to be intelligible to him, but what he saw spoke louder than any words. Toolboxes filled with hand saws, axes and rope. An open tailgate on a nearby pickup, ready to receive the aftermath of the task they appeared ready to perform. "Que pasa," he whispered to one of the onlookers near him. "What are they trying to do?"

The man turned to him. "What does it look like?"

"They plan to cut it down? I thought everyone wanted the tree saved."

The man shook his head. "Si, but those men say it cannot be saved. Some believe that, others do not."

Tristan's brain raced, thinking of all that Ángel had told him. If the tree held as much spiritual value as the little well did, they couldn't just hack it down like this. It may still have life in its roots. He needed time; time to put his design into action, and to put a stop to this ham-handed way the workers planned to execute their task. "You can't do it with those tools," he shouted.

Heads turned to the sound of his voice. "Pardoneme, senor?" one of the workmen said.

"You'll never get through the size of that trunk with those. And safety precautions must be taken, so that no one is injured. This is a public place, there are rules."

"How would you know these rules, senor? You're not from Zaragoza."

"No, but I am an engineer; and there's a better way to deal with this. A proper way."

"It's a tree. How many ways are there," another workman scoffed, brandishing his ax in demonstration. Expressions of outrage rippled through the crowd.

"We can save it," Tristan called out. "I can save it."

The crowd quieted as he spoke. "Indeed, senor. And who are you?" the first workman asked.

"He is El Milagro," a voice rang out, much larger than the person it belonged to. Ángel stood at the back of the group, still gripping the wheelchair's handlebars. "He can do anything. He built this wheelchair for my mother. He fixed the well. He can save El Guardián."

More voices rose from within the growing crowd. "Milagro?" muttered some. "Impossible!" cried a few. "Let him try," said others. The workman shouted over the din. "We have orders from the city council to remove it by the end of the week, senor."

"Then let me speak to the council," Tristan said. "If they disagree with what I have to say, then by all means, swing your axes." The gathered townsfolk clapped and whistled their approval. "Do we have a deal?"

With a nod from the head workman, the others began to pack up their tools. "The council may not have time to see you today," he warned. "But I can direct you to the town hall."

"I'll take my chances," Tristan answered, and made his way through the crowd toward Ángel. The boy looked sad, but awestruck at the same time. "I'm sorry Ángel, but I think you'll have to go on home without me. I have to get to the town hall as soon as possible."

Ángel nodded. "I knew you would stop them," he said. "I'll tell my mother you were too busy saving El Guardián to come to supper." He maneuvered the chair away from the crowd and back onto the sidewalk. As he walked away, he looked back over his shoulder and flashed a broad smile. "She will love you even better!"

Folding his arms, Tristan watched the boy move down the street while he waited for the men to escort him to the town hall. Now he was certain a plot was afoot; to somehow hook him up, to spark some romantic interest in him for Senora Ibanez. A widow, huh? That explained a lot. Don Giorgio was very forthcoming with that information. He recalled Ángel's mother being pretty enough, even as she leaned on her cane at the well ceremony. He felt pity for her, but these two unlikely matchmakers would be very disappointed. His romantic interests were already sparked, bursting into flame, and building to an inferno in his very soul.

Committing to yet another 'miracle' project would further keep him away from the source of that fire; but he couldn't back out now. He had to put his money where his big, egotistical mouth was; though he'd much rather be putting his mouth on the soft lips of Marlena Sanchez…and every other part of her body. He wiped his brow as he trudged to the town hall under the searing heat of the sun. This country had taken hold of him in ways he'd never imagined since that crazy night with Ariel at the cantina; and apparently it wasn't about to let him go.

Chapter Thirteen

"Pencils down."

Marlena did as her teacher commanded, breathing a long-awaited sigh of relief as she slapped the yellow wooden stick to the desktop with the flat of her palm. Finally. It was done. The last exam she'd ever write inside this school building. She was free.

Turning in her test paper felt like a weight off her shoulders. One less obstacle between her and her dream. But how to make the dream a reality? The days since the bullfight brought nothing but uncertainty. Tristan had not returned to the villa to seek her out; and though Ernesto had come to finish the pig barn, she carefully avoided having to speak to him.

Today however, she'd not be so lucky. There he stood by her locker, waiting for her, just as he did every day at the bus stop. For that reason, she'd purposely chosen a seat away from him on the bus, and today, opted to walk to school. She pictured him waiting for the bus this morning, pacing and looking about, wondering where she could be. Marlena sighed. Now was as good a time as any to cut the apron strings between them; even if it meant slashing the very fibers of her friend's heart.

He turned toward her, one nervous finger pushing his dark-rimmed glasses up the bridge of his nose. "Marly!" he called.

"Hi," she answered without inflection. She opened her locker and pretended to rummage through it, though she'd emptied it of its contents days ago. Only one item remained.

The packed traveling bag she'd hidden there this morning. Ernesto mustn't see it.

"Are you not even going to talk to me?" he asked, breaking the icy silence.

"Why should I?" she answered, shielding herself with the locker door. "You've made your position clear. You expect to own me; push me around like a bad child. I already have parents. I don't need you acting like one."

"I'm trying to apologize," he said. "I've been apologizing all week. Can't you even listen to me for one minute?"

"Apologize all you like, but I'm leaving. Get it through your head. You and I have no future."

"Don't say that," Ernesto replied, his voice choked with denial. "We have our whole lives ahead of us. Everything can change."

Marlena turned, finally looking her childhood friend straight in the eyes. "You can do what you love best, which is to stay here forever, but I'll be going to Madrid. And yes, everything will change. It already has."

Ernesto looked back at her as though she had two heads, his mouth gaping open in disbelief. "It's like I don't know you anymore," he said, shaking his head. "Who you are. You're not the Marly I grew up with."

"That's just it," she said, exasperation in her voice. "We're all grown up now, Ernesto, both of us. We're not children any longer, and I am who I am. Who I'm going to be."

Ernesto's square, stern jaw worked back and forth, grinding up his next words like grain in a flour mill. "It's because of him, isn't it? That Flynn. What's he done to you?"

"Nothing," she answered. It was only partly a lie. "Except to show me that a different kind of life is possible."

"Don't listen to him Marly. He'll hurt you. He's not right for you."

"And you are?" she rounded on him. "Embarrassing me in front of all those people? Telling me what to do?"

"I'm only trying to protect you."

Marlena shook her head. This conversation was going nowhere; the argument pointless and unnecessary. It would only leave bad feelings between them forever. She didn't want it to end that way, knowing the possibility that she might never see him again. Her voice softened. "I know that. Because you care for me. I care for you, too, Ernesto; I do. I just don't need protection. I don't need you."

The look of hurt on the sweet face she'd known all her life stabbed at her heart, but she couldn't take back the words. She meant them.

"Then what do you need, Marly? Tristan? A foreigner who can't possibly understand you, or our way of life? You don't know him, or what he's capable of. He's practically a stranger."

"I didn't say I wanted him. I want the kind of freedom he has. Anyway, I don't have to answer to you, or anyone else."

"Not even your mother? Does she know you're planning to leave?"

"That's none of your business." Marlena hadn't broached the topic of leaving, or any topic really, with Bianca, aside from telling her she would be going shopping after school today. She felt guilty lying to her mother, but it was too late for regrets. The bag hidden in her locker held clothes, makeup, and money for bus fare. No one could stop her now. She was leaving directly from school. Ernesto didn't need to know that. "Right now, it's you who needs to leave. As in leave me alone. I want to clean my locker."

Ernesto backed away from where they stood. "Fine," he said coldly. "If that's how you want it. Have a nice life. But when it doesn't work out, don't expect any help from me."

She watched him walk away, his back straight and his

shoulders squared atop his slim frame. He didn't look back. And neither would she. When he was out of sight, she grabbed her bag and slammed the bent and pitted locker door, along with her childhood life, shut with a bang.

*

Digging the trench was a slow process. The water table beneath the well became significantly lower the closer they got to the town square; too deep to dig a direct line to it with the manual tools at Tristan's disposal. But with enough pipe and fittings scrounged from various suppliers he would be able to connect the wellspring to El Guardián. However, it meant burying the pipe underground, to ensure a downward flow and to protect it from traffic damage.

With each strike of his shovel, Ángel worked alongside him scooping away the dislodged earth with a bucket. "This hard work," the boy exclaimed between scoops. "But it bring life to El Guardián, yes?"

"It should," Tristan said. "You see, the vitality…la vida… of any plant or tree is in its roots, not its leaves. That is, what's below the ground is more important than what's above."

Ángel laughed and nodded. "Like people. What is underneath is who they really are. Not what they say or how they look."

"Exactemente," Tristan said, straightening from his bent-over stance to mop the sweat from his face with a well-used red bandanna he kept in his back pocket. The kid was perceptive beyond his years. He could not help but apply the observation to the object of his affection. Marlena Sanchez kept a cool surface, but Tristan felt certain her blood ran hot beneath the smooth, fair skin. Her kiss was proof of that, and he wanted to bring it to boil, have it spill over with passion, even if it burned him in the process. And he couldn't do that from the business end of a shovel. He plunged the implement into the ground with renewed force, determined to get the job done as soon as possible.

"I think that is true of you, Senor," Ángel continued. "You don't talk about yourself. You are mysterioso."

"There's no mystery to me," Tristan laughed. "I'm a penniless student doing the classic student thing; trekking across Europe just for the experience. See new countries, meet new people."

Ángel kept at his task for a moment before speaking again. "How come you not married?" he asked suddenly.

"Oh, I'm not ready for that," Tristan scoffed. "I have nothing to offer a wife. No job, no home. And I'm way too young."

"You old enough," Ángel replied.

"Yeah, so you've said. You think I'm a crippled old man," Tristan reminded him. "Besides, I haven't met the right woman yet."

"But you've met lots of women here. Every woman wants to get married," Ángel said.

"Is that so? Like who?" Tristan's thoughts again focused on Marlena, even as the words left his lips. His attraction to her felt irresistible, indecently so; but marriage? Christ, she was only eighteen. She'd never left home, or her family. Did she dream of marriage? If he continued his pursuit of her, surely marriage would be expected. He'd better re-think his intentions and cool his randy jets before things got out of hand. But that would be like throwing a pitcher of water at a raging fire. He might slow it down, but would never quench it. The vision of her nude body sprawled beneath him in a moment of passionate lovemaking resurfaced in his mind more often than he wanted to admit.

Ángel kept his head down, continuing to scrape away the mounds of sandy soil with his bucket. "Like my mother," he said. "She needs a husband."

Tristan jabbed at a fresh patch of dirt with his shovel, ramming it into the earth with all his might. Ángel's statement answered a lot of questions, except the obvious. "She is not married to your father?"

"He died. A long time ago." Ángel cast a shy glance upward. "You would make a good husband for her."

Tristan paused and leaned on the handle of his shovel, returning the boy's expectant gaze. How to tell a ten-year-old he had no interest in his mother, without hurting his feelings? "I'll take that as a compliment," Tristan said. "But like I said, I'm not ready for anything like that."

Ángel's lips pouted in thought. "When you think you be ready?"

Tristan had to laugh at Ángel's persistence. "Not for a long time." He crouched down to the boy's level. "Listen, Ángel. I like you. And I'm flattered that you think of me as good husband material, but I have many things to do yet with my life. Things to accomplish."

"Like what?"

"Like this pipe, for one. And other things…big things. Like buildings and bridges." Tristan smiled and slapped Ángel lightly on his arm before rising to his feet again. "So, c'mon, let's get back to work. Trabajo!"

"After that you get married?" Ángel asked hopefully. "That sounds like a long time. You really be old by then. Maybe no woman want you."

Tristan laughed again. "Maybe so. But at least I'll be able to afford a wife, even if I don't get one." The idea of marrying Marlena floated perniciously in his mind. And then he remembered Ernesto. Did his designs on Marlena extend to marriage? Were they already lovers? He didn't appear to be much older than she. Perhaps it was just puppy love, that would fade over time; but perhaps it wouldn't. It might grow and mature and…his line of thought cut off and headed in a new direction. Would he be able to go off and build his dreams, and expect the girl to still be here? Still waiting? With his rival still in the wings? Hardly. He'd be damned if he let someone else have her. He would have to come to terms with his feelings for her; and if his desire ran as deep as his fantasies, the time to make a move was sooner rather than later.

Soon, Tristan's shovel struck something hard. The roots of El Guardián! He looked up, noting they were perhaps thirty feet from the tree's dying, brittle trunk. The root system had grown massive, seeking the ever-scarcer life-giving nourishment from the earth. He dug deeper and faster, creating a sloping channel in which to lay the last section of pipe that would deliver the needed water right to the giant, subterranean heart of El Guardián.

Tristan and Ángel backtracked several yards to the previous section of pipe they'd completed, which he'd closed off with a valve made from a garden tap. Sweating but spurred on by the prospect of finishing the task, Tristan laid the last piece of pipe into the trench and connected it, a rusty hose clamp having to serve as a flange. It would leak, but any escaping moisture would filter into the surrounding ground, which would only help other vegetation along the way. Breathless from heat and exertion, he turned the valve and rose to his feet.

"What now?" Ángel asked.

"We wait for the flow to build up. Let's go see," Tristan said, practically running to the open end of the pipe they'd just laid. Ángel scampered close behind. Peering into the open trench, he saw the soil turning dark with moisture around the pipe's opening, and then the formation of a small puddle. Soon, a visible trickle of water emerged from the end of the pipe.

A tired, but grateful smile creased his dust-covered face. He reached out and ruffled Ángel's dark, bedraggled hair on the top of his head. "Muy bien, well done!" he shouted. The boy responded by wrapping his arms around Tristan's waist in a hug. They stood and watched the pool of water grow and deepen for several moments. The pipeline was a success, but the rest was up to El Guardián. It might be months before any new growth would be seen. He'd explained that to the town council when they gave him permission to proceed, as well as how the tree would need severe trimming in order to spur new growth.

But for today, their work was nearly done. Tristan and Ángel backfilled the trench with the displaced earth and returned to where he'd parked the old blue van, tossing their tools into the cargo area in a gesture of triumph. "I think this calls for a celebration," Tristan said as he closed the rear doors of the van. "Want to come along? Maybe get some ice cream?"

Ángel nodded enthusiastically. They climbed into the van and drove to the confectioner's shop where Tristan treated the boy to a triple scoop cone and himself to a cold bottle of beer. "I still wish you would marry my mother," Ángel said between licks of ice cream as they left the shop. "Then I would have a new father, too." The boy looked at Tristan, his dark eyes brimming with undisguised honesty and longing. Tristan stooped to one knee and gripped Ángel by the shoulders.

"Now, that would truly be a milagro," Tristan said. "Someday, you may have a new father, Ángel; but you know, a man doesn't have to marry your mother to be one to you. A father is someone who teaches you, shows you wrong from right, protects you, cares about you; and loves you no matter what."

Ángel considered this as rivulets of melting ice cream dripped over the lip of his cone and onto his small hand. "Do you love me, Milagro?"

"I do, Ángel. I care about you and you can always count on me as long as I'm around."

Ángel smiled. "Then, you are my father," he beamed. "You do all of those things."

Tristan returned the smile, knowing he'd stepped into that one with both feet. But if Ángel thought of him as a father figure, what was the harm? The kid certainly needed one, so why not himself? "You go on home now," he said. "I have to get back to the church. I'll see you tomorrow, okay?"

"Okay," Ángel said, and skipped away with his ice cream, waving a cheerful goodbye with his free hand. Tristan got to his feet and pulled the grimy bandanna from his pocket again. Wiping the caked-on dirt and dust from his face he climbed into the van with the satisfaction of a job well done. It remained to be seen if El Guardián would truly recover; but with roots like that, the tree stood a good chance. No miracles required.

He started the engine and headed toward his own, at least for now, home at the Gracia Immaculata, looking forward to a bath or at least a quick duck under the garden hose outside the church. Turning off the main street, he slammed on the brakes. It couldn't be. A slim but shapely silhouette with long brown locks stood at the bus stop. Tristan nudged the vehicle forward, riding the clutch until he pulled up alongside the girl. She whirled an about-face as his squealing brakes brought him to a full stop, her hair swinging out in a brunette fan as she turned. He loved that hair, his fingers aching to touch its dark silkiness. "Hi," he called through the open passenger window.

"What are you doing here," Marlena asked, her captivating eyes widening in either surprise or fear. Perhaps both.

"I was about to ask you the same thing. Shouldn't you be at school?"

"School is finished," she said, with a regal lift of her chin. "Shouldn't you be at the church?"

Tristan smiled, running a hand through his own hair that must look like a wild blond bush by now in a futile attempt to look presentable. He wished he weren't so filthy and sweaty. He probably smelled like shit, too, but couldn't stop himself from speaking his next words. "Well now, seeing as we're both where we're not supposed to be, can I give you a lift?"

Chapter Fourteen

"I'm going to Madrid," Marlena said. His offer of a lift seemed too little too late. He knew she wanted to go there; they'd talked about and planned it, but he hadn't shown up in days.

"What a coincidence," he said, smiling through the grime on his face. "So am I."

He practically leapt from the driver's seat to open the door for her. He looked tired and sweat-soaked, but still handsome in spite of all that. The magic moments of their kiss came back to her as though they were still happening. Her heart began to pound, and felt heated blood rushing to her face, threatening to burst out in an embarrassing blush of pink.

Her mind spun. The bus would stop at every dusty crossroads from here to Madrid, picking up not only passengers but probably dogs and chickens on the way as well. She would get to the city far sooner driving with him. The open door to the van beckoned like a portal to another dimension; a time machine that could transport her to another world, one she'd craved and dreamed about. She'd come this far; she couldn't go back. It was all or nothing now. Squaring her shoulders, she lifted her bag and stepped as daintily as she could manage into the cab.

Tristan closed her door and sprinted around to the driver's side. "I need to stop at the church first, but we can get on the road right after that," he said, sliding behind the wheel and shifting the vehicle into gear.

A wave of panic swept over her; she hadn't counted on any delays, or the possibility of seeing anyone else she knew before leaving. Least of all the local Pastor who would obviously question them, or worse, report back to her family, whether intentionally or not. On top of that, any extra minutes she spent in her home town were that many minutes to change her mind, or lose her nerve. "Oh. I thought…we could just leave straight from here."

Tristan looked at her, his intense blue eyes seeming to penetrate into her thoughts, her soul. With all that had happened, with everything her tía said, and the way she felt in his presence, she would never be able to keep secrets from him, for all her efforts to distance herself. They were linked in ways she had yet to understand. He would find her out, one way or another.

"I should tell Don Giorgio where I'm going; and I want to get cleaned up," he said, switching his gaze forward and pulling away from the curb. "You're not exactly catching me at my best," he chuckled.

"Then let me out. I'll take the bus," she said, her voice rising in pitch. "I don't want to miss it."

"What's your hurry," Tristan asked, throwing her a sidelong glance. "I only need a few minutes. We'll still get there faster than the bus."

"No. I mean, it's alright. You have other things to do. Please let me out."

"Marly…"

"Don't call me that," she scowled, her fingers wrapped

around the door handle. Only one person called her Marly, and she didn't want to think about him, or the fact he'd likely be skulking around her family's villa within the hour, looking for her. She needed to leave. Now. With Tristan or without.

Tristan pulled over. "Isn't that what most people call you? Sorry if that's too familiar, but it's a long drive to Madrid. Don't you think we should drop the formalities?"

"You can call me whatever you want, just not that."

"Why? Because it's your lover's pet name for you?"

Marlena glared at him. "He's not…we're not…" she broke off and shook her head. "I've told you. It's not like that."

"What is it like then, between you two? Because if he's not your lover, he puts on a pretty good imitation of it," Tristan said, a tinge of anger in his voice.

"It doesn't matter. I'm leaving anyway." She pulled on the handle, the rusted door opening with protest. Tristan grabbed her other wrist.

"Then leave with me," he said. "Please don't get out. We'll go now, if that's what it takes to get you away from him." His words were firm, commanding, but she didn't mind it coming from him. It seemed right. She dared to look into his blue gaze once more. His features softened into a smile. "If you can stand the smell."

Only when Marlena pulled the door shut again did he release his hold on her arm. "I'll try," she said, returning a teasing half-smile. She was used to the odor of hard-working men; there were many of them in her mother's employ. It didn't bother her. All that mattered was that she was on her way.

"So, I asked you a question," Tristan said, after pulling back into traffic. "What exactly is your relationship with Ernesto? And don't say it's none of my business."

Marlena sighed. "I've known him a long time. Since I was born, it seems. But things have changed. At least for him."

"So, you are not lovers."

"No!" she practically shouted. That implied she and Ernesto had…she couldn't imagine it. Had sex? It had never occurred to her, and did not really know what sex would be like, but the idea of Tristan thinking she was not a virgin bothered her even more than his bold question. Of course, she was a virgin! Weren't girls in his country virgins at her age? Doubts flooded her mind. Maybe that wasn't normal where he came from; perhaps he'd think her an oddity for being so. This man made her question almost everything about herself; what she knew, how she felt. He unnerved her at the same time he fascinated her. "A gentleman wouldn't ask such questions," she added.

His smile flashed unnaturally bright against the tanned and dirt-tracked skin of his face. The devil's own smile, Marlena thought; but irresistible for all of that. "You'll have to make do with me," he said, glancing out the side window as he made a turn, his obtuse answer clear enough. The idea he didn't consider himself a gentleman sent an alarming thrill up her spine and another bout of familiar buzzing beneath her panties. "If you say you are not lovers, then I believe you," he went on. "I'm glad, actually."

"Why is that."

He took his eyes off the road long enough to train them on her for a full second. "Because I don't think he's right for you."

Marlena laughed. "He said the same thing about you."

"Well, he's wrong." Tristan returned his attention to the road. The city of Zaragoza began to disappear behind them as they drove. "I'm exactly the right man for you."

"How do you know that?"

"I think we both know that. Don't think I didn't notice how you kissed me."

"What can you tell from a kiss? Maybe I kiss every boy like that."

His mouth dropped open for a split second, then he shook his head. "You don't," he argued. "I know you don't. You know you don't."

A blush rose again to her cheeks, and she crossed her arms to hide her nipples as they tingled and tightened beneath her blouse. He knew her. Better than she knew herself, it seemed. Her body had become like an untrained farm animal around him, plainly displaying every urge and stimulus she felt with no warning or control. It couldn't be right. But it wouldn't stop, and she didn't want it to. She was on her way now, to her own life and her own destiny. Why shouldn't her body be as free as her spirit?

They drove on without speaking for a time. When nothing but open hills and plains filled the view all around them, Tristan spoke again. "Are you staying with family in Madrid?" She shook her head no. "Have you booked a room, or an apartment?" Again, she shook her head. His brow wrinkled in concern. "Why are you, I mean we, going then? It will be almost dark when we get there."

"I have an appointment."

"Where? For what?"

"A job."

"Oh. When do you start? It must be soon if you're in such a hurry."

"I haven't got the job yet. I'm going to apply when I get there."

Tristan plied the brakes and brought the van to a stop on the shoulder. "Does your mother know you're going to Madrid?" he asked, turning to her.

"Please," she said, her eyes turning tearful. "This is my only chance. I have to do this. If I don't get there soon, it may be too late."

"Why? Too late for what?"

"There's a company, who will train me and everything. I

don't know how much longer they'll be taking applications. Can you just drive, please? I have to get there. I can't go back now."

Tristan looked at her as though alarm bells were sounding off inside his head, but he said nothing. Her tearful, pleading glance seemed to have silenced his objections. There was no turning back for either of them. What lay ahead would involve both of them, possibly for life. "Alright," he said, moving the gear back into first. "We'll go."

*

"This is it," Marlena said, glancing from the torn piece of newsprint in her hand to the in-need-of-repair glass entrance door in the middle of a commercial block of businesses they'd pulled up in front of. Aged and crumbling stucco cladded the exterior, and the darkened windows revealed nothing of what might lay behind.

"Are you sure," Tristan said, sounding unconvinced. "It doesn't look much like a place of business to me. Let me see that ad." He reached for the scrap of paper she held. In a flash, she crumpled it into her palm.

"I'm sure," she said, taking a deep breath to quell the anxiety rising in her chest. She'd come all this way; the last thing she needed was someone to question her decision, or worse, talk her out of it. The place did look empty and a little forbidding, making her mouth go dry despite the perspiration she felt forming on the back of her neck and under her arms. It was only for the interview anyway, she reasoned. The training facility could be somewhere else entirely. And if she was too late, there was nothing she could do about it; but if it wasn't… the ticket to her dreams could lie just a few steps away. There was only one way to find out. She moved to exit the van.

"I don't like it," Tristan muttered. "Something's not right

about this. Don't go in there." He grasped her forearm, but Marlena shook free. "At least let me go with you," he pleaded.

"No." if she wasn't accepted, or if the applications were closed, she didn't want him to witness her failure. But it wasn't the only reason. It occurred to her that her whole life she'd been supervised, guided and accompanied in everything by others. Her mother. Her church. Even Ernesto. For once, she was going to do something alone and independently. "I don't need an escort, or a bodyguard," she argued. "Just wait here."

She saw Tristan's stubbled jaw tighten, and his blue eyes take on a leaden hue. "Count on it."

Chapter Fifteen

"I'll leave the doors open," Tristan said. "I might go get us something to drink, so if I'm not here when you come out, just get in the van and wait, okay?"

"Claro," Marlena said, clambering out of her seat. Stepping onto the crumbling concrete curb, she paused. "I don't know how long I'll be."

Tristan shrugged. He'd wait. He didn't want to let her out of his sight; certainly not here, in what looked like a seedy neighborhood. But he had to let her go. "Doesn't matter. I'll be here." With trepidation, he watched her swing open the dingy glass door of the building and disappear into the darkness beyond it. He felt as though the place had swallowed her, that she might never come out. He shook the irrational fear from his mind and looked around. Near the end of the shabby strip of businesses on the block, he saw a launderia that had coin-operated public showers. He wanted to clean himself up more than ever, so he shoved the gear into park and got out of the van. If he hurried, he could be in and out in ten or fifteen minutes.

The launderia was small but bright inside, and thankfully no line-up for the showers at the back of the shop. He fished out enough coins for the shower as well as for a tiny, guest-sized bar of soap from a vending machine on the wall. Preferring not to think too much about who or what might have used the facility before him, he undressed inside the small, humid enclosure. The clink of his coins dropping into the meter immediately launched an almost blistering-hot stream of water from above, but it felt good, nonetheless.

His aching parts were soothed, his muscles eased by the flow of water as he let it cascade down his neck, shoulders and back. He'd liked to have stayed in the comfort of it for an hour, but knew the meter would run out in mere minutes, if not sooner. He soaped up his sweaty skin, his hand lingering over his cock and balls as he spread the suds over them. The image of a naked Marlena sharing the space with him entered his mind, the rising steam not only from the dribbling water, but their passionate exploration of each other. Damn, if he had more coins he'd be tempted to relieve the tension in his awakening cock.

Sitting next to the girl for more than two hours on the road had been both ecstasy and torture at the same time; God, she was beautiful. He didn't want the trip to end. They'd planned to come to Madrid to see museums and architecture, drink in the Spanish culture; now that they were here, it seemed silly to about-face and go all the way back to Zaragoza. Perhaps they could stay the night, find a modest hotel somewhere nearby. Oh my, what would her mother think then?

With a metallic snap, the comforting flow of water came to an abrupt halt and put and end to his runaway thoughts. He dried and dressed quickly. Sadly, fresh clothes were not an option but at least his body felt clean beneath his soiled and smelly threads. By the time he returned to the van, carrying two bottled sodas from a nearby convenience store, dusk shrouded the street. He hoped to see Marlena's silhouette inside the cab as he drew nearer, but those hopes were dashed when the empty passenger seat greeted him. The interview must have gone longer than expected; but from a job-seekers perspective that was usually a good sign.

He climbed into the driver's seat and set the soda bottles on the dash, then turned the ignition on to fiddle with the radio dials in hopes of raising a decent frequency. He hadn't thought to check out whether the radio even worked before he bought the thing. When he finally coaxed some crackly strains of folk music through the speakers, he sat back and surveyed the street. No movement near the door that Marlena had entered, and with a start, he realized the whole place was completely dark inside; no lights on at all. It didn't look right. Didn't feel right.

How long had she been in there? He drummed his fingertips on the wheel, wrestling with his better judgment, the tension in his muscles, acid beginning to swirl in his gut. Glancing down, he noticed a crumpled ball of paper on the floor. He reached for it, realizing Marlena must have dropped it in her hurry to get out. Careful not to tear it, he unraveled the sorry-looking wad and flattened it against the dash.

*

Tristan was beginning to act like Ernesto, Marlena thought; exerting his authority under the guise of concern and protection. Did men in every country do that? If so, it was becoming tiresome. Wasn't being held back by tradition and government bad enough, without every male in sight getting in the way, too? She almost felt relieved to step through the storefront door and leave Tristan's company behind, but still nervous as to what she might find inside.

Her eyes adjusted to the dim, and beneath a slow-moving ceiling fan, an overweight, dark-haired man sat behind a solitary desk. He looked up as she approached, pulling a lit cigarette from between his lips and exhaling smoke. "Si?" he asked as the foul-smelling wisps rose upward into the fan's circling blades. His dark eyes traveled up and down her height, but seemed to hold no glint of interest toward her. Even so, she felt paralyzed under his steely, apathetic gaze.

"I'm here to answer this ad," she began, but realizing the old news clipping she'd had in her hand was gone; she must have dropped it. She swallowed hard and gathered her courage, lifting her chin and speaking clearly. "About models being needed? And training provided?"

The man stubbed out his cigarette in a tin tray on the desk, adding to a sizeable and disgusting pile of old butts. "We are no longer taking applications for that," he said, his voice deep and gruff. "You should go on home."

Marlena's heart fell. "Oh no," she said aloud. "I know the ad was from weeks ago, but…I couldn't get here until now. Can't you let me audition? Please? I've come a long way, and I know I'd be good at it, if you give me a chance."

He turned in his swivel chair and looked her over once more, his lower lip protruding in a doubtful manner. "How old are you?"

"Eighteen," she said proudly.

"You have ID on you?"

Marlena dove her hand into her traveling bag. "Yes," she said, pulling out a card and handing it to the man. She didn't own a driver's license, but her school ID had her birthdate on it. She looked hopefully at him while he scrutinized the card. When he looked up, his expression seemed more agreeable than before, and his eyes wandered over her again.

"We may have something," he said, gripping the arms of his chair to lift himself to his feet. "If you think you're so good. A moment." He turned down a short hallway that was curtained off at the end. He parted the drape just enough to stick his head through. "You want to look at another one?"

he said, gesturing with his chin back toward where Marlena stood.

"Yeah, sure," came a man's voice from inside.

The man turned around and motioned for her to come. Marlena moved down the hall toward him. He stopped her as she reached the curtain. "You can leave that with me," he said, nodding to her bulky bag. Marlena hesitated. "I'll keep it safe," he assured her. "You won't need it in there."

She didn't want to ruin her chances by being difficult; this could be her big ticket. Surely they weren't going to steal her belongings. She smiled and handed the bag over. The man held the curtain aside.

Marlena passed through the opening into a dimly lit space. It smelled of dust and stale smoke. As her eyes adjusted, she saw electrical cables snaking across the floor and what looked like lighting equipment in the center of a black-draped room. The same male voice echoed from the surrounding darkness. "Well, hurry up. Stand on the mark."

She scurried forward to stand over a crude letter X taped on the floor between the metal light stands. She noticed a camera fastened to another, three-legged stand. "My name is Marlena," she said into the shadows. She sensed movement from off to one side, and with a snapping sound, the little space flooded with light from all sides. On reflex she blinked and shielded her eyes with one hand.

"Yeah, sure," the voice said from behind where the camera stood. "We don't have all day, Marlene. Let's get on with it."

"Marlena," she corrected. He didn't sound very friendly. But maybe he'd had a long day, just as she had. It seemed an eternity ago she'd stood at the bus stop; and she might not even be here now if it hadn't been for Tristan. She pictured him waiting outside for her already, and for some reason that comforted her, despite her earlier impatience with him.

"Are you gonna smile, or what?" the man said. Marlena

straightened and put on her best smile. "That's good," he said as the camera's shutter clicked in rapid-fire succession. "Now turn around." Her smile faded a little, but did as he said and turned her back to the camera. It clicked some more. "Okay, turn around and take the dress off."

Marlena stiffened. Did she hear him correctly? Take her dress off?

"Hey. Like I said, haven't got all day, Marlene."

His tone of voice made her start to panic; she was annoying him with her hesitance. This was a business, after all; and hadn't she already prepared herself to do whatever was asked from behind a camera? Just do it, her brain whispered. She reached behind her neck for the zipper's tab and pulled it downward. The soft material skidded off her shoulders and fell to her waist.

Marlena's heart pounded as the cool air brushed her exposed skin. With shaking hands, she pushed the dress past her hips and let the dress fall around her ankles. She stepped out of the ring of fabric and stood there, clad only in her plain white bra and panties. Her arms wrapped protectively around herself. Doing a thing was much harder than imagining doing a thing, she realized. Instead of beautiful and confident, she felt as awkward as one of the newborn lambs on her family's farm, and just as scared.

"Arms down," the voice snapped. She dropped her arms to her sides, lowering her eyes to the floor. The voice clucked in disdain. "You want the job or not? Look at the camera, doll."

Marlena's head snapped up. The spotlights glared in her face, the heat radiating from them doing little to stop her shivering. "Yes, I want the job." The camera sputtered multiple shots. Gooseflesh rose all over her body and her nipples hardened, straining against the cups of her bra; only this time it was not pleasurable like before.

"That's a good girl." The voice seemed to soften, and

lowered in pitch. "Yeah. Keep that look." More camera clicks. "Don't stand like you've got a pole down your back. Feet apart; put one hand on your hip." Marlena relaxed a bit, feeling more comfortable the more she moved around; feeling like a model. She posed as he directed, striking the same stance facing away from the camera. This wasn't so bad. And after all, how else would they know if she was model material if she didn't show her body? Still, she wished they would finish soon. She wanted to put her clothes back on.

"Okay turn around. Lose the bra."

"What?" The question slipped from her lips before she could stop it.

"Don't pretend you don't understand. Take it off. Show us your tits."

Marlena felt frozen, unable to respond. His words shocked her. So crude and vulgar. How dare he speak to her like that. "No," she finally said, shaking her head. "I can't."

"Don't waste my time, little girl. We're done here." Panic rose again. She'd blown it; the very thing she didn't want to do. It felt so wrong, what he asked; but she couldn't afford to say no. Not now. Not when she'd gone this far.

"I'm not a little girl," she said, her voice barely above a squeak.

"Prove it. Show me your tits, or get out."

Chapter Sixteen

Ernesto pushed through the doorway of the Sanchez villa, practically knocking Consuelo over before she could step back. "Is Marly here?" he asked, his voice breathless and strained. His mind replayed the moments he'd last seen Marlena, the harsh words he'd spoken. He didn't mean them, and regretted all of them.

He'd waited for her after school, to apologize and set things right again. Even if it meant parting ways, he couldn't live with this rift between them, and would do anything to repair it. When the school bus had departed and still no sign of Marly, he searched the nearly-empty school hallways and classrooms for her. She had simply vanished. He trudged the miserable distance home, and though he wasn't to take it without permission, immediately jumped into his father's work truck and drove to the villa, feverishly hoping she'd gotten there some other way.

"No, Senor Allesandro. She not here," Consuelo answered brusquely, clearly indicating her indignation with his unseemly entrance. "You were not expected. What is it you want?"

Ernesto exhaled in exasperation, running one hand through his unruly hair and adjusting his glasses that had slid down the sweaty bridge of his nose with the other. "I must see her mother. Is she at home?"

After a stiff appraisal of his appearance, Consuelo gave a curt nod. "I tell Senora Bianca you here."

Ernesto paced the brick and stone foyer until Bianca appeared. "Ernesto. A surprise to see you," the lady of the house began, pausing as she took in his demeanour. "Whatever is wrong? You seem upset."

"I can't find Marly. She wasn't on the bus home, and I'm worried. Do you know where she is?"

"I believe she wanted to do a little shopping after school," Bianca said. "She had some money saved up and asked if she could buy some new clothes. We hope to hear from the modeling school any day now." Bianca smiled and leaned toward him a bit. "She wants to be a model, you know."

Suddenly, the tension in Ernesto's body released, leaving him feeling boneless and a little embarrassed. Of course, there was a logical explanation; he'd jumped to conclusions again, like he'd been doing a lot lately. Ever since that British gringo had arrived, it seemed. But he found it hard to be logical where Marlena was concerned. His feelings for her had always been strong, and they were increasing day by day; changing, growing desperate. He nodded his head and gazed down at the floor. "Yes, I…she told me. But she never said anything about going shopping today."

Bianca chuckled and placed a hand on his shoulder. "Well, women can't tell their men everything, you know. We always need a little mystery to keep the good ones around." Ernesto raised his head, her words lighting a tiny flame of hope. "Do you want to wait here for her?" she asked.

As much as he wanted to do just that, Ernesto didn't like the vision of what Marly might think when she saw him waiting around for her like a lost puppy. He was stronger than that, and he had to show it. "Thank you, but no. I've intruded here enough, Senora. I'll call later."

"It's no intrusion," Bianca said, releasing her touch. "I'll tell her you were here."

"No, don't do that. I mean, she probably knows I'd come by," Ernesto said, disguising his anxiety with false bravado. "Sorry to trouble you. Goodbye, Senora Sanchez." He left the house and strode to his truck as though iron was in his spine. If Marly didn't tell him her plans, there was a reason. Clearly, she didn't want him hanging around; or at least hanging around while she picked out dresses and shoes. That, he could understand. But her attitude had been more hostile than that.

He rolled the other parts of their conversation around in his head. "I'm going to Madrid," she'd said. That wasn't news; they'd even talked about going there together. Recalling that fact sent a stab of remorse through him. She'd given him that chance, and he ignored it. Now she'd be going without him. Alone.

Or maybe not alone.

Could she have meant that literally? Going to Madrid… today? He started the engine and put the gear in reverse, backing down the long driveway at full throttle, ignoring the bone-shaking bumps. If she wasn't alone, he had a good idea who might be with her. He had to know.

In minutes, Ernesto braked to a hard stop in front of the Gracia Immaculata. He raced up the steps and burst through the main doors into the sanctuary. The Pastor would be in his office or the rectory, and against his upbringing, ran full speed up the center aisle and toward the back rooms of the church. "Pastor Giorgio," he called ahead.

His head swiveled as he entered the rectory, looking for the man. The Pastor stood in the doorway of his small office, responding to all the ruckus. "Ernesto," Don Giorgio said, a look of concern on his face. "What brings you here, and in such a rush?"

"Is Tristan here?" he asked point-blank.

The Pastor shook his head. "He is not. And I'm becoming concerned. I hope there wasn't an accident."

"An accident?" Ernesto said, blinking through lenses that were fogging from his heavy breathing. "What do you mean?"

Don Giorgio stepped closer toward him, spreading his hands wide. "He went to work in town today, doing some excavating for a project with the town counsel. He wasn't sure how long it would take, or even be successful, but hasn't yet returned. Digging is hard, risky work. I hope he hasn't been injured."

"He's been gone all day?" To Ernesto, that meant two possibilities. He had either been occupied, and therefore not with Marlena; or, used the project as an excuse to be away for the entire day with her. "Where in town?"

"Somewhere near El Guardián. I believe it was to do with an irrigation plan. He took young Ángel with him as a helper. Why are you looking for him?"

Ernesto hadn't thought as far as having to explain his reasons. He'd hoped to find Tristan at the church and confront him directly, but now the question hung in the air. "Senora Sanchez asked me to find him. I was coming to town anyway, and...there's a...mechanical problem she thought he could help with." He cringed at having to lie to a clergyman, but decided to keep going with it. "Who is Ángel?"

"A little boy from town. Ángel Ibanez. He lives with his mother on Calle Verdugo. I'm afraid he's rather taken with our Senor Flynn; been spending a lot of time with him. Misses his father, I expect." Don Giorgio folded his arms as he cast his kindly gaze over Ernesto. "Why don't you sit down. You seem out of breath, my son. What troubles you? Do you wish to talk about it?"

Ernesto sank onto one of the benches at the rectory table. He didn't want to talk about it, exactly; but he was running out of ideas. If he could talk to anyone, surely a church Pastor would be a good choice. "I'm sorry, Padre. I wasn't entirely honest with you. I've come for a different reason." He took a deep breath. "Marlena is missing. We thought…that is, I thought… Tristan might have…they might have run off together."

The Pastor looked taken aback; his brows rising in surprise. Then he shook his balding head. "I think you're mistaken. Why would you say such a thing?"

"Because he wants her," Ernesto blurted out. "Don't you see that? He has from the beginning."

Don Giorgio uncrossed his arms and brought his palms together in a calming gesture. "I cannot confirm or deny any such thing. Be that as it may, you say Senorita Sanchez is missing? That is serious. How long has she been gone? Oh dear, her poor mother must be distraught."

Ernesto flinched inwardly, realizing that the only person feeling distraught was himself. Marly's mother wasn't the least bit worried; and he had only his own jealous suspicions to go on. "When Marlena wasn't on the school bus home I got worried and went to her house. Her mother thought she had gone shopping after school, but had not yet come home."

"Well, then, perhaps that's all there is to it."

"You don't know Marly like I do; and you don't know what's been going on between her and…and him. I just feel something bad has happened."

"Why don't we go and see?" Don Giorgio suggested. "Let's walk into town and have a look in the shops. If she's there, that will set your mind at ease, yes?"

Ernesto nodded in resignation. If nothing else, he could talk to her. She wouldn't brush him off with the good Pastor in tow.

"And I may also find out what has become of my miracle

worker," Don Giorgio continued, reaching for his cloak. "Shall we go then, Senor Alvarez?"

Chapter Seventeen

Tears of humiliation welled in Marlena's eyes as she reached for the closure on her bra and unhooked it. She dropped the white lace thing to the floor, her nude breasts in full view and nipples standing to attention. The camera clicked rapidly.

"Good girl. You want to be in movies, don't you?" The voice was smooth now, low and quiet. "Speak up, so I can hear your voice."

Movies? The ad never said anything about movies. "What do you want me to say," Marlena asked, staring blankly ahead, forcing back tears.

"Say how you like to be touched."

She wasn't sure what he meant. "Touched?"

"Yeah. How your boyfriend likes to touch you."

Of all the questions she could be asked, that wasn't one of them. It occurred to her they never asked her name; she'd provided it willingly. They didn't ask her to fill out any forms or if she had any experience, and now they were talking about movies. Had she made a mistake…a terrible mistake? A dark wave of remorse began to engulf her. She was trapped in this awful place, naked and vulnerable and above all, ashamed. She wished she'd never seen that newspaper.

"Well? Cat got your tongue?" he demanded.

"I don't have a boyfriend."

The voice went silent for an agonizing minute. Her face blushed hot with embarrassment. Dios, she wanted to crawl away and hide. "A pretty girl like you? Don't lie. Touch your breasts and imagine its him touching you."

Marlena squeezed her eyes shut, as though seeing nothing would make everything not real; make everything she'd done and would do next be like it never happened. Afraid to hear what the voice might say next, she raised her hands to her chest. She remembered standing at the bullring with Tristan's arms around her, and how her breasts had tingled to life against his strong body. Her fingers brushed the hardened nubs of her nipples, and it made them tighten even further. Her panties felt wet, just like that day in her bedroom. No, not here. Please not here.

"That's good. More. Squeeze those tits. Tell me how it feels." The tears she'd been holding back spilled down her cheeks as she cupped her breasts, hiding her throbbing nipples. "Does it feel good?" the voice prodded. She shook her head. "Mierda! Don't cry. Only little girls cry. Little girls don't star in movies. You're still just a little girl, aren't you?"

"No," she sobbed.

"I don't believe you. Just a little girl from the country, right?"

"I'm a grown woman," she cried, her blubbering only serving to prove she was not. She felt frightened and miserable. She sniffled a wet breath, sounding more like a child than ever.

The man fell silent again while she stood there trembling. "Take off your panties and prove it," he finally said.

*

Tristan kept his eyes on the dark glass door, but saw nothing. It had been close to an hour since Marlena had passed through it, and he was getting angry. The yellowed newspaper clipping had been so mangled, he could barely make out the print. His knowledge of Spanish was improving, but not enough to understand all the half-obliterated words. From the few that he recognized, the ad did appear legitimately seeking applicants. Modelos, he presumed meant models, since Marlena had talked about going to modeling school.

But what kind of modeling? Clothes? Jewelry? Posing for painters or sculptors? The latter made him even more uneasy; he remembered the art students at university sketching nude models in the studios. He hoped it was fashion modeling, but even that made him think of lingerie ads in clothing catalogues. He shifted uncomfortably in his seat, keeping an anxious eye on the blackened glass door for another long minute. Frustrated, he decided to get out of the vehicle altogether.

Dark had nearly fallen, making the heat even more claustrophobic than it was in broad daylight. He looked up and down the deserted street. Odd that no pedestrians were about, and virtually no other cars had driven down this way. He'd seen bad neighborhoods before, and as the shadows deepened, knew this was one of them. He walked around to the curb side and leaned on the passenger door of the van. His stomach churned with foreboding, the emptiness of the street further heightening his suspicions. Even thugs and pickpockets didn't seem to frequent the area.

Tristan was okay in a fight; thoughts of he and Ari in that backstreet cantina ran through his mind. Ironically, the incident had been nearly two years ago, and the place might only be a mile or two from where he stood now. He'd know what to do if a lone attacker tried to jump him, but what if a whole gang of them suddenly showed up? He had no weapons on him. He thought of his tools in the back of the van, and stepped around to open the rear doors. Two shovels. A steel tape measure. A plumb bob and line. He smiled as his eyes fell on a pipe wrench. He hoisted the heavy tool to his belt.

As he closed the van, he caught a flash of something moving behind the entrance door of the building. He leaped across the sidewalk and grasped the handle, startling the figure on the other side as he wrenched it open. "Mierda," it cussed, stepping back. "Who the fuck are you, we're closed."

"Not yet," Tristan said, shouldering his way in. "A girl came in here. Where is she?"

The lights were off, but he could make out the man's dark bulk in front of him; a stocky body, shorter than himself. The smell of stale cigarette smoke radiated from him. "There's nobody here," he grunted. "Get out, I'm closing up. You're trespassing."

"You can call the cops after I find my friend. Where is she? What kind of place is this?"

"I don't know your friend," the man's gruff voice said. "This is my place of business, and my business is none of yours, amigo. Get lost."

Tristan stepped closer to the man, his grip tightening on the wrench's handle. "She came in here an hour ago. I'm sure you couldn't miss her; pretty, long brown hair."

The man laughed, an ugly, guttural sound, and mirrored Tristan's advance. No more than a few inches stood between them. "Lots of pretty girls in Madrid, amigo," he said, his tone low and suggestive. "Why don't you go find one at Senora Roja's place on the next block…she'll show you a good time."

New voices sounded from somewhere deeper inside the dark space. A man's harsh voice, then a woman's…a woman crying. Instinctively, Tristan swung the wrench at his opponent's head, catching him on the side of his skull with a sickening crack. He pushed past the man's falling body and moved toward the voices. His eyes had adjusted to the light enough to sidestep the few obstacles in the room and head down a tunnel-like hallway. A sliver of light shone through a slightly parted curtain straight ahead.

He broke into a near-run as the woman's cries echoed louder from behind the curtain and ripped it aside as he reached it. He blinked at the sudden glare of light from the center of the room, and then his guts went cold. With spotlights trained on her, Marlena stood in the harsh cone of light, almost completely naked. Her body trembled as she sobbed uncontrollably, vainly trying to cover herself with crossed arms. A dark figure stood just outside the circle of light, his features vaguely outlined by the glare. As Tristan burst into the room, the man's eyeglass lenses flashed a reflection as he turned toward him.

"Get away from her, you perverted fuck," Tristan shouted in a feral growl.

"Nico!" the man screamed, obviously calling for his associate out front.

Tristan rushed forward. "He can't help you," he snarled. "I said get away from her!"

The man backed up, crashing into the lighting stands and knocking them over. "Fuck!" he cursed as he stumbled, briefly revealing his face in the bobbing light, but turned away as he scrambled to his feet and ran from the room.

Marlena had backed away from the skirmish and into the shadows, her sobbing turned to anguished wails. Tristan stepped over a camera and tripod that had also collapsed into the heap of upturned equipment. "Are you alright?" he said, his heart pounding and his breath ragged as he went to her.

She sat huddled in a fetal position, hiding her face. "No! Get away," she cried between sobs. "Don't touch me. Don't look at me." Tristan averted his gaze, and saw her clothes in a heap near were she'd been standing. He reached for them and brought them over.

"I won't look. Here. Are you alright? Did they hurt you?" He crouched a few feet away, his eyes lowered. He realized he still held the heavy wrench in his hand, and wondered if 'Nico' was still out cold, or worse. Had he killed the brute? He didn't want to find out. They had to get out of here, fast. He shoved the wrench handle inside his belt. The photographer had fled backstage; hopefully there was another exit besides the way he'd come in.

"No," she blubbered, sniffing up her tears. "They said something about being in movies. I thought it was a modeling school, and it would just be photographs…"

Modeling. Tristan thought back to the shred of newspaper Marlena had dropped. It was all a scam. Offering modeling classes, then luring innocent, naive young girls into makeshift porn studios on that pretense. It made his blood boil; God only knew what they did after they took the pictures. Drug them, maybe…hold them captive; make them unrecognizable to anyone who might be looking for them. He'd heard his former workmates talk about pornographic films that were beginning to flood the theaters now that Franco's iron fist was weakening its hold on the populace; and the seeds of evil were sprouting from between his failing fingers.

"Shhh," he quieted. "It's okay. It's over now." While Marlena dressed, he quickly picked up the fallen camera then returned to help her to her feet. "We have to get out of here, fast."

Chapter Eighteen

Marlena choked back a sob and allowed Tristan to lift her from the floor. Her fingernails dug into his strong forearms as he did so, not only to hold on, but to stop her limbs from shaking. No time to think now, about fear or shame or embarrassment; the need to escape from this place was all that mattered. As he led her in the direction the photographer had gone, Marlena clasped Tristan's hand like a lifeline, shutting out everything from her mind except the warmth of his grip, blindly trusting he would get them both to safety.

What if the photographer jumped them in the darkness? And what about the man in the front office? Surely he'd heard all the commotion. Whoever they were, those two men knew the building, and neither she or Tristan did. She prayed there was a back door of some kind and they would find it quickly without running into either of them. Suddenly, Tristan changed direction and nearly jerked her arm out of its socket. "There," he whispered.

Wincing against the pain, Marlena saw a dim square of light ahead, and was pulled toward it. As they got nearer, the shape became recognizable as a grimy window set into a heavy door. Tristan threw his weight against it and the pair of them stumbled out into a darkened alley. Humid air carried the fetid smells of garbage and human waste to their nostrils, but she didn't care. It was the smell of freedom.

"Come on," he said, ushering her away from the building and down the narrow alley. They emerged on the main street, and she saw their rusted blue van parked several yards away. The area was deserted, with no sign of either man from inside the building. Panting for breath, Marlena's knees buckled and felt herself slipping to the ground. Strong arms went around her waist and held her to stand again. "We have to keep going," Tristan whispered, his voice hoarse with urgency. "Just a little farther."

He half-dragged her to the van and quickly deposited her inside, tossing the wrench and the camera in the back. In a flash he was behind the wheel, the vehicle lurching away from the curb and speeding down the street. Marlena huddled in the passenger seat and turned her face toward the window. The emotions she kept at bay while escaping now filled her all at once; shame, embarrassment, relief, remorse. She couldn't face Tristan like this.

She'd been estupid. Stupid enough to believe a vague ad in a newspaper, stupid enough to believe everything she read. Even the torn magazine she kept under her mattress she'd accepted as truth. In addition to feeling duped, Marlena suddenly felt small, a tiny, insignificant thing that knew nothing at all about the world. How did she expect to succeed, to rise above her life that she considered so mundane, to want more than what she had? Perhaps there was nothing more for girls like her; become someone's wife and have no ambitions except to cook, clean and have babies. She was foolish to think otherwise. But she felt dirty, now. Soiled. Ruined from even having that kind of a future.

"Are you sure you're alright?" Tristan asked, breaking the silence that filled the cab of the van.

Marlena curled her body up even tighter. "Yes." She was physically alright, but her pride had been wounded beyond repair. She could barely speak. What did he think of her now? All the feelings he'd stirred within her with his kiss, with the closeness of his body…whatever had begun to grow between them seemed lost, just as any chance of living the life she'd dreamed of.

"Here." Tristan offered her one of the sodas, the glass bottle sweaty and dripping with condensation. "I'm sorry," he said after an uncomfortable silence. "Sorry that I didn't go in there with you. I should have gone with you."

Marlena had only her own naivete to blame. If he hadn't come in when he did, she might still be there, at the mercy of those horrible men. She took the bottle with shaking hands, and raised it to her lips. She should be grateful; he'd rescued her, yet he was apologizing. She felt worse than shamed; she felt shameful for not even thanking him, but the words would not come. She took a sip of soda to ease her throat. "I told you not to," she finally said, the statement coming out more harshly than she intended.

"I did as you asked, against my better judgment," he said. He slapped the wheel angrily. "Flaming hell, why didn't I stop you. I had a feeling that place meant trouble." She could feel him turn his gaze on her, hot and accusing. "What did they say to you? Did they threaten you? Make you do whatever they said? Or do you just take your clothes off for anyone who asks?"

Marlena's cheeks burned, with more than embarrassment. Anger flared inside her at his words. "I do not," she spat. "I was being professional. It's what models do."

"That was not modeling. Did you not see what was wrong with what they were asking you to do? They took advantage of you."

"I don't want to talk about it," she cried, tears returning to her eyes.

"I think that was a porn ring," Tristan continued. "Do you realize what could have happened? They could have drugged you, beaten you. Made it so that you didn't even remember your name or where you came from. Then filmed you being… doing…" He broke off, leaving the sentence unfinished. "You'd have disappeared, never saw your family again." She looked away again, her misery deepening. "Or me," he added. "And I don't think I could bear that."

She let his words sink in as she watched the streets of Madrid slip past through her tear-blurred eyes. He hated what she'd done, but he didn't hate her, even after she'd made the biggest mistake of her life. That's what friends did. But is that all he wanted? To be her friend? At that moment she realized she wanted more than his friendship; that a bigger mistake would be to turn away from this man. Her inner voice spoke clearer, louder; validating what she felt deep down. They'd met for a reason, their fates inextricably bound together.

"Let's get you home," Tristan said, interrupting her thoughts. "Your mother must be beside herself with worry by now."

Marlena bowed her head. Go home? The idea made her heart pound and her stomach twist. What would she say? What would her mama say? How could she explain any of this? Her mother had never punished her for anything before, but she'd never given her reason before. Her grandmother had beaten Aunt Juliana without a second thought; perhaps Bianca was capable of doing the same. Her limbs began to tremble.

"No! I can't go home. Not now, not yet," she said. "Please don't."

Tristan looked at her. "You have to go home. Where else can you go?"

"I can go with you. Please. If you want to go back to the

church, I'll go with you; just don't take me home. I can't face them."

Tristan sighed but kept driving. "It's three hours or more, at night," he said. "We're tired. I think I know a place we can stay, get something to eat, if I can find it. It's been awhile since I've been there."

"Where?"

"A small place. Near the edge of town. The rooms are cheap, and…"

"It sounds fine. I have money." Even as she said it, she realized her bag had been left behind. Her ID and her money. She couldn't even offer to help pay for lodging, or food. Her stomach rumbled. Nether of them had eaten since they left Zaragoza.

Tristan shook his head. "Don't worry about that. You just need to rest, and so do I."

They drove on in silence, the city thinning as they moved farther from its center. The paved streets turned to cobble, and then to dirt. Not even streetlights seemed to exist this far out. Marlena looked upward, seeing with wondrous clarity the stars of the infinite cosmos overhead, and felt very small, indeed.

Tristan slowed as he made one last corner and pulled to a stop alongside a low roofed adobe building, with rounded windows carved out of the walls and its clay-tiled roof missing several tiles. Strings of bare light bulbs hung just under the roof line, the only illumination on the exterior. A small neon sign flashed in one of the porthole-shaped windows, alternately displaying the words 'Cantina' and 'Open'.

"Doesn't look like it's changed much," Tristan said, shifting into park and killing the engine.

"How do you know this place?" Marlena asked, glancing warily at the run-down exterior. Nothing about it was welcoming. But it did seem an appropriate place for hiding out, jammed in among other similarly questionable establishments and backing on to a narrow alley.

"I stopped here once before; shortly after I arrived in Spain." He paused. "It's where I first saw your Aunt Juliana." Marlena looked at him in surprise. This is where it happened, all the things her tía had told her about. They were true! "Come on, let's go inside."

"I can wait here," she said, uncertain why she felt so hesitant. She'd been in a far worse situation just hours ago. Perhaps it was a feeling of foreboding, of mal suerte, since hearing her tía's story.

"Not a chance," he replied, shaking his head. "I'm never letting you out of my sight again." Marlena shivered, even as the hot, humid night air settled on her skin. Walking inside a place with such bad history was far more desirable than the humiliation of returning home, or being left alone. She never wanted to be left alone again. Tristan hurried to her side of the van and opened the door, his strong hand closing firmly yet gently around her wrist. "I'll take care of you."

She looked into his eyes and saw strength, trust and something more; something meant only for her. The glow from the dim strings of bulbs illuminated his curly blond hair like a halo around his head. Angels wore halos. With sudden clarity, she realized she'd met her own guardian angel. She clasped his muscled bicep with her other hand and willingly slipped from her seat to stand firmly on the ground next to him. "I know," she said.

Chapter Nineteen

The bed was small and sagged a bit in the middle. A patchwork quilt, clearly handmade with its random squares of mismatched fabric, draped over it. Only a single chair, a rickety bedside table and the lamp sitting atop it comprised the remaining furniture in the room. "It's not much," Tristan said. "But it's private."

A wisp of night breeze slipped through the open porthole window and caressed Marlena's forehead. Her apprehension had dissipated the moment Tristan helped her across the threshold of the room. Something about it, about being with him, made her feel safe and relaxed. It felt like a sanctuary. The traditional crucifix hung above the head of the bed seemed to validate the thought. For all her railing against tradition, this simple wooden icon suddenly brought her peace, and tears to her eyes. She'd made so many mistakes this day; so many wrong turns and unfortunate consequences. Yet redemption was always just a prayer away.

"Hey," Tristan said, his voice quiet and compassionate. His arms went around her and drew her close. She rested her head against his solid chest. "I'm sorry about the room. I know it's pathetic. I'd take you to a five-star hotel if I could."

His words reminded her of all Tía Juliana had said. "Like the one you used to run? On the coast?" she murmured into his shirt.

"How did you know about that?" he asked.

"Tía Juliana told me everything. Well, nearly everything. That she used to be a dancer here, and that two men fought over her and you stopped them. Then she came to your hotel looking for work."

"El Mirador," Tristan said, his whispered words seeming full of regret. "Yes, she came there."

Silence hung between them for a moment. Marlena could hear the steady, comforting beat of his heart inside his chest and smell his scent. An earthy, fresh fragrance like leaves on a forest floor after a rain, overlaid with the smell of soap and unlaundered clothing. Again, a fluttering sensation gripped her stomach, and a tingling ache began at the tips of her breasts.

Her arms went around his waist and she pressed herself harder against him, fitting her womanly curves into the hard planes and hollows of Tristan's fit body. They were alone, with no one to object or judge them. No one to say what should or should not happen between them. Not even God. She'd felt shame at being naked before those awful men, but knew she would not feel that way here, with him.

She lifted her head and brought her lips close to his. A stubbled growth of beard scraped her chin. "I don't need a five-star hotel," she said, her voice soft and breathless. "I need to grow up. I'm tired of being treated like a child. Can you show me? Show me how to be a woman?"

"If you're asking what I think you're asking," he said, his lips brushing hers, his arms pulling her even deeper into his embrace. "I'm not sure I can. Not like this, not after what you went through today. God, if you'd only asked me a week ago, a month ago…"

"A month ago, I was a disobedient, naïve little brat who

didn't listen to anyone but her own stubborn, ridiculous ideas. I don't want to be her anymore."

"You can't blame yourself for what happened," Tristan sighed, his lips trailing soft kisses across her cheek, under her ear and against the spot on her throat where her hot blood pulsed in rapid tempo. She could hear his breath coming heavier, faster, heating her skin with each tight exhale. "What did they do to you," he murmured between kisses, the hardness below his belt growing and pressing into her belly, "…to make you say such things?"

Marlena felt an uncontrollable spasm ripple through her abdomen and settle between her legs, releasing a delicious slickness over her tender privates. She wanted his touch there, between her moist folds, to bring again that dark, overwhelming and indescribable sensation of joy rushing over her, the need achingly sharp. "They made me see what a foolish, silly girl I was. They told me to go home. I wouldn't listen. I begged to stay. I trusted them, total strangers," she sobbed. "More than I trusted you, or anyone who cared about me."

Tristan cradled the back of her head with one hand and framed her cheek with the other, locking their faces close to each other. "I care about you, Marlena Sanchez," he said, his voice raw and crackling with emotion. "If you don't care for me, or don't trust me, then I'd better take you home right now. Because I don't think I can hold you like this another second without making love to you…"

His words were lost as she moved first, claiming his lips in a searing kiss that left no question of her trust unanswered. He responded with equal heat, matching the passion that poured forth from her, their tongues seeking and exploring, the flames of desire fueled by an energy drawn from the very depths of their souls.

"Say you want this," Tristan whispered, breaking their

burning kiss, his hands finding the zipper tab of her dress and pulling downward. "Say you want me, Marlena."

"I want you," she gasped, her fingers diving into his mass of curling blond locks. "I want you to take me away, and to be with you, always," Her lips found his again, emphasizing her words and trapping his groan in his throat with her fervent kiss. He untangled her fingertips from his tousled mane and lowered her arms to slip the dress down over her shoulders. His palms caressed the nude skin of her arms as he slid the garment downward, dropping it to the floor as she lifted her hands out and away, only to have them fly to the buttons of his shirt and begin to work them free.

As the last button gave way, their bodies separated of one accord, pausing to drink in the sight of one another. Marlena pushed the material of his shirt aside, her hands exploring the smooth, muscled contours of his chest, breathing out a sigh of wonder. Months of physical work had sculpted his body into hard perfection, from his rounded pectorals to the washboard ripples of his midsection. He closed his eyes for a moment, his head tilting back slightly as her touch flowed over him before he reached for his belt and began pulling the buckle free. She watched in fascination as he popped the rivet on the waistband and split the zipper of his jeans open, releasing the stiffened mass that had pressed so urgently against her.

She wanted to touch it but before she could, Tristan opened his eyes, his blue gaze deepening to an intense, ultramarine hue that seemed to penetrate the very core of her being. He cupped her breasts with both hands, exploring their firm texture with gentle but urgent fingers. Her nipples swelled to aching hardness beneath her bra, and the place between her legs vibrated wildly with need. "You're so beautiful, Marlena…you have no idea what the sight of you does to me."

His words only added to the desire she felt bursting within, and arched into his touch as she reached behind and released the closure of her brassiere, allowing the cups to spring free in his hands. He whisked the skimpy garment away and took full possession of her naked breasts in his palms, rubbing the diamond-hard tips of her nipples with his thumbs. "Dios mio," he whispered, as he bent his head to take one hardened brown disk into his mouth. She felt the warmth of his tongue as it circled her aching nipple, and gasped in sweet pain as he sucked it deep into his eager mouth.

Her body ignited with the multiple sensations of his hands and lips on her breasts, his wiry blond hair and rough beard brushing her heated skin. Her panties were soaked with a renewed gush of her excited juices. She whimpered in helpless submission. "Tristan…"

As she said his name, he released her breast. She shivered visibly as cool air met wet flesh, the round orb of her breast glistening in the muted light of the tiny room. "Trust me," he murmured into her ear. Then he bent and lifted her slight body off the floor, moving them both toward the sad but available bed. He laid her down on it, her dark tresses fanning out over the single pillow. She lay still, looking up at him as he stood above her, his eyes shining with undisguised desire.

"Let me see you," she whispered. "All of you, as you see me…as God made us. Show me what a man truly and fully looks like."

His lips curled in a wry grin, and shrugged his opened shirt off his shoulders and onto the floor. Marlena tilted her head as it rested on the feather-stuffed pillow, admiring what she saw, the soft light reflecting off every line and curve of his upper body, from broad shoulders to bulging biceps. When he shoved his well-worn jeans downward, she marveled at the flex of muscled thighs and the sinewy working of tendons. Her questions of the male physique were now answered in full, and she drew in a breath as his aroused cock was revealed; rigid, swollen and rippled with veins.

Tossing the denims aside, Tristan stood still before her in all his naked male glory, allowing her a moment to observe as she wished, and satisfy her curiosity. Her eyes took all of him in, and her tongue darted out to moisten her lips in anticipation of what was to come next. All the mystique and secrecy she'd been indoctrinated with her whole life about men and women, about sex and marriage and decency and the sanctity of her virginity felt like so much rubbish now. There was nothing to fear or be ashamed of here. She wanted this man and he wanted her. Nothing could be simpler or more beautiful.

"Do you like what you see?" he asked playfully, echoing the words she'd spoken to him in the kitchen in what seemed so long ago.

Marlena nodded silently, and reached out for him, beckoning him nearer. He strode to the side of the bed, where she took his stiff cock in her hands, stroking its tight skin and hardened ridges, exploring every inch of its surface. Tristan groaned and stilled her hands. "Wait."

"I'm sorry, does that hurt you?" she asked, worried that perhaps she'd done the wrong thing. The stretched and reddened skin looked painful to her.

"No," he chuckled, shaking his curly head. "Far from it. But you're going to kill me if you keep doing it," he said. "I'd die a happy man, but if I'm to die of happiness, I want it to be inside you, making love to you." He removed her hands from his body and lowered himself to the bed, lying partly on top of her. A thrill rushed through her, starting between her legs and rocketing up her spine. He kissed her again, his tongue thrusting deep inside the wet, warm cave of her mouth. Her pussy began to ache.

Tristan worked his kisses downward, from her lips to her throat to her breasts, licking and sucking each one in turn until she thought she would explode with desire. As his tongue swirled and flicked each rock-hard nipple, his hand stroked her belly, moving downward in soft circles until he reached her panties. She gasped out loud as he placed his hand between her legs and palmed her sex, the wet fabric pressing against her pussy as he rubbed and squeezed.

"It's alright," he whispered. "Let yourself go, I've got you; I'll take care of you."

Marlena's heart thudded in her ears and her breath came short; she could hear herself panting, wild with lust. Tristan slipped his hand beneath the waistband of her soaked panties and tugged them down as he kissed a path down her belly and abdomen. She lifted her hips on instinct, allowing him to slip the last barrier between them out from under her and down the length of her legs.

At last they were both naked, skin to skin. It felt wonderful and natural; how could this ever be thought of as sinful? Everything she'd been taught about sex was completely untrue. It was breathtakingly beautiful. Tristan rested his head on her belly as his hand traveled back between her legs, stroking the sensitive skin of her inner thighs, urging them apart. She spread her legs, wanting nothing more than to open to him completely. She was his, body and soul.

His fingers plied her wet folds, teasing the sensitive bud near the top of her labia. Marlena's whole body jerked as he worked it in tiny circles, then up and down, side to side. The mysterious, powerful rush of sensation she craved more of began to build with each move of his fingertip. "Dios," she moaned.

"You're so beautiful, Marlena," he murmured. "I want this to be so good for you. You feel so good, let yourself feel good. Don't fight it." He slipped his finger inside her soft entrance as he spoke his sweet words. Her eyes went wide, and her private muscles clenched around his finger as he moved it gently in and out. When he pulled it free and touched her bud again, the beautiful wave she'd felt from afar rushed forward and overtook her in a storm of ecstasy.

"Tristan!" she cried aloud. Her mind blanked, every thought drowned in the deluge except for him, his name; knowing that he was with her, ushering her lovingly through this forbidden heaven.

"That's a girl, let it come, baby," he urged, maintaining his erotic touch, nurturing her throbbing bud forward through orgasm. As the waves began to recede, her tender privates still convulsing, he drew his body overtop her once more.

He raised one of her legs so that her foot rested in the small of his back, the tip of his engorged cock poised at her virgin entrance. She sucked in a breath and dug her nails into his muscled arms. "I love you, Marly," he whispered, his handsome face level with hers, his clear blue eyes full of tenderness and truth.

She'd never heard those words spoken to her; never heard the name Marly sound so right as it did coming from the lips of this man. She surrendered to him completely, and felt a gentle pressure as he breached her outer lips. His fully primed cock pushed deeper, stretched her untried walls when suddenly, a searing sting raked through her lower body. She let out a strangled cry at the sharp yet sweet pain.

She was his, now and forever.

Chapter Twenty

Ernesto awoke to the sounds of birds chirping in the murky dawn. For a moment he felt disoriented, his surroundings unfamiliar, but soon recognized the features of Villa Sanchez. He raised his upper body from the wooden bench on which he'd slept, paying no mind to the stiffness in his back because of it. He rubbed his eyes and peered all around, seeing nothing in the quiet dimness, but felt certain he was not the only one awake. Senora Sanchez had likely been up all night.

He'd returned to Marlena's home when his search of downtown with Pastor Giorgio turned up fruitless. They saw no sign of her on any of the shopping streets and no-one they spoke with had remembered seeing her. Unless she'd somehow snuck into the villa while he was asleep, she was still missing, and his heart felt as though twisted and squeezed into a bloody pulp with worry. He'd asked permission to stay and stand vigil near the front doors. Though there were other ways to gain entry to the house, it was unlikely she had returned without him knowing.

He sat up fully and gazed out the window. Even the dogs were still asleep. No other vehicles besides his own sat parked outside. He could not even imagine Marlena staying away from home overnight, or how she could have lied, even to her mother, about her true plans. Worse thoughts began to grip him; what if she'd been abducted? By someone else entirely? Tristan's disappearance might have been coincidence. But Ernesto didn't think so. He and Marly were together somewhere, he was sure of it.

Ernesto wandered into the kitchen and sat down. A bowl of fruit was laid out in the center and he helped himself to an orange to ease his growling stomach. He wanted to search the house to be certain she hadn't come home during the night, but it was not his place to do so. As he bit into a juicy section of orange, he heard footsteps on the stairs. He turned to see a pale, anxious version of the normally vibrant, elegant Bianca enter the kitchen. Her eyes seemed hollowed from lack of sleep and her body language spoke of nervous exhaustion.

"Ernesto," she said, managing a small smile. "Did you really stay the whole night?"

"Si, Senora. I didn't see or hear anything, but I did fall asleep. Have you heard anything?"

Bianca shook her head. "She's nowhere in the house. Her bed hasn't been slept in. Everything in her room is just as she left it." She joined him at the table and exhaled in a defeated sigh. "Where could she be, Ernesto?" How could she lie to me?"

He swallowed his piece of orange with difficulty, thinking of how he could voice his suspicions to her. "Perhaps she didn't," he said quietly.

"What do you mean?"

He shook his head. "I don't want to worry you even more but, it's possible she was abducted."

Bianca's tired eyes widened. "You mean kidnapped? By whom? Why? For money?"

"Not for money. For something more precious."

Bianca straightened in her chair. "What are you saying,

Ernesto," she said, her voice low and quavering. "If you know something you must tell me."

Ernesto took a deep breath. "I think Tristan Flynn planned this. He wants her, Senora; I'm sure you know that. I think he took her and went to Madrid."

"That cannot be," Bianca gasped. "Senor Flynn is an honorable young man. If he was interested in my daughter, he would have asked my permission to call on her, and Pastor Giorgio would certainly know his whereabouts. And Madrid? That's a long way away from here, why would they go there? Why would you say such a thing?"

"Honor!" Ernesto scoffed. "That's what he wants, Senora… to take her honor, her innocence!" He could not bring himself to say it more plainly. "I'm sorry but with respect, you don't know what's been going on. I've seen them together. They were holding each other and kissing," he said, spitting out his last word like an olive pit. "He's the farthest thing from honorable. He's a wolf among sheep." Bianca looked horrified. Finally, perhaps someone would look at Tristan in the same light that he did. "With your permission, I could go after them," he suggested.

She only stared at him in disbelief. "No. We need to go to the police. Where would you even begin to look? You don't know for certain what's happened," she said.

Ernesto doubted the police would take any action. Marly was eighteen and couldn't be considered a missing person until a day or two had passed, but he could see her mother was distraught. Perhaps she even doubted Ernesto's ability to help, and had more faith in the police than in himself. He wanted to find Marlena more than ever. "Call the police if you want, but I'm going to look for her anyway. Thank you for allowing me to stay the night."

He rose from the table and left the house, feeling angry, hurt and frustrated in addition to worried sick; but Bianca had a point. Where would he even begin to look in a big city like Madrid? He didn't know his way around. He wasn't even sure he could afford the gas it would take to get there, and it would be hours away in any case. But he had to do something.

He went outside where the first rays of sunrise struggled to emerge from behind a cloudy horizon and got into his truck. He drove out of the Sanchez property, not knowing where to go and uncertain of his next step. As he reached to road that led to town, he could think of only one thing. He remembered the Pastor mentioning a young boy that had been helping Tristan. Perhaps he knew something. Clinging to that idea, he headed back toward town and the Gracia Immaculata, hoping Don Giorgio was an early riser.

*

The sky had completely clouded over by the time Ernesto followed the Pastor's directions and arrived at a small dwelling sandwiched between two similar adjoining ones on Calle Verdugo. The overcast conditions made the entire town seem gray and desolate, and a perpetual dry wind caused by the relentless drought whistled through the streets, stirring up dust and debris. His stomach felt as barren as the windswept townscape before him. He'd eaten nothing but that orange since yesterday, but couldn't worry about food right now. He knocked on the sagging wooden door of the house, and was met by a thin boy with dark hair and wide eyes. "Are you Ángel Ibanez?" he asked.

"Si. Do you wish to see my mother?"

"No. Pastor Giorgio sent me to talk to you. Have you seen Senor Tristan Flynn?" The boy looked him up and down, a hint of suspicion on his face. "My name is Ernesto, and I'm a friend of his," he added. The term of friend was a bit of a stretch, but he had to at least introduce himself and gain the boy's trust.

"Si. I saw him yesterday," the boy said. "He lives at the church."

"I know that, but he didn't return there yesterday, and Don Giorgio is very concerned. Do you know where he might have gone?" Ernesto saw a figure come into view behind the boy, and was shocked to see a frail blond woman appear from the shadows, seated in a wheelchair. She moved herself to the boy's side.

"May we help you, senor?" she asked in a quiet, pleasant voice.

"He's looking for El Milagro," Ángel said to her. "No-one has seen him since yesterday."

"Verdad? Is that true? I do hope he hasn't come to any harm. Such a nice man; and he's been so good to us."

"El…Milagro?" Ernesto asked doubtfully. "Why do you call him that?"

"Don't you? He fixed the well; he built this wheelchair," Ángel answered, patting the handlebars of the contraption. "He's saved El Guardián, too. He can make miracles."

Ernesto's blood began to simmer. Nearly everyone he'd spoken to thought of Tristan as some kind of folk hero. Why didn't they see the Welshman for what he really was? An opportunist and a cad. He decided to ignore the boy's last comment. "Well, he's missing. Do you know where he might have gone? Did he say anything to you when you last saw him?"

Ángel thought for a moment. "He said, see you tomorrow."

Ernesto's brow wrinkled. See you tomorrow? That implied Tristan had no intention of leaving. It didn't make sense; but then, what else would he say to a young boy who obviously idolized him? He'd hardly disclose his illicit plans to him.

Ernesto opened his mouth to speak, but closed it quickly as a sudden whirlwind of dust blew across the porch, smattering his face with grains of sand and dirt. "Come inside, por favor," the woman said. Ángel's small hands gripped Ernesto's arm and dragged him forward. He stumbled inside and closed the door behind him, the last gasps of the wind causing curtains to flutter and papers to scatter. He wiped the grit from his face with his sleeve.

"This weather," the woman sighed. "I've never seen such a dry, hot summer." Ernesto rubbed the last of the dust from his eyes and looked in her direction. She gave a warm smile as she backed her wheelchair into the center of the room. Ernesto saw an ancient stove and wooden washstand on one side of the room, and a curtained-off bed in the opposite corner. The single open room appeared to be all the space they had. "Welcome, I'm Carolina Ibanez. You've met my son, Ángel. What is your name?"

"Gracias, senora. I'm Ernesto Alvarez."

"Well, Senior Alvarez, it looks like you may be stuck here for awhile until that wind dies down. Will you have something to eat?"

Despite its meagre appearance, the small abode smelled wonderful; of cinnamon and ginger and newly-baked bread, and Ernest's stomach grumbled once more. He really was hungry, and had run out of ideas on where to find Marlena short of driving to Madrid. His shoulders slumped as he exhaled in resignation. "Si senora," he nodded. "I'd like that very much."

Chapter Twenty-One

"I wish we could stay here forever," Marlena sighed as she lay next to him, her head on his chest and their bodies tangled together in the tiny bed. Morning light beamed in through the porthole window, and the faint sounds of street traffic drifted to Tristan's ears as he wrapped his arms more tightly around her. The only thing he wanted forever was to have this girl in his arms, his heart and his life.

"Surely not here," he murmured into her hair.

He felt her warm body wiggle with laughter. "I meant here with you. Away from everything and everyone."

"Ah, so you're embarrassed to be seen with me, is that it?" he teased. Her hand caressed the taut muscles of his abs. Her touch aroused him instantly, and he felt ready for another round of lovemaking. If his cock had anything to say about it, they could very well be staying here forever.

"Not embarrassed," she said. "Just…"

"Just what?" he prompted, stroking her soft black tresses that were only slightly mussed from their wild, wonderful night. He smiled at the recollection, how she'd melted to his touch, writhed in ecstasy beneath him and cried out his name.

He'd taken the gift of her virginity she'd given freely. He would honor that, and her, for the rest of his life.

She turned her head to look into his face. "You know what will be waiting for us in Zaragoza. My mother, and Ernesto, and the whole villa. Waiting for an explanation; maybe even to punish me."

Her brown eyes, so lovely and full of wide-eyed innocence, gazed into his and seared his soul. Punish her? Did she mean physical punishment? No wonder she didn't want to go back; the idea seemed unthinkable but painfully underscored his position as an outsider. His cultural sensibilities did not apply here.

With a stab of guilt, he realized he was responsible for this, no matter how much she had agreed to their union; no matter that it was her decision to leave without telling anyone. She'd trusted him, and he'd made the situation worse. He'd protected her and saved her from an unimaginable circumstance, but had still failed her in his own way. He wouldn't be seen as her rescuer. He'd be seen as a villain, and she as a victim. "They will be worried, yes, but we've done nothing that you should be punished for." He traced the curve of her cheek with his finger. "We've chosen each other, and they'll have to accept that."

"I want to believe that," she whispered. "But where does that leave us? If we're scorned by my family, by society, we may never be happy here. You can go back to England, but I..."

"Shhh..." he put his finger across her lips. "I will never leave you, Marly. Trust in that. If I return to England, it will be with you by my side. I won't be apart from you, ever."

She kissed his fingers as they brushed across her lips. "How can you be so sure," she said. "You don't know this country; what can happen here. This is not England."

Tristan smiled. "No, it's not. But I assume the law here still allows two people of age to marry each other, does it not?"

Marlena's eyes went wide. "Marry?"

"Matrimonio…that is the word, si? You've heard of it?" he joked; but his intentions were no joke. He would marry this girl, in any country. Nothing would stop him, not family, not politics. "Then we could live in either country, any country; any one you'd like."

She blinked as though clearing her vision of a mirage. "Are you asking me to marry you?"

It wasn't the most romantic proposal, he realized, but he wanted nothing more in the world. "Marlena Sanchez, yes I am. I'd get down on one knee, but there seems to be this beautiful girl lying on top of me. The only girl I want. I hope she'll say yes."

Her brow wrinkled a little, and a smile teased the corners of her mouth. "That's not how it's done here," she said. "You would have to ask permission from my family, and I never said I want to be married. I wanted…"

He pulled her up to his level and kissed her, stopping the words he didn't want to hear from coming out. His lips crushed against hers, and his tongue pressed open the seam of her closed mouth, demanding entry. She surrendered to his sweet invasion, allowing him to explore her wet depths and responding with equal eagerness, her tongue dancing with his and her lips drawing every ounce of passion from his soul.

With difficulty, he broke their kiss, just enough to let her know he understood. "You want a career…as a model, I know. You can have that Marly, I promise you. I'll help you. I would never hold you back, but I will marry you." He dove back into their kiss as though to add an exclamation point. His cock reached full mast again, and with his arms around her, rolled them both over so that he was on top. His hardness pressed against her mound, and her legs parted, inviting him in. He groaned in helpless desire, settling his groin in the warm cradle between her thighs.

She raised her knees, accepting him fully, and his heart pounded as the tip of his cock plied her waiting entrance, reveling in its soft wetness before plunging home. He wanted her answer, wanted her unconditional acceptance of what he already knew in his heart and soul, that their joining was beyond marriage, beyond any permission or sanction, because they were fated to each other, irrevocably.

"Say it, Marly. Say you love me. Say you'll marry me." He felt the rapid rise and fall of her lungs beneath him as she panted in and out, as heated with desire as he. Her soft brown eyes had darkened into needful pools of dark chocolate.

"Only if you promise to make love to me like this every day," she gasped. "That it will always be like this between us."

"I promise," he whispered, cupping the underside of her breast and massaging it gently. His cock eased forward then retreated again, teasing the slick, hot tissues of her sex.

"Oooh," she groaned, writhing in anticipation. "Make love to me, now, please…"

"Is that a yes?"

"Yes!" she squealed, her fingernails digging into the meat of his shoulders like cat's claws and her hips bucking upward, begging for more of his throbbing cock. He didn't disappoint her, a smile on his face at her answer. He thrust deep inside her, again and again, just as he'd imagined all those months ago. The girl who haunted his dreams was real at last, was his at last; and would be his from this day forward. He needed no priest or judge to pronounce that.

*

A haze hung in the air and stretched across the midafternoon sky, the relentless sun paling behind it as Marlena and Tristan began the journey back to Zaragoza. They'd stayed far longer than intended, consummating their mutually pledged union a few more times before admitting it was time to leave. Tristan was as uncertain as she on what awaited them on their return home, but they'd made their choice and no power in Spain or anywhere on Earth would separate them nor defeat them.

They enjoyed some tapas in the cantina before officially checking out of the seedy but nostalgic establishment. Tristan saw no-one in the place that resembled the gypsy behemoth that had attacked Ariel on his fateful last visit here, and no-one appeared to recognize him; just another faceless gringo in the crowd. Joints like this rarely cared where or who the money came from as long as your drinks and lodging were paid for.

With full bellies and a carton of sodas for the road, they set off for home. The van's gears ground and the suspension squeaked as he backed onto the cobbled lane behind the cantina to turn around. The place looked even more neglected in daylight than it did at night. Of all the places he could have returned to, this shabby bar was not on his list; but now that he had happy memories of it to wipe out the unpleasant ones, it would always remain special.

He glanced over at Marlena seated on the passenger side, to find her gorgeous brown eyes already staring back at him. He'd never forget this day, or how beautiful she looked despite everything they'd been through. The day the rest of their lives would begin. "What?" he said, smiling at her deliberate gaze.

"Tell me about Aunt Juliana," she said. "About what happened here. About your friend."

Tristan shifted the van into drive and the vehicle jolted forward. Of unpleasant memories, El Mirador certainly topped the list and wouldn't make for very pleasant conversation. The images he still held in his mind were horrific at best. He wasn't sure if she was ready to hear the whole truth, but it was a fair drive to Zaragoza, and she did ask the question.

As he navigated to the main highway leading out of the city, he thought about how to begin, how he could put aside the image of Juliana's now-scarred body and tell of the beguiling, spirited girl that had set such unthinkable events in motion. "I remember her red hair. You couldn't help but notice her with that flaming red hair," he said, a smile forming as he pictured her at her most beautiful.

Marlena smiled and nodded. "Yes. Everyone noticed that about her."

"I was hitchhiking, and my friend picked me up on the highway just outside Segovia. I'd been looking at ancient architecture there. He drove a fancy car, and I could tell he had money. He was flashy; a big talker. He wasn't afraid to tell me about himself and his business."

"What was his business?"

"Tourism, I guess you'd say. He owned a few properties on the north coast, and was on his way to the Costa Del Sol where he'd just bought another venture. I think you know the name."

Marlena nodded. "El Mirador. Mirador means a place you can see out from. A viewpoint."

"Yes, it was all of that. A beautiful view of the sea. But it was a long drive, so we ended up stopping at the cantina. We had a lot to drink, and suddenly there she was, her red hair flashing as she danced a flamenco. Ariel couldn't take his eyes off her."

"His name was Ariel?" Marlena asked, her eyes widening.

Tristan nodded. "Ariel Torres."

"My tía wouldn't say his name; only that he was handsome, and he tried to grab her."

"I think he attracted people more with his personality than

his looks. It was magnetic, and impossible to ignore. You could fill a room with his charisma."

"What did he look like?"

"Black hair, well-groomed, a moustache and tanned skin. About six feet tall, and dark eyes that held you hypnotized in their gaze."

"It sounds like women would find him irresistible. No wonder my tía fell for him."

Tristan chewed his lip for a moment. There was an attraction, certainly, but in the end, a fatal one. He wasn't entirely sure how deep Juliana's feelings went, considering how cruelly she'd jilted Ariel in the end. "But he got very drunk and put his hands where they didn't belong. She left the dance floor, but Ariel followed her out back. I told him to stay put, but he wouldn't listen. I went out the front entrance and circled around into the alley. That's where I saw this hulking big gypsy rag-dolling him around, about to pound the life out of him."

"You mean a Romani. They don't like to be called gypsies. What did you do?"

"I wasn't any match for the…a Romani his size. I hadn't any weapons, but my backpack had a steel frame and was full of all my gear, so I slid it off my back and swung it at him from behind. It caught him in the head and he staggered sideways before falling to the ground. He'd let Ariel go, so I grabbed him and we legged it."

"When did you see Juliana again?"

"Not for a few months. We drove through the night to El Mirador. I thought we'd part ways at that point, but he offered me a job, more or less. We got on well, and he was grateful for what I'd done. He wanted to train me in the resort business, and open up a casino inside the hotel. He even talked of becoming partners but…" he let out a bitter chuckle. "It wasn't in the cards, so to speak." He looked over at Marlena, who had turned her head to gaze out the passenger window. "Things went really well for awhile," he went on. "I helped with repairs and such, and business was good. A lot of jet-set money flowed through there, celebrities and rich tourists. Then one day, this redheaded girl showed up, begging for work. Ariel recognized her right away, despite how thin and pale she'd become, like the fire had gone out of her."

"She was ill? Was she injured?" Marlena asked in alarm.

"No. I just think she was starving. Ariel took pity on her and gave her a job as a dancer in the hotel nightclub. It wasn't long before they were lovers."

He glanced at Marlena for a reaction. She nibbled nervously on one of her fingernails. "Did he ever plan to marry her?" she asked.

"I don't know, but he was certainly besotted with her. He hired her to dance, but became more and more jealous whenever she performed in front of a crowd. She didn't like that, and…"

"Is he Jorge's father?" Marlena interruped, her full attention turned to him. "This man?"

Tristan tightened his grip on the wheel. Now that he'd actually seen the baby, he had no doubts that was true; but Ariel would have had no such assurances. "In my opinion, yes. Jorge looks very much like him."

"Then what happened? Why did he not protect her from harm, if she was carrying his child? What kind of monster was he?"

He didn't blame her for the anger he heard in her voice. Juliana had suffered terrible injuries, but her family didn't have all the facts. "I mean no disrespect to your Aunt, but she had other lovers. No-one could be certain who the father was. Ariel, he couldn't see past his jealousy or his feelings of betrayal. The night it happened, he caught her in bed with another man. Their bed. In their room. He went crazy with rage."

Marlena swallowed hard. "Go on."

"He couldn't control his anger. I followed him into the basement, where there were a lot of gas fumes, and…he had a blowtorch in his hand. I tried to reason with him, I begged him not to…" Tristan broke off, his words seeming to die in his throat, choking him into silence.

Marlena reached out and gripped his arm. "Are you saying…he set the fire himself? Deliberately?"

Tristan nodded. "When I knew I couldn't stop him, I ran. I had to save her, save her baby…" Recalling the awful ordeal again in such detail left him sweating and anxious. He rolled down the window for some fresh air, but a ferocious blast of wind made him recoil inside the cab. Dark clouds had gathered overhead, roiling and churning like slow boiling water and blocking out the sun, the daylight taking on a strange, greenish hue. Marlena's face looked paper-white against the gloom, and he couldn't blame her for paling at the story he'd just told. He took a deep breath as he closed the window. "His uncontrollable passion destroyed everything, including himself."

"Incendio," Marlena murmured.

"What?"

"Incendio. It means fire. That's what my Tía Juliana said, Incendio; and that I'd end up like her, consumed by flame, because I told her I would brave anything, even fire, to become a famous model." Her voice wavered as she spoke, then put a hand to her forehead.

"It's just words, Marly; nothing like that will ever happen to you. I'll be with you, keeping you safe." She nodded and wiped at her face before looking up at him. His heart clenched at the sadness and fear in her deep brown eyes that glistened with tears, and he knew he'd give his life, his immortal soul to protect this girl; his girl, his future wife. The van swerved slightly, buffeted by the wind. Tristan gripped the wheel and steered them back on course. The weather seemed to be worsening as they drove north. "Let's get home," he said. "There's a storm coming."

Chapter Twenty-Two

"I really must be going. Thank you for your hospitality," Ernesto said, rising from his place at the Ibanez' small wooden dinner table. The meal had been satisfying, as had the company; but nothing would be solved by his staying any longer.

"De nada, you will always be welcome here, Senor Alvarez," Carolina said. "I hope you find your friend Senor Flynn; it would be terrible if something has happened to him. Ángel has grown very fond of him."

Ángel beamed a smile across the table. "He teaches me things, and cares about me. That's what a father does," he said proudly. "I wish he'd come back."

Ernesto raised his eyebrows at the boy's comment. "I'm sure your own father cares about you, Ángel," he said.

The boy dropped his gaze. "Ángel's father passed away when he was very young," Carolina explained, rubbing Ángel's shoulder gently. "We are grateful for Senor Flynn's help."

"Then, I'll have to look extra hard to find him," Ernesto said, forcing a smile. There seemed no use in fighting it. Flynn had bored his way into the very heart of their town like some parasitic worm. He imagined squashing that worm under his boot when he finally did find him.

"Ángel, see Senor Alvarez out, por favor," Carolina said, gathering the dishes into a stack as she remained seated in her chair. He gazed at the wheeled contraption, noting its construction. He could have easily built something like it himself if anyone had asked; but they had not asked. Once Flynn was gone—and Ernesto was certain he would be gone as suddenly as he'd arrived, leaving everything and everyone he'd touched high and dry—he could take his place. He could play El Milagro as well as any man, maybe better, because he belonged here.

"It was nice to meet you, Senor," Ángel said, hopping to his feet. "Come again, any time."

"Gracias," Ernesto said, and turned to follow Ángel. As they reached the door, an ear-shattering crack of thunder rocked the house, rattling the dishes and silverware on the table. The boy dropped to the floor in fright, covering his ears.

"Ángel," his mother called, wheeling her chair toward him.

Ernesto crossed to the nearby window and looked out. A darkened sky threatened overhead, and rapid bursts of lightning flashed from behind the thick clouds. His pulse quickened as he thought of Marlena caught in the oncoming storm somewhere. Was she safe? Was she frightened? He wanted nothing more than to protect her, but was helpless to do so under the circumstances. He felt angry at his own inabilities, his lack of bravado and ambition; all the things that Marly seemed so to admire and did not find in him.

Another resounding crack of thunder shook the floorboards beneath his feet. He shifted his balance just in time to avoid being speared by shards of glass as the window suddenly shattered. He heard Carolina scream, and turned to the sound. She held Ángel's head in her lap as he kneeled next to her chair, her eyes wide with fear. "Can you help us, senor," she said. "Take us somewhere safe?"

"It's just a storm, it will pass," he replied, unsure where he could take them. Surely it was better to remain indoors rather than venture outside, especially with Carolina's mobility issues. He gazed in shock at the broken window. "I'll clean up this glass," he offered, spying a straw broom in a corner of the kitchen. As he moved toward it, a nasty gust of wind blew through the opening, forcing more glass out of the frame and a plume of dust into the room. The thin curtains flapped wildly. He turned to the frightened boy and his mother. The humble dwelling had not even a partition behind which they could shelter. "Is there something we can use to board up that window?"

Carolina shook her head. "What you see is all we have."

"Any tools? A hammer?" he asked.

"No, nada."

Ernesto sighed and looked around, his eyes falling on the solid wooden table. He lifted the stacked dishes and placed them on the floor, then upended the table and dragged it to the window, bracing its broad flat top against the opening. "I'm sorry, but this will have to do for now." It didn't cover the window entirely but was enough to keep out the wind. He picked up the broom and began sweeping the glass into a pile.

"It's all right, thank you, senor," Carolina said.

Ángel had risen to stand next to her. "It will get cold in here," he said anxiously. "And what if it rains? Cold and wet is not good for my mother."

Ernesto looked at him and pushed up his eyeglasses in frustration. "If your roof is solid, it should keep out the rain. Turn on your stove and open the oven for heat," he suggested. "I don't know what else you can do."

"Take us to the church," Ángel pleaded. "There is plenty of room, it's warm and it's made of stone. We'll be safe there."

"Ángel," Carolina said, taking her son's hands in hers. "We can't ask that of Senor Alvarez. I'm sure he wants to get home to his own family."

Ernesto thought of his family, his farmhouse with warm, comfortable rooms and plenty of food, in contrast to the mother and son in front of him who had little except each other. He hadn't thought to tell anyone where he was going since he'd left home yesterday. His kin would be just as worried about him as he was worried about Marlena, and a stab of guilt sliced through him for not considering them. In fact, he hadn't considered anything except his own rampant emotions for days. The Gracia Immaculata would be right on his way home, and there was nothing to be served by staying in town. He'd exhausted his options to find Marly. He couldn't help her, but he could help these two people. "It's a good idea. I can take you to the church," he said. "Ángel, help your mother to the door while I bring my truck."

Ángel nodded as Ernesto turned to leave. The front door groaned with the pressure of the wind against it as he opened and hastily slid through it. The wind's force took him by surprise and nearly knocked him off balance as he stepped out. It whistled through the thick curls of his hair, lodging sand and dust against his scalp. He saw food wrappers and other garbage fly past him down the street as he staggered around the corner to where he'd parked. It seemed like Mother Nature was having a temper tantrum and taking it out on the world around him. He heaved himself into the truck's cab to escape her wrath.

The engine came to life without difficulty and as he drove around the corner, Ángel was already watching for him through a crack in the door. He came to a stop in front of the house and jumped out to open the passenger side of the truck. Ángel held his mother's arm as she attempted to step out onto the street. Ernesto ran to her other side. "Por favor, we must hurry," he said, lifting Carolina into his arms and depositing her into the cab.

"She needs this," Ángel shouted over the howling wind, trying to yank the wheelchair over the threshold.

"I've got it," Ernesto growled, returning to grab the metal contraption with both hands and practically hurling it into the truck bed, irrationally annoyed that he had to rescue his rival's little invention along with the boy and his mother. Ángel scampered inside the cab next to Carolina and pulled the door shut. Shielding his face with one arm, Ernesto moved to the driver's side and got in. "Is everyone all right?" he asked.

"Yes, we are fine," Carolina said, but her pale face and worried expression seemed to say otherwise. "We are sorry to be such trouble."

Ernesto shook his head, inadvertently sending dust flying as it shook loose from his hair. "It's no trouble, senora. You'll be safer at the church, and perhaps Pastor Giorgio will have some news." He pulled away from the curb and started back though town the way he had come. They saw few people about, and those they did see were hurrying for shelter, bracing themselves against the unruly winds. The clouds had turned an ominous blue-black, giving the tortured streets a ghoulish, surreal cast that turned day into night.

A jagged finger of lightning stabbed through the sky, and a ripping crack of thunder followed, audible even inside the truck, the reverberation enough to jostle the vehicle itself. Carolina ducked her head as Ángel clung to her. "Why is there no rain?" the boy asked suddenly.

Ernesto's lips tightened as he considered the question. He'd never seen a storm quite like this one. Heavy cloud cover, with lightning and thunder almost always brought a torrential, even if brief, downpour. Everything about this storm was unusual, even with the extended drought that had gripped the Zaragozan plains of late. As they reached the town square, El

Guardián's stark white trunk and barren branches stood out against the dark backdrop of sky, as jagged and forbidding as the bolts of lightning that flashed all around it.

He stepped on the brake to make the turn for the church, when one of the streaks of lightning seemed to lash out like a giant sword and slice the tree's helpless, brittle arms. Sparks flew as a felled limb snapped and crashed to the ground. The three looked on in horror as smoke and a flicker of flame rose from the charred stump left behind.

"Don't stop," Ángel cried.

Ernesto had no intention of stopping and hit the accelerator hard, his tires spinning as the vehicle careened through the turn and Carolina's chair slammed hard into the wall of the truck box. If there were no rain soon, the relentless wind might carry those sparks aloft, and he didn't want to picture where they might land. Everything around the tree, including shops and homes and fences, would be ready, ripe targets for a hungry fire.

Soon, the silhouette of the Gracia Immaculata came into view and he pulled the truck to a stop in front of its main doors. "Ángel, go open the doors and I'll bring your mother in," Ernesto said.

"There's a back door," Ángel said, pointing around to the side of the building. "It will be easier, and I'm sure the Pastor will let us in."

Ernesto hadn't ever been through the back door, and kicked himself mentally for not remembering there was one. Although he was certain he could do it, carrying Senora Ibanez up those stone steps, as light and petite as she was, would be difficult as well as unsafe. He steered the truck around the side Ángel indicated.

At the back of the church was a small gated yard that connected to the cemetery. As Ernesto pulled up, Ángel leapt from the truck, pushed open the unlocked gate and hurried up the path to knock on the wooden door at the rear of the building. They were sheltered somewhat from the wind back here, but the menacing clouds still roiled overhead.

In a moment, Don Giorgio appeared. "Why Ángel, what brings you here young man?"

"There's a storm coming," Ángel replied, his young voice breathless and full of urgency. "It blew the window in at our house, we needed to come someplace safe. Can we stay here?"

Don Giorgio placed a calming hand on the boy's head, then looked past him toward the truck, his weathered face lined with concern as he noted the occupants. He nodded at Ernesto. "Of course. You are all welcome here; please come in."

Ángel scurried back to the truck to help Carolina climb out. Ernesto unloaded the wheelchair and placed it near her. The Pastor ventured down the path toward them, glancing upward to the darkened sky. "This is most alarming. I've never seen anything like this weather," he said. "Is everyone alright?"

"We're fine," Ernesto said, holding the chair steady as Carolina settled into it with Ángel's help. He frowned and glanced up to meet Don Giorgio's eye. "But Marlena is still out there somewhere."

The Pastor shook his head and turned to Ángel. "Go on, take your mother inside. I must speak with Senor Alvarez."

Carolina reached out to touch Pastor Giorgio's arm. "Gracias, Padre."

Don Giorgio gave a warm smile in reply as Ángel began to wheel her inside. Then he spoke quietly to Ernesto. "I have no news of either Senorita Sanchez nor Tristan. Did Ángel know anything?"

Ernesto shook his head miserably. "No. He hasn't seen him since yesterday."

The Pastor sighed. "I presume you are still harboring your original suspicions, then?"

"I can't help how I feel, Padre."

"Well now," Don Giorgio chuckled. "Can't blame you for that. We wouldn't be human without our feelings, would we? Unfortunately, there's nothing we can do but wait. You've done what you could, son. Come inside and rest. Have something to drink. Pray if you want to."

"I can't stay, Padre, but we may need your prayers. Something far worse may be happening, and I have to go see. Help if I can."

"What are you talking about?"

"On our way here, we saw lightning strike El Guardián and catch flame. "I'm afraid the town may be on fire."

Chapter Twenty-Three

Flashes of lightning illuminated the forbidding black clouds like bombs bursting inside them. Broken tree branches lay strewn across the road, ripped free by the fierce winds that seemed to blow from all directions at once. Twigs and other debris struck the windshield as they drove forward. Tristan held the van on course, his knuckles showing white as he gripped the wheel hard.

The city of Zaragoza loomed up ahead, its skyline obscured by a sickly gray haze. Marlena kept her eyes on the strange tableau before them, and gasped as streaks of lightning lashed out from the clouds and skittered across the horizon in a wild, jagged pattern.

"Holy shit," Tristan muttered, bracing himself for the expected report of thunder. Marlena covered her ears in the same anticipation. None came. "This is so weird," he said after a moment. "Lightning but no thunder; clouds but no rain. And the wind is warm, not cool. It's like no storm I've ever seen."

The inside of the cab had grown chokingly hot, the windows having been rolled up for almost the entire trip. Sweat clung to Marlena's neck and rolled in between her breasts; her dress felt stuck to her skin and her legs bonded to the cracked vinyl of the seat. By the time they reached her villa she'd look as bedraggled as a stray cat, and give her family all the more cause to suspect the worst. "How much longer until we get there," she asked, wiping her brow with the back of her hand.

"Maybe a half-hour," he said. "To the city limits. We'll have to cross town to reach your villa or else go around somehow."

"Whichever is the fastest," she said, wondering if the storm had already hit the outskirts of town and wreaked havoc on the farm. Suddenly she was more worried about her family than herself; and felt guilty that she'd not been there to help. Perhaps she'd never get away from this place, never be free of family responsibilities to live the life she truly wanted. But Tristan had changed all that irrevocably. She had to move forward, not back. By her own actions, the new course of her destiny had been set, even if it wasn't quite the way she'd imagined it.

Mile after anxious mile passed, until they were near enough to the city to realize the murky haze than hung over it was not cloud, but smoke. Its acrid smell permeated the inside of the van, sneaking through any and every available crack or vent hole. Marlena put a hand over her mouth. "Incendio," she said. Her mind raced, bits of her conversation with Juliana coming back to her in flashes, as menacing as the lightning now ripping the sky, the runaway train of her thoughts arriving at a single destination. "I've brought this…I'm the cause of this," she moaned.

"What?" Tristan said, his eyes breaking from the road ahead and flicking over to her. "What are you talking about?"

"I told you what my tía said. I would end up like her. Consumed by flame. Because I asked for it, dared it to try and stop me from reaching my dream. And I've brought it down on all of us, on everyone!"

"That's crazy," Tristan said. "We don't even know it's a real fire, it could be just someone burning brush, or…"

"It's not!" Marlena cut him off. "You don't know my tía. She sees things, knows things. We have to get to the villa, now! Please!"

"Okay, calm down," Tristan replied. "We'll cut around the city on side roads, there might be traffic or blocked streets if we try to go through."

"Just hurry," she cried, leaning forward and gripping the dash.

Tristan turned onto a dirt road that veered to the east, only slowing enough to make the turn before accelerating even faster than they had been traveling on the highway. The vehicle's rusted springs protested as the two of them were jostled wildly about by the rough, unpaved surface beneath their wheels. "Hang on," he said unnecessarily. "I'm sure everything and everyone at your villa is fine," he added. "And it's ridiculous to blame yourself. Fires don't start spontaneously by divine wrath, or whatever you may think is at work here."

Marlena turned on him. "Haven't you read the Bible?"

Tristan blew out a breath. "Yes, okay, I get your point. But its not very likely that the hand of God reached down and struck a match, now is it?"

Marlena bit her lip and decided to say no more on the subject. They could discuss religious beliefs another time, and his flippant remark made her wonder if that would be something to come between them in future. She'd bucked against tradition, but it didn't mean she would abandon her beliefs entirely. The van hit a deep pothole and tossed her upward to bump her head on the ceiling of the cab. "Ow!" she cried, and grasped about for another handhold as she came down again.

"I did say hang on," Tristan said as he gained control of the wheel again. "Are you okay?"

"Fine," she grumbled, rubbing one hand on her head. "I don't care if you think my beliefs are silly. I just know I'm part of these events, just as you think you know I'm not."

"I'm not questioning your beliefs. And I do know your tía, by the way. What do you mean about her 'knowing things'? Are you saying she's some kind of clairvoyant?"

"Everyone in the family says it. She has visions, premonitions."

Tristan stayed silent for a moment. "She didn't seem to have a premonition about El Mirador," he finally said. "She'd have gotten out on her own if she knew something bad was about to happen."

"Maybe she did know," Marlena said, thinking back on other conversations with Juliana. Was it possible her aunt had felt she deserved to die by fire? And made no attempt to save herself? It felt too horrible a thought to contemplate; and if fire had come to their villa, would Juliana feel as though the flames had returned to collect their due after she escaped the first time?

"What?" Tristan asked.

"It's in the past now," Marlena said, then raised a finger to the window. "Look, the smoke is getting thicker."

Tristan nodded. "And it's not coming from out in the country. Seems more like...oh, bloody hell!" he exclaimed as they neared an intersection with another unpaved road that pointed north toward town. He slammed on the brakes to make the turn, the force of it throwing Marlena against the passenger door. "It's coming from the town square!"

Marlena righted herself and brushed away a stray lock of hair from her face. The square. The markets, the shops, the church! All of these stood within blocks of it. The months of drought had made everything ready tinder, and this surreal lightning storm provided just the match to ignite it. It would only be a matter of time before it spread to her home, if it hadn't already.

"I'll take you home," he said. "Then I have to see what's going on, Don Giorgio might be in trouble."

Marlena felt panic rising, but not because of the danger that might lie ahead. She needed to get home, yes; but if Tristan were to just drop her off, it would be like a repeat of the day he brought Aunt Juliana home, only worse. Tongues would wag even more viciously, and he wouldn't be there to defend her honor, explain what happened and his intentions. He'd look like a villainous cad who would be reviled and never accepted or trusted again. That might be worse than not showing up at all. "Then I'll go with you," she said.

Tristan looked her way again. "I thought you wanted to get home. And you should. We don't know what we'll find in town."

Marlena gazed back at him, hearing his words, but not listening. She took in his roughened appearance, his days-old clothes, his piercing blue eyes and wild blond hair; his lean, slightly dirty hands on the steering wheel. Wondrous hands, full of strength yet capable of exquisite tenderness. He would always protect her, and thought he was doing so by taking her where she'd be safe. But by staying with him now, she could protect him, too. From suspicion and rebuke, from rejection by her family. She could protect their future. "I know. But we will face my family together, not apart. And whatever we find in town, we'll face that together too."

A tired smile lit his handsome face. "We will," he said, nodding, then turned his attention back to the rutted track ahead of them. The few scattered farm sheds and outbuildings they passed alongside the road indicated they were nearing town. The smoky haze continued to descend, reducing visibility and obscuring their path forward. A railway track bordered the town, and after they'd crossed, followed a back road that skirted past the square and led them in the direction of the Gracia Immaculata, its stony silhouette barely visible until they were almost upon it.

Tristan pulled around to the back of the building and got out. Marlena didn't wait for him to come to her aid, and jumped out of the passenger side. The air, thick and sharp with smoke, stung the back of her throat as she breathed in. She covered her nose and mouth and hurried through the gate to the church doors, with Tristan right behind her.

He pushed the door open and ushered her inside, quickly closing it behind them. The darkened rectory lay empty except for a few plates and cups on the long table. From the sanctuary she heard voices, one at least she was certain of. Don Giorgio's. Tristan's hand slipped into hers and pulled her toward the sound and the church's inner sanctum.

Don Giorgio stood on the dais leading a prayer. Several people seated on the pews nearest the front bowed their heads and repeated after him, as well as a woman sitting in what looked like a wheelchair directly in front of the dais. Together, she and Tristan moved forward down the center aisle. The Pastor signed and concluded his prayer as they drew near. Reflexively, Marlena dropped Tristan's hand and repeated the sign. He glanced at her and then up at Don Giorgio.

"Tristan," the Pastor said, a relieved smile crossing his face. "Thank goodness you've returned…and Senorita Sanchez as well. It is very good to see you both."

All heads turned to them, and among them Marlena saw the faces of her mother and aunt in the front pew, with Jorge cradled in Juliana's arms. She rushed forward to embrace them all. "Mama, Tía!" she exclaimed, throwing her arms around them. "I'm so sorry. Are you both alright?"

Juliana cast a knowing eye over her, and then over Tristan. She gave Marlena a small nod, but kept silent, turning her attention to the gurgling infant in her arms. Bianca, her face pale and eyes reddened from crying and likely irritated by the smoke, reached out to stroke Marlena's cheek. "Cariña, thank God you're safe." Her expression held no anger, only relief and gratitude.

"I'm fine. Tristan was with me," she said. "He helped me get home." Bianca's gaze drifted over Tristan, then back to her daughter.

"So, it's true you were together," she said. "Ernesto insisted that you were."

"I'm sorry, Mama, for lying to you, and not telling you where I went. But I started off alone; I hadn't planned on being with anyone. Tristan only happened by and offered to help. Ernesto couldn't have known anything about it."

"Ernesto cares for you, he always has, you know," Bianca said. You worried him as much as us. He went looking for you everywhere. You should apologize to him as well."

"Where is he," Marlena asked, glancing around at all the people gathered in the church. Ernesto was definitely not among them.

"He went back to the square, to see what was happening and try to help. He said that lightning struck El Guardián and it caught fire. He saw it."

Marlena put a hand to her mouth. Her nightmare had come true, and she was the cause of it. The drought-ravaged town would go up like a torch, and the fire could spread to the open grasslands if not caught in time. "What are you both doing here? Is the villa safe?"

"Yes, it's fine. José and the boys dug trenches just in case, and will use water from the livestock troughs if we need to. We came here to pray for your return," she said.

A heartbreaking sob echoed in the high-ceilinged sanctuary and all eyes turned toward the sound. The blond woman in the wheelchair held her face in her hands, her shoulders trembling, with Tristan crouched by her side.

"Poor thing," Bianca said. "As though life hasn't been cruel enough to her already."

"Who is she," Marlena whispered, watching Tristan as he spoke softly to the woman and put a hand on her shaking shoulders. Then he stood and walked toward Marlena, his face laden with concern. He took her hand in his as he stepped close, then turned to acknowledge the other women.

"Senora Sanchez," he said to Bianca with a nod, and another to Juliana. "I'm sorry I can't stay and talk. I want you both to know that your daughter did nothing wrong, and is a strong, courageous girl. I'm grateful to have brought her home safely. Please take care of one another until I return. We can answer all your questions then."

"Where are you going," Marlena asked in alarm. This wasn't the plan; they'd promised to face everything together from now on.

"I'm going back into town," he said, squeezing her hand gently. "I have to find someone. He could be in danger."

"Ernesto's gone there," she said.

"I know; that's why I have to go. Ángel ran off after him, and hasn't come back."

"Ángel?"

"That woman's son," he said, gesturing to the woman in the wheelchair. "He's only ten years old, and he's all she has."

Marlena looked over at the blond woman, obviously distraught over her son. "How will you find him? Do you even know what he looks like?"

Tristan exhaled deeply, then nodded. "He's one of the first people I met here. He asked me to build that wheelchair for his mother," he explained. "She can't lose him, and neither can I. He's my friend."

To Marlena's surprise, he leaned in and kissed her full

on the lips, right there in church for all to see, including her mother. Oh, there'd be hell to pay later; but what did appearances matter now? He was going to save a little boy, and Ernesto, maybe the whole town, and why not? He'd saved her already. That's what heroes did.

Chapter Twenty-Four

Tristan drove the van as near to the town square as he dared before pulling over and continuing on foot into the chaos of the main street. The sun had long set by this time, but the smoke and dust hanging in the air blocked any view of the moon or stars overhead. He took the shovel that was still in the van along; if necessary, he could use it to dig a firebreak or smother runaway sparks with dirt, or worst-case pry someone or something free from under a collapsed structure.

He made his way into the square, and saw for himself what Ángel's mother said was true. Flames billowed up from the naked branches of El Guardián, searing them into a spindly spiderweb of glowing, red hot twigs. Rivers of fire flowed out along the tree's gnarled roots and snaked across the cobbled pavement in multiple directions, fueled by the fierce wind setting flame to dried leaves and litter. Shops on every side of the square had already caught fire, flames licking at their cloth awnings and searing their doors and windows black. Where was the bloody fire department, he wondered?

He coughed, and shielding his nose and mouth, strode forward. A moment later, he was relieved to see some flashing lights through the thick veil of smoke. Thank Christ, at least some kind of aid had arrived. He made his way toward the lights, and found a small crew of men moving around an emergency vehicle, pulling hoses and connecting to a nearby hydrant. "Hey," he called out to them. "Can you use some help?'

A man who appeared to be in charge turned to him, the angled features of his moustached face illuminated in the glow of flames. "Senor, stay back please. You can help us best by keeping yourself and others away from danger."

"I understand," Tristan said. "but you need able bodies. I'm volunteering."

Unwilling to spend time arguing with him, the man strapped his hat tighter to his head and gestured to the adjacent street leading out from the square. "Clear those buildings," he said, make sure no-one is trapped inside. The wind is carrying the smoke that way."

Tristan nodded and hurried in the direction he'd pointed. He looked back over his shoulder at the blazing firebrand that was El Guardián. His efforts to try and save the historic icon had been in vain. With bitterness, he realized he should have let them cut it down; perhaps this whole event could have been avoided. He'd wanted to build something beautiful in this land, and here he was doing nothing but destroying it.

He pushed aside these thoughts, and forged ahead down the street the fireman had indicated. He soon understood why. This street was lined with homes and apartments. Through the smoky haze he glimpsed a sign that read Calle Verdugo. As he shouldered his heavy shovel and trudged forward, he was suddenly almost knocked to the ground by something or someone barreling into him from the side. He stumbled under the impact and lost his grip on the shovel.

"You!" The man shouted. "What are you doing here? What have you done with Marly? If you've laid a hand on her I swear to God..."

Tristan recognized the voice immediately, despite the rasping hoarseness caused by smoke inhalation. Ernesto. "She's at the church," Tristan shouted back before Ernesto could finish his threat. "She's with her mother, and Don Giorgio, and others. She's safe."

"What did you do to her? Where did you take her?" Ernesto carried on as if he hadn't heard a word, pouncing on him as he tried to regain his footing and knocking him fully to the ground.

"Stop," Tristan yelled, rolling to one side to get up, but Ernesto landed on him with his full weight and pinned him down. The breath was squeezed from his lungs, and he gasped like a suffocating fish, with nothing but smoke-laden air to inhale.

"I'll kill you if you hurt her in any way," Ernesto snarled. "Or maybe I'll kill you just to be rid of you." Tristan gagged for air while struggling to throw his assailant off. Ernesto's slight build wasn't heavy, but with his lungs starving for oxygen, Tristan couldn't budge him. He'd underestimated the depth of the man's resentment for him.

He groped for the handle of the shovel he'd dropped. He didn't want to injure the man, but had to do something to bring him to his senses. Ernesto lunged for his outstretched arm and tried to restrain it, but Tristan's fingers had already closed around the smooth wooden handle. He dragged the instrument toward him and swung it upward. The bottom side of the blade caught Ernesto in the shoulder. He grunted and was knocked sideways. Tristan rolled loose from under him and got to his feet, staying in a low crouch and holding the shovel crosswise in front of him.

Ernesto staggered to his feet, seeming dizzy from the blow but not seriously injured. His glasses were nearly off and hanging from only one ear. He straightened them as he rose to his full height, his chest heaving as he too, gasped for breath.

"Are you crazy," Tristan shouted. "If you really want to kill me, you'll have to do it later, assuming we don't both die by fire first, you idiot."

"Where did you take her," Ernesto asked again between coughs as he advanced on Tristan again.

"Nowhere she wasn't already going," Tristan answered, bracing himself to take Ernesto's weight as he lunged clumsily toward him. Tristan drew the shovel handle up to chest height and forced Ernesto back with a quick outward thrust of his arms. Ernesto swayed on his feet but kept his distance, too short of breath to continue. "She's not your concern anymore, amigo."

"What do you mean?" Ernesto spat.

"She's made her choice. If you care for her, you'll respect that. Now listen to me; Ángel is missing. Have you seen him?"

Ernesto stood back, a stunned look on his face and his shoulders sagging like a man too beaten down to resist any further. He took a few wheezing breaths. "He's at the church, too. I took him there myself. You were probably too busy ogling my girl to notice," he sneered, still stubbornly combative despite the situation.

Tristan shook his head. Arguing with the man was pointless, and a waste of precious time. "Ángel isn't at the church," he shouted over him. "His mother told me he ran out after you. Now, have you seen him, or haven't you?"

Ernesto seemed to regain his wits. He pushed his glasses up the bridge of his nose, their lenses coated with ash and dust. "No, I haven't seen him," he replied. "I've been at the well, with others, to try and bring water from there, but it looks like you fucked that up too. There's barely anything coming out."

The mention of the well triggered Tristan's mechanical brain. He recalled the painstaking work he'd done to restore the well's flow and then diverting some of it underground to almost this very spot. It had only been a trickle at the start, but perhaps it had gained pressure since then, and would explain why the flow at the well itself had lessened. Buckets would likely not fill fast enough for the carriers to do much good, if hauling it by hand was what they had in mind. If he could release the water pressure in the underground pipe, it might be enough to at least keep the ground moist and slow down the fire's spread; but the idea would have to wait. "I have to find him. The fire officials asked me to evacuate the homes on this street," he said, pointing with the blade of the shovel.

Ernesto looked in that direction, his mouth forming a grim line. "Ángel's house is on that street."

"Bringing water from the well by hand will take too long. I have a better idea. Help me clear the street and look for Ángel. Then I'll show you."

Ernesto ran a hand through his curly hair, shaking loose a cloud of dust, then wiped his brow with his sleeve. "I'll take the side with Ángel's home. You take the other," he said.

They separated, and Tristan quickly checked all the houses on his side. Most were empty, but the few residents who remained heeded his order and left. He doubled back to meet up with Ernesto, unable to see more than a few feet ahead. His eyes, nose and throat felt as thought they too, were on fire. They couldn't breathe this air much longer. "Ernesto!" he called, his voice stifled by the smoky, acrid air. He kept his feet moving and called Ernesto's name again.

"Here!" he finally heard in response.

Following the sound, Tristan came to a small abode with its window smashed and its door wide open. He stood on the small porch and peered in. "Ángel! Ernesto!" he called. Footsteps crashed toward him, and Ernesto appeared out of the dimness.

"He's not here," he said, pushing past him to get out onto the street.

"Where would he go? Any ideas?"

"How should I know? You're his damn fairy godfather," Ernesto said. "I only met the kid today."

Tristan bit back a retort. He hadn't done anything intentional to make Ángel look up to him, but certainly got the impression that Ernesto now felt he had to compete for the boy's affection as well as Marly's. He began to understand the man's frustration. How would he feel if the situation were reversed? Bloody pissed off, he imagined, but now wasn't the time to be adversarial. "We'll keep looking," he said. "But we have to move on. If we don't get that fire under control, everyone is in danger, not just Ángel. I have a plan, and I need your help. Let's get back to the square."

Ernesto didn't look at him, but nodded in agreement. "What's your plan," he asked gruffly as they began to jog side by side back to the heart of the disaster.

"There's another way we can use the well water," Tristan said. "A few days ago, I set up a pipeline leading from the well to El Guardián. It's underground about a foot, but we should be able to dig it up. The flow wasn't much at the time, but passing through a small-bore pipe would have built up the pressure by now. Let's hope it's enough."

An unholy glow filtered through the veil of smoke as it hung over the square. The two hurried their steps, short-cutting their way through narrow alleys to reach the open area surrounding El Guardián. As he watched the flames curling up its trunk in a fiery spiral and billowing outward along its thick lower branches, Tristan realized that the place where the pipe ended was much closer to the tree than he thought.

The fire crew's efforts seemed to be focused on the buildings that surrounded the square, leaving the tree to burn unhindered. Indescribable heat radiated from it, singeing his skin right through his clothing as Tristan raced across the square with Ernesto on his heels. The brightness of the flames lit the entire square, and he had no trouble locating where he'd last buried the pipe; but as he got near the spot, his steps slowed. The backfilled earth he'd laid down just days ago had been disturbed, scraped away in a haphazard pattern, as if dug by bare hands.

Ernesto nearly piled into him as he stopped short, and then a shriek of terror raked his ears, audible above the roaring din of fire. Tristan looked up, and to his horror there was Ángel, terrified and clinging to a sagging telephone pole, it's base charred and weakened by the fire. It could collapse any minute, and the urgency of excavating the pipe suddenly seemed secondary. He didn't know how or why the boy got there, but someone would have to climb up and get him down. "Ángel!" he called out. "Hold on, I'm coming!" He took a step toward the pole and was quickly jerked back by a firm grip on his arm.

"You've got the shovel," Ernesto said, his dirty eyeglass lenses eerily reflecting the menacing flames. "Do what you came to do. I'll get the kid."

Tristan stared at him for the space of a heartbeat, then nodded. "Go." He watched him dash toward the pole, and then turned away. He had no choice but to trust Ernesto's agility and strength to rescue Ángel, no matter how much he wanted to do so himself. He gripped the shovel and dug furiously in the face of the flames that were quickly advancing on their position.

The firemen were doing a good job suppressing the burning buildings, but until they quashed the source of the fire they'd still be at risk. He worked faster, until he felt his arms shudder as the blade of the shovel struck something solid. He started scooping the dirt away like a madman, widening the trench to get at the pipe and create a path to direct the water.

Sweat seemed to stream from every pore of his skin as he began chopping at the makeshift pipe to split it open. The heat was tortuously oppressive. He could barely see or hear anything, but sensed movement nearby. As he looked up, Ernesto appeared out of the smoky haze, carrying Ángel in his arms. *Thank Christ.* He set the boy down and he immediately scrambled toward Tristan. He laid his shovel aside for an instant as Ángel threw his arms around him. "I knew you would save me," he cried.

"It was Ernesto who saved you," Tristan said, wanting to hold on to his lanky little body but prying himself loose because of the intense heat. "What in God's name were you doing here," he admonished, trying to sound stern but not quite managing it. "You should have stayed at the church!"

"I wanted to help! I tried to follow Sr. Alvarez but I couldn't find him. I remembered the pipe I helped you make," he said. "I thought I could dig it up and make the water go out on the street. But my hands got tired, and I had to get up high to get away from the smoke."

"So, you climbed a telephone pole," Tristan scolded.

"Come on, let's get this thing open," Ernesto interrupted. He dropped to his knees and began clearing away more dirt with his hands. Ángel tried to help, though his hands were nearly raw. Tristan chopped at the pipe one last time, and the casing burst open. As though his prayers had been answered, streams of water spewed forth from the broken pipe with all the forceful pressure he'd hoped for.

The trench they'd cleared funneled the water outward, spilling out onto the ground and then reaching the super-heated brick pavers of the square. Steam rose and mixed with the smoke, the 'holy' water snuffing out everything in its path as it raced toward El Guardián. Tristan gave a shout of triumph and looked about for his tiny apprentice, only to find him clinging to his new hero. He smiled and stood back, ignoring his protesting knees and aching back to watch the flames smother and start to die.

Then he felt something land on his head. On reflex he

swatted at it, thinking it may be a spark that would set his hair on fire. Then he felt another on his arm, then another. Something trickled down his scalp. By God, it was starting to rain. "It's raining!" he shouted needlessly, spreading his arms wide and welcoming each drop as it struck his skin. He basked in the cleansing sensation of it as the rain increased, regretting his sarcasm about the wrath of God. Ángel may call him El Milagro, but they had all just received a true miracle, literally from on high.

Chapter Twenty-Five

Baby Jorge gurgled happily as he lay snug in his mother's arms. Marlena smiled at him, but could feel Juliana's unwavering stare fixed on her, rather than her son. She met her aunt's intense gaze, a knowing glint in Juliana's green eyes that said she knew everything Marlena had done since yesterday, and felt a shiver course up her spine. She could also feel her mother's quiet wrath settling upon her, for her actions, her deception, and most of all, the very public kiss she'd just enjoyed.

Bianca interrupted her and Juliana's wordless exchange. "Sr. Flynn said he helped bring you home, Marlena. Home from where?" Her tone seemed to balance somewhere between concern and condemnation. Marlena faced her mother. How would she explain this without Tristan here to back her up?

"Madrid. I went there to see about a job."

"A job?" Bianca asked, as though not hearing her daughter correctly. "What sort of job?"

"A modeling job, and the ad said I could only apply in person. I had to go, mama, I just had to."

"Why couldn't you tell me this? Instead of making up lies?"

"I didn't think you'd let me go if I told you. And, if I got the job," Marlena paused and lowered her eyes. "I wasn't coming back."

Bianca stayed silent for a long, uncomfortable moment. "I take it that didn't happen," she finally said

Marlena shook her head. "No. They…were no longer hiring," she said, wincing inwardly at yet another lie, but it was better than the truth.

"And how is it that Sr. Flynn found you?" her mother persisted.

"I was going to take the bus to Madrid. He saw me at the bus stop, and offered to drive me instead." Marlena looked up again, sensing Bianca's disapproval. "It would have taken hours and hours on the bus," she said in defense.

Bianca regarded her intently before speaking again. "Then why did you not come home until today?"

"It got late," she said. "We stayed in a hotel in Madrid."

Bianca's jaw dropped in disbelief. "You…" she began, but couldn't seem to find any further words.

Juliana placed a hand on Bianca's arm. "It is all right, sister," she said. "I foresaw this. It was meant to happen. You needn't be upset, nor worry."

"But, that… just isn't done," Bianca gasped, then closed her mouth as several people cast curious glances her way. She leaned in, and lowered her voice. "We'd planned for you to go to modeling school, not run off at the first chance you had. How could you do that to us? To yourself?'

"I can't wait for the school to make up its mind. I can't stay here forever, mama," Marlena pleaded. "I want to make something of myself, and I want to do it now. For me, for you, for Jorge." She glanced at Juliana. "I'm sorry, Tía Juliana. But you know what will happen here. He will always carry your shame; be denied opportunities because of what he is. I don't want that for him."

Juliana diverted her gaze to her baby, and they all fell silent. Working up her courage, Marlena knew she had to say the rest. "Mother. There's something else. Tristan wants to marry me."

Bianca looked into her daughter's eyes. Behind their dark irises, so much like her own, Marlena saw a storm of emotions; shock, confusion, sorrow. But there was also happiness. Taking in a long breath, Bianca pulled something from her purse. "This came for you today," she said, handing it to Marlena.

Marlena took the slightly creased, white business envelope from her mother and looked it over. It wasn't very thick; perhaps only a single sheet of paper inside it. Then she noticed the return address; from the Escuela de Modelaje, and she nearly stopped breathing. The modeling school had replied! A bittersweet stab of agony sliced through her. If she'd only stayed at home one more day; if only she hadn't been so impatient, she wouldn't have caused everyone so much grief. But if she'd stayed, she'd never have found her destiny with Tristan. He said he'd never hold her back, but would this letter change things?

She tore it open and pulled out a sheet of crisp letterhead. She forced her hands to stop shaking as she unfolded the letter, and got as far as the first line before squeezing her eyes shut.

Dear Sra Sanchez. We regret to inform you…

No. No, no! It couldn't be. After all this waiting, she was being rejected? Disappointment bubbled up in her throat until she felt it would choke her. As she sat there wishing away the words on the page, a pattering sound began overhead, amplified in the tall space of the sanctuary. It grew stronger, and heavier. She opened her eyes. The people began to stir, looking upward and murmuring prayers of thanks. Pastor Giorgio went to one of the windows and opened it. Praise the Lord, it was raining.

Suddenly, the doors to the sanctuary burst open, and all eyes turned to the intrusion. In the archway stood Tristan, and behind him Ernesto, who carried a young boy in his arms. All three looked as though they'd been through a war; sodden and covered in dirt.

"Ángel!" the woman in the wheelchair cried, holding her arms out. Clearly this was her missing son, the boy Tristan went to find; but it was Ernesto who brought him forward, carrying him several steps before setting the boy's feet on the floor. He ran to his mother and collapsed into her embrace. Their joyful sobs echoed in the stillness of the church while murmurs of relief rippled through the small crowd.

The two men hung back, then slowly approached the front of the church. Ángel's mother lifted her blond head to greet them as they came near. "Thank you, thank you both," she said, her voice choked with emotion.

"He's alright, Carolina. Just a few scrapes. He might have a cough for a few days," Ernesto said, gently ruffling the boy's hair. Marlena watched the scene, struck by how different Ernesto seemed with his clothes and face tarred with soot and the purposeful confidence in his stride as he had come forward, playing the role of hero. Suddenly she no longer saw him as the boy she'd grown up with; he was a man in his own right, and he deserved better than the way she'd treated him, no—used him—in the last few months. She regretted it deeply, and hoped he'd find his own path, the path he was meant to follow, and be happy. If that still meant staying in Zaragoza, working for his family and in the community, then that was all she could wish for him. His choices were his own, and not up to her. She had no right to pressure him.

Tristan walked toward where she sat on the pew behind her mother and Aunt Juliana. Marlena caught his gaze, his sparkling blue eyes hollowed and red-rimmed, but still reflecting the warmth and deep meaning of what they'd shared. Tía Juliana had known from the beginning, that he would bring great change, for both good and bad; but all of it was right, for her, for him, for her home town, even though it might be already razed to the ground. Incendio.

"What's happening?" she asked as he stood over her. She set the letter down as he reached for her hands and pulled her to her feet.

"The fire is under control," he said evenly. "But we lost El Guardián, and a lot of the surrounding buildings. It will take a long time to repair."

"Perhaps it takes destroying some things, to make way for better ones," she said, thinking not only of the town, but of her crushed dreams. He threw her a curious look, then pulled her close and cradled her head against his chest.

"Yes. Sometimes that is what it takes. No-one was hurt, but it's a huge loss for the community. Things will never be the same again. That's why I have to help."

"You've done all you could. It's not your responsibility," Marlena said.

"Yes, it is. I was drawn here for a reason; for many reasons. I know it now more than ever." He rested his chin on top of her head and held her even tighter. "That's why I'm going to stay."

"Stay? At the church?" she asked.

Tristan chuckled, the warm vibration of his chest tickling her cheek. "I mean here in Spain. Unless you have an objection."

"I don't," she answered, her mind a jumble of excitement, apprehension, uncertainty. What would this mean to their relationship? "But what about England? Your family?"

He grinned and stroked her hair. "I told you when I came to this country, I didn't know my purpose; what I would do with my life. But I began to see what was possible, and now I see what is inevitable. I'm needed here. To build. And rebuild. And to be with you."

Marlena felt tears welling as he spoke, realizing in that sliver of a moment that becoming a model was not everything; that what she also wanted was to be with Tristan, in the place she knew her heart would always call home. Still, it was not that simple. "You can't sleep in Don Giorgio's shed forever. Where will you live?"

"Where will we live," he corrected her. "To know that, there's someone I need to ask." He released her from his embrace, and focused on Bianca, who had been watching them intently. Marlena wasn't sure if her mother looked pleased or horrified, her face seemed so pale and her eyes like crystals of black ice. "Senora Sanchez. I said I would answer any questions you have; but would you be so kind as to let me ask one first?"

Bianca and Juliana exchanged glances, then Bianca gave a nod.

"I wish to marry your daughter," he said. "And you should know that she has already said yes and I'm going to marry her regardless of your answer, but I'm told it's traditional to ask your permission. May I have it?"

Marlena drew in a sharp breath. She wasn't expecting him to just blurt it out like that. She held the air in her lungs as she waited for Bianca's reaction. Aunt Juliana averted her eyes, seeming very pleased with herself as her lips formed a satisfied smile. Onlookers had started turning their attention to the scene.

With practically the whole church watching her, Bianca cleared her throat, then proudly lifted her chin. Her eyes ticked back and forth between Marlena and Tristan, and a smile tugged at the corners of her mouth. "You may have it, Senor Flynn. Welcome to our family."

Marlena exhaled, and re-filled her lungs with a breath of

joy. Applause and congratulations flowed from all around them, and she and Tristan kissed again in full view of everyone present, including the Pastor and Ernesto. When their lips separated, she caught a glimpse of Ernesto over Tristan's shoulder. He stood near the little boy and his mother. The film of dirt on his lenses hid his eyes from her, but his facial expression seemed blank, resigned.

She'd plunged the final dagger to his heart, and it looked as if he was too numb to even feel it. "What happened between you and Ernesto?" Marlena asked, whispering in Tristan's ear amid the many voices all around them.

"I hit him with a shovel."

"You what?"

"We had a disagreement," he continued. "But we saw eye to eye in the end."

"You got in a fight?"

"Just a small one. It didn't last long. 'Only a fool fights in a burning house,' as they say, or in this case, a burning town." His expression sobered. "Pretty much the whole square was on fire, we had to move fast. We worked together despite our differences. He's a good man, Marly."

"I know. And I've hurt him so much," she said, shaking her head. "I need to apologize. He didn't deserve the way I treated him."

"You told him the truth. That's what good friends do."

Yes. He had always been her friend; her rock. She had to be that for him now. Ernesto stood, rigid and unmoving as she strode toward him. "Ernesto," she said softly.

Ernesto didn't move. "I'm glad you're safe," was all he could say.

Marlena's heart recoiled at his coldness; he seemed like a stranger, not the lifelong pal and confidante she'd always known. "I'm sorry for all the pain I've caused you. You know you will always be in my heart, just not the way you'd hoped. If you no longer feel friendship for me, I understand."

Ernesto shook his head, and gingerly removed his glasses. The look in his eyes, so full of tenderness, pain, and longing, nearly broke Marlena's heart. "That isn't possible," he said. You are part of me, Marly. That will never change. I love you. I've always loved you; but if all you have to give me is friendship, I will gladly accept that."

Marlena felt her heart twist at his words. They could not be plainer. He loved her; and loved her enough to let her go. She would never have a better friend. She wrapped her arms around him and hugged him tight, not caring about the dirt and ash that covered nearly all of him. "Thank you," she said.

Epilogue

September, 1973

Tristan stopped working long enough to appraise and enjoy the vision before him; marveling at the delicate curves of her cheekbones and the arch of her brows; her flawless skin and sleek dark hair. He drank in all her loveliness, knowing he would have a lifetime ahead to appreciate it. It made him smile.

"I brought your lunch," Marlena said, setting a basket down on a makeshift workbench that consisted of a sheet of plywood straddled over sawhorses. Tools and plans littered its surface, and construction materials lay everywhere around them, lumber, sheeting, concrete blocks, wire and conduit. The repairs to most of the storefronts in the square were progressing well, and the construction company Tristan had started was lining up more and more work every day. Even after the repair work was completed, they'd be busy until the end of the year. It was a small venture, but Tristan knew it would lead to something much bigger. The name Flynn Enterprises had been floating in his brain and had a nice ring to it. Someday he'd incorporate it.

"You are an angel of mercy," he said, clearing a spot on the temporary workbench.

"No, I'm the devil of details," she replied, unwrapping the basket. "I still want your opinion on the flowers and invitations for our wedding; but since you hardly have time for me anymore, I'm stuck with the decisions. I hope this isn't a pattern for us going forward." She flashed him a disapproving glare, but a wry smile curved her luscious lips that he couldn't wait to be kissing again. In private. Or not.

It's true he'd been busy, but it was all for their future. One day he'd have armies of workers under him and would take his soon-to-be bride on trips around the world, spending as much time with her as she'd allow before getting sick of his doting attention. "I trust your judgement completely," he said, then turned and whistled across the piles of lumber and over the noise of power tools. "Ernesto! Lunch!" He turned back to Marlena and reached for a sandwich from the plate she'd laid out on a tablecloth. "Aren't you due at school soon, young lady?"

She handed him a napkin. "Not until Monday," she said. "They've only just received the enlargements I sent. I'm lucky that the letter said my application had only been put on hold until I submitted my full-length portfolio pictures."

"We're lucky there were some useable pictures in that camera," Tristan said, taking a bite. Although it represented an unpleasant incident, they decided to develop the film taken from the fake studio in Madrid. The first few shots of a clothed Marlena were actually pretty good. They had them made into 8x10s and destroyed the rest; they even got a decent price for the camera at a local pawn shop.

Ernesto joined them at their temporary table, doffing his hardhat and gloves. Tristan had been very impressed with Ernesto's natural aptitude for carpentry. After seeing his work on some of the farm buildings at the Sanchez villa, he asked him to join his construction crew for the town repairs. He'd shown himself to be a reliable, fast worker who took on responsibility readily. With formal training, he'd be an even greater asset to the little company; which wouldn't remain little for very long. Tristan envisioned it growing far beyond Spain's borders.

"This is wonderful, Marly. Thank you," Ernesto said as he looked over the lunch spread.

Tristan watched him say a silent grace before helping himself to the food. A good man, to be sure; gracious enough to let the best man win, and smart enough to grasp opportunity when it presented itself. It seemed like the right time to pitch the idea he'd been mulling around. "Ernesto, would you be interested in becoming more than a carpenter?" he asked.

Ernesto pushed up his eyeglasses and regarded Tristan for a moment. "I suppose so. Why do you ask?"

"Because, I was thinking you'd make a great project manager, maybe even a design engineer."

Ernesto seemed taken aback. "Kind of you to say, Tristan, but I'm happy being exactly what I am. Just ask Marly," he said, throwing her a shy smile. Marlena tilted her head and returned the smile. It didn't bother Tristan that hers and Ernesto's friendship remained solid. He might be possessive about certain things, but not this. He admired and respected them both too much to interfere with their choice of friends.

"I'm glad," Tristan said. "But, if the opportunity to study engineering came along, wouldn't you be interested? With a degree in your pocket, you could work for any company, anywhere in the world."

"My world is here," Ernesto replied. "And I could never earn a degree. Who would accept an application from an uneducated, self-taught carpenter like me?"

"Oh, I don't know about that. If you had a sponsor, say an alumni of a respected engineering school in Wales, you could be accepted quite easily. And when this job is finished, you'd have enough money for tuition. What do you say?"

"You're offering to sponsor me?" Ernesto asked, repositioning his glasses again. Marlena squealed and clapped her hands in delight.

Tristan looked around, to his left and right and over his shoulder. "You see anyone else blathering?" he asked.

Ernesto blew out a breath and shook his curly head. "It's a lot to think about."

"While you're both thinking so hard, why don't we all take a walk after you've eaten and talk it over," Marlena said.

"Good idea," Tristan said, wolfing down the last of his sandwich. Marlena packed away the remains of their lunch, and the three of them strolled around the square, discussing the extent of the damage and the progress of the many repairs. Ernesto asked questions about the university and Tristan answered them, but said he wanted more time to consider the opportunity.

"The offer is open whenever you decide," Tristan said. They eventually came to the center of the square, as though saving it for last. Tristan still found it hard to look at the blackened, sawn-off stump that was all that remained of the once massive, flourishing tree. He smiled as he thought of Ángel and his declarations that the tree would never die, and that it was older than any of the people who lived here. The boy had taught him much about life here, despite his lack of years.

"It was a very old tree," Marlena said. "But I believe that old things must die, if there is ever to be room for the new. Don't you agree?" She looked over at both men.

"Yes, I can see that," Ernesto said, his gaze lingering on her, his interpretation of her statement painfully clear.

Tristan filled his lungs with the sharp autumn air that still held the bitter tang of destruction. Incendio. He remembered

Marlena's words. Consumed by flame; just like his heart in his desire for her. "I agree," he said, considering the omnipresent conflict between old and new. Between ancient trees and newly planted forests; between old traditions, and new ways of thinking. "It's happening all around us. Not just to El Guardián or this city, but across the country, with your own government; and the change will be welcome."

Marlena crouched down to examine the remains of El Guardián more closely. "Look!" she said, pointing to a spot on its flat-topped stump. He and Ernesto leaned in for a closer look, and to his astonishment, Tristan saw that a tiny green shoot had erupted from somewhere deep inside the ancient sentinel that refused to give up its life. Its spear-like tip defiantly awaited its moment to unfurl into a fully formed leaf.

He shook his head in amazement. The new, rising from the ashes of the old. It fit. This hot-blooded land he had embraced in all its passionate glory would experience a new beginning, forged from the rich depths of the old, just as he himself would; with a new family to cherish and an empire to build.

- The End -

INCENDIO

Spanish Seduction Book Three

From the Author

*Thank you for reading my Spanish Seduction Triology..
I sincerely hope you enjoyed it, and if so, the favor of a
customer review would be appreciated.*

Keep the passion going!
Read other books by Jean Maxwell:

*The Witch Doctor
(Nine Lives Chronicles Book 1)*

*Winter Symphony
(Overtures - Book 1)*

Short Stories:

The Last Hallow's Eve

The Terminatrix

*

Yours in words,

Jean Maxwell